The Telepathy Office

By Keith Gell

Ordering Information:

Quantity sales. Special discounts are available on quantity purchases by corporations, associations, and others. For details, contact the publisher at the email address above.

ISBN: 978-1-9160302-0-6

Acknowledgements.

Thank you to:

Lucy Wintle and Heinrich Kley for the cover art.

Victoria Fergusson, Teria and Loula Shapanis, and Penny Gell, for beta reading my novel.

Matt Davey, Tracy Newton, Linda Wintle, Jane and Lucy Paterson, Fiona Daly, Hanna Jackson, and Tony and Heather Flood for your support and encouragement.

From Keith Gell

1

Magic is dangerous. Every goblin knows this. Even the lunatic werewolves howling at the three moons know it. So how could he be so irresponsible?

'He' was the very eccentric Grand Master Emmanuel Scribble and his weakness was a reckless love of books. He spent hours reading them through his bone framed glasses, and his particular interest was the subject of magic.

He owned a bookshop, and riddled the basements under it with lots of pan-dimensional passageways. Every passage led to yet more book-filled rooms, each in its own small pocket dimension. These were stuffed with so many books they overflowed even the abundant shelf capacity, with excess tomes piled floor to ceiling. It was a necessary expense to magically carve out compartments of space-time because he had to isolate dangerous books in such a way that they could be stored safely.

Some of his books were so hazardous that simple possession of them was illegal under the city's strictures on magical hygiene. Certainly, that would be the case under sections 4 and 17 of the Dangerous Spells Act 1865, and probably section 9 of the Demon Act 1845. Casting any of the evil spells contained within them would amount to a most serious criminal offence. But by the prudent use of pan-dimensional magic, he cunningly circumvented these laws by putting the books outside the city limits, and therefore out of metropolitan legal jurisdiction. Yet the simple fact remained that many of his books were dangerous because of their subject matter, which was black magic and demonic invocation.

Although Scribble hated to see any book destroyed or damaged, even ones that any vaguely safety-conscious goblin would throw on a bonfire without the slightest sentimentality, he was not by nature a reckless goblin. He guarded them day and night. In fact, to the best of anyone's recollection, he never left his basements. Rather, he remained vigilant and below ground at all times, casting his diligent eyes over the entrances into his tunnels. He was a powerful magician and a formidable watchman.

As he preferred to spend his time reading, he hired helpers to relieve him of the day to day running of his bookshop. They worked the floor as sales assistants and ran errands at his behest.

Scribble sat on his favourite Chesterfield armchair. He reached over for the smoking box that he kept on a coffee table. He opened up the box, took out his pipe and charged it with the last of his kobold weed, and started smoking.

Better send for more weed, he thought to himself. He picked up a small brass bell from the table and rang it. The bell was not loud, but it was a magical bell, and its sound reached the ears of whoever the ringer had in mind while ringing it, no matter how far away that person might be. On this occasion, Master Scribble sought the attention of one of his shop assistants, a certain Mr. Apocalypse Broadhead.

Scribble began reading a draft government report entitled, *'The Municipal Weather Machine'* by Jeroboam Nettlebed, who was the Chief Municipal Weather Wizard and a good friend. Nettlebed had asked him to review the paper for the forthcoming lecture on weather magic and manna pollution at the Imperial School. He found Nettlebed's ideas fascinating and was enjoying himself, but soon wanted another pipe full of weed, and it irritated him that Mr. Broadhead had still not responded to his summons.

What has become of Apocalypse Broadhead? It is unlike him to take so long, he thought to himself. In agitation, he laid his pipe on the ashtray, rose out of his armchair and made his way to the spiral staircase that led to the shop floor above. He was about to go upstairs for the first time in decades to fetch Broadhead in person when he noticed something odd; there was no noise coming from the shop floor. No chiming tills, no customer chatter, no footfalls of shop staff running about the place - just silence.

What can the matter be? Thought Scribble.

He had long been conscious of the dangers should one of his wicked books fall into the wrong hands, and he knew in his bones that something was awry.

As a precaution he cast a spell on himself called **A Wizard's Image Removed**. From a casting point of view, it was a relatively simple spell, so he did so without the noise or dramatic hand gestures that a lesser mage might need to generate extra power. The effect of the spell was to move his image ten feet away from where he actually stood, which in this case was to the other side of the room. His sigil was to fill the room with the smell of old books, but in his basement, it was not noticeable.

His fears were justified. The blood-drained corpse of Apocalypse

Broadhead tumbled down the spiral staircase, soon after two goblins and three goblinettes followed. They all had pale white skin, the colour of chalk, and two of them had some blood on their clothes from feasting. Goblins infected with vampirism.

Fooled by the spell, the first vampire to reach the bottom of the stairs launched itself at Scribble's image only to fall through it. It crashed into the table and tumbled to the ground.

The invisible Scribble took off down the corridor, his false image following ten feet behind him. The vampires gave chase.

He ran into a small room, and slammed that door shut too. He locked himself in. Outside he heard the commotion of the vampires. He knew that one visual illusion alone was unlikely to trick them for long, as vampires have good hearing and sensitive noses, especially for goblin blood.

The wooden door was strong but had no resistance to magic. He heard a vampire cast a spell on the other side of the door. Soon fungi sprouted from the door's paneling. The wood crumbled away, and as it did the room filled with the smell of bad eggs. As fast as he could, he ran out of the opposite door, locking that door in turn, hoping for a few minutes of precious extra time to make his defence.

He rushed to yet another room, and again he locked the door. He removed a revolver from the bottom drawer of a small desk. Wheezing and sweating, he emptied its bullets onto the floor. The air in the room started to smell, he knew the door would give way soon. He opened a box of vampire rounds, and loaded them into the chambers of the gun. He turned just in time, as a vampire was almost on him. With a deafening bang he shot the vampire in the head, and it burned to ashes. In an instant, another one charged him, he shot again, hitting the creature in its knee. It fell to the ground howling in agony, black blood spurted out of its wound. A second shot burned it to a pile of ashes.

Scribble looked up for the next target, but in the split-second before he could level his revolver to fire, strands of magical silk flew out from its fingers, which wrapped him in a sticky cocoon, and glued him fast to the wall. He was bound and helpless, unable to raise his weapon or move very much at all.

The vampire ambled over to Scribble. She was a tall goblinette, perhaps 5 feet 2 inches high. Her cruel facial features had assumed an evil aspect that reflected the malicious thoughts she long held in her heart.

3

'Master Emmanuel Scribble I surmise. I would like to purchase a book from you,' she said, in a gentle voice laced with menacing undertones of well-honed spite.

'Well, you seem to have me bound up, which gives you something of a negotiating advantage. Which book did you have in mind?'

'The book I am looking to purchase is, '*Keys to the Dark Gate*', you have a first edition copy' said the vampire.

'Ah, *The Keys*, a dangerous book that is why it never got to a second edition,' said Scribble.

'Well, I am a dangerous and impatient vampire, so please tell me where you keep it.'

'I am afraid it is not for sale, Madam.'

The vampire circled her arms and clenched her hands into fists, 'Tell me where you keep your copy,' she said as she cast the spell called **Command the Subservient Soul.** A stink of rotten eggs filled the room as the magic took effect.

Scribble braced all of his mental strength to resist the command, which he only just managed to do.

'You are a strong-willed old wizard, so let's weaken you a little. Cornucopia my dear, please drink some of Mr. Scribble's life from him, enough to make him see reason, but not enough to kill him yet.'

Cornucopia curtsied to her mistress, bowing her head in deference. She walked over to Scribble, and tore away the shirt covering his right breast. After pulling two of the strands of silk aside, she inserted her fangs into his flesh and drank his blood. He experienced no pain, but he felt his life, strength and will ebbing away as the vampire bled him. After he weakened, she stood aside, awaiting further instruction.

'Master Scribble, I command you again: Tell me where you keep your copy of Keys to the Dark Gate.'

Now he lacked the strength of will necessary to resist this magical command. 'Room 31, bookshelf 87, the ninth book from the left,' he mumbled, half conscious.

The mistress turned to her servants. 'Watch him, do not kill him yet. Not until I have the book in my hand.'

She left the room and returned with *The Keys*.

'Cornucopia, drain the last drop of lifeblood out of Mr. Scribble; and Prudence you watch and go thirsty.' The vampire queen spoke with gleeful malice.

She left the room for the last time.

Cornucopia gloated at Prudence, relishing the thought that while she would feast, Prudence would crave blood. Prudence looked back at her, then she stared deeply into her eyes.

Cornucopia was transfixed. After a minute, she left the room without drinking Scribble's blood or harming him. She was in a magically induced daze.

Prudence was now alone with the helpless old wizard. 'You are lucky it's me, Mr. Scribble.'

Finally, she left, leaving him alone bound in the magic web. He was exhausted and confused, but against all expectations, he was still alive.

2

Manna is magical power captured in physical form.

Excerpt from **Magic Theory and Practice 4th** Edition by Grand Master Emmanuel Silverwings, Emperor Phoenix Press.

***

An escape pod, battered and scorched, floated in the vast inky waste of deep space. Four orkish pirates slumped inside. They looked as defeated as their tiny capsule. The air had long become stale. The pod's thin metal skin was now the only protection from the suffocating vacuum of space. Unless their luck changed, death would come soon.

They were survivors of a lost battle who had jettisoned from a burning raiding ship two days ago. Two of the orks were fresh to war, Lieutenants Victor Mandrake and Oskar Mortimer. Their uniforms were dirty but still new. They were uninjured and had no battle scars. Both showed more fear from the past trauma of battle than a good ork should; and the dangerous company they now kept.

The third ork was Sally Sting, a pirate princess. She looked both fierce and beautiful. The irregular stitching to the deep wounds to her thigh and shoulder, showed they had been sewn by an amateur. She was unconscious and pale with blood loss, and would be the first to die if help did not come soon.

The fourth ork was the infamous Captain Jack Coffin. He should not be on the lifeboat. He should have stayed on his destroyed ship and burned with it. That was expected of a commanding ork. Everyone knew it, Coffin most of all.

Coffin could never return to Caragula now. He was a disgraced orkish war captain, who had taken to a pod rather than die in battle. He had abandoned his ship, and with it his duty and his honour, all thrown away to rescue his beloved princess. And she would soon be dead.

He bled from a painful stomach wound that without medical treatment would slowly kill him in the days to come. But he did not show the slightest sign of discomfort or fear. Jack Coffin was stern and terrifying, even in defeat.

There was still air to breathe, but it was old air that tasted of sweat and ignominy. They had finished the last of their food and water, and even the uninjured orks would soon die of thirst if they did not suffocate beforehand.

Lieutenant Mandrake was trying to stitch up the belly wound of Captain Coffin with the wrong kind of needle. It was the needle and thread that Mandrake kept in the inside pocket of his tunic, in case a button fell off.

It must hurt him when I sew his flesh? The young officer thought. He was terrified of Coffin, and it was all he could do to stop his hand from trembling.

Coffin noticed the youngster's fear, he grunted, 'If you make a messy job of that stitch, I will make you unpick it and do it again.'

Mandrake finished sewing; he sat down, relieved that he had completed the task.

Oskar Mortimer looked at the reluctant surgeon, summoning up the courage to speak to Coffin, 'The orkish war manual states that at times of food shortage, it is customary among ork warriors to kill the weakest', pointing to the near-dead princess, 'but given our esteemed company, would you agree to draw lots as to who we eat Sir?'

Without hesitation or spoken reply, but with a clean and graceful action, Coffin leaned over to Mortimer, and snapped the young ork's neck with a sickening crack. He turned to Lieutenant Mandrake, then pointed to the fresh corpse, 'If you are hungry eat Mortimer'.

They sat together for an hour more with the dead Mortimer and dying Sting when an extraordinary thing happened. A thought from another's mind entered Coffin's head, *'My name is Starcatcher, and I am a Star Dragon Prince of the city of Salin. Greetings ork.'*

Jack Coffin had heard of telepathy, and he knew high elves and minor gods, and some species of dragons could communicate using it. But he had not experienced it before. He knew that if the dragon could put thoughts into his mind, then he could also have been reading it for some time. But he was an ork, not a high elf, and he had no protection against the invasive telepathy of a star dragon.

'Why would you want to assist a dishonoured ork pirate?'

'We have similar problems you and I, and we could solve them together. Tell me, would you go to the afterlife itself to rescue your beloved orkess?' projected Starcatcher.

'I would.' Coffin thought back without hesitation.

'In return for your rescue from abandonment in space, would you bring back the soul of my beloved lady dragon?'

'I would want more than that,' Coffin replied.

'What more do you want?'

'I have dishonoured my clan; those that I am responsible for will lose their rights and liberties on Caragula. If you can help them, I ask that you do.'

'I agree, so we have a deal in principle Captain Coffin. I will ask to have the contractual paperwork drawn up. It will be ready for you on arrival at the Goblin Metropolis.' The dragon concluded in a business-like tone.

Captain Jack Coffin felt the pod speed up. The dragon must be pulling us along now, I must be going to the Metropolis.

3

Oubliette Prison is the only jail in the Metropolis; it houses all the city's convicts. It is a massive structure, 13 stories high in places, and built of dark starstone. The colour of its walls gives a foreboding look that brought even the bravest goblin to the brink of terror. It is home to thousands of criminals. Within it are gateways to small pocket dimensions used to house the most dangerous offenders. There is no record of a goblin having ever escaped from Oubliette. It is common for goblin mothers to threaten their children with incarceration there, so as to frighten them into obedience and eating their greens...

Extract from **The History of Metropolitan Life**, Goblin Press

***

Goblins can be bullies. And Police Constable Babylon Pinch had good reason to feel persecuted. Sergeant Witchson gave Pinch the nastiest jobs, volunteered him for the most dangerous missions, and sent him out on the worst of nights. Tonight, the manna fog lay thick over the streets of the Metropolis. Pinch stretched out his hand, and as he did, he could not see his fingers. The fog in the Metropolis is magical and dangerous, made from the droplets of water found in natural fog, mixed with particles of manna pollution from the city's thousands of magical workshops and factories. This made it magical, and on still nights it swirled around the city like a shroud that sparkled with spectral hues.

He knew the health consequence of walking his beat in this unnatural atmosphere, he could mutate. Or grow a huge nose or glowing ears. Or burst out in colourful warts all over his skin. He could even develop magical abilities himself, and that was not necessarily a good thing. *I cannot wait for the weather machine to blow this filth away* thought Pinch, in anticipation of its imminent commission.

A police whistle sounded in the distance. Following his standing orders, Pinch made his way towards it as safely as the poor visibility would allow. It had come from Scribble's bookshop. He crossed under the rope of the police cordon. Sergeant Witchson had assembled a party of officers, so he joined the group and awaited his orders from his superior and oppressor.

'This is a vampire attack my good goblins, so given the risk, I have called for a wizard. Keep the area surrounded until he comes. Any questions?' asked Witchson.

'Which wizard?' Asked a policeman who had not been working for Witchson for long.

'Grand Master Pharaoh Henry,' Witchson scowled.

A fearful silence fell over the officers. Everyone in the Metropolis knew of Henry's reputation as a fanatical demon hunter. They knew of the enthusiasm by which he threw himself and others less fortunate, into battle with the most dangerous and evil devils. Despite his many exploits against the forces of Hell, he had never come away with so much as an infernal scratch. The same was not true for his underlings, who were invariably maimed body and soul. Working for Pharaoh Henry was the most dangerous job in the whole of the Metropolis, and no goblin in his right mind would want to do it.

Henry emerged from the thick manna fog, and as he did, he instilled into Pinch an ominous sensation of unspecified dread.

Nowadays, most metropolitan wizards dress garishly, in clothes magically dyed with eye-catching effects and colours, but not Pharaoh Henry. He looked like an old academic goblin, plainly dressed in mundane blue and grey robes, with a silver broach of a snake on his lapel.

'I understand there has been a vampire attack. Who is in command?' When Henry spoke it betrayed the fact he was modest, unassuming and lethal.

'I am Sir, Sergeant Witchson at your service. I thought it best for a wizard to arrive before sending anyone inside.'

'Very wise Sergeant. Vampires are exceedingly dangerous. I need one of your goblins to go inside with me. Your best officer, a brave and fearless soul willing to face the unremitting horror of vampirism. Could I have a volunteer?' Henry asked the assembled officers.

Every police officer remained silent, each standing as nonchalant as he could so as not to attract attention to himself.

'Come now, I need a volunteer, send one in after me please sergeant.' Henry stepped into the bookshop, and as he did he almost looked as if he was enjoying himself.

'PC Pinch, you are the volunteer, so follow the wizard,' ordered Witchson. He burst into a cruel laugh.

'Why me sergeant? Why do you always give me all the dangerous jobs? What did I ever do to you?' protested Pinch.

'Well if I am going to bully someone, I like to think I can make it worth everyone's time.' Witchson's humour had infected the other policemen, who also started laughing. Only Constable Pinch failed to see the lighter side of the situation.

Shaking with fear, Pinch reluctantly followed Henry into the bookshop. The shop lights were still bright, and they showed up the corpses scattered across the floor. Each of their pale blood drained faces was contorted with terror.

'Follow the bodies,' said Henry with a friendly smile. Pinch made his way through the dead, stepping carefully between them.

Two goblin corpses straddled the serving counter. 'It seems the vampires made their way downstairs to the basement. They may still be down there, so you take my revolver and cover me. It is loaded for vampire,' said Henry.

Henry made his way down the staircase, with PC Pinch close behind. Scribble's chair and table lay upturned; the shards of his ashtray and his broken clay pipe were strewn on the floor. The drained corpse of Apocalypse Broadhead lay near the bottom of the stairs, its blank dead eyes were open, and seemed to stare back at Pinch. Pinch felt the knot of terror in his belly. He wanted to leave, but disobeying Pharaoh Henry was also dangerous.

'Do you think I might stand at the top of the stairs in case one creeps up behind us?' Said Pinch.

Henry considered Pinch's proposal for a second, then said, 'What's your name?'

'PC Pinch Sir,' the pitch of his voice aquiver with fear.

'I like your initiative Pinch, but we should stick together, I have lost too many brave goblins by splitting up, and this situation looks treacherous.' Henry made his way down the corridor through which Scribble had fled.

Pinch followed him, in desperate need of the toilet. They came to the door of the room in which Scribble had tried to take shelter.

Henry inspected the door frame where the rotted door had been, 'Decayed by magic eh? Scribble must have shut and locked the door to keep them out, I have seen spells that decay wood like that.'

He picked up the door's lock from the floor. He inspected a splinter of decayed wood and smelled it.

Henry gave the wood to Pinch, 'What can you smell?'
'Smells like rotten eggs,' Pinch screwed up his face.

'A sigil of the caster,' said Henry.

'A sigil?' asked Pinch.

'A harmless side effect of a spell unique to its caster. The vampire was also a magician, and her sigil is the smell of rotten eggs, and I know that sigil is peculiar to a wizard called Ephemeral Wormsong. She was once an ornithopter pioneer. Now she is a vampire queen.'

The two goblins followed the book-lined corridor that led to the office where the vampires had caught up with Scribble. He was stuck against the wall by spider's silk, held motionless and silent.

'Poor old Scribble must be dead', said Henry.

'What are these piles of ashes?' asked Pinch.

'Well, they were vampires. Scribble must have hit them with vampire rounds, so he had prepared himself for the eventuality of such an attack,' said Henry.

'Vampire rounds?'

'Yes, rounds especially made to destroy vampires; cast from silver and bathed in holy water for a year and a day,' said Henry.

Pinch noticed a tiny glint of light in the ashes of one vampire. *Something metal? A belt buckle or brass button perhaps?* He bent down and brushed away some ashes to reveal a brass key. He picked it up and gave it to Henry, 'Is this any use to you?'

'It may well be,' Henry inspected the key carefully. It seemed commonplace enough, and he could not feel any discernable aura from it. He placed it in his pocket.

Scribble let out a moan.

'He is alive?!' Henry was most surprised.

Through his fatigue Scribble mumbled away out of shock. 'I feel exhausted but I am not in any pain. I remember vampires attacking me, sticking me to the wall by a web and threatening me with death. Then my memory goes blank, can't remember any more after that.'

Henry checked Scribble for fang marks and found them on his chest. 'You're bitten my good goblin, never mind though, we will get some holy water on it, then you will be as right as rain.'

Henry removed a small glass jar of water from his jacket pocket, then dabbed it onto the wound. 'They let you live? Well that is unusual. Vampires aren't known for their compassion. How did you survive a vampire attack?'

'A very good question, they were going to kill me, but they didn't, and I cannot remember a thing past a certain point.' Even Scribble could not figure it all out.

'Why did they attack you, any idea?' asked Henry.

'A book called **The Keys to the Gates of Hell**. A book on black magic that contains a grimoire of evil spells. One spell is entitled **'Mirror Gate to the Dark Lord's Realm'**, which makes a doorway to Hell. It also contains an even stronger spell that needs a group of emotionally sympathetic souls to power it. That spell opens up a permanent gateway, one that would allow demons to come through in greater number.'

'Hell, eh?' Henry's interest was whetted, 'Please tell me about these doors to Hell.'

'It's been a long time since I read the book, but a pair of mirrors seems to ring a bell. It works by aligning them so they reflect into each other recursively. After that you can walk into the reflection of one of the mirrors and into Hell,' said Scribble, 'Always worth having a cat nearby when dealing with portals, they can see across dimensions in time and space you know, at least some of them have been known to.'

'Well thank you for that,' said Henry, 'Do you recognise this brass key?'

'It is not mine.'

'Glad to hear that,' said Henry.

'You are not going to leave me here glued to a wall are you Pharaoh?'

'Don't fret Sir, it is vampiric magic. The spell should wear off when the sun rises at around ten to six in the morning. Besides you should count yourself lucky you are not dead,' said Henry.

Henry and Pinch left the basement with poor Scribble still stuck in a web. They left the bookshop and rejoined Sergeant Witchson.

'Thank you for your assistance Pinch,' said Henry.

'Not at all Grand Master,' said Pinch, who felt he could breathe more regularly now, and his heart stopped beating so hard.

'Well, I am glad you feel like that Pinch.' Henry turned to Sergeant Witchson, 'Could I borrow PC Pinch to work with me for the whole case?'

Pinch felt his stomach hollow out with apprehension, and his heart started to thump again, now as hard as a dwarf's hammer.

'The Metropolitan Police would be more than happy to lend one of its officers to you for this dangerous mission,' said Witchson. He screwed his eyes a little as he struggled to conceal his amusement at the thought.

'Sir, journalists are asking about the case,' said a police officer, 'they want to know who is in charge.'

Witchson looked at Henry, who shook his head sternly.

'Tell them, Police Constable Babylon Pinch is heading the investigation, he's the best we have,' said Witchson. He gritted his teeth as hard as he could to stop himself laughing out loud.

4

Goblinette: *An unmarried goblin lady.*
Etymology: *First used in the popular guide '**Chanson's Instructions on Modern Etiquette and Good Manners'**.*

Extract from **The Goblin Dictionary** New Edition 1896, City University Press

Contrary to popular misconception, Virginia Chanson is not the third daughter of the Viscount of Lauderwood; in fact there is no such goblin family of that name, and if there were it would certainly not be a reputable one.
She was a fishwife from the less desirable end of New Basilisk Street, who developed the ability to speak with an aristocratic and authoritative voice because of an accidental and unforeseen side-effect of a spell I miscast. I was experimenting with a translation spell. I targeted a seagull, with the intention to render its squawks into the goblin tongue; but I was distracted at a critical moment in the cast by a dribbling, who pulled at my coat trying to sell me a plate of jellied eels. This caused me to target Mrs. Chanson in error.
I did try to apologize to her for the accident, but she was very happy with the outcome. The popularity of her book, 'Chanson's Manners' (as the guide is popularly referred to), and the royalties it generates, has afforded her the finances needed to feign aristocratic lineage. At the date of writing, 'Lady' Chanson has still not been rumbled by her readers; or by anyone else for that matter. On the contrary, she is currently a popular lifestyle and society columnist for the prestigious newspaper, The Fashionable Intelligencer.

Handwritten notes on the word '**Goblinette**', penned by Noah Bentley, 5th October 1898, found inserted in his dictionary.

***

Every Goblin needs protection from demons. Admittedly there may be a few foolish goblins who think worshipping Lucifer is a good idea, though as to why has eluded the intellects of the finest philosophers. Never-the-less, insane demon worshipper's aside, the Goblin King's commissioning of the Municipal Demon Ward to protect the city from infernal attack is widely thought to be a most sensible idea. And its role is to stop demons boring their way through the fabric of space and time to enter the Metropolis directly from Hell.

Demons can still enter the city from other parts of the universe, and then make their way in by stowing away on pan-ships or manifesting themselves in the countryside outside the city then travel in by road, canal or foot. But in all cases, the ward aids wizards by strengthening spells to vanquish them, and weakens the infernal might that they might employ to pester and plague an innocent goblin going about his or her daily life.

Miss Mercy Beanstock was one of the shift supervisors for a team of witches operating the ward. She was a warding witch by profession, and she thought she had the best job in the whole of Goblindom. Her mother was very proud of her, after all a warding witch was a socially prestigious, well paid and highly skilled position, most suitable for any socially ascending goblinette.

The ward was a well-designed and powerful machine. It had been so successful in its role that it had been years since any demon had managed to get past it. In practice Mercy earned good money while she did next to nothing. Typically, she spent her eight-hour shifts drinking tea while engaging in deliciously scandalous gossip with her crew, all the while sitting around waiting for demon alarms that never came.

None of the crew had ever experienced a demon attack, but they had trained and drilled for this very eventuality and knew exactly what to do, in the unlikely event it did happen.

Quite unexpectedly, the demon alarm sounded.

Miss Heavenly Sweetluck silenced the alarm. She sat down at the controls to feed manna into the ward field generator. She tapped the instrument's meter with her left hand, then she adjusted the feed control with her right. Her job was to stop the ward malfunctioning, or spewing out too much magical pollution into the sky, all the while maintaining a strong warding field to keep the demons out.

Miss Clemency Potion sat at the controls to track the strength of the warding spell, and to measure the infernal might of any demon trying to get into their world.

'Seven demons are entering the world. The warding field strength is at five Henrys. One demon appears to be manifesting somewhere in Dragonfair,' said Clemency who could hardly believe what she was seeing.

'Increase the field strength to 7 Henrys.' Mercy stiffened with apprehension.

'Warding field at 7 Henrys but it is still coming through,' said Clemency.

'Increase to ten Henrys,' instructed Mercy.

'Increased to ten Henrys the field is holding the demons, but they have not retreated,' said Clemency.

'Approaching machines safety limits,' said Heavenly.

'One of the demons is coming in harder, with a small imp in its wake. Why is it not retreating, how is it managing to defy the ward?' said Clemency.

'Increase the warding field to twelve Henrys,' said Mercy.

'There are seven demons trying to enter, a major one, and six lesser ones. It must be getting magical help somehow,' said Clemency.

'The machine is straining, exceeding the safety limit. Current manna rate of burn is 2 queens, six Rooks and 4 pawns per hour' said Heavenly, her voice raised in fear.

'Stay calm everyone. Increase to fifteen Henrys,' said Mercy, who was not calm herself.

'The demons are retreating; no wait, two are coming through again,' said Clemency, who could not understand how this could happen.

The warding machine was buckling under the strain, its dials were in the red and the tortured sound of whining cogs filled the control room. Mercy knew that if she kept running it at this intensity it would break down, and that would be catastrophic.

'The machine might fail any time now. We need to decrease power,' said Heavenly.

'The demon is coming through to our dimension; we will need to increase power to hold it,' said Clemency.

Like a fisherman who had too large a catch on his line and so cut it loose, Mercy realised she would have to let this one go, regardless of the dangers that entailed for the Metropolis. 'Reduce power to one Henry.'

'Power is reducing. Two demons have entered the city,' said Clemency.

'What is the machine's state?' asked Mercy.

'The operating conditions exceeded the machine's specifications, but it is still working and is now cooling down. It appears there is no lasting or major damage,' said Heavenly.

There was an uneasy silence in the control room. They knew they were the first crew to allow demons into the city since the ward's construction. They were all terrified of the consequences of their failure, but Mercy felt rather faint.

'What do we do now Mercy?' asked Clemency.

'I must report the invasion to Henry. He will want to talk to me as I am responsible, but he will ask you two some questions also. We need to make a report of exactly what happened, what we did with the machine, and how much manna we used.'   Mercy Beanstock no longer thought she had an easy job, in fact she thought that after she had submitted her report to Grand Master Henry, Constable of the Municipal Demon Ward, she might not have a job at all.

Mercy made an entry of the demon attack in the log.

'Please take control while I am gone Heavenly. Clemency please come with me for a moment,' said Mercy.

Clemency led Mercy into the lady's rest room. Mercy was in a cold sweat of fear and breathed heavily.

'Will you be alright Mercy?'

'I am frightened I may lose my job, Clemency,'

'Would you like me to come with you? I could explain it is not your fault,' said Clemency.

'That's kind of you, but you had better stay here with Heavenly in case there is another invasion.'

Mercy put on her coat and hat, then left the building. She walked across the bridge to Avonbridge Street and caught the number 64 tram to Dragonfair, from where she alighted on Troll's Bonnet Street.

She walked into Oakensoul's College, where she spoke to the receptionist, 'Sir my name is Mercy Beanstock. I am a senior warding witch for the Municipal Demon Ward, here to make an emergency report to the Grand Master Wizard, Pharaoh Henry.'

The receptionist mumbled to a colleague to cover for him on the desk, then rushed off to find Henry. He was back much sooner than

Mercy had expected.

'Master Henry will see you at once by the tree, follow me please Miss,' said the receptionist.

She followed him to the green in the centre of the college. Grand Master Henry was sitting on an iron bench.

'What happened.' Henry asked with a stone face.

Mercy explained that two demons had got past the ward. A major demon, and a minor one, and that she let them in rather than damage the ward.

'Well this is troubling,' said Henry. He began to pace up and down, deep in thought. 'I wonder how it managed it?'

Mercy remained silent.

'Have you ever seen a demon attack Miss Beanstock?'

'No.'

'I have seen far too many. The worst was back on old Draska. We were attacked as we tried to make our escape.'

'You were alive at the time of old Draska?' said Mercy, amazed at Henry's age. Goblins can be very long-lived, and can stay as young as they want by means of rejuvenating magic.

'I was with the Goblin King. Of course, he was not a King at the time, but he led many goblins to safety here; and together we the built this Metropolis. Many goblins escaped, but not all, demons managed to catch many of our friends. It is a terrible sight to see what demons can do to a mortal Miss Beanstock. I hope you do not see too much of it.' Henry looked at Mercy with the look of a goblin that had seen horror and feared its return.

There was a long uncomfortable silence. Henry eventually spoke.

'Miss Beanstock, I think you made the right decision. I would rather allow a limited number of demons into the city than compromise the ward. If the demon ward is failing there must be a good reason. From my investigations I have reason to believe there may be a door to Hell, and that is amplifying the power of an invocation spell. I must find it, in order to make the demon ward work again. Go back to the ward and be sure to keep me informed of any further developments. I like to hear bad news promptly; do you understand Miss Beanstock?' Henry looked very grave.

'Yes Sir.' Mercy gave Henry a deep and respectful curtsy, before turning and making her way out. *Well I still have a job.*

5

*The **Law of Essential Nature** states: **The ideal defining property of an entity cannot be changed by magic**. This is understood from Plato's suggestion that concrete entities acquire their essence through their relations to 'Form', which are abstract universals logically or ontologically separate from the objects in the world of sense perception.*

Socrates was able to recognize two worlds: the apparent world, which constantly changes, and an ideal unchanging and unseen world of forms, which may be the cause of 'what' is apparent. The most popular definition of magic among wizards of the Socratic philosophy is: Magic is the use of one's mind and soul to the manipulation of the world of forms, which in turn changes the apparent reality of our sensual world.

From **Magic Theory and Practice 4th Edition**

*'**Mundane**' describes any goblin or object that is without magical ability. A goblin that is magical is referred to as 'gifted'; most goblins are at least a little gifted by the time they reach adulthood.*

Extract from **The History of Metropolitan Life**, by Isiah Manna, Goblin Press

***

Goblins love to read, which is why there are so many newsagents across the Metropolis. Wizards read about magic and ideas, other goblins about the news and events around the city or across the galaxy, but Miss Euphoria Fireheart preferred scandal and fashion. And she had lots of magazines to read because she sold them for a living.

At 21 years old, she stood 4' 3" tall, which was average for a lady goblin. Her skin was the colour of vanilla ice cream, her eyes midnight-blue, and her thick hair a rich burgundy red. All in all, she was an exceptionally handsome goblinette, and eligible for marriage, but she had no interest in common suitors as her sole ambition was social advancement.

Most goblins were snobs, but she was discerning about such matters. She knew goblin history: High elves created goblins to do their menial labour. From this premise, she correctly deduced that: With the exception of the Goblin King, any goblin claiming to be an aristocrat could not be, and the likes of Lady Virginia Chanson must be imposters. Further, she reckoned the only true upper classes had to be elves. And so, with this incontrovertible conclusion in mind, Euphoria set about the undoable task of becoming a member of elfin high society.

She read 'Society Elf' magazine voraciously, collecting every picture she could find of Draskan princesses. She spent idle hours picturing her elfin self in her mind's eye, typically escorted by a handsome elf prince or two. Of course, they all doted on the Princess Euphoria.

But it was not done to entirely ignore goblin society. So, she kept up with metropolitan events by reading the Fashionable Intelligencer. She took a keen interest in the centaur races, the opera, the Festival of Illusions, and most importantly, the Great Goblin King's Ball.

Her work usually kept her busy, but now and then there would be a lull in trade when she looked at pictures of elfin ladies. She noticed that their postures were different from goblinettes. She studied the picture of Princess Clio, noticing how she held herself. She tried to imitate it, holding her chin higher, and her back a little straighter.

A goblin punctured her fantasy by the demand, 'Metropolitan Herald, please Miss.'

Euphoria passed him a Herald in silence, irritated at having her daydream disturbed for a newspaper. She glanced at the headline, which read: **'Vampire Attack on Scribble's Bookshop – Constable Pinch to Head Investigation!'**

She hoped this Pinch would deal with the vampire problem, as she felt that undead infestations brought down the tone of the neighbourhood. In her opinion the Herald was a respectable enough newspaper; not as interesting as the Intelligencer, but a step up on the City Gossip. The paper she hated most was the clandestine Revolutionary Goblin, a scurrilous and subversive paper printed for underground distribution to the worst kind of upstart. Unfortunately, its editor and printer was her socialist father, Mr. Zebedee Fireheart. Needless to say, she found his political eccentricity acutely embarrassing.

As she stared across the square, she saw a goblin walking on bird's feet, which was obviously a result of magical transformation from the manna fog. Some goblins evolved to giftedness with unsightly physical side effects. The thought of mutation worried her of late.

She had not yet experienced magical transformation which was unusual for a goblinette of her age. The reason being was that she had enjoyed a kind and contented upbringing, and so lacked the distress necessary to trigger magical evolution. She had been exposed to as much manna pollution from the city fog as any other metropolitan resident, and was brimming with magical power. But to date, she remained stubbornly mundane. Yet the fact remained that she itched with magic; a veritable powder barrel of magical energy waiting for some small spark to explode her into someone new and sorcerous.

'Morning Tattle', requested a customer.

Euphoria handed him a Tattle, and as she did, she caught sight of the postman making his way across the square to her shop. She had waited for days for the response for her job application as a trainee newspaper correspondent.

'Good morning Miss Fireheart,' said the postman. He handed her five letters. She thanked him and gave him her father's mail to post.

The postman looked at the envelopes with suspicion. All the stamps had been stuck with the head of the Goblin King (printed on all goblin stamps) upside down. He shot Euphoria an accusing glance.

'I stuck the stamps on in the dark. I do apologize for any offence I may have caused,' she said lying her little pointed ears off.

She knew it was one of her father's many silly acts of rebellion against the monarchy and the oligarchy of wizards. *Daddy will get himself in trouble one of these days!* She thought to herself.

She placed the letters behind the counter to read when she had a spare moment from serving customers, which seemed like forever. Eventually, a lull in trade gave her the chance to look at them. Two were for her father, three for her.

She carefully read the reverse of the envelopes. The first had the return address as Assyria Neepfield, C/O The Benevolent Society for Poor Goblins, 42 Great Goblin Street. *Great Goblin Street is just around the corner,* he could have saved himself a stamp. The second had a return address of Lady Virginia Chanson, Society Correspondent, The Fashionable Intelligencer, Upper Cripplegate, and the third was from Dr. Apricot of Cat Fishing Street.

She felt so excited that the Intelligencer had replied to her job application, and that Dr. Apricot had replied to her request for magical cosmetic medicine, but in keeping with the goblin adage of 'saving the best until last', she decided to open Assyria's letter first. *It's another of his stupid poems,* she thought. It read:

Across the swaggering crowns of a stormy sea
In the bird's melody from the morning hedgerow
Within the careless innocence of my schoolboy hymns
And the music of Star Dragons played out in purest thought
I hear your song

While walking a seaside promenade on a boiling summer's day
And in the sweaty air of a thundery night
Over the white roasting sands of desert dunes
And through steamy green jungles dark and dank
I feel your warmth

In the pregnant orchards of imagination
And in radiant colour frozen into crystal truth
Guided by the still whisper of conscience
Cradled safely in the faithful arms of justice
You hold me safe

Within the easy laughter of old friendships
Through the fragrance of roasting cinnamon
Over the happy purr of my contented cat
And between her claws, and petite fangs
I call out to you

In the heart soaring wonder of discovery
And in the tender amnesties of encouragement
By the unspoken oath in a lover's gaze

On liberty's vibrant wings
I seek your heart

In the radiant harvest of creation
Within the misty tenderness of fraternity
And in the golden bubbles of joy
Rising softly in a glass of happiness
I touch your soul

She liked the poem; what she did not realize was that it started to set down roots in her. It began to grow in her mind in more ways than she imagined. She knew all too well, upward social mobility is far more important to a goblinette than silly romance, so she put all thoughts of Assyria Neepfield and his foolish poems aside. But the poem was not going to put her aside, it was a magical poem, and it had plans for Miss Euphoria Fireheart.

She opened her second letter, from Dr. Apricot's surgery. It read:

Dear Miss Fireheart

As you are aware, his majesty the Goblin King has made funds available to heal sick and poor goblins who could not otherwise afford medicine.

You have applied for these funds to pay for cosmetic magical surgery to look like an elf.

From this, I infer you are too poor to pay for the surgery yourself. Looking like a goblin does not make you sick, so you do not fulfil the necessary criteria of being both a sick and poor goblin. You are simply a poor goblin with aspirations that exceed your position in society. Accordingly, Dr. Apricot has refused your application for pro bono medicine.

Please do contact us in future should you either fall sick or come by money.

Yours faithfully

Mme. Deliria Grimbrow, Receptionist (1st class) to Dr. Apricot.

She was cross at the tone of Mme. Grimbrow's letter, especially at being referred to as poor. But she still had the most important letter to read, which gave her hope. She eagerly opened up the letter from the newspaper, praying in her little goblin heart that she got the position she had applied for:

Dear Miss Fireheart

Thank you for your application to be my assistant, with a view to train as a society correspondent at the Fashionable Intelligencer. You tell me you work at your father's newsstand and read the Intelligencer every day. I commend your good taste in reading material, and applaud your desire for social advancement; but coming as you do from such humble stock, I cannot help but think that as a daughter of a newsagent, you would have more chance of success in life were you to stick to selling newspapers rather than trying to write for them.

I must reject your application for this position, and wish you every success in a career more suited to your breeding and origin.

Yours sincerely

Lady Chanson, Society Correspondent, Fashionable Intelligencer.

Euphoria felt a hollow in her belly and had to stop herself from crying. *Will I ever get on in life, or will I always be as common as cobblestones?* She thought to herself.

A tall gentlegoblin interrupted her misery. From his fashion sense, it was clear to her that he was a goblin of standing. He wore an ochre jacket with a white collar-less shirt and a green silk cravat.

After the humiliation of the letters, she really needed a moment to herself. She decided not to serve him. She looked away from him, and when she did, from the corner of her eye she saw a demon. It was a fleeting thing, and therefore almost certainly an illusion, but in that brief instant, his face was all fangs and insect's eyes.

'May I enquire if you are Miss. Euphoria Fireheart?'

'What is it to you?' she snapped, still angry at the rejection letters, and frightened at the momentary apparition.

'I have a letter for Mr. Assyria Neepfield, may I give it to you to pass to him?'

'You may.' Euphoria snatched the letter.

'I hear that Mr. Neepfield writes poems to you Miss Fireheart. If this is the case, I would like to buy one,' said the stranger.

Euphoria wondered how a strange goblin had found out her business. She did not like the idea that he knew she received poems from Assyria, but she did need some money for a new dress. She had seen one she liked in the shop window of Ambrosia Woodstock's haberdashers on Great Goblin Avenue.

'Which poem did you have in mind?'

'I will pay you fifty pounds for the letter containing the poem entitled *The Hubris of Draska.*' He counted out ten crisp five-pound notes and placed them on the counter. It was a vast sum.

'Done,' said Euphoria without hesitation. She kept her correspondence in the pages of her favourite copy of *Society Elf*. Pulling out the pile of poems, she searched through them for the 'Draska', handed it to the toff and took the money quick.

'Thank you, Miss. Good to do business with you. I wish you good morning,' said the posh fellow.

Mercurial Frostdrop entered the kiosk with a cup of cocoa for her friend just before the goblin left, 'I do not like the look of that one Euphoria,' she said.

'Well he did strike me as an odd fellow, but £50 is not to be sniffed at.'

6

*An **Arcane Connection** is a magical link from one object to another object, or person, by the Law of Contagion. Possession of an Arcane Connection facilitates spell casting on the entity it connects to. For example, the possession of a clipping from a goblin's finger nail, or an artist's favorite paint brush, makes it easier to affect the goblin, or artist, with magic.*

The Law of Contagion: *Put simply, 'Once together, always together'. Objects and people which were once part of a whole, or are emotionally or creatively connected, remain magically connected to each other after separation. By this principle arcane connections are made.*

Excerpts from **Magic Theory and Practice 4th Edition**

***

Pharaoh Henry stopped walking. He stood stock still in the street, paralyzed by a wave of guilt. The lady goblin he was about to visit needed his help, but he had been too busy to assist her. Now that he needed her help, he found the time. She was a good goblinette and he was wrong to treat her that way.

He slid his hand into his coat pocket to feel the key Constable Pinch had found in the ashes. He frowned on the realisation that the vampires who stole the book must be part of a satanic cabal. The book **Keys to the Dark Gate** could open up a gate to Hell itself, so he needed to find the coven before demons invaded the city.

He planned he could use the key to locate Ephemeral's lair. His reasoning went: Every key has an associated lock. This key belonged to the vampires and will fit the lock somewhere in their nest. If the association between the key and the lock is strong enough then an arcane connection will have formed between them. Therefore, he needed to find someone with the right magical skills to divine which lock belonged to that key, and then in turn, he would have the door to the vampire's nest.

He hurried down Troll's Bonnet Street to the business premises of the diviner he had in mind. Every shop in the Metropolis had a sign, and most were painted in magical pigment and well looked after. The paint of number 32 was flaked and shabby, but still legible, it read:

Miss Vanilla Catchpenny.
Professional Wizard. Auguries and soul migration divination undertaken to the customer's satisfaction.
No job too small or fiddly.

The dirty shop sign read 'Open'. He pushed the door; it was locked. He looked through the window, but could not see through the glass, which was grimy with the residue of manna fog. *Poor Vanilla is on her way down*, thought Henry. He banged on the door and waited for 10 minutes, then he banged again. No-one came, so he kept banging.

After what seemed like an age, he spotted the small shape of Vanilla from behind the dirty glass. She unlocked the door; he opened it, which creaked for want of oil, to let himself in.

She slumped down in a chair, exhausted. At 4' 1", she was a hauntingly beautiful goblin lady, in a ghostly sort of way. Her skin was a pale whitish-blue, and her face expressionless. She looked altogether lifeless. Today she wore her purple-coloured dress uncorseted, it was the same unwashed dress she wore yesterday. She slouched over her dusty table supporting herself with her elbows, her frail skeletal frame bent over.

It was Vanilla's eyes that were her strangest features; they seemed to be black, or at least a very dark shade of blue, flecked with tiny dots of silver. They looked like deep seas of darkness dotted with tiny specs of light. Her eyes had mutated because of an accident with the mind-altering drug called alapania. It had caused her to see the entire galaxy in her mind in a single instant, which had driven her mad for a while. Now Vanilla's eyes had no whites, or pupils or irises. Instead each contained an eye-sized image of the galaxy, which is most unsettling to any unprepared goblin who looked into them.

On hearing of the accident, Henry had paid for magical doctors to restore most of her sanity. Still, to this day, Vanilla remained a burnt-out husk of her former self, and only came to life when drugged with yet more alapania.

Alapania, the augurist drug extracted from the gnomescap mushroom, and it is sucking the life from Vanilla, thought Henry. 'Villy, you are taking too much.'

'Just tell me what you want, Grand Master, then please go and leave me alone,' she slurred through her foggy stupor.

'I need your help Villy.'

'My help? Don't you have magicians to help you? Elijah Pencil and that pretty goblinette, Condolence some-one-or-other, I can't remember her name.'

Henry looked away to hide his expression of guilt. 'Both dead,' he said.

'You always manage to get goblins to help you some way or other. You have your ways. Don't you have anyone?'

'Yes, I have Joseph Hightower and Enigma Oates.'

'Then ask them to help you.'

'I sent them on a mission to investigate vampire attacks, neither of them has reported back yet.'

'God help them,' said Vanilla.

'Well I am sure I will hear from them soon,' said Henry.

There was a long and strained silence. 'So Pharaoh Henry, how can a burned-out husk like me help you with your noble cause today?'

'Can you tell me if this has an arcane connection?' Said Henry, as he held out the brass key.

She took the key, held it in her hand, then closed her eyes in concentration. 'I cannot feel anything. Perhaps if I had some, but I have none, nor money to buy any.'

Henry had come prepared for this predictable response. He opened his satchel, and removed a small tin filled with alapania, and placed it in her outreached palm. She brewed up a pot of the narcotic, then poured the mauve tea into an unwashed teacup and drank it down thirstily. It was good; apothecary grade, not the cut black-market product she was used to. In moments, the fog cleared from her mind, and some of her life energy returned to her. Her body straightened and her face animated.

Vanilla held the key in her hand again, but this time her fingers showed practice to them, 'You are in luck Pharaoh. I sense a strong arcane connection now.'

She took a street map from her shelf, blew off the dust, laid it on the coffee table and unrolled it. Then she threaded a silver chain through the key to make a pendulum. As she moved the key over the map it started to swing in a circle, locating the position of the lock that was linked to it by the arcane connection.

'Peccadillo Street. That is where you will find the lock for this key.'

'Can you be more specific?'

'No, not unless I physically go to the road on which the building stands.'

Henry nodded assent, so she put on her cloak and hat. She locked her shop door, then linked onto Henry's arm and together they walked up Troll's Bonnet Street, up Great Goblin Street, across The Great Wish Road, to reach Peccadillo Street.

As they passed number 17, she felt the key vibrate very slightly in her hand. In silence she shot Henry a glance to indicate the location of the vampire's nest.

'Can you tell me anything else?' asked Henry.

Vanilla stood stock still in concentration.

'It's terrible! There is a torture chamber in the basement, some sort of pit. They are in intense pain. You must help them,' she said, her face screwed up in distress.

Henry held her up, supporting her lifeless body to help walk her away from the source of the agonizing psychic link.

'That's far enough. I need to sit down,' she said.

Henry carefully sat her down on a doorstep, where she started to sob.

'Are you going to be alright,' Henry asked.

Vanilla did not answer. She looked exhausted.

'Villy, how long since you last ate?'

'Forgotten.'

'I am going to have to take more care of you. Otherwise, that drug will have the better of you.'

'It has me on the mat already Master Henry,' she said, then let out a resigned sigh.

Henry held Vanilla's hand, and led her into the Green Dragon Café, where they sat at a small table at the back. Vanilla had not washed for days and was too unkempt for this establishment. Still he wanted her to eat something.

The waiter glanced at Henry, his involuntary expression revealed his dilemma: A dirty and bedraggled goblinette would bring down the reputation of the café. On the other hand, he knew who Henry was, and could not ask the couple to leave.

The waiter rushed over to serve them, not knowing quite what to do.

Henry thought that diplomacy was best. 'Two bowls of porridge with ochreberrys and honey, and two pots of tea please, and could you move us to a private table somewhere out of the way?'

'Certainly Sir,' said the waiter, who looked relieved at getting this smelly goblinette away from his regular respectable clientele. He led Vanilla and Henry to a small private room, from where he dashed off to get their order.

'Villy, that drug is killing you the way you take it. I need to intervene in your life for your own good. From now on, each day I will make sure there is clean pure alapania at Oakensoul's College for you. But you must also wash and eat while you are there.'

Vanilla looked thankful, but then an aspect of weariness came over her again. The alapania was starting to wear off already. *She has built up too much dependency on the drug. I have lost her when I should have taken care of her,* thought Henry.

7

If there were no hopes or tears,
Nor music from the spheres,
There would be no tunes for an angel's ears.

An ancient saying dating back at least as far as the primordial elves. Modern magical philosophers cannot agree as to its meaning.

***

Prudence spun around violently.

Dizzy and confused she realised Cornucopia had grabbed her by her shoulder and turned her, 'You are to report to the pit immediately.'

Prudence froze. She had been given a direct order, passed down senior vampire to a subordinate. Panic filled her unbeating heart. *Am I to be thrown in?* Awful images shot through her mind of the pit, a dark stinking hole of torment. Undead corpses wailing in agony, writhing together in filth, feeding off each other, and being fed off. Sent insane by their thirst for blood. *Will I be there soon?*

Thoughts of escape raced through her mind. She glanced to the front door; its guard looked back at her knowingly. He was one step ahead of her. There was no way out.

'Now,' commanded Cornucopia. She smiled her special smile that foretold of cruelty

Prudence made her way to the lowest basement. That was where the pit was, and beside it stood the great bronze statue of Lucifer. A faint smell of incense persisted in the air around the summoning circle. Her clever vampire nose could even tell how long ago it had burned. *They have been worshipping the Devil recently. They must have visited the nest just before midnight, and had left a couple of hours later,* she thought. *Mortal Luciferians in a vampire's nest?* That was unusual.

A living goblinette stood by the pit's edge. She had been captured earlier in the evening, and was now bound up in magical silk.

The entire nest had assembled to watch what was to happen, and before them stood Ephemeral Wormsong, Queen of the Vampires.

They are here to see a spectacle, I must be going in the pit, thought Prudence. Her stomach felt hollow with fear.

'Stand by the goblinette,' ordered Wormsong, while looking at Prudence.

Prudence caught hold of the captive's arm as she staggered, *Exhaustion from lack of blood.*

'Remove the cap.'

The heavy bolt that secured the pit cover gave out a metallic creak. She put her fingers under the rim of the cap. Her goblin frame struggled to lift its heavy weight, and after she had opened it so the putrid stench of the necrotic bodies filled the room. The cries of the victims penetrated into her soul.

'Now throw my captive in,' ordered Wormsong.

Prudence was unable to move. Transfixed by the horror of her mistress's order.

'Throw her in,' commanded Wormsong, carefully and calmly.

Prudence stood motionless, disobeying her mistress for what seemed like an eternity. She imagined that Ephemeral Wormsong's heart would seethe with anger at her insubordination, but she did not show it. Rather her queen remained perfectly calm and composed, without the slightest expression on her face. *What was going on in the mistress's mind? What will she do to me?*

'Cornucopia, throw the captive in,' said Wormsong.

Of course, Cornucopia obeyed without hesitation. The goblinette let out a miserable whine as she fell into the terrible hole.

The pit fiends below growled and howled at the fresh living blood. All the spectator vampires laughed, except Prudence and Wormsong. Prudence did not laugh as she knew she would be next, and Wormsong did not because she was more interested in Prudence.

Then something unexpected happened. Wormsong approached them both, and as Prudence braced herself, Wormsong threw Cornucopia into the pit instead of Prudence.

'Well Cornucopia did not expect that!' said Wormsong with a smile.

Wormsong watched as Prudence stiffened with fear, she wanted to cry.

'Are you going to sob my poor Prudence?'

Prudence was too afraid to respond. Wormsong slapped her

hard across her face.

'Come on Prudence sob for me. If you cry, I will throw you in the pit too,' said Wormsong with a look of glee, 'You're weak Prudence! It amuses me to see you so afraid. Replace the cap.'

This time Prudence did as she was told.

'Hurry up.'

Prudence summoned all her strength and closed it.

'Come with me,' said Wormsong.

Prudence followed Wormsong, who led her out of the colony house. When they reached the corner of Peccadillo Street and Great Goblin Street, Wormsong threw Prudence against a brick wall. Her body tensed, arching away from her queen and persecutor.

'The captive now enjoying the hospitality of my pit was one Miss Enigma Oates. She was a demon hunting wizard who worked for our enemy, Pharaoh Henry. Have you heard of him?' asked Wormsong.

'Yes Ma'am,' said Prudence.

'I thought that Cornucopia had disobeyed me, and had let Emmanuel Scribble live. Now I am not so sure. I commanded her to tell me what she remembered from the raid. She told me that she had not killed the bookseller, nor could she explain her disobedience. She got the pit, despite showing such promise, because I needed to make an example of her. But I am starting to think she was not responsible, and I will get to the bottom of this,' said Wormsong, 'It was you who let Scribble live was it not?'

'Yes Ma'am,' said Prudence.

'You showed a mortal compassion, why?'

Prudence could not answer.

'Before I became a vampire queen, when I was still alive, I flew. I competed to develop, build and race pioneering ornithopters. But I was never so naive as to be a sporting goblinette. When I wanted to win, I cheated. I put other goblins down to make sure they were below me, even when it would have been easier to spend that same effort to raise myself up. I enjoyed sabotaging their flying machines more than improving my own, and swindling them out of business greater than winning contracts fairly. I want to be better than others, and prefer to do so by putting others down. Then one day out of the blue it happened; I became the first vampire in the Metropolis. Initially I resented my awful disease, so I set about spreading it to others, to ensure they were as cursed as I. I like to harm and humiliate and particularly I dislike you Prudence because you just do not seem nasty enough. But vampirism is not a disease, it's a blessing. Cruelty and the domination of others is truth; compassion is the lie. And now you tell me that you, a vampire showed compassion to a mortal. Actually, it's rather funny. Well you cannot be kind. It is not possible for a goblin in your position. You are the hunter of goblins, and the hunted of wizards, you must kill to feed, and that is the lesson you must learn.'

'Yes, Ma'am,' said Prudence.

'Compassion is not for you now Prudence. You are a vampire. Power over others is your goal, if it is not then you will remain at the bottom of the pyramid, and be the bitch of every vampire above you. Do you want that?'

'No Ma'am.'

'Do you know what the forces of goodness will do to you if they capture you? Have you any idea what Pharaoh Henry is capable of?'

'He will torture me?'

'You are a vampire who kills to feed, he will destroy you. And if he has time, if he captures you undestroyed, he will torment you.'

Prudence felt the fear of Pharaoh Henry wash over her.

'If you want to remain safe in the colony, I want to see an end to your foolish notions of compassion, do you understand?'

Prudence nodded.

'So, let's see a bit more cruelty from you Prudence. I know you can do it. Keep your eyes peeled for the law,' said Wormsong.

'Yes, Madam Wormsong, I will,' Prudence whined, instantly feeling ashamed of her own subservience.

Wormsong caught Prudence by the throat, 'Yes, Madam Wormsong, I will,' she said in imitation. 'I don't want to see you at my nest until first light.' She threw Prudence backwards, releasing her grip; then she turned and walked back down Peccadillo Street with a strut that told the world she owned it.

There was no wind tonight, and the fog lay thick and smooth, blanketing the cobblestones. Prudence caught sight of a strange breeze that ruffled the fog. It was gentle enough, but there was something paradoxical and unnatural about it, especially on this still morning.

Goblin costermongers began to gather around the corner of Great Goblin Street and Arcadia Square. She looked over at the traders unloading their barrows with boxes of fruit. She wished she could still be part of the mortal world again, but knew that for her there could only be oblivion.

Across the square stood the tower of the Society of Alchemists. Its huge illuminated clock showed five thirty-five, *10 minutes before sunrise,* thought Prudence. *Perhaps I should wait until dawn and just die, it would be quicker than the pit. What existence do I have? I am without hope. But if I die at sunrise will I go straight to Hell?*

She understood her position very well. She was a vampire, separated from the shelter of goblin society, without protection or liberties under law. Even her eternal salvation was lost to her. She felt nothing but the fear that ate her mind.

But Prudence did have a friend; a chocolate-coloured cat called Lampwick, and tonight he would save her soul.

Lampwick meowed from the shadows then sped along the wall to meet her. His orange eyes glowed especially brightly. She tried to stroke him, but he arched his back and meowed a complaint.

'What's wrong with you Lampwick?' asked Prudence.

Lampwick stared directly at her face, his marmalade eyes met her black irises, and when he did, his soul locked with hers.

'Pay attention Prudence, this is an urgent matter,' Lampwick projected.

Prudence almost jumped in surprise. *'Lampwick, you are a telepathic cat!'* She thought back.

'Goblins are closing in on you - Hunters. They know you are a vampire. They will destroy you'.

'Who is coming Lampwick?'

'Wizards and soldiers. Lots of soldiers and they will kill you and your kind. You must go down into the tunnels quickly. I will follow and help you escape. No time to explain. Hurry Prudence, run. Go now!'

She scanned Arcadia Square. If there was a threat, she could not see it. No wizards or soldiers or anything else untoward for that matter. *But is something hiding in the fog? What can Lampwick see that I cannot?* Without further ado, she raced to the nearest tunnel entrance and flew down its stairs.

Once at the bottom, she came face to face with a goblin policeman coming the other way. He jumped in surprise, and looked more afraid of her than she was of him. She ran past him.

A pistol cracked loudly form behind, the shot shattered white porcelain wall tiles to her front. Fear gripped her. On she ran, faster than she thought she could. The rhythmic tramp of marching goblins told tale of soldiers ahead of her. *They will kill me.* There was a small side tunnel ahead, *can I escape down it?* It was her only chance, but it meant running towards the soldiers.

The marching became louder until she could see them, three abreast, blocking the way ahead. They stopped. The first rank levelled their muskets directly at her.

'Don't shoot, you could hit me!' shouted the police officer from behind her. His voice quivered with fear that echoed down the underpass.

When Prudence got to the entrance of the side tunnel, the line of bayonets were just feet away. Turning on the spot, she fled down the dark passage. From behind her an officer barked orders.

As she ran, from behind her came the sound of heavy footfall and rattling equipment. Soldiers were chasing her. She heard a yowl of a cat, a crackle of musketry, and the clatter of accoutrements from tumbling soldiers.

She did not look back. On she sped, going deeper; following the darkest and narrowest tunnels whenever she could. Eventually, she found a place to crouch in a dark narrow cul-de-sac, where she hid in the dense fog, as would a frightened creature, watching, waiting and listening.

Lampwick's reflective orange eyes shone bright, even through the fog.

'*Prudence, do you know Fireheart's the newsagent in Arcadia Square?*' Lampwick said with his mind.

'*I do.*'

'*I will take you to him. You must tell him a fib. Tell him that you are a revolutionary goblinette escaping political persecution, so he will hide you and keep you safe.*'

'*Thank you Lampwick, you are my only friend.*' Prudence rubbed her pale fingers into his deep chocolate coloured fur.

8

The Principle of Creativity:
There is an old wizard's adage (often misattributed to Grand
Master Jeremiah Seelykin) that captures the meaning of the
principle of creativity: 'Both magic and creative works alike
spring from the mind and the soul'. The corollary to this
principle is, of course, that good art is itself magical, which is
why every painting, song, and story of worth, casts its own
spell.

Excerpt from **Magic Theory and Practice** 4th Edition

***

Euphoria woke up too early. She felt longings for Mr. Neepfield, and knew it would come to no good. Worse still, her urges kept her awake.

She got out of bed, took a shower, and put on her new dress. She looked at herself in her full-length mirror, posing as an elf. She liked the iridescence of the dragon green colour, an effect only recently made possible since the advent of modern magical dyes. Euphoria Fireheart was fashionable, even by the competitive standards of a young goblinette.

Assyria Neepfield's poem had ensorcelled her with a love charm, but she did not know it. For that matter, neither did the poem's author and spell caster, who was unaware he could even cast a spell. Assyria had simply written her a poem to express his love for her, and now she could not get either him or the poem off her mind. The poem had woken Euphoria up at 4:30 am, forced her to dress; marched her out of her home; and set her to search the city for him at some ungodly hour before sunrise.

She navigated her way across Arcadia Square, past the costermongers dressing their barrows for their day's work ahead.

'I'll thank you for a bag of fairyfigs and four ounces of gnomenuts,' she said to a barrow boy.

'That will be thrupence Miss,' stammered the young goblin, who was so enamoured with Euphoria that he gave her extra.

From the corner of Great Goblin Street and Peccadillo Street, she glimpsed a pale goblinette fleeing down a tunnel entrance, followed by Lampwick, the chocolate-coloured cat who lived at her father's newsagents. Euphoria's doll-like face broke into surprise at the scene, 'Lampwick! Come here!'

Lampwick ignored her completely; after all, he was a cat. She watched as he chased down the tunnel after the goblinette, from where the sound of a shot rang out.

She worried if either the goblinette or Lampwick had been injured, but decided any investigation would be far too dangerous. Instead, she pressed on down Great Goblin Street, her destination was the Benevolent Society for Poor Goblins. She found Assyria in a line of ragged goblins queueing for rootneep soup.

He was a tall goblin fellow of almost 5' in height, with short cut brown hair and purple eyes. Many goblinettes considered Mr. Neepfield to be a handsome chap (at least when he tidied himself up a bit); but tonight he was lifeless; as if his misfortune had washed the very life and soul out of him.

Euphoria pulled on Assyria's arm, but he resisted leaving the queue. She tugged at him, until he reluctantly gave up his long-established (and important) place for soup, a place immediately filled by the next hungry goblin.

To be out of earshot of the crowds, the outraged Euphoria marched her despondent Assyria to a quiet spot.

'Mr. Neepfield you're begging shall doubtless cause me vicarious social disgrace as seen from our well-known association. I am distressed by the very speculation of who saw this, and the adverse social consequences it might have on my once exemplary reputation!' complained Euphoria.

'I lost my job; I need something to eat.'

'Hardly justification for the embarrassment you have caused me Mr. Neepfield, but given the gravity of your unjustifiable disregard toward proper social principles, I am forced to intervene, even at the risk of being implicated as a pauper's associate, by taking you in. There are some rooms in the deep caves under my father's newsagents where you can sleep for now. I have some fruit and nuts for you to eat until breakfast time when we will eat porridge.'

'Thank you so much,' said Assyria.

To keep up proper appearances, and not to be seen by all and sundry with a penniless goblin, she led him to her father's newsagents by the most discreet route possible. They went through the deepest of the tunnels, which were dark and almost empty at this time of the early morning.

Deep tunnels could be dangerous and Euphoria felt afraid of what might be hiding in the murk. Some nights Euphoria had heard the eerie howls of werewolves' echoing from miles away down in the abandoned caves beneath. It unnerved her.

Before they could reach Fireheart's newsagents, they found their way blocked by two heavily loaded carts. One was pushed by an ogre, the other drawn by a donkey led by its goblin owner, and they argued. Fearing some accident or altercation, Euphoria pulled Assyria into a side alley to get out of the way until the traffic cleared.

As Euphoria stood in the cover of the tunnel, hidden by a curtain of magical fog, Assyria put his hands around her slender waist and kissed her. Needless to say, she was taken aback by this scandalous act of affection from an unknown poet. Indeed, it was such a shock to her sensibilities that she found herself inadvertently responding to his improper advances in a most embarrassing and awkward manner. It took some ~~minutes~~ moments before Euphoria gathered her wits about her to break free from his outrageous embrace.

'I demand you desist from that at once, Mr. Neepfield! You are not behaving as a gentlegoblin,' reproached Euphoria in a state of hot flustered excitement.'

'Please forgive me Euphoria. I could not help myself,' said Assyria.

When the carts cleared, they made their way down the last few yards to the deepest underground entrance of Fireheart's newsstand. Later on, it would be busy down in the tunnels, because this was where the newspapers and books were delivered to Fireheart's from Great Goblin Railway station. But it was now just after sunrise, and there were few goblins around this early, so it struck Euphoria as rather odd to see light creeping from around the edges of the service door.

Not knowing what to expect, Euphoria unlocked the door and opened it. To her surprise, her father was standing in the cellar talking with Lampwick the cat, who had shape changed into goblin form. With them was the very same pale goblinette Euphoria had seen dashing away on Peccadillo Street earlier.

'Ah Euphoria there you are, this brave young lady's name is Prudence Pepperhill. She is a sister revolutionary escaping the royalist police. We are going to keep our new fellow socialist safe,' announced Zebedee Fireheart with the happy smile of a political zealot.

As an aspiring socialite, Euphoria found her father's socialism awkward. But she knew she was not going to win an argument about politics with that stubborn old goblin, who despite being a successful businessman, knew nothing of modern polite society.

'Well, this is a revelation. Did you hear the shot ring out from the tunnel off of Arcadia gardens?' Euphoria asked the goblinette.

'They were shooting at me. Lampwick helped me escape,' said Prudence.

This was all too much, Euphoria thought, *Shots in the night indeed! The wrong kind of goblins live in the neighbourhood nowadays, they don't have any sense of decorum; it brings down the tone of the whole borough!* This gave Euphoria an idea. She saw an opportunity to use this situation to get Assyria Neepfield under her all too socialist fathers' roof.

'They shot at our poor Sister Prudence! Indeed, I witnessed it all as I endeavoured to rescue Brother Assyria. The police almost apprehended him too. He has been writing political poems you see, becoming a thorn in the side of the oppressive wizards. So many activists arrested tonight, a roundabout so to speak. It is so awful the way they persecute the working goblins who fight for liberty and justice.'

Zebedee Fireheart fell for it.

'Oh, that's terrible Assyria,' said Zebedee, 'You will have to stay with us a few nights until things calm down. You and Prudence can keep each other company while you hide with us. Are you hungry my young hero? I must ask Mercurial to send down some porridge for you and Prudence. That will warm you up. You can have the room next to Prudence, just down the hallway.'

'Thank you, Mr. Fireheart. You are most kind Sir,' said Assyria.

'Call me Brother Zebedee.'

Zebedee looked into Euphoria's face, and said 'It is so nice to hear you take an interest in the cause Euphoria, you have spent far too long on trivial matters such as gossip and fashion.'

Euphoria smiled back at her father with an expression of unblemished innocence on her face, and said nothing.

9

Think of the dimensions of the universe we live in: Length, breadth, height and time. It is huge beyond our imagination. So big it would take billions of years for a beam of light to cross it. You are all training to become dimension wizards, and create 'little pocket universes', each with their own limited space and time. You will soon find out the difficulty and expense needed to build even these, and then you will realise how great God is to have created our universe.

Opening statement from the **Christmas Lecture on Dimension Magic**, delivered by Grand Master Absalom Gentlespell.

***

As Ephemeral Wormsong threatened Prudence on the corner of Peccadillo Street and Arcadian Gardens, neither of the vampires imagined that three wizards were eves-dropping on their conversation with deadly intent. Their spy point was a small balcony on the tower of the Society of Alchemist's, on the opposite side of the Square. Although some distance away, the wizards could hear everything said and done by means of a spell called **Voices on the Wind.** It carried the sounds of Prudence and Wormsong on a gentle breeze that ruffled the manna fog, and confused Prudence.

One of the wizards was Pharaoh Henry. By his side stood Reverend Noah Bentley, who, as well as being a wizard, was the congenial vicar of the church of All Souls in the Wardrobe, member of parliament, and a prolific vampire hunter to boot. He dressed in a vicar's dog collar and black jacket. He walked with a limp for which he needed a walking stick, which doubled as a sword-stick, its silver blade discreetly hidden. Carrying swords in public has long been out of fashion in goblin society, not to say uncouth, so his stick enabled him to mingle with polite goblins, yet still dispatch a vampire should need arise.

The third wizard was Emmanuel Scribble.

'That pale goblinette, I have this half-formed memory about her,

I cannot remember the detail. Possibly she saved my life,' said Scribble.

'I have never heard of a vampire showing compassion, why would she let you live?' said Bentley.

'That would be an interesting question to put to her if we could capture her, but all units are in place and it's too late to change the order: Destroy all vampires on sight, no exceptions,' said Henry.

'Who is helping you tonight Pharaoh? Are Joseph Hightower and Enigma Oates with the soldiers?' asked Bentley.

'Still missing.'

'Oh no. You are losing too many goblins Pharaoh.'

'I only have a policeman to help me now, PC Pinch, and he worries me. He wanted us to split up when we investigated the vampire attack at Scribbles,' said Henry.

'Hmm, sounds like a goblin with more courage than sense to me.' Bentley's expression betrayed his exasperation at the stupidity and recklessness of inexperienced hunters.

'You are right; still, we need more demon hunting wizards. I have permission and funding from the King to recruit some. The attack on Scribble's book shop has caused quite a stir in political circles,' said Henry.

'Glad to hear you have the money, but where will you find the volunteers? Who wants to fight demons anymore? There are easier and better ways to make a living by magic.' said Bentley.

Pharaoh Henry looked back at Bentley with a heavy look of guilt. He had sent many good goblins to their deaths. But what else could he have done? Demons and vampires must be fought.

As the three wizards watched the vampire goblinettes from afar, it was clear who had the whip hand.

'Pretty young girl that goblinette, no doubt one of Wormsong's minions, it seems a shame to destroy such a thing of beauty,' said Scribble to Bentley.

'She wouldn't look so handsome watching her suck the last drop of life from your veins.'

The magical breeze conveyed the sound of the voices of Wormsong and Prudence from across the distant and noisy square: 'Keep your eyes peeled for the law' Wormsong threatened, 'Yes Madam Wormsong, I will,' whimpered the goblinette.

She seems too timid to fight. Best dispatch her quickly and compassionately, thought Henry.

'It is time for me to go Noah. I will be invisible and silent, so don't let some half-witted ogrebrain shoot me or run me over with something,' said Henry.

Pharaoh Henry was not by nature a tidy goblin, but he recognized good organization was essential for a raid where stealth and timing were critical.

With this in mind he had carefully planned the logistics of the raid with Noah, and laid out the equipment he was going to need for his mission on a table. On his check list was a rope, a single action revolver loaded for vampire, a box of 36 extra rounds of ammunition, eight flasks of holy water, a watch, a bottle with its stopper, the brass key found in the ashes, another magic key, a small dimension box, some cloves of garlic, and a flight feather from a speckled phoenix. Lastly, and perhaps most important of all, his silver knife.

He carefully placed the rope, revolver, ammunition, water, garlic and dimension box inside his satchel. He found his satchel indispensable for his everyday life, as it had a pocket dimension incorporated in its design. This pocket had the capacity to hold a vastly greater volume of things than physically possible from its mundane size. Retrieving items from it was also aided with magic, all he had to do was put his hand inside, think of the item he wanted, then pull it out.

He took the small bottle, stopped it with its cork, then placed it inside his jacket pocket. Stopping the bottle activated the spell of odorlessness on him. Until the bottle was opened or smashed, Pharaoh Henry had no smell, even his blood could not be sniffed out by a vampire's clever nose.

Henry placed the phoenix feather in his cap, which magically silenced him. Many wizards nowadays need to cast spells in a booming voice and flamboyant gestures so to add power to them. As impressive as loud and dramatic spell casting might appear to mundane goblins, noisy magic is something of a handicap in situations where stealth is necessary. Henry, through years of hard practice, could cast a spell in silence, using only the most subtle of hand gestures.

Hanging on the door was an invisibility cloak. He threw it around his shoulders and disappeared from sight. Lastly, he picked up his sharp well-used knife, and held it in his hand, ready for action.

Now undetectable to any mundane senses, he made his way

down the stairs with great care to avoid accidents.

He looked at the huge clock face on the tower behind him, and checked the time, it was 5:35 am, and today the sun would rise at 5:45. The soldiers should all be in place, sunrise will be in 10 minutes, time to start the attack. The battle had begun.

Invisible and in silence, he approached the goblinette on the corner intent on dispatching her. She looked around her for a threat she could not see or hear. He was almost on her, just about to slit her throat, when without warning or reason, she darted towards the tunnel entrance on Great Goblin Street, followed by some small dark animal. Henry chased after her a little way, but she was faster. She dashed down the stairs into the subway.

He let her escape. *What spooked that one? How did she know I was coming?* thought Henry, *'Better leave her to Pinch'.*

Seconds later a shot rang out from inside the tunnel.

Well, that's her dealt with, shame in a way, she was a handsome one, but Bentley is right, we must destroy vampires, he thought.

Henry pressed on down Peccadillo Street until he reached number 17, the house of Ephemeral Wormsong. Outside a vampire goblinette was keeping watch. This time his target did not run away, or display any suspicion of what was about to happen to her. He stabbed her in the heart. Only in the last instant of her existence did she express fear. She erupted into a flame of blue fire, then crumbled to ashes.

He took the key from his satchel, inserted it into the lock and opened the door. *We are in the vampire's nest, now the real fight begins!*

The entrance hall led onto a parlour where seven vampires sat in armchairs. They sipped blood from small expensive wine glasses. The former owner of the blood was Joseph Hightower, who lay curled in a foetal position on a rug, too exhausted from blood loss to move.

'You will die tonight, the question is whether our mistress wants you back as one of us, or not. Of course, worse still she could throw you in the pit,' a beautiful vampire goblinette said to Joseph.

'Ah the pit, full of thirsty vampires feeding on each other. Our mistress might throw you in there, and your pit mates will drink the last few drops of your blood. You will become as they are, forever thirsty, having to drink their sour vampiric blood, as they drink yours. You will suffer the never-ending torture of thirst never satiated, without the relief of final destruction,' gloated a suave young male vampire.

Henry walked past the group undetected, then made his way to the staircase, where he descended to the kitchens below. The kitchen staff were not vampires. Weakness caused by heavy blood loss prevented them from escaping, and collars around their necks acted as magical alarms, and would alert their masters should they try to leave the kitchen.

A vampire guard sat in a chair to watch over them. Henry dispatched it quickly and quietly. The staff looked around. They were too dazed, weak and apathetic to appreciate what was happening.

Henry took off his magical cloak and removed the feather from his cap, so as to become visible and audible. He silently led the staff into a small pantry. Out of his satchel, he took five garlic bulbs and two flasks of holy water and gave them to the goblins.

'Eat a bulb of garlic each, and splash on some water. It will help keep you safe. Be quiet and do not open the door,' whispered Henry. He shut and locked the door.

Will that pantry door hold against the ravenous hunger of the tortured pit fiends? He thought.

He donned the cloak and feather again and took the stairs further down to the lowest basement. He saw the large iron cap of the pit, beside a bronze statue of Lucifer.

On the opposite side of the room, the floor was tiled to make a summoning circle, which was illustrated with pictures of demons, their names spelt out in Enochian letters.

Next to it was a table, on which lay a book-sized object wrapped in a black silk sheet, a letter, and a dagger with a black obsidian blade and a wormwood handle. He took the items on the table and placed them in his satchel.

In a third corner of the room stood two mirrors, each askew from the other.

The pit cap, was well secured with three padlocked bolts. He used his magic key to unlock the padlocks, then he opened the trapdoor. It was so dark inside that he could not see into the pit, but there was a wretched cacophony of tormented souls. He held his breath, then tied one end of his rope to a spike on the wall and threw the coil down the pit. He ran up the stairs as fast as he could. When he got to the parlour, the seated vampires now knew something was wrong as the stink of the pit had reached their nostrils and agonized cries their ears. They thought the same thing: *They have escaped the pit!*

In panic some vampires dashed out of the front door, where the sound of musketry reports and screams signalled their doom.

The soldiers got them! thought Henry. He picked up the limp body of Joseph, and carried him to a broom cupboard.

'I cannot do this work anymore, Henry' said Joseph.

'Try not to speak,' said Henry as he daubed holy water on his wounds.

He locked Joseph into the broom cupboard. Then he made his way upstairs, to a hallway of panicking vampires.

'Who opened the pit?' asked one vampire, before another pushed him aside. It was Ephemeral Wormsong herself. She looked right at Henry. She could not see or hear the stealthy wizard but she was a mage, and could tell something was there. She muttered a spell and threw out her hands in gesture. Thick strands of silk grew out from her fingers and flew towards him. They covered the wizard in a sticky web that held him fast against the wall. Grand Master Pharaoh Henry was now helpless.

'There is an invisible wizard in that web, kill him' Wormsong ordered a vampire.

The underling drew his dagger then moved towards Henry, but he hesitated at the sound and smell of the approaching pit fiends, who were making their way up the stairs. His hesitation saved Henry's life.

'Do it!' shouted Wormsong.

The vampire approached again, but before he could kill, fiends from the pit, crazed with bloodthirst, sprang onto him from the stairwell. More wretches came up, rushing the vampires in the hallway. Shots rang out, and some of them ignited into flame, but there were many more following behind them until they overwhelmed the vampires.

Trapped behind the web Henry could see the massacre. He also saw Ephemeral Wormsong escaping up the stairs to the roof. The ravenous pit fiends drank from the fallen vampires.

Henry could do nothing. The fiends sniffed at the air for more blood, but they could not smell or see Henry, had they been able to they would have torn him apart.

In an instant, the strands of the web melted. *It must be after sunrise*, thought Henry, inferring this from the fact that the web spell had worn off. He could not see the sun as the windows were shuttered.

Soon enough, Henry heard the sound of goblins outside, who were putting up scaffolding. The pit vampires, now enraged with the smell of blood, did not have the sense to realize that the shutters on the windows were about to be torn off. Sunlight entered the house for the first time in decades, and as it touched the pit fiends they howled in pain. Some of them burned to ash on the spot, others fled down the stairs, but there was no-where to escape to, as the ground floor was also bathed in sunshine.

Henry took off his cap and cloak. The fiends were scattering in all directions, but one looked familiar to Henry. It was Enigma Oates. Henry opened his dimension box and tossed it at her. The box expanded and opened, and sucked her inside. When the box closed it returned to its original size, imprisoning Enigma within.

He retrieved the box and made his way downstairs. The windows were open and light flooded the hall. There were no vampires now, just piles of ash where they had been. Babylon Pinch and Noah Bentley entered the hallway with a small group of soldiers.

'Greetings my fine chaps. You may want to rescue the goblins locked in the pantry and broom cupboard,' said Henry.

'Yes Sir,' replied Babylon Pinch.

'Did any vampires escape?'

'Two Sir, one got onto the roof, and flew off on an ornithopter, the other escaped into the tunnels before the attack started,' said Pinch.

'The ornithopter pilot will have been Madam Ephemeral Wormsong. Enigma is in the box. Protect her from the sun and lock her in a dark room, so feed her some blood as soon as possible,' Henry said to Bentley.

'Henry, journalists are here, do you want to speak to them,' asked Bentley.

'Certainly not, I must keep my name out of this,' said Henry.

'Well someone has to speak to them,' said Bentley.

'You do it Pinch. Say it was you who killed all the vampires,' said Henry.

'But I don't have the authority to say such a thing, I'm just a Police Constable,' said Pinch.

'I will speak to the Chief Constable to clear your story, but you must go and take care of the press. I repeat: You killed the vampires, do you understand? Keep your story straight and simple. That's an order, now I must go as I have work to do,' said Henry.

Henry reached into his magic satchel to retrieve the sheet of paper and book he had taken from the basement. The book was **Keys to the Dark Gate**. On the paper was a letter from Assyria Neepfield to Euphoria Fireheart, and it contained the poem, *The Hubris of Draska*.

10

'Fool that I am, I attempted to do a good deed for that good for nothing of a poet, Assyria Neepfield. Mr. Neepfield is impoverished, a situation for which I am sure he is entirely to blame. I naively tried to rescue him from the indignity of being in a soup queue. In return for my kind charity, he tried to hold me and kiss me in a most improper manner. As you can imagine I was unsettled, I was trembling all over with ~~moisture~~ butterflies under my tummy.'

Excerpts from the **Diary of Miss Euphoria Fireheart**, 27th March 1898.

At the date of publication, the Metropolis is home to 574 wizard's colleges. In these colleges wizards live work and study magic together, and in many cases serve one or more of the city's many magical needs. The Warding Witches have the unenviable job of stopping demons entering Metropolis. Needless to say, it is a difficult and thankless task.
The Municipal Demon Ward, as its official name suggests, is a large magical machine designed to keep demons out of the Metropolis. It does this by creating a powerful city-wide warding spell, that repels demons and forces them back to Hell. Of course, this requires the warding spell to be greater than the demon's magical might.
The 'ward' as it was colloquially known, is housed in a tall narrow tower on a small rocky island on the river Bone. It is manned every hour of every day, by three crews of three goblins, each working an eight-hour shift.

Extract from the **A Report into the short-comings of the Municipal Demon Ward.** Chaired by Rev. Noah Bentley of the *Bentley Commission.*

The Telepathy Office

The remarkable thing about Mr. Assyria Neepfield was not how handsome he was, or how he earned a living (or rather failed to), but instead his ability to sense and convey in words the beauty in a goblin's short existence. It was a singular talent that set him aside from all but the most sensitive and creative of goblins. But he was a penniless goblin rich in artistic sensibilities, who lived in a city where it was the pennies that count, and most goblins could not distinguish between moving verse and a catchy jingle.

The aspiring poet stood by a sunsand lamp in his new accommodation. He turned up the dial to light up the room. Euphoria Fireheart was somewhere where she should not be, asleep in Neepfield's bed. He tried not to stare at her as she lay naked on the white linen sheets, but he could not help himself. Her burgundy hair flowed across on her porcelain white body as she turned over to find a more comfortable position. The sunsand light cast coloured reflections across her skin. Her dainty stub of a tail, so fashionably docked, protruded two inches into the air. He thought to himself that she was the most beautiful sight he had ever seen in his life.

'Could you ever love me Euphoria?' he asked as she woke.

She rubbed the sleep from her eyes. 'Mr. Neepfield. Isn't it enough that you take advantage of my good nature to ravish me? Do you have to wake me with your foolish nonsense about love as well?' She said half-asleep.

Euphoria arose from his bed; she walked to the chair where she had left her clothes. She reached into her bag, and from inside the leaves of a copy of the Fashionable Intelligencer, she took out a letter addressed to Assyria.

'The reason I was looking for you last night was to give you this. It is a letter to you Assyria, from a lady by the smell of her perfume,' she said, as she held the letter out of Assyria's reach.

'Keep the letter Euphoria; you are the only goblinette for me,' he said. Now it was hers, Euphoria opened it without asking further permission. Enclosed with the note was the business card of Delilah Twotemples of Golemaker Hall. The card was printed on treated expensive magical paper to make it glow.

'This must have cost a fortune. This Miss Twotemples is not short of money I can tell you that,' she said, while slipping the business card in her clutch bag.

'Let me read it to you, I am sure you have lots of other girls after you because of your soppy poems,'

Dear Mr. Neepfield.

I would like to meet you to discuss an artistic project. If you are available, please could you meet me at 1pm on the 27th March at the Green Dragon Cafe on Riddle Street.

Yours sincerely Miss Delilah Twotemples, Golemaker Hall, Northminster.

'Golemaker Hall, Northminster eh? Artistic project? Well it's the first time I have heard it called that. Sounds to me like you have pulled a posh piece of skirt this time. Would you do an artistic project for me Assyria? A small love poem perhaps? Or a quickie more like.'

'I would like to write a poem for you Euphoria, you know I would, but I haven't been very industrious recently. I love you Euphoria.'

Euphoria purred in appreciation. She furrowed her deep red eyebrows in a sweet gesture of affection, 'I can't be faithful just to you Mr. Neepfield because I aspire to elevation, and all you fuss about day in and day out are your plays and poems, and you don't care in the least about social propriety and getting on in the world. You don't have a ha'penny to your name.' Assyria looked dejected.

'Don't be sad. I tell you what, I'll give you sixpence to buy some soup. That should cheer you up. And I would very much like you to write a poem about me, but you must be sure to describe my elegance and refinement. I won't worry too much that it's not very industrious, just as long as it reflects my unaffected sophistication. You could enter your love poem about me in the Royal Poetry Contest, I am sure it would win because poems about glamorous elfin debutants such as myself are all the rage.'

'Elfin debutant? But Euphoria, you are not an elf,' said Assyria.

'I soon will be,' said Euphoria, as she held up Delilah's business card.

11

'The Pawn is the smallest measure of manna. There are 12 pawns of manna in a Rook, and there are 12 Rooks to a Queen.'

Extract from **A Guidebook to Magical Weights and Measures**, by Ramases Stickleback, Green Dragon Press.

***

Number 73 Cat Fishing Street is an elegant building of eight stories high, constructed in the moon elf style. Its stonework is faced with powder pink star coral, and its main entrance is a black double door that gleams as only magical paint can. To the left of the door is a shiny polished sign, carved from a single scale of a red dragon, etched with the words:

Dr. Obadiah Apricot, Skilled Practitioner of Magical Healing and Cosmetic Surgery. Physician to the Goblin King.

Dr. Apricot skills were much sought after among the financially affluent goblins of the Metropolis. Goblins wealthy enough to afford cosmetic procedures, modified their bodies back and forth, often at great expense, to keep in step with the whims and fancies of goblin fashion. At this time, impractically long, pointed ears were all the rage in society circles, and many aspiring goblinette debutantes came to Dr. Apricot to have their ears done.

Euphoria entered the surgery with her best friend and confident, Mercurial Frostdrop. Mercurial hardly spoke to anyone except Euphoria, Lampwick and Zebedee, which is a good thing because she rarely had anything sensible to say. In fact, Mercurial was most noticeable by her taciturn behaviour, and expressionless appearance. Euphoria appreciated her silence because she liked to talk for both of them.

They both wore elfin style gowns that Euphoria had had specially tailored, with some of the money she had made from selling Assyria's poem, *The Hubris of Draska*. The design of these had been copied from a picture in 'Society Elf' magazine. It was of the same style of dress worn by Princess Salonicha to the opening of New Draskan Opera house, differing in so much that Salonicha's was yellow, and Euphoria's dress was an indigo that exactly matched the colour of her eyes. Mercurial's was a metallic shade of mermaid-scale green.

They strutted up to the desk trying to look as aristocratic as they could, and largely succeeding. Euphoria fraudulently introduced them both to the receptionist, 'My name is Miss. Delilah Twotemples and this is my maid Mercurial Underling, I have an appointment with Dr. Apricot regarding my letter to him,' she lied.

Euphoria passed the receptionist a business card. Of course, it was not Euphoria's business card, as she did not have one. It was the business card of Miss Twotemples' that she had purloined from Assyria Neepfield.

The receptionist studied Euphoria and Mercurial carefully. They certainly dressed well enough to be rich young ladies, maybe a little too much make-up, but never the less; the pair still gave a plausible appearance of upper-class goblinettes. The receptionist gave a deep and deferential courtesy, and then said: 'Please take a seat ladies, the doctor will see you presently.'

At the receptionist's request, the painted goblinettes sat down in the waiting room of Dr. Obadiah Apricot, where Mercurial noticed a large lizard was looking at them. As is the custom of the vast majority of wizards, Dr. Apricot had a familiar, in his case a large green lizard by the name of Ogilvy.

Ogilvy crouched in the corner of the waiting room, under a strange alien shrub, and stared intently at Mercurial and Euphoria. He exhibited the complete absence of expression only possible from a reptile, which had rather unsettled Mercurial. Little did she know it, but Mercurial's dragon like stare was unsettling for Ogilvy in much the same manner.

'He is looking at us,' Mercurial whispered to Euphoria, referring to the lizard. Mercurial always spoke quietly in public, on the rare occasions when she did speak at all.

'Oh Mercurial, don't be so *alrey*, it's just a stupid lizard, it cannot speak or think except to think of worms to eat,' said Euphoria.

'*Alrey?*' asked Mercurial.

'Yes Mercurial, *Alrey¹*, it's a high elf word, used by aristocrats such as myself, and it refers to common or stupid behaviour by goblins such as you. You really should try to use more elfin words if you hope to fit into Elvin society as I do. After the surgery, our bodies will be transformed into that of lady elves, so you need to start acting like one,' said Euphoria, raising her nose in the air slightly on the word *aristocrats.*

'When we become elves, we will be taller, slenderer, and our physical features will change. I had dresses especially made so they will magically alter themselves after the transformation to our exact measurements,' explained Euphoria.

A nurse opened the door into the surgery and said, 'Miss Twotemples and Miss Underling, Doctor Apricot will see you now.' Mercurial and Euphoria followed the nurse into the surgery.

'Ah Miss Twotemples, you have come with your maid to be changed into elves I see,' said Dr. Apricot reading Euphoria's letter.

'Exactly so, doctor.'

Apricot looked at Mercurial sternly.

'Are you sure this is what you both want? You haven't been pushed into it by anyone have you?' Apricot looked at Mercurial sternly.

'No doctor.' Mercurial replied simply and without giving any clue as to her feelings, 'I want to look like Miss Twotemples. We will be elfin ladies together.'

Privately Dr. Apricot was very sceptical about this whole idea, but he did not show it. In the Metropolis it was generally a good strategy to show deference to a goblin lady, and Miss Twotemples was clearly of high social stature as far as he could make out.

'Well magical cosmetic surgery is not something to be taken lightly, so I need to be sure you have properly thought this through. I shall need to look into this one, to see if it is ethical. I don't want to break my Hippocratic Oath and all that,' said Apricot.

'Well we want to know how much it will cost to get the job done, both for myself and Mercurial,' explained Euphoria.

The mention of money engaged Apricot's greed, and he became too blinded by it to catch onto the ruse. He made a quick calculation in his head. He would need flesh manna and change manna, about a

---

[1] 'Alrey' is the word for 'window' in the Draskan dialect of the Elvin language, the author cannot guess the source of Miss. Euphoria Fireheart's confusion as to the meaning of the word.

rook of each, which should be enough for the two goblin girls.

'Well the cost of the materials for the cosmetic surgery would be one hundred pounds, and I would add another sixty pounds each for my spell casting fees,' said Apricot.

Inside Euphoria's heart fluttered at such expense, but she concealed if perfectly. After all, she was not the one who was going to have to pay it, and it was far too late to back down from her fraud now.

'The price is satisfactory, would you prefer I send one of my servants to pay it, or would you want to send one of your runners to pick it up from Golemaker's Hall?' asked Euphoria.

Dr. Apricot knew about Golemaker's Hall over in Kingsfield. It was the town house of Samuel Golemaker, wealthy owner of the demon bottle factory on Phoenix Street.

'I could send a runner to pick it up tomorrow morning, would that be acceptable Miss Twotemples?' said Apricot as he tried to show a calm face, while inside he was boiling over with avarice at the idea of making so much profit so quickly.

'It would,' said Euphoria, 'Now that we have dispensed with the money, the question arises as to when would you be able perform to the surgery?'

'As it happens, I already have enough manna in stock, so as soon as you could bring me pictures of what you want to look like I can perform the magic. The whole thing should only take half an hour,' replied Apricot.

'I am very glad you said that doctor, I would like you to do it now. I want to look like the elf in the pink dress, and Mercurial wants to look like the elf in the yellow dress,' explained Euphoria as she passed Apricot two pictures cut from the **Society Elf** magazine. One of the pictures was of the Princess Salonica, the other was of Princess Davini, both of New Draska.

Dr. Apricot led the goblinettes into a private room behind his surgery. He had plenty of manna, but he hated using the freshest manna on a mere servant, so he scraped the remains of some old creation manna for Miss Underling from an old jar, and used the freshest manna he had bought that morning for Miss Twotemples. He mixed up a rook each of creation and flesh manna in two separate bowls. He then sprinkled the manna over each of them, while chanting the spell called **Change the Body's Form**.

'Close your eyes ladies, and imagine in your mind the bodies you

56

want to have,' said Dr. Apricot as he cast the spell.

The magic took just over ten minutes to take effect. They slowly became taller and their features more gracile as their goblin bodies transformed to elfin ones.

Euphoria and Mercurial stood in front of each other, now with the bodies of elves. Unable to stop themselves, Euphoria and Mercurial giggled like dribblings.

****

Dr. Apricot felt very pleased with himself for making so much money so quickly, especially from clients from the higher echelons of society. In high spirits, he called to the receptionist to send in the next patient, who was a large goblin man.

'Mr. Abel Goodhalf I see. What can I do for you Sir?' asked Dr Apricot. He did pro-bono healing work for poor goblins in order to get royal approval from the King. He could also claim his manna back; and he cheated as to how much he used. But he did not like curing poor goblins because he made more money from the rich who wanted cosmetic magical surgery.

'I broke my fingers at work. I am feeling very weak too doctor. No life in me what so ever. And I have a terrible itch on my shoulder,' said the goblin.

'Well let's have a look at you.' Dr. Apricot inspected the fingers, they were broken alright; but they were easy to mend with a healing spell and some of the manna he had used on Euphoria.

Then he looked at the offending shoulder; where he found a red patch of skin that was causing the itch. In the middle of the rash were two small puncture wounds.

'Mr. Goodhalf, can you tell me how you got these wounds?'

'No doctor. I cannot.'

I wonder if there is still a vampire about, but if there is, why didn't it drain him to death? And why doesn't he remember being bitten? thought Apricot.

12

'Nothing goes out of fashion like fashion.'

Quote from Clemency Drinkwater, War Correspondent for the Fashionable Intelligencer

The **Law of Correspondence** *is a* **sympathetic magical doctrine** *that describes how a magician can influence a target by creating something that resembles it. The better the resemblance captures the essence of the target, the stronger the correspondence will be.*

Excerpt from **Magic Theory and Practice** 4th Edition

***

The Green Dragon Cafe on Riddle Street is famed citywide for three sound reasons: delicious cocoa, delightful soup, and most importantly to its owner, the wealthy clientele who can afford its prices.

Assyria Neepfield sat alone on an outside table.

His worn-out coat made him conspicuous. He had never frequented the Green Dragon before and was uneasy at the daunting prospect of the bill. He had spent the sixpence Euphoria gave him on a ream of paper and pencils; now he was destitute again. If Delilah Twotemples, his mysterious benefactor, did not show up and pay him an advance, he would have to wash up for the coffee. He sipped very slowly to delay paying the bill. Things were looking bad, it was now almost half-past one, and his cup was finally drained.

Fearing the waiter might demand immediate financial settlement, he hid as best he could behind a copy of The Daily Goblin, given to him by Mr. Fireheart. The headline read: ***Vampire Nest Raided, Hundreds of Bloodsuckers Destroyed - Babylon Pinch the Hero!***

The waiter prided himself on his keen eye for spotting poverty but this time he had been remiss. He dropped Assyria a glare of suspicion, angry at the belated realisation that he had been tricked into serving a vagrant.

Assyria's attention was drawn to a goblin lady who emerged out of the crowd. She strolled up to Assyria with swagger. At 5' 1' Delilah Twotemples was an exceptionally tall society goblinette. She wore a simple, but expensive scarlet dress, daringly cut short at the knees.

'Sir, are you Mr. Assyria Neepfield, author of the poem Hubris of Draska?'

Assyria nodded, momentarily entranced by her elegant beauty.

'Please accept my apologies for the dramatic vagueness of my letter, and for my late arrival. May I sit with you?' said Delilah. She effortlessly conveyed the urgency of her busy schedule without compromising her cultivated poise.

Belatedly Assyria remembered his manners and sprang to his feet to pull her chair back for her.

'Allow me to introduce myself. My name is Delilah Twotemples. I am an opera singer and music composer. I so adore your poetry, as does my sponsor. I am working on a new opera, and that is the matter I wish to discuss with you.'

'Thank you, Miss,' Assyria looked away bashfully, which is improper manners for a goblin when responding to a complement, but he was unused to it.

'Please call me Delilah.'

'Thank you, Delilah. Your new opera, may I ask what will it be about?' said Assyria, who was adapting to his new social setting, now he looked Delilah in the eyes.

'The fall of Draska. My patron had in mind the same name as your poem the **Hubris of Draska.** At least that's the working title. Of course, should you accept the commission we would welcome your input on all creative matters, including the title. I will take the main role of Queen Anatitia of the High Elves.'

'And what do you want me to do?'

'My proposal is to offer you a commission to write the words for the songs. I want you to be my librettist for this work. I shall write the melody myself. Do you consider £200 commission to be fair? All finances to cover your service have been approved,' said Delilah. Her relaxed demeanor suggested that £200 was not as much money to her as it was to Assyria.

'£200 would be most acceptable, but my circumstances force me to make an awkward request.'

'I am keen to have you onboard, and remove any obstacles to

that end, please tell me what it is.' She said.

'Could you give me a small advance?'

Delilah opened her clutch-bag. 'I am afraid I only have £30 on me, and I need a few shillings for the cab fare. Would £25 suffice?' She said.

It was enough for Assyria to live on for a year. 'That would be plenty.' He said, relieved at his new-found solvency.

'I am so glad we have managed to get the financial side of things out of the way. I find haggling over money like common merchants to be so vulgar. As a fellow artist I am sure you agree with my sentiment,' said Miss Twotemples. She took out five large white £5 notes from her purse and gave them to Assyria, 'The opera will be performed at the Grand Opera House in Arcadia Gardens, with an initial run of three months. I intend to start writing tomorrow, and have rooms at my patron's house set aside for our work Please could you be there at 10 am tomorrow morning? I am afraid I cannot stop as I have a pressing engagement with an agent charged with hiring an orchestra. Do you have any further questions Assyria?'

She called me Assyria, how familiar, thought Neepfield, *such a free-spirited lady.* 'Who is your patron Delilah?'

'He is Mr. Solomon Golemaker. And I hope to see you at Golemaker Hall tomorrow. Now I am so sorry but I must dash. Good day to you Assyria.' She held out her hand for Assyria to kiss as he bowed.

Assyria bade Delilah farewell and she rushed to a waiting horse drawn cab.

For the first time in his life he had some spare money. It was a novel but liberating experience. *Haggling over money like common merchants is vulgar? If she knew what it is like not to have money, she would stoop to haggling alright,* he thought.

Assyria's confidence grew with his new wealth; even the suspicious waiter knew that he had turned the tables on him. He intercepted the poor goblin by waving one of his five-pound notes under his nose, 'A large bowl of fairybean soup and a crust of buttered bread please waiter.'

13

The Royal Mint holds reserves of manna used to back the goblin currency. The goblin pound is convertible to creation manna. 1 pawn of creation manna will be exchanged for 10 pounds on demand. An elfin pound is exchangeable for comprehension manna, both the dwarven crown and gnomish gilder for material manna, and an orkish dollar for destruction manna; each at the rate of 1 pawn per 10 pounds, crowns, gilders or dollars. Needless to say, that exchange rate would only be available on the home planet of the respective race.

Goblin currency is more complex than that of other races. There are 4 crowns or 20 shillings to a goblin pound, and twelve pennies to a goblin shilling. In most other currencies, including dwarven, elfin, and gnomish, there are 10 shillings or 2 crowns to a pound or gilder, and 10 pennies to each shilling. Clearly the exchange rate between currencies changes with the price of the manna type they are each based on in any given market.

From **Manna and Economic Theory**, by Velocity Goldenleaf, Phoenix Press.

***

Captain Sebastian Valancy was a high elf. He dressed in a green frock coat with long tails and bright gold buttons, which was the dress uniform of the 3rd Draskan Dragoons, the regiment in which he had formerly served.

He was now stationed in the Goblin Metropolis, where he held the position of senior telepath, and bore the heavy responsibility of establishing the city's Telepathy Office. He did this on his own, which meant he was a busy elf.

He had purchased a suitable building on Arcadia Square, and now he stood in its main foyer to oversee the goblin decorators who were painting the walls. Outside the building, labourers unloaded carts of furniture in anticipation of when the decorators had finished, so they could do their job. It was all a huge muddle.

He had a business sign painted to advertise the Telepathy Office's services, but had yet to hang it on the front wall. It read:

The Municipal Telepathy Office
**Messages Sent Across the Galaxy by Elfin Telepaths.
Reasonable prices. Confidentiality assured. Messages
Large or Small, Private or Business. Enquiries Welcome**

So far only one room was finished, his office. It was necessary for him to have a desk and filing cabinets in order to deal with all his paperwork, so he had it done ahead of the others. His office also contained his all-important telepath's couch, because telepathy was best performed in comfort. To enter a trance some elfin telepaths preferred to sit in an armchair, but Valancy liked to lay on his well-worn chaise longue.

To recruit mundane staff, as was the custom in the Metropolis, he listed his vacancies on a blackboard mounted on the wall outside the front door of the building, it read:

Goblins Wanted:
**1 Office Manager £ 2/10/4 per Week[2]
12 Runners £ -/18/- per Week (Might Suit Dribblings on
Bicycles, or Spritely Kobolds)
3 Receptionists £ 1/2/6 per Week
4 Tea Makers and Cleaners £ -/12/6 per Week
Free Uniforms. Meals Provided for Goblins on Shift**

A large and colourful queue of job hunters had formed in the street. It included pretty goblinettes dressed up to the nines, veteran goblin soldiers in scarlet tunics and medal ribbons, dribbling's with their tiny bicycles and kobolds with their lime green scales and diminutive dragon-like wings.

But how was he going to select an office manager? He knew

---

[2] The goblin notation for currency was the amount in pounds first, separated from the shillings by a '/', and the shillings were separated from the pennies by '/'. So £2/10/4 means two Pounds, ten Shillings and 4 pence. A '-' means none of that denomination is present, so -/18- means 18 shillings.

nothing about goblins.

The recruitment of mundane staff was a job in progress. But, more crucially he still needed a second telepath.

In his mind's eye he saw an image of a dove fluttering in the air. It was the emblem of Miss Urania Rego, his superior on New Draska. Valancy quickly made his way to his office, where he lay on his couch to take the communication.

'*Please report on progress,*' projected Urania.

Valancy thought there was a sternness to her. He gave her the details of recruitment, advertising, and office preparation.

'*The company directors need faster progress given your expenditure,*' projected Urania.

'*I am proceeding as fast as I can, I am on my own here,*' replied Valancy

'*The offices are fully operational on orkish Caragula, gnomish Sterwyck, and dwarven Mannaheuval. So together with New Draska, the rest of the telepathic communication network is up and running. I need to report to the directors that the office at the Goblin Metropolis will join the network by the 1ˢᵗ April. You are the last link. Can you do it?*' Urania was very business-like.

'*That would be a very tight schedule. Is there any news on my co-telepath,*' projected Valancy.

'*We are sending you Aristotle Vim, you linked while serving together in the Cavalry,*' projected Urania.

'*We served in separate units. We linked as cavalry officers, in preparation for an action that never came, so never had the opportunity to telepath in the field.*'

The word 'linked' in the context of elfin telepathy has a very specific meaning. It is a common misconception, that high elves can readily enter into telepathy with any other of their kind. This is largely untrue, although 'random linking' has been known to happen on rare occasions. Usually in order to communicate by mind, telepaths have to consciously and deliberately 'link' to each other. It is achieved by two elves entering full-face, eye-to-eye contact while unmasked. Having linked, they can then communicate over huge distances, and across dimensions.

Linking is considered socially familiar in elfin society, and is not entered into lightly. To prevent unwanted linking, elves wear masks while in public, and only removed them when alone, or solely in familiar company. In this context, 'familiar company' means elves that are already linked.

Of course, female elves would never attend a social gathering of any sort without a mask, but do bear their faces to have their pictures taken, as there is no danger of linking from a likeness.

'*I can vouch for his telepathy in the field. I received his projection myself, and he is wonderfully clear, even over vast distances of pan-dimensional space,*' projected Urania.

'*When can I expect him?*'

'*He is en-route from New Draska to the Metropolis aboard the Golden Phoenix as we telepath. The Phoenix is scheduled to arrive in four days' time. He has never been to the Metropolis before so it would be best if you pick him up from the docks, or arrange for someone else to do it,*' projected Urania.

'*I will see that he is met.*' But Valancy did not know how he was going to find the time to do it himself, and he did not have anyone he could ask.

'*We will telepath tomorrow to check on your progress, until then, goodbye,*' projected Urania.

Valancy did not know where to start with all the things he had to do, he needed help. The first problem was how he was going to deal with the queue.

Goblins respected queues. They disliked it intensely when upstart goblins tried to push in front, rather than do the decent thing and join at the end. But of course, there are exceptions to this, and one of them is if the queue jumpers are elfin telepaths. Euphoria and Mercurial marched straight past the patient goblins, and up to Sebastian. No goblin objected because they all thought they were lady elves.

'Captain Valancy Sir, please may I have your attention,' said Euphoria.

Valancy was astonished to see a pair of elves standing in front of him. He was unaware there were other high elves in the Metropolis, especially female.

'Good ladies, how may I assist you?' he said. Valancy felt embarrassment at speaking to lady elves without masks. To an elf, it is more unsettling than being naked.

'My name is Euphoria Fireheart and I have come to ask for a job as a telepath's assistant, and so has my associate, Miss Mercurial Frostdrop,'

Valancy was intrigued, 'A telepath's assistant, but we are not advertising such positions. I am a telepath, what had you in mind as to how you would assist me?'

'By showin' the pay in' customers to your rooms, preparing 'em, giving 'em cups of tea, and of course, most importantly, taking their money,' explained Euphoria with such excitement she dropped her upper-class pretensions and broke into her working-class accent.

Valancy was a little taken aback by Euphoria's forthright request, so much so he wondered if she was serious. He studied Euphoria carefully, she looked rather like a beautiful china doll of an elf lady. She clearly knew what she wanted, and he liked that.

Euphoria's companion, Mercurial Frostdrop, was 4' 3' tall; she was the same height as Euphoria, with bluish black hair, green eyes and pale skin with just a faint tint of blue. However Mercurial differed in her mannerisms; whereas Euphoria was candid and outspoken, Mercurial was as silent and expressionless as a dragon cutting a deal. *This Mercurial is so quiet and thoughtful, she must be very clever,* Valancy mistakenly thought.

'I need someone to interview the goblins in the queue, and recruit the best of them,' asked Valancy.

'We can do that,' said Euphoria.

'I need someone to organise the painters and decorators, and put the furniture in the correct places.'

'Consider it done.'

'I need to advertise the services of the Telepathy Office to prospective customers.'

'We will advertise in all the best newspapers, and organise an opening ball, that should do the trick.'

'I need someone to greet my co-telepath Aristotle from the pan-ship docks in four days' time.'

'I'm your elf,' said Euphoria.

'But are you actually elves?' Valancy asked.

'We look like elves, so we are,' said Euphoria.

Her outrageous suggestion stunned Valancy into an amazed silence. He looked at the two little goblins before him, first Euphoria, and then the stone-faced Mercurial. He half expected them to wink and admit the ruse, but they were not joking. This was a serious business offer.

He pictured the future Telepathy Office. Each telepath assisted by, a lady who to all intents and purposes was a high elf, or someone who looked very much like one to the uninitiated, (which was everyone in the city who was not in on the trick). The more he considered it, the more it seemed wonderfully subversive, even humorous, and so the more he liked it. The high elf women back on

New Draska would be most offended if they found out they were being impersonated by a pair of common goblin girls. In particular, Urania Rego would be incandescent with indignation. Euphoria's proposal appealed to his sense of sedition. He knew then and there that Euphoria Fireheart and Mercurial Dragonface were going to be so much fun to work with!

'Anything else we need to discuss,' said Valancy.

'We need to discuss my favourite subject,' said Euphoria.

'And what is that?'

'Money,' she said.

'I don't think that will be an issue,' said Valancy, 'We need to open for business by the 1st of April, let's get to work.'

14

The maximum penalty for using infernal manna is death.

Section 18.3(7) of the **Magical Sanitation Act** 1857.

***

After a brief knock, Deliria Grimbrow entered Dr Apricot's surgery.

'Doctor, a messenger has sent you instruction from Grand Master Pharaoh Henry,' said the receptionist.

'Please read it to me Deliria,' said Dr. Apricot. He was quite distressed at the very thought that the crank Pharaoh Henry was even communicating with him.

Please go to number 376 on Huntingdon's Housing Estate immediately. A patient of yours by the name of Mr. Goodhalf is under demonic attack. The hand you treated has mutated into a demonic claw. I shall see you there presently. Yours Pharaoh Henry.

'Call the coach and horses immediately, Miss Grimbrow,' said Dr. Apricot.

Dr. Obadiah Apricot knew he was about to meet the most infamous wizard in the Metropolis, the firebrand demon hunter, Grand Master Pharaoh Henry. He shuddered in apprehension.

Dr. Apricot's carriage clattered along the cobbles as he hurried to Huntingdon's Housing Estate, home to thousands of worker goblins. He raced up the stairs to the Goodhalf's apartment and ran inside a door that had been left open.

'Oh, I am so glad you came quickly. You fixed Mr. Goodhalf's hand earlier, but he has come over all peculiar,' said Mrs. Goodhalf.

She led Dr. Apricot into her small bedroom. Mr. Goodhalf lay in bed, where he did not look right at all because there was a large disgusting hairy claw where his right hand should be. The claw festered with sores, each oozing a filthy yellow puss, which stank of an unnatural corruption.

As Dr. Apricot approached the patient, the claw, which had a mind of its own, snapped at him with menace.

Apricot was terrified, so he wisely retreated out of the bedroom and shut the door. The good doctor was to blame; he had administered medicine to a goblin's wounded hand that had now become possessed. Worse still, the hot-headed demon hunter Pharaoh Henry was on his way to see him soon, and questions would be asked as to what had happened. Dr. Apricot had a profitable position, so the last thing he wanted was scandal to besmirch his fine reputation.

'Mrs. Goodhalf, I ask that when Grand Master Henry arrives, that you let me do the talking,' said Dr. Apricot.

'You want me to show him where Mr. Goodhalf is lying down, and after that not to say anything to him,' she replied with a touch of defiance.

'Madam, I must impress upon you that the Grand Master Pharaoh Henry is the most feared wizard in the city. He is a fanatic, a dangerous madgoblin! So please don't get me too involved with him,' said Apricot, who started to tremble with fear.

'I'm sure he's not that bad. Most goblins are nice if you are nice to them first. What's so different about this wizard?' said Verity Goodhalf.

'He's a maniac with no regard as to the safety of others that is what's different about him. He is a demon hunter. That's what he does, and it's what he wants everyone else to do too, regardless of the peril, and he won't tolerate the slightest difference of opinion on the matter. Have you any idea how many promising young goblin wizards have died horribly fighting his wild crusades against the forces of Hell? I have a medical practice to run Madam. I am the physician to the Great Goblin King himself; I have a blossoming career in front of me. The last thing I want is to be dragooned into one of Pharaoh Henry's suicidally dangerous demon hunts. So please, I beg of you Madam, for the love of the one true God and our Lord Jesus, please let me do the talking.'

There was an ominous knock on the door; Mrs. Goodhalf answered it. Pharaoh Henry entered the flat accompanied by Babylon Pinch and Vanilla Catchpenny.

Pinch walked a few steps behind Henry and Vanilla. The policeman struggled to make his way through the flat with a four-foot-high demon bottle tied to a set of trolley wheels.

Mrs. Goodhalf reported the incident to police after her husband had grown a dangerous claw in place of his left hand. The claw demonstrated a vindictive and spiteful will of its own.

'Do I have the pleasure of meeting Dr. Obadiah Apricot and Mrs.

Verity Goodhalf?' asked Henry.

'Yes, indeed Sir, so glad you came so soon Sir. Shows great professionalism for a magician of your high standing to show such concern for the likes of us working goblins Sir,' blurted Mrs. Goodhalf, before Dr. Apricot could get a word in edgeways.

'Not at all Mrs. Goodhalf, your safety from the claws of Hell is my foremost concern. So please show us to your husbands' sickbed without any more delay,' said Henry enthusiastically.

Verity led the group into the Goodhalf's bedroom. The claw immediately lashed out at Henry, who sidestepped it with the agility of a dancing pixie. Henry grasped it and held its pincers shut.

'Pinch, hold this claw closed and keep it still for me,' said Henry

Pinch did as he was told, but it was not easy. The claw had a demonic physical strength all of its own, and the weeping puss made it slippery and difficult to grip. But he held on tightly, even while he was getting covered in its repulsive filth.

'Hold the claw firm Pinch, while I tie it to this hook on the ceiling,' said Henry as he took a rope and secured it.

With the threat from the claw diminished, Henry turned to Mrs. Goodhalf and said, 'Madam, could I put upon you to make us all a nice cup of tea?'

When Mrs. Goodhalf left the bedroom, Henry asked Apricot 'So how did you treat this patient of yours Doctor?'

'He had caught his fingers in a machine accident at the demon bottling plant, breaking two of them and cutting off the tip of the other, so I administered a poultice on the wound to heal the breaks and grow his fingertip back.' said Dr Apricot.

'What did you put in the poultice?' asked Henry.

'Three pawns of creation manna, two pawns of flesh manna, a phoenixwort leaf, and a pinch of salt,' replied Dr. Apricot.

'When did you do this?'

'Lunchtime today.'

'Do you have any manna from the same batch with you?'

Dr. Apricot opened up his case and handed over to Henry two small glass vials each of which contained finely ground manna; one powder was white, the other brown.

'Please would you test the manna,' said Henry to Vanilla.
She took out a small silver spoon from her clutch bag, and poured a little of the white powder onto it. The silver spoon turned black in colour the instant the powder touched it. Vanilla nodded to Henry.

'Kindly open the demon bottle Master Pinch,' Henry asked his apprentice. Henry carefully placed the white powder back into the vial, and then placed the vial into the demon bottle. Vanilla wiped the spoon carefully; then she poured some of the brown powder onto the spoon, but this time the spoon remained silver. Vanilla handed the brown vial back to Dr. Apricot.

'Yes, for the creation manna, but the flesh manna is safe,' said Vanilla.

Henry drew the sheets off of Mr. Halfgood, who was sweaty and feverish. He looked carefully at his body, inspecting it inch by inch.

'Did you notice these two puncture wounds Dr. Apricot?' asked Henry, pointing to the sick goblin's chest.

Apricot examined the two delicate puncture holes. 'I have seen a lot of these recently on many of my patients. Not sure what they are,' Apricot admitted sheepishly.

'Can you help me Sir?' Mr. Goodhalf whispered painfully.

'Of course, I can help you Sir. Get you sorted out in no time,' Henry reassured the sick goblin with absolute sincerity.

'Dr. Apricot. The creation manna you used in the poultice was infernally tainted Sir,' said Vanilla.

'Infernally tainted Madam? To what extent?' Apricot knew the penalty of using infernal manna very well.

'Yes Sir. Infernally tainted Sir, to the extent that it is the worst I have ever come across Sir,' said Vanilla.

'Presently I shall ask you to go to your surgery, and test your stocks of manna for demonic contamination. Any tainted manna you find you will depose of safely in the demon bottle. But before you go, I ask that you prepare a fresh poultice for Mr. Goodhalf with pure clean manna, then remove this claw and re-grow the gentlegoblin's hand. You must dispose of the claw carefully by placing it in the demon bottle. As I say, please use my creation manna, not yours, but your flesh manna is uncontaminated so you can use that,'

Henry took a vial of white powdered creation manna from his satchel and gave it to Apricot.

'Before you leave good Doctor, when and where did you obtain your tainted manna from?'

'I bought the manna myself at 6 am this morning, a rook of creation and a rook of flesh manna, from Graves and Inglewood, at the Municipal Exchange.'

'As I said, you will need to go back to your surgery and get rid of any tainted manna immediately. Master Vanilla Catchpenny will help you test it and compensate you for your loss. One last thing Doctor, please keep checking your patients for puncture wounds. Let me know if you come across any patterns,' said Henry.

'Patterns Sir? What kind of patterns?' asked Apricot.

'Patterns such as, are the patients with the punctures male or female. Where do they live or work? Are they of similar age, interests, social class? Give it some thought and get back to me if you come up with anything,' said Henry.

Pinch, please take Vanilla and kindly visit Graves and Inglewood at the Municipal Manna Exchange. Go at once and with haste, stop them selling any more creation manna until I get there.'

'Yes Sir, certainly Sir, goodbye all,' said Pinch, who hated being near the demonic claw, and could not wait to get away.

Pharaoh Henry then looked deeply into Mr. Goodhalf's eyes. He cast a spell to see into Goodhalf's memory and when he did so the pupils of the wizard's eyes became slits, like a lizard's eyes, which was his sigil. He found the memory of the accident. He went to older memories. He could see his recollections of walking through the caves. Then, Goodhalf was drinking beer with friends at the Star Dragon's Rest public house. Henry ran through memories of him going through his routine, day by day, until he came across an incident with a goblinette in a tunnel. He ran through this memory repeatedly, time and again. She wore a black dress, and her skin was as pale as moonlight. She wore a single small scarlet flower in her hair. But try as he may, he could not catch sight of her face through all the memories of Mr. Goodhalf's lovemaking. Nor was there any memory anywhere of a bite. *A strong and distinctive memory* Henry thought to himself, *but there is something not quite right about it.* He ended his spell, and stood up straight.

'Two pieces of advice for you Mr. Halfgood: Firstly, say your prayers more often, there's a nice church near here called All Souls in the Wardrobe, which I highly recommend. Secondly, keep away from prostitutes, especially that lady goblin with the white skin, there is something odd about her.'

'I shall have to leave you now with the patient, but there is one very important outstanding question in my mind,' said Henry to Dr. Apricot.

'What is that Sir?' asked Dr. Apricot.

'Who else has been polluted by this infernal manna?'

'Oh, golly goblins, I treated Miss Delilah Twotemples!'

****

Euphoria woke up next to Assyria who was still fast asleep. She climbed out from under the blankets and went over to his desk. She read the lyrics he had been working on for his new operatic commission. He must have been working late.

Still sweaty from her earlier lovemaking, she took a shower. She enjoyed feeling her hands on her new elfin body as she sponged herself with soap and water. She washed her front, and then started to wash her back when, to her surprise, she noticed that her tail had grown back.

How bizarre, she thought to herself. She could not see her tail, but it was long, and it has a strange feel to it; not like skin, a different texture, with a bump on the end.

She reached out to the sink where Assyria kept his shaving mirror, and used its reflection to look at her tail. It was bright red and scaly, and it was barbed, like a little devil's tail. She was horrified.

Surprise eh sweetheart came a thought, and it was not Euphoria's thought either; rather it came from an unpleasant mocking creature that had managed to get inside her head. Whatever it was, it was repugnant and female.

'Who are you?' said Euphoria.

Never you mind, get back into bed with that goblin of yours, commanded the creature.

'I certainly shall not. Who do you think you are telling me to do such things!'

Every devil in Hell knows who you are you jumped up little tart. What makes you think you are important? Get back to that bed and do it with him!

Euphoria felt an urge for physical love overcome her. Not particularly with Assyria, but with any goblin, he just happened to be the closest available. She tried to resist it, but it was too strong. She ran to the bed, woke him up, and mounted him. Her rampant desire soon wore Assyria out, but although she had climaxed several times, she was not satiated.

'Assyria save me! Something has entered my mind and engendered lascivious cravings within me,' said Euphoria. She started to sob.

Stop whining; thought the creature; *you are going to throw yourself around with a lot more goblins than him before I am finished with you...if I finish with you.*

15

High elves are known for their telepathic ability. The act of putting an idea in a recipient's mind is called 'projecting'. The idea of listening to a thought from someone else's mind is called 'reading'. By use of telepathy, high elves can 'project' their thoughts instead of speaking, and 'read' instead of listening.

Excerpt from **Sentient Races and their Abilities.** Proceedings of the Royal Xenological Society, September 1888.

***

In a part of deep space known as the 'Orkish Marches', an elegant pan ship named the Golden Phoenix lay at anchor by the goblin war fleet. Behind it lay a vast glittering nebula of dust that the Draskan elves had named 'The All-Seeing Eye'.

An elf sat in an observation room, located at the rear of the Phoenix. It was furnished with four beautiful green armchairs, made from dragon wood and upholstered with moonreed cloth. The room was lit by sunsand lamps that reflected a spectral bluish light against the metal inside of her hull. The light gave the cabin a ghostly feel which Aristotle found hypnotic and relaxing. The room's single window was a large crystal canopy, that afforded its passengers a magnificent vista of the nebula. He saw the goblin battleships silhouetted against it, they looked tiny and insignificant.

The elf stared out of the window, entranced with this vision of the deep expanse of creation. He stood 5' 2' tall, and had the sharp chin, high cheekbones and pointed ears so typical of his species. He had made the best use of the observation room during his voyage from New Draska. Since anchoring, he had watched the shuttles fly between the Phoenix and the war fleet, picking up passengers and dropping off supplies and mail.

His acute elfin ears heard the docking bay close for the final time, which meant the shuttle had finished loading. The Phoenix would soon set course once more for the Metropolis.

He heard light footsteps coming along the corridor; a small lady goblin entered the room.

'I see this is the observation room. May I join you Sir? We will be flying past the star dragon's migration route shortly, and I have always wanted to see them,' said the goblinette.

'Please do join me Miss, and allow me to introduce myself, my name is Aristotle Vim, on route to the Metropolis.' Vim got to his feet and pulled back a chair for the goblinette to sit on.

'Harmony Honeyhill Sir, War Correspondent for the Fashionable Intelligencer, we shall be together the whole voyage, and I must say how exciting it is to have the company of an elf. Are you a moon elf or a common elf Sir?'

'A high elf.'

'Golly goblins! You are my first high elf. If you do not mind me asking, are you travelling for business or pleasure?'

'Business, I shall join one of my elfin colleagues in a new venture to provide a telepathic communication service for the city', replied Aristotle, 'We intend to make it possible for a goblin, to send a message to any other telepath anywhere in the known universe. All at the speed of pure thought, which is of course, infinite'.

'And do you offer your telepathic services commercially now? I do so urgently need to send a message to the Metropolis you see. I can pay you. How much do you charge?'

'I shall be working at the Municipal Telepathy Office, which has not opened yet, but I should be happy to oblige you, and I can do this without payment.'

'Oh dear Mr. Vim I must insist you take my money, just give me a receipt so I can claim it back from the newspaper. The opportunity to send a story by telepath is wonderful luck.'

'What would you like to communicate and to whom Miss?' said Aristotle.

Harmony reached for her notebook and started reading aloud.

'This news is sent to you from Harmony Honeyhill, assigned to the goblin war fleet on the orkish marches. Two days ago, on the 25th of March, tiny specks of light were seen against the backdrop of the 'Eye of God' nebula from the command decks of the goblin battleships. They were the tell-tale signs of a fierce fire fight between the dwarven ironclads of their grand fleet, and the orkish raiding boats of Princess Sting and her lover, the infamous pirate Captain Jack Coffin. Intercepts of messages from the dwarven fleet claim a decisive victory, and the destruction of Coffin's ship 'Star Thunder'.

It would seem that Sting's orkish fleet in the marches has been defeated in detail.'

Aristotle sat motionless in his armchair to cast a telepathy spell:

> *Across time and space I cast my mind*
> *By the strength of my Soul*
> *I send my conscious thoughts*
> *My mind forms ideas, ideas project magic*
> *Across time and space I cast my mind*

Once he had entered a telepathic trance, he saw the mind of Captain Sebastian Valancy through his third eye. He locked minds with him.

'*Nice to share minds with you Vim,*' Sebastian projected '*Your clarity is as impressive as I had hoped.*'

'*Most kind of you to say so Sir,*' Aristotle projected back.

After receiving the message told to Aristotle by Harmony Honeyhill, Sebastian projected back: '*Well that is astonishing news. I shall send a kobold messenger over to the Intelligencer right away. When word gets out that news of a battle was related to the Metropolis days before any other source, everyone will want to make use of our telepathy service. Please be sure to invite Miss Honeyhill to our opening party on Thursday evening. There will be no charge for the message*'

'*But she insists on paying Sir.*'

'*Oh, does she? Alright, the standard rate then, same payment as in New Draska'.*

'*Aristotle, when you get here I will send someone over to meet you. We are hiring goblins now to help staff the office, so it will probably be one of them,*' projected Sebastian.

Something is amusing Sebastian, thought Aristotle. He thought of peeping into Sebastian's mind to see what the joke was, but he dismissed the impulse immediately. Sebastian would probably have blocked the mental intrusion, and mind-reading without permission is considered most impolite in elfin society.

'*I will ask the goblin to meet you at the docks and escort you to the Telepathy Office. She is to be your personal assistant in future. I look forward to seeing you in person soon,*' projected Sebastian.

Aristotle came out of the trance.

'I sent your message Miss Honeyhill, it will be at your newspaper within the hour. Captain Sebastian Valancy invites you to the opening party at the Telepathy office in four days' time, just 12 hours after our arrival in the Metropolis. Please feel free to bring a companion should you choose to attend,' said Aristotle.

'Why thank you, I should be delighted to attend. Will this be your first visit to the Metropolis Mr. Vim?'

'Yes, it is. I'm so looking forwards to staying in the largest city in the history of the galaxy,' said Vim.

'When a soul loses interest in the Metropolis then it is time for a fresh reincarnation, or so the saying goes,' said Harmony proudly. 'It has changed so much in the last 28 years that I have been alive, and is still on the move. In fact, it's changing faster and faster. There are triple-decker trams above ground, trains below ground, free magical medicine for anyone sick, plenty of vegetables to eat, lots of housing, lots of jobs and opportunities for business, even municipal baths. My young nephews and nieces can swim, all of them! But the biggest improvement will be the Municipal Weather Machine.'

'The weather machine?' enquired Aristotle.

'Control of the weather by a magical machine. It will no longer rain, except at convenient times, and then just in localized spots to water the parks and gardens, and it will always be warm, whatever the time of year. Little black clouds will put out fires.'

'Well I look forward to exploring your great city,' said Aristotle.

'Are you travelling alone Mr. Vim?' said Harmony.

'Please call me Aristotle. Sort of alone, but I do have a battlecast in the hold.'

'A battlecast? What is that?'

'It's a golem created for war. The other passengers seem to like him because he keeps the ogres on their best behaviour.'

Harmony knew a golem was magically created from inanimate matter.

Aristotle became distracted by the strange dots off the nebula he had noticed earlier.

'Excuse me Miss...'

'Please call me Harmony.'

'Harmony, please forgive me for changing the subject, but what are those dots and how far away are they?' Aristotle asked as he pointed through the crystal canopy at the dark specks in the distance.

'Oh, they are the star dragons I have been looking for, and they are relatively close too, only about 5000 miles away', said Harmony.

The dragons looked like specks of ground black pepper against the purples and pinks of the 'Eye'.

'They have been navigating these lanes for millions of years. I never thought I would see them.'

How could Dragons use wings to fly in a vacuum, what do they gain traction on? thought Aristotle.

Perhaps some elves understood dragon flight, but Aristotle was a telepath and a mentalist wizard and knew next to nothing about Xenozoology. Everyone knew star dragons were huge creatures, the largest known species of dragon in fact, but they looked so small against the backdrop of the pan-dimensional space lane. Then a notion came to him, he wondered if by means of telepathy, he could listen to their songs? Aristotle re-entered a trance, and to his surprise through his mind's eye, he could hear them sing. Undistorted across the distance of hyperspace, a beautiful sweet melody played out in projected thought.

'I can hear their songs with my mind Harmony. It is so beautiful.'

'Please sing the tune to me, Sir,' said Harmony.

As he listened, he sang out, and as he sang, Harmony jotted down the tunes on her reporter's notepad.

Who is the mind that listens to our song? The thoughts entered directly into his mind from a distant star dragon.

He was taken aback. This was the first telepathic communication he had ever had with a creature that was not a high elf.

Hesitantly, he introduced himself by telepathy, *'My name is Aristotle of the house of Vim, I am a high elf of the Draskan line, and I hold the rank of lieutenant. I am travelling to the Metropolis to work as a telepath. May I ask who you are Sir?'* responded Aristotle in thought.

'My name is Starcatcher, and I am a star dragon prince of the city of Salin. I am returning with my clan after a hunt, to the roosts near our city. We have not had the pleasure of communicating with a high elf for a long time, not since the fall of Draska.'

'Such are the dangers of demon bottles,' replied Aristotle.

'The ship you are on does not have such a dangerous device, but only yesterday I sensed the telepathic raging of a vicious demon called Vebizel. He projected his fury from inside a bottle that drove a goblin battleship; even from inside the pocket dimension that imprisoned him. But I must change the subject to a pressing matter, would you be willing to help save the lives of some orks, Lieutenant Vim?' asked Starcatcher.

Aristotle had never met an ork before and knew they were an unruly, warlike race of creatures. But they were sentient none the less, so Aristotle would not want to see them die if he could help it. *'I will help if I can what would you have me do?'*

'I came across a battle-damaged orkish warship that had escaped from

the battle with the dwarfs,' Starcatcher explained. *'Before it broke up, it ejected a lifeboat; I sensed it had four orks on board. The lifeboat is tiny and will run out of oxygen soon. I have been dragging it for hours, and the orks still left alive will soon suffocate unless I teleport them to your ship. To do that and minimise the chance of a bad teleport, I need to lock onto your mind, are you willing to let me do that?'*

'Of course, send them Sir'.

From the canopy Aristotle saw a speck leave the flight. It grew in size until it appeared as a huge and wondrous dragon. From the tip of his snout to the end of his tail it was at least ten times longer than the Golden Phoenix, and his wingspan was greater still. His scales were an iridescent violet in colour. The dragon tugged along the small metal cylinder which was the orkish lifeboat.

As Starcatcher passed over the ship, with a loud popping of displaced air, four orks materialised onto the deck.

'I bid you Goodbye for now elf. I do hope to contact you soon,' Starcatcher projected, *'Remember how to share minds with me. I would like to speak to you soon. You can use my scale as an arcane connection to make the telepathy easier.'*

'It would be an honour Lord Starcatcher, prince of the star dragons,' Aristotle projected, *'I will remember your mind's door. I am your humble servant, Aristotle Vim'.*

Aristotle came out of his trance. He rushed over to the orks, checking them in turn for signs of life. Next to the bodies of the orks, was a diamond-shaped dragon's scale.

A fierce old warrior ork, came to consciousness. Looking at Aristotle, he said, 'Is she alive?'

'No Sir, she is dead.'

16

'It seems I have some sort of magical disease, doubtless contracted at the insanitary surgery of that quack Dr. Apricot; and it would be only just and proper to take him to court to claim back all the money I defrauded him out of. The symptoms are that I am in some sort of mind sharing with a nasty demoness by the name of Pandamonia. She constantly exhorts me to do such unladylike and improper things. She is a dirty promiscuous creature, and has taken quite an improper interest in the orkish pirate, Jack Coffin.'

Excerpts from the **Diary of Miss Euphoria Fireheart**, 29th March 1898.

***

As the Golden Phoenix descended towards the metropolitan dockside Aristotle Vim admired the vista of the whole city from its observation gallery. Aristotle's mother, who had been born in the wondrous city of Draska, had told him of its majesty; still he was astonished at the sight of the goblin capital. Draska may have once been the most beautiful city in the history of the known universe, but the Goblin Metropolis is the biggest and the most industrious city that was ever raised, and it is still growing fast. Set on the Avon and Bone rivers, it is a city of countless busy workshops, each of them creating the magical artefacts traded across the furthest reaches of the galaxy.

To the North, the huge blades of the Municipal Weather Machine turned gracefully. It was so far away, the largest magical device ever built to stand on a planet's surface appeared rather small. It looked like some marvellous metallic blue-winged insect, set against the white snow-covered hills on the Northern horizon.

To the East, the sky scintillated with the spectral colours of magical pollutants as they blew out of the city and over the mutated forest of Ecclesdown.

The Golden Phoenix landed gently at the Southern Dockside; a gangplank extended out to the stairs.

The orks were off first. Jack Coffin and Mandrake carried the wooden boxes that contained the bodies of Princess Sting and Lieutenant Mortimer off the ship. Then they waited for Aristotle at the dockside.

Aristotle knew that any orkish pirate worth his share of loot could spot a dwarven merchant ship when he saw one, and he could see Coffin had spied a large one being unloaded.

'A dwarven captain is misrepresenting his golems,' Coffin said to Aristotle.

'How so?'

'Starsteel is how.'

'That dwarf has imported 100 starsteel golems. Military-grade starsteel, so they are not worker golems, they are battlecasts. I know all about them, some were teleported into my ship in a space battle. Their armour can deflect a four-pounder cannon shell,' said Coffin.

Aristotle looked over at the golems being unloaded from the dwarven ship.

'Why would anyone import 100 battlecasts into the Metropolis?' said Aristotle.

'Not for any good reason I'd wager. If you can, I suggest you let the authorities know about them, and they might consider arming the city guards with troll hammers,' said Coffin.

'I shall let Sebastian know,' said Aristotle.

'I am grateful for your rescue, and hope that one day I can repay my debt to you,' said Coffin.

'Not at all; if there is any other way in which I can assist you, please let me know. You can find me at the newly opened Telepathy Office at Arcadia Square, Dragonfair,' replied Aristotle.

After his communication with Sebastian during the voyage, Aristotle had given some thought as to who he was to meet after landing. To his surprise, it was a high elf lady in miniature. He had no idea there were any elfin women in the Metropolis. Her thick hair was a deep auburn, which flowed over her shoulders. She dressed in classical elfin style, identical in cut, but not colour, to the yellow kimono worn by Princess Salonicha during her recent engagement ceremony to Prince Archimedes, except in this case, it was a stronger and more magical shade of indigo. Perhaps her most distinctive feature though was that she was completely unmasked.

'You must be Lieutenant Vim, very pleased to meet you', she said in ungrammatical Draskan, laced with a heavy Goblin accent, 'My name is Euphoria Fireheart, newly employed at the Metropolitan

Telepathy Office. I am honoured to make your acquaintance Sir.'
Euphoria gave Aristotle a small polite curtsey, Aristotle replied with
a bow.

'I am your servant Ma'am', said Aristotle. He tried not to show
disquiet, but he was quite taken aback by her slightly odd facsimile of
elfin beauty and manners. This goblinette was a perfect illusion of
an elf lady, except when she spoke or moved, then she betrayed the
unmistakable hallmarks of a goblin.

'I am a Miss, not a Madam, and please call me Euphoria', she
corrected in the common tongue, having exhausted her meagre
Draskan, 'Sir you must be tired and thirsty after your journey, would
you care for some tea?'

Aristotle introduced the orks to Euphoria. Pandamonia, who was
in Hell, shared Euphoria's mind. She saw, heard and felt anything
Euphoria could, and she took an interest in Coffin on sight. *I want
you to get into bed with that one*, thought Pandamonia directly into
Euphoria's mind.

Euphoria felt Pandamonia's lust for the ork; sharing her
excitement, and her body to respond in a most awkward and
embarrassing manner. *Stop it you dirty lascivious demon*, Euphoria
thought back.

'Miss Euphoria, please could you tell me where I could find an
undertaker, and where I could sell some manna,' asked Coffin.

Given the distraction that excited her body, Euphoria had to get a
firm grip of herself to pay attention to the orks questions, which she
only just managed to do. 'Isaac Cripplegate on Riddle Street is well
spoken of, and he is not far from the manna exchange on Phoenix
Street, you can buy and sell manna there. You could hire a kobold to
show you the way. You can also hire a hand cart and porter for your
crates,' as she pointed to a party of kobold guides.

'Thank you miss, and thank you Aristotle,' said Coffin, and with a
deep bow, and to Euphoria's relief, he went on his way.

The dockside was full of café's and small restaurants, where
travellers could refresh themselves in the open air. Euphoria invited
Aristotle to sit at a small table, and ordered a pot of elfin tea, with
two plates of kobold nuts and berries.

Aristotle found the tea and small meal to be most refreshing.

'While the underground trains are fastest, and horse-drawn cabs
the most comfortable, the most informative way to see the city is
from the top deck of a triple-decker tram. May I suggest we travel

that way?' said Euphoria.

'How will Clockheart find his way to the telepathy office?' asked Aristotle. Referring to his battlecast golem, who was far too heavy for the tram.

'Just hire a kobold to guide him there; it should only cost you a penny.'

Aristotle and Euphoria made their way to the stop for the number 48 triple-decker tram that runs from the pan ship docks to Dragonfair. They climbed the stairs to the top deck, and as luck would have it the two front seats were vacant, which gave them an eye-catching view of the city's landmarks they passed on the way to the telepathy office.

17

Two infernal mirrors are to be used. Move one of the mirrors over to almost the centre of the conjuring circle, and the other mirror to face it exactly. The reflections in each mirror are reflected into the other, creating an image of a mirror in the other mirror, and so on, and so on. In one mirror there will be an infinite number of reflections, but not in the other. Rather in the centre of many nested reflections, will be a small black rectangular door; the door to Hell.

Excerpt from **Keys to the Dark Gate** 1st Edition

***

Two of the Metropolis' most important buildings are the Royal Mint and the Municipal Manna Exchange, both of which are situated in the borough of Northminster. They stand opposite each other on Phoenix Street, and are served by the Royal Western Line's 'Exchange' underground railway station, and the number 57, 112 and 38 tram routes. The underground is fastest, so given the urgency of the developing peril, Henry boarded a train from near the Goodhalf's home, and arrived at Exchange just 30 minutes later.

The Manna Exchange is two stories high, with several large archway entrances through which large numbers of goblins, of diverse magical professions, scurry in and out to buy and sell the commodities that power their trades.

Henry entered the archway marked 'gate 12', over which the exchange management had hung one of the many warning signs, each of which was prominently displayed in large letters that read:

<u>DANGER!</u> *High Magical Aura and Volatile Manna*
<u>SPELL CASTING STRICTLY PROHIBITED</u>

Henry was sensitive to magic; he could feel the strength of the aura. Every sensation experienced inside the exchange was sharper, more intense, and paradoxically more real than it should be from its mundane nature: Colours sparkled, smells were more distinct, and sounds felt as if they did not need to go through your ears to get into the middle of your head.

This effect is of course due to such a large amount of manna being stored in such a relatively small area. Manna, the physical manifestation of magical power, had magnified the magical aura of the exchange. Even the weakest spell cast within such an aura would be greatly amplified in power, and might easily run out of control. It would be like trying to move a cart at the top of an icy hill, where even the smallest movement would set it into a dangerous slide.

The Manna Exchange was a crowded ant's nest of activity. At its heart was the central auction, where importers brought in raw manna by the queen from all over the known universe, and then sold it on to the wholesalers.

The wholesalers then sold the manna on to retailers and other large consumers. The end-users were magicians, apocatharies, doctors, artefact makers, and all manner of other artisans and professionals from across the city. All of them involved in the production of magical goods and services and who needed to buy manna for their trade.

Henry was looking for one wholesaler in particular, namely of Graves and Inglewood. He found their stand at the North end of the Exchange, where Vanilla and Pinch awaited him. Above the stand was a bright purple sign advertising their enterprise in large letters:

Nimrod Graves and Canaan Inglewood Wholesalers of Finest Quality Manna.

'Vanilla found the infernal creation manna, so I stopped them selling it Master Henry sir,' Pinch said before Henry could ask.

'Good man Pinch, that's the spirit!' Henry replied heartily.

A small queue had built up and its members were waiting to be seen to by the salesmen. Henry addressed the salesmen and the queue, and said, 'Stop what you're doing everyone, I need to speak with the wholesalers.'

Murmuring spread along the queue.

'Here, who do you think you are? I'm trying to run a business,' said one of the salesmen.

'My name is Pharaoh Henry. I am a High Constable of the city and a Grand Master wizard.'

The crowd knew the name Pharaoh Henry and feared his reputation, everyone in the Metropolis did.

The prospective customers dispersed immediately before any mention of getting invited to a demon hunt could be suggested. Pinch kept especially quiet, and tried to look as inconspicuous as possible just in case Henry wanted to dragoon him into doing something dangerous.

The salesman had also heard of Henry, and the things he got up to, and made other goblins do. Now they looked afraid, 'Mr. Henry, I don't want any disagreement, but please...' the salesman was unable to finish his sentence before being abruptly stopped by Henry, who had cast a discreet but powerful magical spell on him by just the slightest finger gesture. Spellcasting, with so much volatile manna about, was of course in direct violation of the exchange's safety regulations, but Pinch was looking the other way at the time, and the exchange guards had hurried off, so it went unnoticed by the law. The spell left the salesman as silent and still as a stone statue.

'May I ask your name Sir?'

Henry asked the second salesman.

'My name is Canaan Inglewood Sir, and I respectfully ask, hoping not to cause offence Sir, in deference to your rank as Grand Master Wizard and all Sir, or to impede you in the duties of your official office as High Constable, but I do object to having my memory read. It's my memory you see Sir, personal to me, its private...' Replied Inglewood desperately.

Henry ignored Mr. Inglewood's plea. His eyes transformed into that of a snake. He transfixed Mr. Inglewood with his stare and then began to look through his memories. Once inside his mind, the first thing he did was search for memories as to who had sold the creation manna; he quickly found who he was looking for. The culprit was a tall goblin man, dressed in an ochre jacket and green cravat. He had asked for £80 for a queen of creation manna; very cheap, suspiciously so. Then Henry searched for who had bought it, and saw the sale to Dr. Apricot.

Henry also found another interesting memory; one unrelated to the tainted manna. It was that of a stern-looking ork. He wore a dirty blood-stained uniform and had freshly stitched wounds that had been sewn up with a needle, rather than healed with magic. Henry knew his uniforms, all nations, all ranks. That uniform was of a Captain in the Orkish Navy, which strictly implied this ork was a pirate.

The ork produced an earring containing five pawns of destruction manna, and a necklace containing a rook of comprehension manna and demanded £15 for it. Inglewood initially tried to bargain with him but was too frightened to press the issue. He knew he could make a healthy profit as comprehension and destruction manna was in such short supply, besides that ork looked very intimidating.

That ork looks like he has just been in battle thought Henry to himself, *what is he doing in the Metropolis?*

Henry released Inglewood, leaving him trembling with fear.

'How much of the tainted manna do you still have Mr. Graves?' asked Henry.

'7 rooks and 3 pawns Sir,' replied Graves.

'You have sold 3 rooks and 9 pawns of tainted manna to four customers, including a rook to Dr. Apricot. Is that correct?' Henry asked Graves.

'The amount is correct Sir. But we don't keep records as to our customer's identities,' said Graves.

Henry gave Graves a long merciless stare, that successfully brought home to the salesman, the intense level of the wizard's frustration at his inadequate response to this most serious breach of hygiene.

'Under the powers invested in me as High Constable, and pursuant to section 12 of the Magical Sanitation Act 1857, I confiscate this manna on the grounds that I have reason to believe it to be infernally tainted. I will pay you eighty pounds compensation. You must give me the remaining tainted manna immediately. If you see any of the customers who bought some, then you are legally obliged to warn them it is not to be used, and instruct them to contact Constable Pinch, who will take custody of it. Pinch will be stationed at Oakensoul's college for the duration of this investigation. Make all goblins aware that knowingly using, selling, or possessing infernal manna is a serious criminal offence under sections s8.1(3), s9 and s11, of the afore mentioned statute, and the penalty is imprisonment at Oubliette, or even death, for the transgression of its provisions. Do you understand the seriousness of your situation my good goblin?' Henry gave Inglewood the money.

Inglewood was already very afraid, but the mention of Oubliette caused him to stiffen with fear, 'Oh yes Sir, we will keep an eye out Sir.'

'I will also buy the earring and necklace the ork sold you. I will give you £20, which is more than you paid for them,' said Henry. Purely out of force of habit, the salesman momentarily thought of haggling with Henry, but on reflection quickly dropped the bad idea. He handed over the jewellery and took the money.

Other than his official Oakensoul's badge, Henry never wore jewellery. He had no interest in it, and knew nothing about it. He passed them to Vanilla, 'Can you tell me anything about these?'

She looked closely at the earring, 'It is of orkish style but of the finest craftsmanship. This was made by a dwarf slave on Caragula,' she said.

'They come from an orkish pirate. Experienced pirates always wear some item of jewellery on their body that contains manna, especially when they go on raids. The reason is that if they are killed in space, and their corpse found, then the value of the manna will cover the cost of a Christian burial,' said Henry, 'Can you detect an arcane connection?'

Eyes closed, she held the earring, and then the necklace, as she attempted to augur if either piece had an arcane connection, and if so, to whom. The powerful magical aura of the Manna Exchange greatly enhanced her divination, 'The earring belongs to an ork, and he is close by. The necklace once belonged to an orkette. She is dead, but her corpse is also near.'

'Most impressive,' said Henry. *Such skill*, he thought.

Henry wondered whether he needed to speak to this ork. Under normal circumstances he wouldn't hesitate, but with so many dangerous things happening he wondered if he could spare the time. After some consideration he decided that he had to find out what this ork was up to, 'Vanilla, do you think you could find this ork and invite him to dinner at Oakensoul's. Please be discreet about it, we do not want the world to know we harbour orkish pirates,' he said.

'I think I can track him down without too much difficulty,' she said.

'Wonderful Villy. Take Pinch with you just in case. After all, he is an orkish pirate, which means he will be dangerous to anyone who upsets him,' said Henry.

Oh no! thought Pinch.

18

A stasis coffin is a magical coffin that, when the lid is shut and sealed, causes time to stop inside it. This effect is achieved by creating a coffin-sized pocket dimension, but without the dimension of time. Bodies inside are perfectly preserved until the lid is opened again, which breaks the spell and restarts both time and the decomposition process.

From **Modern Funerary Practice**, by Isaac Cripplegate, Happy Kobold Press.

***

Captain Coffin knew full well that Lieutenant Mandrake would make a run for it sooner or later. He did not blame him really, after all, they were not in space anymore; and by abandoning his ship, Coffin had relinquished his authority as Captain.

Coffin had ordered Mandrake to go with the bodies to Cripplegate's the undertaker, and request they be preserved in stasis coffins. They were to meet there again when Coffin had sold some manna at the Manna Exchange to pay for the interment of the bodies.

He had not been long, half an hour at most, but when Coffin entered the undertakers Mandrake had gone. Coffin tapped the bell on the counter.

Isaac Cripplegate appeared from behind a curtain. He was a rather small goblin, dressed in a black frock coat and a top hat half as tall as he was, and looked appropriately sullen as was befitting his trade; 'How can I of be of service good Sir?'

'Did my colleague speak to you about putting my dead comrades in stasis coffins?' asked Coffin, in his very direct manner.

'He did indeed, the crates containing the corpses have been placed in the workshop, and we will transfer them to coffins as soon as we have received your payments of ten pounds each Sir,' replied Cripplegate.

Coffin placed four five-pound notes on the counter, 'Do you know where the Lieutenant went?'

'I am afraid I do not, he just left your deceased beloved here to be interred and he went.'

Coffin could guess where he had gone, and it would not be good for him, 'How long does it take to walk to the Orkish Embassy from here?'

'About a twenty-minute walk, sooner by cab.'

Coffin knew Mortimer did not have money for a cab, but that still did not leave him much time to hide from the orkish authorities. As a dishonoured captain the ambassador would, at the very least, have him kidnapped and sent back to Caragula. More probably he would be assassinated. He needed to find somewhere to lay low and find it soon. He thanked Cripplegate for his service and left.

He made his way down Phoenix Street towards the Manna Exchange. At six feet two inches tall, Coffin stood out in the crowd, but the sun was starting to set, so he hoped he would be less easy to spot in the dark. Up ahead he saw a small and painfully thin goblinette, escorted by a police officer who was unaware of what was going on around him. She looked directly at him; she was seeking him out.

The goblinette took a necklace from her bag, and held it up for Coffin to see. It was Sally Sting's necklace that he had just sold to pay for her funeral. He also saw a group of goblins hiding in the crowds; they were circling the goblinette, nasty vicious-looking creatures. Vampires!

One of them drew a revolver and shot at the goblinette at close range. He felt conflicted as to whether to intervene, as he did not want to draw attention to himself, but he did not have much time to act either. Most goblins in such a situation would hesitate, but Coffin was not a goblin, he was an ork, so he did what orks do in situations of uncertainty, he attacked.

***

Villy fingered the necklace in her clutch bag as she made her way down Phoenix Street; she felt its aura and followed the arcane connection it had to its former dead owner. From the direction it took her she correctly deduced that the owner's corpse was located at Cripplegate's the undertakers.

She let go of the necklace, and tried to sense the aura of the earring. She could feel its owner was close; she saw him, an ork standing a few yards in front of her.

How was she to invite him to meet with Pharaoh Henry? She removed the necklace from her bag and held it up, offering it to him.

Then the ork dashed towards her. He moved so fast. He was not running at her, but something near. She looked around and saw there were eyes on her; cruel spiteful eyes that meant her harm; vampires were about to kill her. One of them had a revolver and shot at her.

Belatedly Pinch drew his revolver, but before he could level it, blood spurted from his arm. He dropped his gun. A vampire with frightening fangs was about to tear into him, but instead, it burst into flames. The nearby crowds of goblins panicked and fled. Vampires were attacking them, and the ork was attacking the vampires, then it was all over. Pinch and Vanilla stood in front of Captain Coffin and around them were piles of vampiric ash.

Coffin picked up Pinch's revolver and handed it to him, 'Yours I believe'.

Pinch was silent, stunned by his wound, and the sudden attack that still left him confused.

'Thank you, Sir, and these are yours I believe,' said Vanilla as she handed him Sally Sting's necklace, and his earring. One of the vampires had shot over four rounds at her and missed.

'You were lucky,' said Coffin.

'Not luck…Magic. Mrs Vanilla Catchpenny, at your service Sir.'

'Jack Coffin, at yours,' he said as he sheathed his fighting knife. Given its effect on vampires, the knife had a silver blade.

He looked at her eyes; black pools with tiny silver specks. She looked so frail and weak.

'I will need to report this vampire attack.'

'Don't mention me,' said the ork.

'I have to. Who else should I say destroyed these vampires?'

'Say it was him,' said Coffin, pointing at the petrified Pinch.

'I request you come to Oakensoul's with me and I will put you up for the night and feed you,' said Vanilla.

'I must go,' said Coffin, wanting to get away from all the unwanted attention, and distrustful of this strange little lady mage.

'Would you like to know where her soul has gone to?' Vanilla said to Coffin.

'How did you know even know she was dead?' asked Coffin

'I told you, I'm a wizard. Come to Oakensoul's and I will track her soul for you.'

19

*It is a criminal offence to induce any of the seven deadly sins into the mind of a goblin by magic. The relevant legislation is the **Seven Deadly Sins Act 1846,** where Section three deals with gluttony, four avarice, five lust, six wrath, seven envy, eight vanity and nine sloth. The motivation behind the Act is that these sins destroy the goodness and charity within a goblin's soul, and so divorce him from God's grace. As spells of this nature are by definition evil, their use is banned with a maximum penalty of four years imprisonment.*

From **Goblin Common Law** by Adam Wensleydale, Green Dragon Press.

***

After Euphoria stopped working at the Fireheart's newsstand to take up her post at the Telepathy Office, Prudence asked Zebedee for her old job. Now she worked the subterranean kiosk with Lampwick. She liked the honest work, as it reminded her of her life before infection, when her veins ran with warm blood.

Her counter was two stories underground, and it served the worker goblins who used the passages to get to the railways that operated in tunnels deeper still. The trains below ran day and night, and the deep rumble of them could be heard periodically. She liked the sound; it comforted her, somehow it reminded her of heartbeats. Now she felt something she had not felt for a dragon's age, freedom. The burden of oppressive terror she had carried at the nest had left her.

She picked up a bundle of papers, and carefully arranged them in the rack beside the counter for prospective customers to view. The headline on the front page of the Goblin Times read: **Valiant Pinch Wounded in Further Vampire Attack.**

Her interest peaked, she stopped work to read the front-page story carefully:

Shortly after sunset, on the 31st of March a large band of vampires fell upon terrified goblins going about their business on Phoenix Street. In the violent battle that ensued, all of these horrifying monsters were destroyed by Constable Babylon Pinch. Pinch is the hero of the previous raid on the vampire nest at Peccadillo Street, so it is speculated that this was a revenge attack.

The stalwart officer was injured in the fierce fighting. However, the prominent physician, Dr Obadiah Apricot is quoted as saying, 'With God's help our Pinch should make a full recovery.' We at the Times feel sure that all law-abiding goblins share our relief that our steadfast protector will be back on duty soon. Thank you, Babylon Pinch!

She let out a sigh of relief. *Am I free, does this mean Wormsong has lost so many of her slaves she can no longer hunt for me?* she hoped. *But what of this Babylon Pinch? He must be a very dangerous vampire hunter; will he catch me; destroy me? At least final death at his hand would be quick and painless.*

Maybe they will forget about me, and assume all the vampires are dead. I could be in the clear. Things are on the up, she reasoned. She went into the kitchen behind the stand and made three cups of cocoa. Then she climbed the iron spiral staircase up to Zebedee, who worked the outlet on the ground floor.

'Thank you, Prudence,' said Zebedee, as she gave him the drink, 'It's good you have adapted to working the night shift, not all goblins get used to it.'

'I like the night best, because there are less government police around,' said Prudence, in a half-truth, 'I must give Lampwick his cocoa before it gets cold.' She hurried off down stairs again to Lampwick.

'Let me see if I understand you correctly, you are not a goblin who has learned to shape change into a cat, rather you are a cat who learned the trick of becoming a goblin?' said Prudence, as she gave him his cocoa.

'That's it, Pru. Not a trick I learned, actually I had no choice in the matter, I just morphed into goblin form,' replied Lampwick.

'An uplifted cat, how incredible!' she said, with an expression of genuine interest.

'Not really Pru. Cats are higher than all creatures including goblins and elves, so I am not uplifted in any sense of the word. Besides, animals and plants in the Metropolis are getting mutated as often as goblins nowadays. But I was a ship's cat, and got changed out at sea.'

'Really? Without the need of manna fog?'

'Some days there is more pollution out there than here in the city. Magical storms occur all the time off of the Bone estuary. Think of all those dense clouds of manna that get blown out to sea from the city's chimneys. They create raging tempests out there you know. It's a real hazard of our times.'

'Do you like being a goblin, or would you rather still be a cat?' asked Prudence.

'Being a goblin has opened up my life to many opportunities otherwise unavailable to me. But as you know I do like to shape change back to feline form to run around the city every so often. I can also assume the shape of something in between, a sort of cat-goblin, which also comes in useful on occasion.'

'Go on show us Lampwick, turn yourself into a cat. Show me how you do the transformation,' said Prudence.

'Maybe later, if I turn into a cat here and now all my clothes will fall off, and then I will have to get dressed again, besides I don't want to get naked in front of a load of passing goblins,' said Lampwick. They both laughed.

'But I'll keep you safe Prudence. I'll keep an eye on you,' said Lampwick, as he held up his goblin hand, he magically extended four intimidating cat claws.

'Ooh lovely claws, but I can defend myself better than you think, Mr. Lampwick,' said Prudence with a wink. 'Do you do it with cats or goblin girls?'

'You know you are the only goblinette for me, Prudence.'

'You are such a tease Lampwick Cat!' she replied with a coquettish smile.

'Though there is a lovely grey queen kitty on the square,' said Lampwick.

A young goblin worker from the demon bottle factory stared at Prudence as he walked by. She gave him a look of warm and inviting interest, which while convincing to the uninitiated as perfectly sincere, it was distinct from the genuine expression that she had given to Lampwick.

'Half-a-crown for half an hour Sir,' she said to the man.

The goblin looked unsure, he liked the look of Prudence right enough, but half a crown was a day's wages as a skilled demon bottler.

'Come on sweetheart, don't be shy, you only get what you pay for,' said Prudence.

The goblin pulled out the money from his pocket. He held out two-shilling pieces and a silver sixpence. Prudence took the money, handed it to Lampwick for safekeeping, then led the goblin by his hand into the dark shadows of the narrow unused passageway opposite.

The tunnel was too dark for any normal goblin to see into very far, but Lampwick was far from a normal goblin. He was a shape-changing cat, and his clever eyes could see in the dark far better than any goblin's could. He watched Prudence with her customer. He stood stock still. She stared up into his eyes, and he down into hers. She unbuttoned his shirt, and put her face against his shoulder as if she was kissing it. The goblin remained still as a statue. After a few minutes, she fastened up his shirt again, and made eye contact for just a little longer, before leading him out of the small alley.

She emerged refreshed, but her customer looked exhausted and drained of life. A smile lit up his otherwise worn out expression.

Is that all? Is that how goblins make love, they just look into each other's eyes for a bit? Seems a bit tame, thought Lampwick.

As Prudence's client staggered away, she resumed her place outside the kiosk.

As if by magic, a tall distinguished goblin appeared at the newsstand. He came out of nowhere. *Where did he spring from?* Thought Lampwick.

He was a very well-kempt gentlegoblin dressed in an ochre-coloured jacket and matching trousers, with a white collarless shirt and green silk cravat.

'Could I have copies of both the Revolutionary Goblin and the Metropolitan Herald please?'

Lampwick gave the upper-class stranger a wary glance, as his request for the illegal paper made him suspicious.

The gent picked up on Lampwick's distrust, 'I know you have a copy of the Revolutionary Goblin, and I can assure you, I am neither police nor informer. If I were you would be under arrest by now.'

Lampwick handed him a Herald from above the counter and a copy of the Revolutionary Goblin from below it. 'That will be thrupence, Sir,' said Lampwick.

The man gave Lampwick a shilling. 'Keep the change,' he said, as he stashed away the illegal paper in his satchel.

'Want some business governor?' Prudence asked the goblin.

He glanced at her for an instant. Then, ignoring her, he turned to the arts section of the Herald and started to read. Of course, she found this act of ill-mannered indifference most unsettling both personally and professionally.

'What's this about that opera the Hubris of Draska, did all the papers give the dress rehearsal good reviews?' The toff asked Lampwick.

'Wonderful reviews last night, and it is a sensation across the city. If you want to catch an open-air showing there will be one tomorrow at 9 pm up at Arcadian Gardens,' said Lampwick.

'What do you want with an opera, when you and I could go in the tunnel over there?' said Prudence, making eye contact with the goblin again.

He stared into the black pupils of Prudence's eyes for a few seconds, and then smiled at her and asked, 'How much to go up the alley with you Miss?'

'Half-a-crown for half an hour Sir,' replied Prudence, her confidence in her charms as a tradable commodity restored.

'Well how about you escort me to the opera next Saturday night, and I will pay you a pound now and a pound after the curtain falls,' said the goblin. He produced a crisp green note and an opera ticket from his wallet, offering it to Prudence.

She felt a shiver; there was something not quite right about this prospective customer. She could not be sure if Wormsong sent him, but he paid well enough. She needed the money, to finance her escape from the Metropolis, but did not feel safe about taking it.

'Allow me to introduce myself, my name is Captain Uriah Buckle, formerly of the Royal Navy, and currently a glassmaker to the most eminent magicians in the city. May I inquire as to your name?' said Buckle.

Prudence hesitated.

'Come on now Miss, I cannot escort you unless I know your name. We can watch the opera from the park,' he said.

Prudence took the pound note and the ticket from Buckle's hand and passed it to Lampwick, 'My name is Miss Prudence Pepperhill.'

'I will see you at the opera.' said Buckle. He gave Prudence a bow then left.

'My inner voice tells me there is more to him than meets the eye, and it is not very nice,' said Lampwick.

'I have my suspicions too, but two pounds is a lot of money.'

Lampwick watched Capt. Buckle disappear up the public stairs to Arcadia Square. 'I'll keep an eye on you at the opera, just in case. We will have to tell Zebedee we are taking the evening off, so he can get staff to cover for us.'

20

When a goblin becomes magical it spontaneously develops a single magical ability without having to learn it. Such skills are called **breakthrough abilities**. *The breakthrough ability, is the goblin's starting point to learn new spells.*

From **Magic Theory and Practice** 4ᵗʰ Edition

***

Euphoria and Mercurial greeted the guests arriving for the opening ball of the telepathy office. The guests came in their assorted carriages, the most expensive and ornate of which belonged to Solomon Golemaker. It was made of crystal mined by dwarven teleporters from deep under the crust of a distant gas giant planet. *That must have cost a fortune*, thought Euphoria. To underline his wealth, Golemaker employed moon elves as his footmen rather than goblins, and the carriage was pulled by golden horses, which is widely known to be the most expensive colour to magically dye a horse.

Golemaker alighted, after which he helped Delilah Twotemples out. Euphoria saw he had a demon clinging to his back; it was a green-skinned ugly brute. She was so taken aback by its peculiar nature that she could not help but stare at it. Unfortunately, it noticed her and stared right back, seemly surprised that Euphoria could see it.

'Can you see that thing on Golemaker's back?' Euphoria asked Mercurial.

'No Euphoria, I can see nothing,' said Mercurial.

'*You can see a demon?*' telepathed Pandamonia the succubus.

'*Yes, I can see it,*' thought back Euphoria.

'*Well you should not be able to, but for your information, it is a demon of avarice sent to torment that old miser's soul, as I am going to torment yours, I know your thoughts,*' gloated the succubus smugly.

'*And I yours*', thought back Euphoria. '*You are tired of Hell. You would prefer to live here, in the Metropolis.*'

'No, I wouldn't,' thought the demon unconvincingly, which was very unusual as normally a demon's lie is entirely persuasive.

'It would get you in trouble if the Devil found out that you had ideas to abscond', thought Euphoria.

'We can help each other', thought the demon. Euphoria felt its fear.

'Are you suggesting I do a deal with you, a demon? Do you think I am stupid?'

'You have the better of me Euphoria, you are too clever, so no deals. I will leave you alone.' Now her fear was all too evident.

'No-one can see through a demon's deception', thought Euphoria.

'A demon can, and you can see through my eyes, so you can too, because our minds are linked,' thought the demon.

'Your name is Pandamonia, and you were mortal once, a long time ago?' thought Euphoria.

'Very good Euphoria, and I would like to be again, but there are difficulties', thought Pandamonia.

'Such as demons being hunted down in the Metropolis', thought Euphoria.

'With Pharaoh Henry guarding your city that is a significant risk. And if I am killed while mortal, I will just get sent back to Hell, only to be treated as a traitor.'

'If you come here as a mortal, and get killed, can't you get reincarnated as a mortal creature?'

'But why ask me? Why don't you just read my mind again to find out?'

'I don't like going into your mind, it's twisted and nasty inside there,' thought Euphoria.

'Well I acquired bad karma as a succubus, so if I just leave it to nature then my soul will just return to Hell. But high elves use a reincarnation machine and send their souls back to a body of their choice. So maybe I could come into the Metropolis and live there peacefully, and over time learn to be good, all the time getting reincarnated into an elfin body while I repair my karma,' thought Pandamonia.

'Not a chance if that old zealot Pharaoh Henry found out about you! Anyway, keep away from me or I will get Aristotle to send a telepathy message across the universe to tell everyone Pandamonia *intends to betray Hell itself. I will put the posters up around the city myself!'* thought Euphoria, after which she felt Pandamonia's fear again.

After the last of the guests had arrived, Euphoria and Mercurial joined the party. The entrance hall of the telepathy office had been transformed into a ballroom for the evening. It was filled with the city's important goblins, and sprinkled with a few dwarves, elves and orks.

To all intents and purposes Euphoria and Mercurial looked like elfin ladies, so the party's hosts, Aristotle and Sebastian had requested they be their escorts for the evening. It was to be Euphoria with Aristotle, and Mercurial for Sebastian.

As arranged, Euphoria and Mercurial made their entrances just as the party had assembled; and when they did every goblin's eyes turned on then, scrutinizing their new elfin bodies, dressed up to the nines in elfin gowns. Their ruse was complete, to the wonder and awe of the unwitting guests.

The elves greeted their escorts with deep bows, replied to by graceful curtseys. Sebastian had taken it upon himself to explain to Mercurial the finer technical points of telepathy, all the while admiring her form and attire from his elevated view over her cleavage. Mercurial hung on to his every word with a most convincing pretence that she understood what he was talking about. She said nothing and remained stock still, which Sebastian found most agreeable on more than one count.

Similarly, Aristotle was taken aback with Euphoria's elfin beauty. Other than being a little small for a high elf lady, she made a convincing facsimile and was far less aloof than Mercurial. He felt sure that Sebastian on the other hand, preferred Mercurial's remoteness.

The orchestra played a sublime and haunting melody that permeated the buzz of the chattering guests.

'I recognize this melody. It is supposed to be Anatitia's song from the forthcoming opera, The Hubris of Draska, but I have heard it before,' said Aristotle to Euphoria.

'The opera opens tomorrow night. Perhaps you heard it in rehearsal?' replied Euphoria.

'No not in rehearsal,' Aristotle's eyes widened when the penny dropped, 'It is the star dragon's song I listened into during the voyage here.'

'Really?' said Euphoria.

'Well I did sing it to Harmony Honeyhill who then wrote it down.'

Euphoria still suffered flashbacks of anger at the condescending tone of the rejection letter she had received from Virginia Chanson of the Fashionable Intelligencer. *Who was plagiarising a dragon song as their own?* she wondered.

'Aristotle my good elf, we must chat. Ladies could you excuse us for a few minutes, I am so sorry but I must take your elf from you for a while Miss Euphoria,' said Sebastian.

In a convincing pretence at good manners, Mercurial and Euphoria made the effort to pull faces of disappointment on being abandoned in the midst of goblin high society, but actually they were happy to be afforded the opportunity for their favourite pastime: Gossip.

'What are you going to do about that demon that torments you?' Mercurial asked Euphoria.

'I don't know. It seems to have gone quiet for now, demons live in fear of demons bigger than them, and that one could be in big trouble, so maybe it has gone for good,' said Euphoria.

The pair of them looked around to see who they knew.

'He is Euphrates Glock, the High Constable of Cuman Hill,' said Mercurial.

'Yes, with Solomon Golemaker, that mean old penny-pinch,' replied Euphoria.

'I wager it cost the old skinflint a few shillings to be with Delilah. That one is highly sort after to go to society events by those goblins who can afford her. She became the talk of the Metropolis for her part in her last opera. But that tightwad can afford her with the money he makes fleecing his workers. Just ask any poor goblin desperate enough to work in one of his factories,' said Euphoria in a vinegary tone.

'He didn't skimp on paying for the opera. Apparently, the demonward was a genuine elfin artefact. Smuggled out of the ruins of Draska, and especially imported for the purpose,' said Mercurial.

'Euphoria, you see that very thin goblin with very pointed ears, that is Grand Master Cornelius Hand, leader of the Green Coat Party.'

'I wouldn't want to be seen on the arm of that grotesque beanpole, not if he paid me a rook of manna, but what is strange about him is he has a demon on his back too. A purple demon, a smug-looking thing, with a very superior expression,' said Euphoria.

That's a demon of vanity, said Pandamonia*, I must say you are getting good at seeing the demons.*

'There are ambassadors here too, both for the orks and the dwarves,' said Mercurial.

Mercurial subtly pointed out Kasper Scratch and Meister Aldergund Roggerbrood, of the orks and dwarves respectively. Each ambassador was surrounded by a small entourage of flunkies dressed in their respective national liveries. They stood at opposite sides of the room, which, given the mutual hatred between their peoples and governments, was generally thought to be wise by all.

A small but energetic looking goblinette approached Euphoria and Mercurial, and said, 'Apologies for my intrusion ladies. My name is Harmony Honeyhill, and I am the War Correspondent on the Fashionable Intelligencer. I have already met one of your escorts, Lt. Aristotle Vim, on the voyage. Please could I ask you your views on the city from your perspective as elfin ladies?'

'Oh, we are not elves. We are goblins with magical cosmetic surgery,' admitted Mercurial.

'Mercurial, you have just given away our secrets and torn up my veil of mystique into tiny little pieces!' said Euphoria, who was still furious about the rejection letter.

'You are goblins? Magical surgery? I knew it! I absolutely adore your look! I must get it done myself. Forgive me for asking, I know it is rude of me, but I simply must ask, as you look so stunning, what do you goblinettes do?' said Harmony.

'We are telepathic consultants,' interjected Euphoria before Mercurial could say anything more truthful.

'Telepathic consultants? How avant-garde!' said Harmony.

'Is the opera's melody from a dragon's song?' asked Euphoria, who knew the answer to her question perfectly well.

'Aristotle told you, yes? We met on a pan ship, and I introduced him to the pan-dimensional club.'

'What's that?' asked Euphoria, who was interested in any club that sounded even remotely exclusive.

'A club for goblins who have engaged in physical intimacy in pan-dimensional space,' said Harmony, to the laughter of all.

'You and Aristotle became members of the pan-dimensional club together?' asked Euphoria.

'Oh no, I am a long-standing member, but he did introduce me to the high elf club,' whispered Harmony, to yet more giggles.

Miss Delilah Twotemples, on passing, heard the laughter and correctly suspected it was down to something spicy, so she came to join in, 'Harmony, you all sound like you are sharing the most scandalous tittle-tattle. Please let me in on it,' she said.

'Let me introduce you to these two ladies. Despite appearances, they are not elves; rather they are goblinettes, and their appearance is due to the wonders of modern magical cosmetic surgery,' explained Harmony, at which they all shared their names.

'I made a good commission on those dragon tunes from the old tightwad Golemaker. The melody goes wonderfully with Assyria Neepfield's lyrics,' whispered Delilah, to yet more hilarity.

'My Assyria's lyrics?' asked Euphoria.

'You know Assyria Neepfield?' said Delilah. 'Such a talented wordsmith, I am quite sure he has a promising career ahead of him,'

Euphoria unexpectedly felt a bolt of jealousy towards Miss Twotemples over *her* Assyria.

'Euphoria I have just confessed to plagiarism to you, can you imagine why? 'asked Delilah.

'I am sure I cannot,' replied Euphoria, her nose stuck indignantly into the air.

'Well Euphoria, a Dr. Apricot sent me a large bill for a magical cosmetic transformation of two goblin ladies into elves. But as you can see, I am still a goblin whereas you look like an elf. From this I infer you are the one who tricked poor Dr. Apricot out of an expensive magical procedure.'

Euphoria now looked worried at being caught in a fraud.

'Do not worry Euphoria. Dr. Apricot can swing for his money as far as I am concerned, and so can old Solomon Golemaker for paying me for a melody I did not write. You see Euphoria, I know your little misdeed, and I told you mine because I want us to be friends. Us goblinettes must stick together, protect each other, and keep each other's secrets,' said Delilah.

'May I suggest I take a picture of the three of you for the newspaper?' asked Harmony.

Euphoria was delighted at the idea, and posed with Mercurial and Delilah while Harmony snapped them with her picturebox.

'This should make the front page of the Intelligencer,' said Harmony.

Euphoria let out a squeal of delight at the prospect of her newly found fame, and gave Harmony a hug.

Euphoria and Mercurial enjoyed the rest of the evening more than any other time of their lives. But the time flew by, and soon the guests started to go; eventually they were alone with Aristotle and Sebastian.

'Shall we go home? It is late,' said Mercurial.

Please stay Euphoria, let's join the high elf club, you know you want to, came the thoughts of Pandamonia.

21

There is no doubt that the Satanic, Luciferian and otherwise infernal books possessed by Emmanuel Scribble, did and continue to pose a terrible danger to our city. Unfortunately, the fact he keeps them in privately constructed pocket dimensions of space time puts them outside of metropolitan jurisdiction, and therefore beyond goblin law. This is most unsettling. Never-the-less, case dismissed!

The Judge's comments from the Case of **Rex vs. Scribble** 1898

***

The Grand Goblin Opera House is a tall white stone building with lots of windows, which is situated at the very centre of Arcadian Gardens.

Paying customers could sit inside the theatre itself, to watch the players on stage, but for those not lucky enough to possess a ticket, the Goblin King paid for the opera company to employ an illusionist mage, who would project the music and spectacle as an image over the Opera House itself. That way people in the park could see the opera without having to pay for a ticket.

As arranged, at 9 pm Captain Buckle and Prudence Pepperhill met outside the Opera House in the Great Goblin Park, and then made their way to a nice spot near some trees. She wore a plain black dress long enough to almost reach her ankles. The contrast of her black dress, black hair with her white skin was only broken by a small scarlet rose in her hair.

Most of the audience members in the park were goblins, but there were two elves from the telepathy office and their battle cast golem Clockheart, some satyrs and centaurs who worked over at the post office, and of course the flower fairies.

Flower fairies rarely missed an operatic performance, and tonight, as was the custom, they were drinking sweetroot beer in silver thimbles given to them by goblins. They chatted to each other, and flew around the park, talking to the trees, that in turn rustled messages back and forth with their leaves. Goblins were generous to fairies because they often blessed kind goblins with some magical good luck, and every goblin likes to live in hope.

Lampwick, now in the shape of a cat, sat on a high branch and looked around for Prudence in the crowd until he eventually spotted her with Captain Buckle. Euphoria and Mercurial also sat near Prudence. Their escorts were Aristotle and Sebastian, so they appeared as four high elves sitting together. Clockheart stood by them impassively, keeping guard.

As 'The Hubris of Draska' started, the crowd quieted down. The curtains drew back and the stage was set in the royal palace of classical Draska, with a huge elfin soul bottle and a Draskan demonward in the background.

Queen Anatitia's role was sung by Miss Delilah Twotemples, and very soon Prudence felt the fine hairs at the back of her neck prick up. Miss Twotemples sang the story of the fall of the great elfin city with her sweet tones.

The whole audience became entranced with the tragedy, and exactly on midnight, Delilah Twotemples sang the final piece, Queen Anatitia's song.

Delilah's sad and beautiful voice carried the melody across the audiences in the theatre and the park, bringing tears to every goblin's eyes. The opera ended in tragedy, as Draska fell to the invading demonic hordes.

When the curtains finally closed the audience roared their approval. The curtains opened again, the cast lined up and bowed and curtsied to the electric acclaim of the audience.

'Miss Twotemples will be the talk of the Metropolis after that performance, her voice was beautiful,' Aristotle said to Sebastian.

'The opera was out of this world! Did you notice the Draskan warding stone on the stage? It looked authentic to me,' replied Sebastian.

'How could it be authentic? Draska is overrun with demons, they could not have smuggled a heavy obelisk out of the city, and transported it here surely,' said Aristotle.

The audience, now tired and emotionally exhausted, started to disperse. They drifted out of the theatre and into the gardens which were empty and silent. As it was now past midnight, even the barrow boys in the square had gone home.

As always Lampwick was concerned with Prudence's welfare, so he watched over Prudence as she and Buckle walked past three ogres. The ogres looked peaceful enough, they were sitting on the grass discussing how much they enjoyed Miss Delilah's singing, but you never can be too careful with ogres.

'Would you like to earn another pound Miss Prudence? Would you walk over to those trees with me?' propositioned Capt. Buckle.

Lampwick had climbed a tree from where he could overhear the whole conversation between Prudence and Buckle; his cat instinct told him there was something wrong with this goblin. He knew he had to keep a good eye on Prudence to keep her safe, and so he followed her by making his way along the branches, tree to tree. As Prudence walked, she noticed the leaves were rustling loudly. The evening breeze was no stronger than usual, so it occurred to her that the trees might be saying something to each other. They rustled their leaves and seemed to be agitated, *what are they worried about,* she thought.

Eventually Prudence and Buckle entered the shadows, until they were almost hidden in the dark.

Prudence started looking into Buckle's eyes as she usually did for her customers, and look inside his mind. But he was not transfixed, unexpectedly he punched her hard in her stomach. She doubled up in pain and fell to the ground, winded and unable to call out. Buckle took out a stick from his satchel intending to impale her through her heart; but before he could, Lampwick raced to the scene just in time to stop him. Buckle leaned over Prudence's fallen body to destroy her, Lampwick leapt onto his back; with his cat claws extended he tore into the flesh of his shoulders. Buckle screamed in pain; then raising himself with unnatural speed, he threw Lampwick off of him and sent the cat spinning through the air.

Lampwick landed on his feet in a way no goblin could, hissing and spitting at Buckle. Captain Buckle was a large powerfully built goblin, but despite his size, he closed on Lampwick with blinding rapidity. Buckle threw a kick at Lampwick, who needed all his feline agility to evade it.

He almost had me, this goblin is too fast, Lampwick thought to himself.

Captain Buckle came at Lampwick again. Lampwick turned and used his claws to quickly scramble up the tree.

Prudence was still winded from the blow, breathless in her tight corset. She tried to crawl away, but Captain Buckle was after her. He was about to impale her again, when Lampwick leapt at him once more. Lampwick's claws tore into Buckles flesh, his blackish-red blood splattered from the fresh wounds. Buckle struck at Lampwick, and this time his punch caught the cat square on the jaw, shattering bone and knocking him out cold.

'Here leave that poor lady alone!' came Clockheart's voice out of the darkness.

Without hesitation, Clockheart threw a left jab into Buckle's face. Now normally goblins are much weaker than battlecasts, but Buckle held his own for a while, each of them trading blows, one for one, until Clockheart, by virtue of his starsteel armoured shell and his indifference to pain, began to gain the upper hand. Then, suddenly and without warning, Buckle disappeared.

Euphoria, Mercurial and the elves had arrived close behind Clockheart. Like most elves, Aristotle and Sebastian were averse to physical violence. 'Master Aristotle please pick up the lady, Master Sebastian you pick up the cat-goblin, we must get them both to safety,' said Euphoria, who took command of the situation.

The goblinettes and the elves carried Prudence and Lampwick out of the trees, and then out of the park, and across the square. Some flower fairies, who had come to investigate the commotion, flew overhead of the retreating party. The elves, Clockheart and Mercurial could not see the now invisible Captain Buckle but the fairies could, and strangely enough so could Euphoria.

The fairies flew over Buckle, and used their dust to magically outline his shape for a few seconds, just enough time for Clockheart to place himself between Buckle and the retreating party, and give the elves enough time to carry Lampwick and Prudence to safety.

Buckle tried to make one last dash for Prudence to kill her, but Clockheart was blocking his path.

Euphoria was now in the centre of the square with Mercurial. She called out to the retreating elves, 'Quickly, take the wounded to the newsstand.'

It was very late, and Zebedee, was just about to go to bed when he heard the shouting outside in the square. He made his way to the door, opening it just in time for Vim and Valancy to carry Lampwick and Prudence inside the cabin. The newsstand door was too small for Clockheart to enter, so he stayed outside on guard. Aristotle Vim put Prudence down, and though she was still winded and in pain, she was able to stagger the few steps before falling to the floor. Mercurial cut her corset laces to allow her to breathe more easily.

Euphoria was still outside the newsagents with Clockheart, she could see Captain Buckle racing to the entrance, and knew he was invisible to Clockheart. Euphoria saw Captain Buckle in a new form, not a goblin, rather he now appeared as a demon, with many eyes and mouths, each full of long fangs.

'Go!' Euphoria commanded the demonic Captain Buckle.

Remarkably, the square flashed with magical colour that lit up the night sky, and butterflies popped into existence before disappearing again. Buckle staggered backwards, he attempted to resist Euphoria's magical command but he could not. Compelled by Euphoria's newly found magical gift, he was forced to retreat across the square and out of view.

'Euphoria, you can ward a major demon now, I'm impressed,' thought Pandamonia.

22

'When all three powers of government: legislature, executive and judicial are given to the same goblins, or band of goblins, then those goblins can govern with absolute authority. The careful separation of powers, and their management by separate institutions, safeguards against such tyranny.'

'No bill shall be passed into law unless it has first been heard in the House of Wizards, and is then approved by a majority of them in a vote.'

Excerpts from **Principles of the Goblin Constitution** by Jacob Firkin. Green Dragon Press.

***

Jack Coffin woke up in a soft bed. As he got up, he saw that someone had magically healed his wound, and cleaned his uniform while he had slept. He took a long hot shower, shaved and dressed. Now he was clean and rested, he felt better than he had done for weeks.

After a tap of tiny knuckles at the door, Vanilla Catchpenny entered the room.

'How did you manage to take my uniform without waking me, I am supposed to be an ork.'

'I am a mage; I can do things undetected. Allow me to introduce myself I am Mistress Vanilla Catchpenny, certified wizard and seer, and I've got a job offer for you whatever your name is,'

'Well you are a certified something, and my name is Captain Coffin to you. I'm listening about the job offer,' said Coffin.

'My boss, the Grand Master Wizard Pharaoh Henry was so impressed at your performance against the vampires that he offers you paid employment as my bodyguard, at twenty pounds a week,'

'And what will this job entail?'

'In the first instance, it will be to protect me and do what I say at all times. You will be a sort of guard dog, my pet ork so to speak,' said Vanilla, giggling.

'Do what for you?'

'Do what I say to the letter. Obey my every command, no matter how preposterous,' said Vanilla, who was enjoying herself and no mistake.

'And what is your first half-baked instruction my petite mistress, put you over my knee and spank you?'

'I'm your guv'nor, so behave yourself ork boy, or I'll thump you,' said Vanilla. She held up her tiny fist to the brute.

'What do you want to do?' Said Coffin.

'Let's find out where the soul of the owner of that necklace has gone.'

'You can do that?'

'Of course, I can, I told you, I'm a wizard. But I need a drug called alapania, and so I need a letter of permission from the government to buy it legally. Your first job is to escort me to the Parliament of Wizards.' Vanilla did not mention that it was only illegal for her to buy alapania because she was registered as an addict.

Vanilla took Coffin to breakfast, after which they made their way to the Parliament by tram.

The Parliament building itself was made of pink sandstone, but not of cut blocks. Rather it had been magically grown out of the ground by ritual magic, and so was made of a huge single piece of stone; despite having huge beautiful windows, and arched doorways.

'What does this parliament of yours do?' asked Coffin, appearing as unimpressed as he could.

'It does a lot of things, but its big job is to pass laws. Laws are made by wizards elected to do the job.' she replied.

'And who gets to elect these members of parliament?'

'We do; wizards vote who gets to sit in parliament.'

'Only wizards vote?'

'Naturally only wizards vote,' said Vanilla, 'we can't have any old hoi-polloi voting. Just wizards like me,' said Vanilla, as she strode up to the main entrance and walked in.

'Stop there, Madam, I need to check your identity,' said the doorman.

'Less of your lip or I'll get my ork to bash you.'

'That's Vanilla Catchpenny, she's a famous wizard,' said a second doorman.

'So sorry Madam.'

'Come on Coffin, quick now or I'll have to put you on a leash,' said Vanilla.

They made their way to the spectator's gallery and sat down. The benches on both sides of the wizard's chamber in the Houses of Parliament were packed with goblins, and between them sat the clerks and the speaker of the house.

'All silent for the esteemed wizard Grand Master Cornelius Hand,' screamed the speaker, as he furiously banged his gavel to demand attention.

Cornelius Hand stood up from the front bench of the House of Wizards. Hand enjoyed expensive clothing, and today he wore a silk suit dyed iridescent green. Green was the colour of the Magical Philosophers Party often incorrectly referred to as the Green Coat Party, of which he was leader. Behind him sat the Transitionalist Sages, his allies. His opponents sat on the opposite side of the chamber, the Wizard's Hat, the Golden Staff, and the Traditional Hermeticists. Between the opposing benches on the speaker's chair, sat a small blue-faced goblin, the esteemed speaker of the House of Wizards, Master Erasmus Rickety. Rickety had developed a penetrating voice and blue face, as a magical mutation brought on by the constant trauma of having to scream at members of parliament who did not listen to him.

Master Hand stood still for a moment until the murmur from the benches had died down. Then when he was sure he had everyone's attention he started his speech:

'Ladygoblins and gentlegoblins of the House, tonight I request you support these much overdue proposals to repeal the outdated and costly section 23 of the Demon Act of 1854. As you know this prohibits the keeping of demons anywhere on the planet. It effectively bans the use of demon bottles within the city limits of the Metropolis. I ask you to vote to allow the use of demon bottles, as a safe and cost-effective alternative to burning raw manna. Demon bottles could power the magical spells which drive the industry of our great city and do so far more economically. Think of the cost of all the precious manna our city wastes! Wind and sky manna to work the weather machine that keeps us warm and the air fresh and clean from pollutants. Matter manna that drives our trains and trams. Flesh manna makes our crops grow in abundance, cures disease and sickness. Energy manna lights our caves and our streets at night. All these things that afford us such comfort and safety, but the expensive manna we waste costs us dearly. Just think how much we could save, thousands of queens of raw manna, year after year, at an exorbitant price.

But we have an alternative to power our beloved city at a fraction of the cost. That alternative is the demon bottle. With the demon bottle it is the demon that does the magic for us and for free. It costs only the manufacture of the bottle itself, plus the price of a captured demon, and as we all know there are thousands of them running around on old Draska. Now I am sure the opposition is going to try and frighten us with tales of how demon bottles brought the downfall of Draska. That they are unsafe and can never be used. I say look at our new powerful spells now available to trap and control demons, and how much stronger the magic needed to do so safely has become. I say we will appoint a Minister for Demon Bottle Safety to give us the assurance that our powerful magic will protect us against accidental demon escapes. Of course, the minister would need to be appointed by our good Goblin King himself, so no party in this chamber can gain undue influence over the safety officer.

Let us not be ruled by fear my Brother wizards, let us elevate our city to even greater heights, let us make the use of demon bottles legal in the Metropolis, I say repeal Section 23 of the Demon Act of 1854!'

Cornelius Hand's final plea was met with a roar of approval from the Magical Philosophers benches, and moans of derision from the wizards on the benches opposite them.

'Order, order! I call the ladies and gentlegoblins of this house to order! Order, order, we must now hear from the head of the opposition to the amendment, the Right Reverend Noah Bentley,' screamed the little blue-faced speaker, while shouting to be heard and banging his gavel in a frenzy.

Bentley leaned heavily on his stick as he stood up. Prior to his injury, he had enjoyed a reputation for being the city's foremost vampire hunter. He eyed the wizards on the opposite benches, and his fearful gaze silenced those rowdy ministers in an instant.

'Fellow wizards, have we forgotten how we came to be on this planet, in our great city? That our goblin ancestors were once created by high elves of Draska to do their menial work? And where is that great city now? Destroyed by demons the high elves had thought in their arrogance, that they could control! Our ancestors fled to this planet and built this safe city to escape that peril.

Any spell that is used to control a demon, and use its power, is an unspoken bargain with the forces of Hell itself. Who here claims they have the wisdom to do so in safety? Demons exist for an eternity, they existed when this universe was cast from nothing by the word of the one true God, and they will be here when it ends. Demons think more long-term than any mortal goblin could possibly imagine, so their motives are obscure to us; what hubris laced soul would dare predict their nature so well they think to ensnare them with a spell? Remember a demon is the very essence of deception, so who would be so imprudent as to allow them to exist in the heart of our home city? When you try to ensnare a demon, it may be the demon ensnaring you, and its prize would be your very soul!

Far from repealing the Act and taking risks with demons, I propose strengthening the prohibition, and to set up a new college to train demon hunting wizards to enforce the Act more rigorously.

Think of the safety of our souls first and our profits second good wizards, I urge you to vote against this motion and keep Section 23 of the Dangerous Demons Act of 1854 in place, and vote for a new college of demon-hunting wizards!'

The house exploded in uproar.

'Order Order!' screamed Rickity, 'Should section 23 of the Dangerous Demons Act of 1854, be repealed? As many as are of that opinion say Aye.'

'AYE' screamed the Magical Philosophers and Transitionalist Sages.

'And of the contrary say Nay,'

'NAY' cried the members of the Wizard's Hat, Golden Staff, and Traditional Hermeticists.

'I think the Ayes have it,' said Master Erasmus Rickety.

Vanilla Catchpenny knew all too well what this meant, after scrutiny by the court of the Goblin King, which was a constitutional formality, demon bottles would be legalised. *What terrible deception will the forces of Hell get up to next?* thought Vanilla.

She made her way to the foyer, and caught Bentley on his way to his office.

'Vanilla, so good to see you looking well. What can I do for you?' said Bentley, who was happy she was off her drugs.

'I need a letter of permission to purchase and use alapania,' said Vanilla.

23

'Bubble and Squeak' is made from yesterday's leftover groundapples, and then fried with greenroots and sourbulbs. It is the height of goblin cuisine. Surprisingly orks (who are mostly carnivorous) relish it. Goblin cooks who know how to prepare Bubble and Squeak are prized as servants in orkish Caragula.

From **Modern Goblin Cuisine** 2nd edition by Miss Elegance Woodheart

***

Captain Joshua Whitechapel felt wronged. The way he saw it was that as a commercial pan-dimensional spaceship operator, he had a right to make a fair shilling in pursuit of his trade. If a bunch of orks, some of them dead, decide to teleport into his hold from the cold vacuum of space, then they must pay their passage like every other goblin! The fact that some do-gooder elf covered their costs was really neither here nor there. He should not have to put up with delinquent stowaways; he wanted redress for his loss and inconvenience, and he had a good idea of how to get it. He was going to report Coffin to the dwarves and claim the reward money for his good public service.

At least that is what Whitechapel told himself. But the truth was different. Old Whitechapel's soul was riddled through with a nasty demon of avarice. It reasoned with him to chase every pound shilling and penny with an uncontrolled thirst that could never be quenched. Whitechapel short-changed his crew, skimped on safety for his ship and cheated his customers whenever he could. But no matter how much money he pinched, it was never enough, he always wanted more, because as the demon on his back hungered for money, so did Whitechapel.

He thought it was his idea to get the reward for the most infamous pirate in the known galaxy, but it was not, his resident demon had thought of it, and planted the seed in his head. Compelled by his insatiable love of mammon, Whitechapel entered the Dwarven Trade Mission and marched upon the receptionist.

'My name is Captain Joshua Whitechapel, master of the Golden Phoenix. I would like to talk to someone interested in the location of a pirate called Captain Jack Coffin.'

The startled receptionist, a diminutive ladygoblin, jumped at the infamous pirate's name.

'I shall pass your message on Sir. I will be right back,' she said.

She hurried through a large double-door, and disappeared from view, then on her return she said, 'Meister Roggerbrood will see you immediately.'

Whitechapel followed the receptionist to the ambassador's offices.

'In there, Sir,' said the receptionist, pointing out the door.

Roggerbrood was short even for a dwarf. He was bald on the top of his head and wore glasses with thick round lenses. 'Mr. Whitechapel, you wish to talk to me about the pirate Coffin I understand.'

'Yes sir. He jumped on my ship and got passage without paying, so I thought if I told you of his whereabouts you would reward me Sir'.

'Ah the reward.' Dwarfs knew all about avarice, and it was obvious to him that this goblin had it bad.

'Yes Sir, a reward for the public service of turning over a vicious pirate into the hands of the dwarven law enforcement so to speak.'

'Did you have a reward in mind?'

'Yes Sir, I do Sir,' said Whitechapel. 'I want one of those hulls you excavate from the core of a star by teleportation, and leave in space to cool for decades. I want a dwarven hull for a star clipper, to be fitted out by gnomes.'

'Well, I shall pass your offer onto the Dwarven Council and get back to you. Please leave your contact details with the receptionist as you leave. Good day to you Sir.' *Surely even Coffin was not worth a reward as large as this goblin wanted*, thought Roggerbrood.

'Good day to you too Sir,' said Whitechapel.

After Whitechapel had left the embassy, Roggerbrood gave the matter some thought. While he felt certain that Whitechapel's extortionate demand would be laughed at by the Council, he needed to cover himself. After all, this was Jack Coffin. He sent a message describing his meeting with Whitechapel back to the Dwarven home world, by means of the newly opened Telepathy Office. Within the hour, his government responded: 'Pay the goblin, get Coffin'.

***

Lieutenant Mandrake was tired out. His body ached with every step he took. He had fought in a losing space battle against the Dwarf Navy, then spent days confined in a cramped escape pod with the most feared and murderous captain in the Orkish fleet.

His mind was confused about everything except the one fact he was sure of: He needed to get away from the unpredictable and savage 'crazy' Jack Coffin. His destination was the Orkish Embassy, but he had no goblin money, so he walked through the metropolitan streets, and asked directions along the way.

Luckily on his route was one of the many public drinking fountains. He placed his head under the spout and drank the cool refreshing water. It was a beautiful fountain, made of a rich reddish coloured metal. On it was inscribed: 'In Memory of Ebenezer Merryfield, formerly an Apothecary in the parish of Fairyfield, who donated this fountain for the goblins of the Metropolis, *whoever drinks of the water that I will give him shall never thirst. John 4:14*' When he had drunk enough, he put his head under the spout and washed it until it stopped hurting. It was a great relief, but he was still weak with hunger and fatigue.

On he marched, street after street until he finally reached the Orkish Embassy. He made his way up its steps, then through the front doors, and limped over to the receptionist's desk.

'My name is Lieutenant Mandrake, of the Orkish Navy, may I speak to the ambassador about Captain Jack Coffin,' he said to the receptionist before collapsing into a chair and sleep.

The Orkish Ambassador to the Metropolis was Lord Kasper Scratch. He was 42 years old, the same age as Coffin, and about the same height and build. But whereas Coffin had a body of muscle and battle scars, Scratch's body showed the history of a peaceful and luxurious life. Scratch was a diplomatic ork, which meant he could match Coffin's courage and ferocity, but only with guile and diplomacy.

'Lieutenant, I am afraid I must awaken you,' said Scratch as he shook Mandrake's hand.

Mandrake stood up and said 'Sir I must report back my intelligence as an Officer of the Ork Navy.'

'Are you wounded?' asked Scratch.

'No Sir,' replied Mandrake.

'Please let's go to my office. Are you hungry?'

'I ate something on the ship that rescued me.'

'You need to tell me what happened,' Scratch led Mandrake to his office, 'Tell me about the battle.'

'We were running silent, but the dwarves detected us. I don't know how. They opened fire from nowhere, then battlecasts teleported onto the ship, Coffin destroyed two of them...'

'He destroyed two battlecast by himself? You saw this?'

'I saw him do it with my own eyes. But the ship was on fire, and we were ordered to evacuate.'

'But Coffin should have remained on board, and you saw him leave his ship, is that correct Mandrake?'

'Yes, but he carried Sally Sting onto the escape pod.'

'How did the pod escape the dwarves?'

'I have no idea, they must have let us escape,' said Mandrake.

'And how did you get to the Metropolis?'

'Again, I cannot tell you. One minute we were in the pod, next we had teleported to a goblin ship called the Golden Phoenix.'

'The Golden Phoenix had a teleporter?'

'No, it did not. I do not know how we teleported. It's a mystery.'

'What about Mortimer?'

'Coffin killed him for suggesting we draw lots as to who we would cannibalise.'

'Mandrake, whilst it is acceptable for subordinate officers such as Mortimer and yourself to take to an escape pod, it is the duty of an orkish commanding officer to die on his ship. You must sleep. When you wake, we will speak again. We must bring Coffin to justice for cowardice and murder. I will personally testify as to your bravery and loyalty to the Ork High Command on Caragula. We must change the story a little, you must take the credit for destroying the battlecasts. I know you might not like to steal his glory, but I ask you to look at the bigger picture, we cannot let Coffin take any credit,' said Scratch.

'Thank you, Sir,' said Mandrake.

24

Good works of art in a magical universe invariably create a corresponding sympathy to the target they represent; for example, the poem 'The Hubris of Draska' by Assyria Neepfield, created a correspondence between the opera of the same name, and the demonic invasion it described. The superb rendition in song by Miss Delilah Twotemples, and the emotion she elicited from the audience strengthened the sorcery, but that was by a different law, the Law of Emotional Elicitation.

From the annual Hermetic Society's lecture of 1899, titled the **Law of Correspondence**, by Grand Master Pharaoh Henry.

***

The manna fog has mutated many of the metropolitan trees in just the same way as its citizens and animals. One such tree, which is an individual from a species of oak that does not grow anywhere in mankind's universe, has changed to such an extent, it has developed a mind and grown a face. The tree's name is Oakensoul, and he was now so wise and magical that a school of magic was named after him: Oakensoul's College.

The college is housed in a three-story high quadrangle building of honey-coloured sandstone. At ground level are the cloisters, so typical a feature of magic schools. At its centre is the courtyard, and at the very heart of the courtyard stood the old tree troll.

Day and night without rest, he listened for the rustle of other trees as they pass news from across the city, and up and down the country, always on the lookout for suspicious characters.

Grand Master Pharaoh Henry was dean of college. He liked to eat his meals on a bench in the garden next to the tree. Needless to say, the bench was made of iron and not wood, so as not to offend the tree troll. It was a very pleasant spot, and, through his conversations with Oakensoul, by means of a magical device called a tree-tongue, he kept in touch with the network of information that passed from leaf to leaf. Treetrolls were Henry's eyes and ears that searched across the whole city and beyond.

It was midnight, and the sky was clear of clouds, but the stars looked huge and bright, their shine swirled into each other in beautiful patterns. According to a theory by Jeroboam Nettlebed, this was a meteorological phenomenon, caused by microscopic manna crystals in the upper atmosphere.

Henry sat under this wonderful night sky to eat after a very long day. He enjoyed a large plate of mashed koboldroots and a delicious bowl of greenleaf stew. Across from him sat Babylon Pinch, with a plate of curried root vegetables, and quite recovered from his wound with the aid of magical medicine. On another bench sat Vanilla with a small bowl of nuts, and Jack Coffin with a bowl of mutton stew and dumplings.

'Pinch, did Miss Delilah Twotemples suffer any adverse consequence as a result of exposure to infernal manna?' asked Henry.

'She did not get magical cosmetic surgery. Two unknown goblinettes impersonated her and her maid. Doctor Apricot was defrauded.'

'Well I hope we find the imposters before they come to harm. Do you know what else is interesting about the Goodhalf case?' asked Henry.

'Everything Sir,' replied Pinch compliantly. His body may have been magically healed from the gunshot, but his mind was still wounded.

To the astute ears of Pharaoh Henry, it was clear Pinch was more interested in avoiding offense than considering the case.

'That's a jolly good answer Pinch. But the aspects I find most interesting are those fang marks. Furthermore, that fellow Halfgood had no memory of what bit him. His recollections of that episode with a goblinette are also very suspect,' said Henry. He wanted to keep Pinch in good spirits, so he did his best to sound as cheerful and unthreatening as a dangerous fanatic could. He failed.

'What does it all mean Sir?'

'That, my good Pinch, is the correct question to ask.'

Oakensoul's great wooden face turned in its trunk, 'Pharaoh, it may be of interest to you to know there has been an altercation in Arcadian Gardens.'

'An altercation Oakensoul? What sort of altercation, and why is it significant?' asked Henry.

'It is significant because one of the combatants is a demon, Sir.'

'A demon eh?' acknowledged Henry with his interest peeked, 'Any reports of injuries?'

'Several injuries, one of some severity I understand Sir.'

'Is the fight still going on Oakensoul?'

'No, the demon has been exposed and banished.'

'A demon exposed and banished! How and by who?' asked Henry.

'By a goblinette using spontaneous magic,' said Oakensoul.

'Really, how intriguing? I cannot wait to meet this goblinette. Thank you Oakensoul.'

'You had better get Dr. Apricot first Pinch, then meet me at Arcadian Gardens please,' said Henry, 'Villy and Jack, you come with me.'

The college was close enough to Arcadian Gardens for Pharaoh Henry and the others to make their way on foot. They arrived within minutes of having heard of the attack. As Henry entered the square, two of the flower fairies, Tulip and Lilly, flew to meet him.

'It was terrible Mr. Henry,' said Lilly.

'Tell me what happened here Lilly,' asked Henry in a relaxed manner, so as to keep the fairies calm.

'It happened after the opera, a goblin man and a goblin lady with chalky white skin went under those trees over there,' said Tulip pointing to the dark shadows.

'Then he punched her in the stomach, and tried to stab her with a stick,' added Lilly.

'Rose saved her, she told the elves and the golem what was happening, and they stopped him murdering her. The golem and the cat goblin saved the pale ladygoblin from being killed by the demon,' said Tulip.

Henry made a gesture with his hands, as he muttered a short spell to create a glowing sphere that floated above his head. It illuminated the area around him as bright as daylight.

As Henry walked over to the shady grove, he spotted the marks on the ground where the fight had taken place. There were splatters of blood on the grass, and on the tree trunks. Vanilla scraped up some blood with her enchanted silver spoon, which was a magical instrument that could not only detect the presence of magic it could also determine its nature.

Under the spoon's spell, the blood showed spots of many colours, all changing to other colours in constant flux. *The blood of a shape changer* Vanilla thought, *not uncommon in this city nowadays.*

She tested some darker blood from another location, and the spoon went black in an instant. *A demon's blood,* she thought, 'The blood is from two creatures, one is a shape changer, the other is a demon,' she told Henry.

'Did you see the demon?' Henry asked the fairies.

'Yes, at first it looked like a man, and then it went invisible, and then it went all green with horrid horns and ugly cow's hoofs,' said Lilly.

'No it went blue with horns,' said Tulip correcting her sister.

'Green horns!' repeated Lilly emphatically.

'The horn colour does not matter ladies, when did it appear as a demon?' asked Henry.

'When a ladygoblin with three eyes commanded it to go away,' said Lilly.

'Do you know where I can find this goblin lady with three eyes?'

'She lives over there at the news kiosk,' said Lilly pointing to Fireheart's the newsagents.

'Thank you so much for your assistance ladies, you have both been very brave tonight,' Henry said to the flower fairies. He headed out to the newsagents to find the three-eyed demon ward. Halfway across the square, he met Pinch accompanying a bedraggled Dr. Apricot. Henry dismissed his magical glow lamp with a small gesture of his fingers.

'It's almost 1 am in the morning Sir. The middle of the night and you got me out of bed,' complained Dr. Apricot.

'The devil never sleeps, so neither may we. Follow me everyone,' replied Henry cheerfully, clearly enjoying his work.

Clockheart and the two elves were standing guard outside the newsagents as Henry approached.

'My dear chaps, that was an awesome demon and you brave lads gave him a hiding. Well done,' said Henry.

'Are you sure we won the fight?' asked Clockheart as he showed Henry the largest of the many dents in his starsteel carapace.

A demon that assumed physical form, and could dent the shell of a battlecast golem? This must be a powerful one, thought Henry.

'With the power vested in me as High Constable, I nominate you as heroes of the city, and reward you five pounds each,' said Henry. He took three five-pound notes from his coat and gave one to each elf and one to Clockheart.

'Thank you kindly, Sir,' said Aristotle.

'Heroes, a credit to the fine name of high elves and their battlecast golems.'

'Fine name of high elves? From a goblin? Is he being sarcastic?' projected Vim to Valancy.

Valancy was the only elf to have spent much time in the Metropolis, and he knew of Henry's reputation, *'No not at all Aristotle, his name is Pharaoh Henry and he is an enthusiastic demon hunting wizard. He is just a bit excited that's all. He gets like that when there is a demon to chase. Not sarcastic, more like overly zealous,'* he projected without sound or facial expression.

Henry knocked on the door. Zebedee Fireheart answered it.

'My name is Pharaoh Henry, Grand Master Wizard and a High Constable of the City. As you know there has been an infernal incident tonight of great severity, and I require you to allow me to enter your place of business.'

Zebedee Fireheart's expression displayed his unhappiness mixed with his forbearance to receive these new visitors. 'Your entry is unwelcome. There is nothing I can do to stop you, but there will come a day of reckoning!' He grudgingly stepped aside for Henry, Pinch, Vanilla and Apricot.

Lampwick was lying on a blanket, he was still conscious but very dazed and clearly in pain.

'Could you see to the poor chap Doctor?' said Henry.

Apricot carefully examined Lampwick's wounds, 'Broken jaw. Badly smashed, looks as if he was hit with a heavy hammer,' He said. He removed a healing potion from his doctor's bag, and carefully administered it to Lampwick's shattered face. As the pain left him the expression on Lampwick's face relaxed, but he was still exhausted. Now without discomfort, he was able to fall asleep, 'He will sleep for a few hours. The bones should fully heal in an hour or two at most.'

'You had better wash that infernal blood off of his claws Pinch. Then sanitise them with holy water,' said Henry.

'How much do you want for that healing potion Doctor?' asked Henry.

'It was very expensive to buy Sir, I must charge you one hundred pounds just to get my money back,' claimed the doctor. Henry held out his hand, and Apricot gave him the potion. The label on the bottle read **Merryfield and Sons, Respectable Apocatharies of**

Fairyfield Lane. Henry paid the doctor and took the potion.

'Sir, there is mention of two ladies, one with pale skin, another with three eyes, do you know where they are?' Henry asked Zebedee.

'They are downstairs. You are a parasite on the back of the working goblin,' he said. His expression showed his resignation at his inevitable capture and imprisonment at the hands of the city authorities.

'Watch the door Pinch, make sure nothing unclean comes back for another attack,' said Henry.

'Another attack?' said Pinch, looking worried.

Henry, Apricot, Vanilla and Zebedee Fireheart made their way down the spiral stairs into the room below.

Mercurial was comforting a weeping three-eyed Euphoria.

Prudence lay next to them wrapped in a blanket. Her corset lay on the floor where it had been cut off. She stiffened with fear at the sight of a Grand Master Wizard.

'Please introduce us Mr. Fireheart,' said Henry.

'Everyone, this is Pharaoh Henry and the others are his assorted lapdogs. He is a wizard and oppressor. Mr. Henry, this is Euphoria my daughter, her friend Mercurial, and Lampwick's friend Prudence, they are honest goblins who work for a living.' said Zebedee. He gave Henry a sneer.

'That is the vixen who claimed she was Delilah Twotemples. She defrauded me out of expensive magical surgery for herself and her friend!' shouted Dr. Apricot, as he pointed at Euphoria.

'Please calm yourself Dr. Apricot I shall restore any money that has been taken from you.' Henry recognised Prudence as the goblinette who had escaped the attack on the vampire nest. He belatedly realised she was also the prostitute he had seen in Mr Goodhalf's memory. 'Miss you do not need to look so frightened, I am here to help,' said Henry, trying to reassure her, but without success. Prudence looked terrified.

Henry turned to Euphoria, 'Please tell me what has happened here.'

'I screamed at a demon to go, and this happened,' said Euphoria, pointing to her third eye.

'That third eye can be concealed with magic, but do not remove it, as it may be very important. But you told a demon to go and it went? I'm impressed. You were able to ward a demon that could defeat a battle cast golem. That is no paltry achievement,' said Henry, 'what did the demon look like when you dismissed him?'

'He looked in pain and full of rage.'

'You can see demons, and that is a powerful magical gift. It will be an indispensable weapon in our everlasting war against the forces of Hell.'

'I cheated him,' she said pointing to Dr. Apricot, 'I owe him £260 for the transformation to make Mercurial and I look like elves. He is furious with me.'

'Dr. Apricot, please confirm it was these goblinettes you exposed to infernal manna,' said Henry, just to be sure.

'Well it was from the same batch yes. But only for that one. I used the old stuff for her accomplice.' *That one,* was Euphoria, and the *accomplice* was Mercurial.

'Have you felt anything strange recently?' Henry asked Euphoria.

'Mercurial is fine, but I am sharing minds with a demon, and it is not very nice as she has an insatiable wantonness to her. Can you help me Master Henry?' Euphoria looked most embarrassed, especially discussing such matters in the presence of her father.

'I cannot, but perhaps you can help yourself.'

'How?'

'You can ward demons, try warding it.'

'And how do I do that?'

'The same way you warded the other demon.'

'*I will be silent, I will leave you alone,*' thought Pandamonia, directly into Euphoria's mind. The succubus was very afraid of the idea.

'Master Henry, have you seen this?' said Apricot holding up a copy of The Revolutionary Goblin he had found under the counter, 'What scum would sell such treasonous filth?'

Henry wagged his finger at Zebedee Fireheart in a gesture of mild disapproval.

Dr. Apricot stood amazed at Henry's indifference to such criminal behaviour.

'Have you properly weighed the gravity of this goblin's misdeeds? He has been distributing vile republican literature around the city. He is a venomous socialist who does not know his place in the scheme of things, and all you can do is wag your finger at him?' Said the doctor, momentarily forgetting his fear of the great wizard.

Zebedee was also suspicious at Henry's indifference to the

serious crime. 'Yes, why are you so friendly? Your kind always have a hidden motive.'

'Your daughter can see and ward demons, which is a rare and valuable skill. So, I want your daughter to be my friend, which in turn means I want to be your friend. That is why I am willing to overlook your relatively trivial crime of distributing treasonous literature. All I ask in return is that Euphoria visit me at Oakensoul's college to discuss how she managed to ward a demon.'

'I don't want to be friends with a bloodsucking aristocratic wizard!' said Zebedee.

'I am not the bloodsucker,' said Henry.

'You are a class parasite. I was speaking metaphorically.'

'I wasn't,' said Henry, he glanced at Prudence.

'Is this a deal? Are you threatening to arrest my father if I do not be your laboratory experiment?' Said Euphoria.

'No Miss. I will not report your father's political activities because I believe that in the scheme of things it is a trivial matter compared to the threat from Hell. But I humbly request you visit me at Oakensoul's tomorrow evening.' Henry passed Euphoria his business card. It was a simple affair, printed on mundane cardstock, and without mentioning Henry's long list of impressive academic and civic titles, it simply said:

Pharaoh Henry, Oakensoul's College, Troll's Bonnet Street.

Euphoria took the card, 'I'll think about it.'

'We could discuss how you could ward your demon,' said Henry.

'There is another small matter, a rather personal one. Perhaps you could help me with.' Euphoria looked very unsettled.

'Into my ear,' said Henry.

'I have a demon's tail,' whispered Euphoria, so no-one else could hear.

'Come and visit me at Oakensoul's, I am sure we can deal with all these issues. Before I go, I need to talk to the lovely lady with the pale skin in private. Please could you escort Euphoria upstairs. And do not, under any circumstances harm that third eye,' Henry said to Zebedee.

Zebedee could hardly believe his luck that Henry was not interested in his crimes. But he was worried as to what the wizard might do to Prudence, 'I hope you are proud of yourself Mr. Wizard, picking on a poor goblinette.'

'I am doing my job Mr. Fireheart,' said Henry. Zebedee took Euphoria and Mercurial and left the room.

Pharaoh Henry turned his attention to Prudence. He picked up her corset from the floor, and showed to her how its steel boning was bent from the force of the demon's punch, 'This may have saved you from destruction, my pale goblinette. Notice I said destruction, not death as I suspect you may already be dead, or rather in that awful half-way state of being undead. I think you are a vampire, am I correct?'

'Yes, and now you are going to kill me?' she said, wrapped in a blanket to cover her naked body

'The thought of destroying you had crossed my mind. It is after all standard procedure for a demon hunting wizard on the discovery of a vampire.'

'If you are a High Constable you must kill me, why don't you do it and get it over with?'

'Well two reasons, firstly, and this may seem pedantic, you are already undead, so technically speaking, I cannot kill you because you are not alive in the strictest sense.'

'You know what I mean. You could destroy me. You have a reputation as an enthusiastic enforcer of the law Master Henry. So why have you not already sent me to oblivion? Why am I still talking, and not a small heap of ash on the floor? Do you intend to torture me with sunlight, or blood starvation? Scorch me little by little with small shafts of light peeping through cracks in a curtain, burning me bit by bit?'

'There is more than one way I can deal with you, but I need to know the facts. I am going to speak to you, and I need to know you are telling me the truth.'

'How can I prove if I am telling you the truth or not?'

Henry moved his hands in the gestures needed to cast a spell. 'Now Prudence, tell me you are a basilisk.'

'But I am not a basilisk,' said Prudence with an expression of mild confusion.

'Humour me. Tell me you are a basilisk, just say it.'

'I am a basilisk,' she said, and as she did green vapour streamed out of her ears.

'That is what will happen if you say something you know to be untrue. It is how I will know you are telling me what you believe to be true,' explained Henry, 'Have you ever killed anyone Prudence?'

'No,' she replied, 'I thought I would be safer if my hosts did not go missing. Besides, it just did not feel right to kill someone.' No green vapour.

'Whoever heard of a vampire that never killed anyone? You must have killed someone,' interjected Apricot with a sneer.

'No,' said Prudence, 'Never. I take goblin men somewhere quiet. Then I pretend I am going to serve their needs as a goblinette of the night. I stun them with magic, drink just enough of their blood to feed, taking care not to permanently injure them. I take their money, and implant a false memory into their minds.'

'What kind of memory?' asked Apricot.

'A memory of exquisite lovemaking that never reveals Prudence's face so that a memory reader such as me would not recognise her,' replied Henry on her behalf.

'That's about the long and the short of it Master Henry, although I read their squalid little imaginations first to find out what they crave, so I know what experience to leave in their head. A memory tailored for each goblin's individual desires, all part of the service.'

'My dear, you are a perfect vampire and a perfect prostitute, when in fact you have never killed anyone. Bravo my dear, Bravo,' said Henry clapping his hands in approval.

'As it happens, I didn't do anything physical with any of them either,' she added with a coquettish smile, her confidence starting to return a little.

'Which only serves to perfect the irony of it all,' added Henry.

Henry laughed, Prudence started to laugh with him, then abruptly stopped short on remembrance of the peril of her situation.

'Did this demon say or do anything that could help me with my investigation?'

'He tried to kill me by putting a wooden stake into my heart, so he knew I was a vampire.'

'And who would have told him that?' asked Henry.

'I assume my former mistress Ephemeral Wormsong.'

'What is her position?'

'Queen of all vampires in the city. And my persecutor before I escaped the Peccadillo Street colony.'

'Well she must want you destroyed. Let me ask you another question and it is an important one. Have you personally ever turned someone into a vampire?'

'No, I did not want to become a vampire myself and I was soon placed at the bottom of the pack that turned me. They felt uncomfortable with me and would have killed me sooner rather than later had I not escaped.'

'I sympathise with the bit about making people feel uncomfortable. I have a similar effect on them,' confessed Henry with a smile.

'What do you intend to do with me Sir?' Prudence asked hopefully, against all the odds that a High Constable would not destroy her.

'Firstly, I am not obliged to destroy you. As you are a vampire, I could destroy you if I thought it was in the public interest, but I do not. I do not consider you a threat because you have never killed anyone, or infected them. I want you alive because a demon and a vampire queen want you destroyed. I say alive, but at least undead and undestroyed. I cannot let you roam around the Metropolis, but I have the authority to give you sanctuary under section 17 of the Undead Creatures Act,' explained Henry.

'Now wait a minute, you have a duty to protect the decent God-fearing goblins of this city from bloodsuckers like her. You must destroy her,' shouted Apricot angrily, quite forgetting who he was talking to.

'Not at all Doctor Apricot. As Prudence has not killed anyone or spread the disease of vampirism, then it is my prerogative to make a judgement as to whether I must destroy her or not, and I choose not. In fact, I do so want Prudence to be my friend. Are you my friend Prudence?' asked Henry.

'Oh yes Sir, very much so Sir.' Prudence stood up and gave Henry a deep polite curtsy, despite only being wrapped in a blanket to ensure her modesty.

'Will you keep Prudence's secret safe?' Henry asked Dr. Apricot.

Apricot knew the dangers of contradicting the judgement of Pharaoh Henry very well. 'I will keep her secret safe Sir,' Dr. Apricot replied without the slightest trace of insincerity. But green vapour billowed from his ears.

'Before I finish tonight Prudence, I ask that you demonstrate your mind manipulation skills,' said Henry.

'On you?'

'Try the Doctor.'

'Excuse me Mr. Henry, I must protest Sir,' stuttered Apricot.

With a flick of his wrist Henry entranced Dr. Apricot with a transfixing spell, silencing and holding him as still as stone.

'Does he intend to reveal you as a vampire to an authority other than myself?' Henry asked Prudence.

Prudence looked into Dr. Apricot's eyes, and searched through his mind for his ideas and decisions. 'Yes, he does, he hopes for social advancement from the Great Goblin King on account of it.'

'And how much did he pay for the healing potion?'

'Fifty pounds.'

'And is the potion high quality?'

The finest brand and so powerful it has been known to bring the dead back to life, if not too long has passed between the final heart beat and administering the dose that is.'

'Then show me how you can wipe clean the memories concerning your vampirism, and while you are at it, those of Mr. Fireheart's political activism. Leave in his memory that he received payment from Euphoria and Mercurial for their cosmetic surgery to look like elves, and also to magically conceal Euphoria's third eye in future. Implant a very guilty memory into his mind of a prurient nature, and another memory that convinces him you are a respectable goblinette who should not be molested. Show me what you can do.'

Prudence went to work. Her beautiful eye's fixed in thoughtful concentration as she stared deeply into Dr. Apricot's. She navigated the intricacies of his mind. She found the recollections of tonight and squashed them, then planted new ones; perverse and wanton new memories.

After she had finished, she turned to Henry and said, 'Done.'

'Let me see now.' Henry looked into Apricot's mind. He found the guilty memory Prudence had implanted, 'My good goblinette that is disgusting! Where in God's universe did you get the idea of such repulsive obscenities?'

'I discovered it in the imagination of one of my clients. As it happens, that's not the worst one I came across either,' she said nonchalantly.

'Not the worst client? Or not the worst memory?'

Prudence thought for a second or two, then she said, 'neither actually.'

'Well, I think the guilty memory was excessive but other than that you have made a very tidy job of memory manipulation. Very well done.'

Her face beamed with pride.

'Prudence, you are not safe here. The demon will return, as will Madam Ephemeral Wormsong. I ask that you come to Oakensoul's college, a place where I can offer you protection. If you remain here it might endanger Lampwick, Mercurial and the Fireheart's, although I must say that Euphoria does handle herself well against demons. I ask you to come with me and be safe? We do need to leave now.'

'Protection and safety? I would like that very much, as long as Lampwick could visit me.'

25

'Our planet has 3 visible moons: Primula, Selonia, and Eridanto. Most werewolves turn when Primula is full, a cycle of 24 days. Fewer werewolves turn when Selonia is full, a 40-day cycle. No case of lycanthropy has ever been associated with Eridanto.'

From **Magical Diseases: Cause, Diagnosis and Treatment**, by Dr Utopia Lovejoy, Emperor Phoenix Press.

*****

Euphoria's long working day at the Telepathy Office had been profitable and interesting, now she felt very tired. She had stayed up late for the last two nights, there was the fuss at the opera the previous evening, and the opening ball before that. And she had awoken early.

Telepathic messaging was an immediate hit city wide, and the office had been busy all day. In particular there had been a great deal of messaging regarding the pirate Jack Coffin, by both the dwarven and orkish authorities.

The Telepathy Office was now closed for the evening, so she could stand on its steps to enjoy the fresh warm evening air and relax before going home and getting some sleep. Clockheart, who was the new doorman, stood twenty feet away from her, to keep her safe and guard the entrance.

Mercurial appeared through the door carrying a wicker tray with three mugs of cocoa on it. She gave the oversized mug to Clockheart, and a goblin-sized one to Euphoria. The cocoa was delicious, even Clockheart thought so, though he preferred to drink mineral oil.

'Are you going to visit that Pharaoh Henry?' asked Mercurial.

'No. I don't want to work for him. I have a job here. Besides, daddy doesn't like me associating with wizards,' said Euphoria.

Mercurial and Euphoria saw two figures approaching the Telepathy office, they were being shadowed by a bird.

When he got close enough, Euphoria recognised one of them, 'That looks like old Henry. Why can't he leave me alone!'

'He is being followed by a coalbird. I did not think they came out at this time of night. It seems to be looking at us very studiously,' said Mercurial. She pointed at the dark rook-like bird that followed Henry.

'It does not look like a coalbird to me. It looks like a little black reptile with wings, with nasty glowing eyes. It looks like a little demon,' said Euphoria. Without another thought, she threw up her arms as if to shoo it away, but to the astonishment of all present, as her hands rose up to gesture, a purple bolt of magical energy shot out from her fingertips at the coalbird, which was really an imp. It disintegrated into black ash. During the spell-casting butterflies popped into existence, before dissolving into thin air again.

'Euphoria what did you just do?' asked Mercurial.

'I'm not quite sure Mercurial, I did not mean to do anything, but I'm rather glad I did it never the less.'

'You're good at destroying demons Miss Euphoria. I'm very impressed,' said Henry.

'Can't you leave me alone! What do you mean a demon?' said Euphoria.

'That bird was an imp in disguise. I could only tell when you destroyed it, but you can see through their deception. Did you know what you can do is impossible according to the standard theory of magic?' said Henry.

'Well I wish someone else had this impossible gift,' said Euphoria.

'I need to know what you experienced while under the influence of this demon. Please tell me in your own words.'

'I'll tell you then you must go away and leave me alone.'

'I hope to persuade you that I can offer you a great deal in return for your gift, but if I cannot, and you choose not to help me keep the Metropolis safe from demonic invasion, I will leave you alone.'

'The demon is female, and I can read her mind as well as she can read mine. Her name is Pandamonia, and she is a wicked lustful creature. Everything I know or experience so does she, and vice versa.' said Euphoria.

'Well that is a worry. Demons can never be trusted. They have spent thousands of years deceiving people, and can easily outwit us mortals when it comes to trickery,' said Henry.

'She asked me why I did altruistic acts, she was curious about that' said Euphoria.

'And what was your answer?'

'I told her doing good is a reward in itself, but I do not think she appreciated it.'

Henry looked thoughtful. 'Let's look at the benefits, not only are you able to see through demonic disguise, you unconsciously warded a powerful demon. What is astounding is that you can see through a demon's deception, which as I say, is theoretically impossible under the standard theory of magic. You are the only goblin ever to be able to do so, therefore your gift is of interest to me. My cause is to fight demons. With the proper training, you could help me. I am prepared to make you a good offer for your services.'

'What kind of offer?' asked Euphoria.

'I am recruiting goblins to train as demon hunting wizards, and I am most impressed with your performance Euphoria against the coalbird and the demon who attacked Prudence. Would you consider joining this year's cohort as a new student?' asked Henry.

'I have a job, a very respectable position as a telepath's impresario,' replied Euphoria.

'I do understand your position Miss Fireheart. I must say I am disappointed though; you might have gone far as a demon hunter, it would have opened up a whole new vista of opportunities for social advancement,' said Henry.

'Go on,' said Euphoria, her interest aroused.

'Go on about what you would learn as a wizard?'

'No, the social advancement bit.'

'Well you would be a wizard, and therefore a member of the new aristocracy. You would have rooms at Oakensoul's, with a salary, and any goods and chattels of the demons and cultists you banish would be legally confiscated and go to you. You could become wealthy and hire servants,' said Henry.

'Well it sounds all very fine, but I am getting to meet important people from my job at the telepathy office.'

'As an Oakensoul's wizard you would meet important people frequently. You would be an important person yourself.'

'Is there any possibility that I could be invited to the Goblin King's Midsummer Ball?' enquired Euphoria, feigning as much casual detachment as she could.

'You could both have my place at the King's table. I get an invitation every year for myself and an escort, but never use them. I am always far too busy demon-hunting, so you could have my tickets. You and Mercurial could go together. Think of the fine dresses you could wear to all the state banquets. I am sure you would be the talk of the whole city,' said Henry.

'I would sit next to the Goblin King!' said Euphoria, snapping to attention like a whippet to a tasty morsel.

'You would consider my offer after all then Miss Fireheart?' said Henry.

'I would sir,' said Euphoria.

'Well no time like the present, would you like to learn a spell right now?'

Euphoria somehow felt that Henry was leading her in the direction he wanted her to go in, but she could not resist her own curiosity. Many goblins in the city dreamed of becoming a wizard, and now she was given the opportunity to learn a spell by a grand master.

'Will it be difficult?' asked Euphoria.

'It is the easiest spell in the grimoire. It is a simple energy spell called *'Moonlight'*. You hold your arms in a circle in front of you like this,' said Henry as he demonstrated, 'then you simply feel moonlight shining through your arms. If you do it correctly, you can read a book by the magical light you create. Watch me.'

Henry held his arms out in a circle, and then silver moonlight shone through them, 'Now you try Miss Fireheart.'

Euphoria held her arms in front of her as Henry had shown her. It took some time, but eventually there was a small illumination, but not enough and it soon flickered out.

'Don't will the light, just feel it come, and let it pour through the circle of your arms. There's a trick to it, well two tricks actually. First, accept that the light appearing is as likely as not, and secondly just assume the spell will work. It's a difficult thing to explain, but when you feel it you will know,' instructed Henry.

Euphoria tried again, her light started to shine, but then receded for a short while; suddenly it relit and shone as bright as if all of the three moons, when full, were pouring their light through her arms. As she cast her spell, butterflies appeared and then disappeared again. 'Oh, that's delightful,' said Euphoria.

'There you have it Miss Fireheart; you will make a wonderful magician. Those butterflies are your casting sigil,' said Henry.

'*Moonbeams*,' read Euphoria, 'This is a lovely spell.'

'Now would you teach me a spell please?' asked Henry.

'You are a grand master wizard, what spell could I possibly teach you?' replied Euphoria.

'How you magically see through a demon's disguise, and how to dismiss a demon back to Hell, you are naturally adept at both I can assure you Miss Fireheart.'

'But I do not know how I do it, so how could I teach anyone else?'

'Your abilities with demons are breakthrough abilities, so you can cast them without theoretical knowledge of magic. But by demonstrating them and then letting me read your mind afterwards, I could see if I could build a theoretical framework around them to cast spells from,' said Henry.

'Do you have a demon I could demonstrate on?' asked Euphoria.

'Actually, my silent companion is possessed. His name is Nimrod Hunt, and he is a werewolf. He turns wolf at midnight, when the moon Selonia is full, which should happen in one minute from now,' said Henry, inspecting his timepiece.

'Can you help me or not Wizards!' shouted the purple-faced werewolf with an angry snarl.

'Mr. Hunt is an angry goblin; anger has caused his soul to become infected with the demon of wrath. He is a lycanthrope,' said Henry.

Nimrod Hunt screamed unintelligible abuse at Euphoria.

'Your soul is infected with a demon of rage Sir, we must ward it,' said Henry, 'Miss Fireheart, please ward the demon.'

Euphoria felt inside her tummy for the same spell she had cast at the imp, and then cast it at Nimrod. As she did a horrifying purple demon sprouted out from his body. It was the size of a terrier dog; a mass of teeth, eyes and tentacles, all periodically growing out from its filthy purple flesh, only to be absorbed back into its body again.

'Euphoria, if you can see it then destroy it!' shouted Henry.

Euphoria's arms and hands clasped the air as she cast a spell of destruction magic at the demon. When the bolt of magic hit, it started to disintegrate. It screamed in fury and pain as its protoplasmic body burned away into ashes.

Hunt fell to the ground and lay motionless; his skin colour had lost its purple tinge.

'Now please allow me to read your memory Miss Fireheart,' requested Henry.

Euphoria acquiesced to Henry's appeal, and when their eyes met, she could feel his mind entering hers. It was embarrassingly intimate, but Henry did not look in the crannies where she kept her delicate secrets, he was only interested in finding out how she felt when she destroyed a demon. As the memory was still fresh in Euphoria's mind, he soon found it, and took a copy of it as his own, for use in formulating an exorcism spell. Henry had fought demons all his working life, but demons are masters of deceit, so it was only from Euphoria's memory of the attack on Prudence, and the coalbird at the telepathy office, that he could see for the first time what one truly looked like in spirit form.

Henry felt Pandamonia's presence, *I could help you if you gave me asylum in the Metropolis,* she thought.

I will not covenant with demons, replied Henry.

What can I get you? thought Pandamonia.

No deals or promises, but bring me a copy of Nomina Vera Daemoniorum, and I will look at your application favourably, thought Henry.

I understand, thought Pandamonia.

'Thank you so much for letting me enter your mind Miss Fireheart,' said Henry.

'Having my memory read was an awkward experience,' said Euphoria in a fluster.

'Now Miss Fireheart and Miss Frostdrop, I would be grateful if you could tell me all you have learned from telepathic correspondences about Captain Coffin.'

'Well that is confidential,' said Euphoria.

26

It is a criminal offense for a goblin to have biblical knowledge of a vampire; furthermore, for a goblin to fornicate with a vampire amounts to necrophilia with a corpse.

Section 43 of the Ungodly Lusts Act 1875.

***

Lampwick arrived at Oakensoul's college at around half past five in the morning, '*I hope Prudence is still out of her coffin and she has not turned in for the day,*' thought Lampwick.

During office hours, Oakensoul's College was as busy as a gnome's workshop, with magicians and staff scurrying around to lectures and laboratories, but at this time in the morning it was silent and empty but for a solitary guard to keep watch.

'Sir I believe a Miss Prudence Pepperhill is staying here?' Lampwick said to the guard.

'You must be Mr. Lampwick the Cat, we have been expecting you. Jevington the butler and Master Henry have anticipated your visit Sir.'

The guard rang a small magic bell, 'Jevington will be with you soon Sir.'

Jevington soon appeared. He walked up to the guard's desk with a slow deliberate gait. He was a distinguished-looking goblin, very tall (at least 5' 4") and he dressed in a butler's uniform with white gloves. He had a mess of blue hair, which most goblins nowadays consider to be old-fashioned and formal, but it befitted his stern demeanour.

'Mr. Lampwick sir, please come with me and I will escort you to Miss Pepperhill's rooms,' said Jevington.

Lampwick followed Jevington down the stairs to the basement, and then down a corridor, eventually arriving at the underground rooms where Prudence lodged. He knocked on her door.

Prudence's voice cried out, 'Come in the door is open'. She was sitting on an armchair. In front of her was a coffee table with a pile of books, and some paper and pencils.

'Mr Lampwick to see you Miss Pepperhill. And may I take your order for breakfast, and perhaps your guest would like to order too,' said Jevington.

When Prudence saw Lampwick she rushed over to him and threw herself into his arms, hugging him tightly, and quite ignoring poor Jevington.

'Miss Prudence I feel proprietary requires me to leave you and your friend alone if you are to be so familiar with each other in my presence, so please could you make your breakfast selections so I can leave promptly,' said Jevington in a starchy tone.

Prudence took the menu from Jevington, and said, 'I would like some porridge topped with broken cocklenuts, dark sugar, diced moonapples and milk. Oh, and two croissants with butter and some indigoberry jam.'

'Anything to drink Miss Pepperhill?' asked Jevington.

'I'll have a pot of golden tea and a pint of fresh warm goat's blood,'

'And for Mr. Lampwick?' asked Jevington.

'I'll have the porridge same as Prudence, two slices of buttered toast with marmalade, a pot of blue tea, a jug of freshly squeezed cold limony juice, two kippers if you have them, but no blood for me thank you Sir,' replied Lampwick.

'Very good Sir and Miss, I shall bring it here. I have been instructed by Master Henry to inform him of your arrival, and that he hopes to join you for breakfast,' said Jevington, before leaving the room.

'Where does the breakfast cook get the blood from?' asked Lampwick.

'There is an abattoir about fifteen minutes' walk away down in the caves. Ogres do eat meat you know. Come to think of it, cats do too don't they?' asked Prudence.

'Actually, I much prefer fish, especially herrings, but I don't like the bones. I must tell you, Euphoria and Mercurial have made the news,' said Lampwick as he showed her his copy of The Fashionable Intelligencer. On the front page was a large picture of Euphoria and Mercurial as Elvin ladies, posing for the picturebox with none other than the celebrated opera singer Miss Delilah Twotemples.

Lampwick read out the newspaper article to Prudence:

A party was held at the Municipal Telepathy Office last night to celebrate its opening. It is the first in the city. Now it is possible to send messages across the galaxy at the speed of thought! The beautiful goblinettes (or should I say elfinettes) shown in the picture are Miss Euphoria Fireheart and Miss Mercurial Frostdrop, who are telepathic impresarios. These ladygoblins are flaunting the new 'elfin look'. This new style, available only from the most reputable magical cosmetic surgeons, is now all the rage in high society. The celebrated Miss Delilah Twotemples is quoted as saying: 'elf style is a la mode, and I will be getting elfed as soon as I can.'

Reported by Harmony Honeyhill, War Correspondent at the Fashionable Intelligencer.

'So good to hear Euphoria and Mercurial have landed on their feet. Isn't Assyria Neepfield Euphoria's boyfriend?' asked Prudence.

Lampwick shrugged his shoulders and said, 'I think Euphoria considers poor Neepfield a bit below her,'

'Harmony Honeyhill's review of the opera by Delilah Twotemples and Assyria Neepfield is very positive,' said Lampwick who then read it out, '*Mr. Assyria Neepfield's lyrics The Hubris of Draska must be considered a masterpiece in contemporary music. The Metropolis' most celebrated diva, Miss Delilah Twotemples, has a divinely crisp voice that must surely now rate her as the finest soprano in the whole city.*'

'Well I must say, I thought it was wonderful, especially Anatitia's song,' said Prudence.

Lampwick picked up the book that Prudence had been reading, and read out its title, '*Magic Theory and Practice 4th Edition* by Grand Master Joshua Silverwings. Do you think it is a good book?'

'It is actually. Old Master Henry has asked me to read it, I am not sure why,' said Prudence.

'Because I am looking for a new intake of magic students for the next academic year, and I want to offer you and Lampwick places,' said Henry who had silently entered the room, unnoticed by either Prudence or Lampwick.

'Well done Master Henry, it is not easy to sneak up on a cat and a vampire,' said Prudence.

'Me a magician?' Lampwick asked in surprise.

'Well you can turn from a cat into a goblin, which is no small ability,' said Henry.

'But Lampwick is a cat, and I'm a vampire, how can we join the Metropolis' ruling class of wizards?' said Prudence.

'A vampire who can manipulate memories better than any magus I have ever known,' said Henry.

'But still I am a vampire, so I will always be an outcast,'

'And it may still be possible to reclaim you from vampirism,' said Henry.

Being cured of vampirism was a miracle beyond Prudence's highest hopes, so she snapped on to Henry's offer like a dwarf to a gold crown; which was of course exactly what Henry had intended.

'I have never heard of someone being cured of vampirism. Is it possible, or are you teasing me? If you are you are being very cruel,'

'Vampirism is a disease of the soul, but your soul has not been corrupted yet, so there is a possibility to return you to the living,' explained Henry.

'How do you know my soul can be salvaged Sir?'

'Because you have never killed anyone. You even saved Emmanuel Scribble from being killed by Ephemeral Wormsong, which demonstrates you have compassion, and compassion can only fruit from a good soul. If your soul is good, it means your vampirism can, in theory, be reversed. We just need to find a cure,' said Henry.

'Would you help me find a cure?' said Prudence.

'Well that is up for negotiation,' said Henry, 'I need you Prudence to become a demon-fighting wizard, I need Lampwick as well. The manna pollution has led to all sorts of problems for the city. Vampirism is rife, and the werewolf packs are growing larger and prowling the deepest caves. The pollution has weakened the very fabric of the space-time around the Metropolis, making it easier to make a hole through to other dimensions.'

'A hole to what dimension?' asked Lampwick.

'A hole to Hell for a start,' replied Henry, 'As we speak there are cultists out there trying to do just that, and they include Madam Wormsong,'

'So how can we help?' asked Prudence.

'I have the authority from the Goblin King to form a college of demon-fighting wizards. I need you both to join,' said Henry

'Why us? There are thousands of goblins who dream of becoming wizards,' said Lampwick.

'None of them want to become demon hunters. It's far too dangerous. Wizards earn far more designing and crafting magical artefacts, or casting spells commercially. Demon hunting is too dangerous to make a living at for most magical goblins,' said Henry.

'How dangerous?' said Lampwick.

'I have lost two apprentices this year, both captured by vampires. Joseph Hightower has resigned, and Enigma Oates is now an insane vampire herself after being tortured in a pit.'

'So why are you asking me to become a demon hunter if it is so hazardous?' asked Prudence.

'Because your only alternative is to remain a renegade vampire, hated by goblins and vampires alike, which is even more dangerous. I admit your missions as a demon hunter will be perilous, but at least you can live here safely, protected by the guards and other wizards. You can study to improve yourself, and I promise to do my best to help cure you,' said Henry.

'And Lampwick, he has a safe existence, why should he risk any of his nine lives hunting your demons?'

'Lampwick wants to keep you safe for a start. Besides, there is no more respectable profession in the Metropolis than that of a wizard. Think of the social advancement, you would even be allowed to vote for your member of parliament. You will live like a society goblinette, for instance I would like to escort you to the Nettlebed lecture tomorrow evening should you care to join me,' Henry said to Prudence.

'I request some time alone with Lampwick to discuss your offer Master Henry.'

There was a knock on the door, which Henry answered. It was Jevington with the food.

'Please enjoy your breakfasts, and do let me know your decision as soon as possible,' said Henry.

After Henry and Jevington had left, Prudence and Lampwick started to eat.

'Golly goblins! The kippers are delicious,' said Lampwick.

Lampwick noticed a coffin in the corner. 'Do you sleep in that?'

'Master Henry had it made for me by Cripplegate's the undertakers, but actually, I hate sleeping in coffins, always have. I much prefer to sleep on a comfortable goblin floatbed. How about we get into bed together and we could cuddle up close, so you could warm my cold undead body?' asked Prudence as innocently as she could.

As Lampwick was speechless; Prudence undressed and stood naked in front of him. Her skin was as white as chalk, and her hair as black as carbon, with a small scarlet rose.

'I think this is naughty. Are we allowed to do this?' asked Lampwick.

Prudence kissed Lampwick, which sparked an extraordinary and unexpected event, her heart, which had been silent since she had become undead, fluttered a few heartbeats.

'Of course we are allowed Lampwick. Physical love between a goblin and a vampire is permitted even in the finest social circles, every society goblin is doing it, in fact it is quite de rigueur,' reassured Prudence, though in truth she was fully aware of the section 43 of the Ungodly Lusts Act 1875.

27

*Even common goblins who possess only a rudimentary knowledge of magic theory know that some physical objects become so intimate to their owners, that casting a magical spell on the object is the same as casting on the goblin in person. In the book '**Magic Theory and Practice**', such items are referred to as 'arcane connections' and exhibit the 'Law of Contagion'. To illustrate arcane connections, please consider the following examples; invariably a wizards' staff is an arcane connection to the magician who owns it. An arcane connection to Assyria Neepfield the writer is his beloved ink pen. When alive Sally Sting owned a necklace made of beads of manna that formed an arcane connection to her. This connection was how Vanilla Catchpenny could divine where her soul had migrated to after her death...*

From lecture notes explaining the **Law of Contagion**, by Grand Master Pharaoh Henry.

***

Jack had been running around the Metropolis all day helping Vanilla with her errands. Now they were back outside Oakensouls' and he struggled to get out of the carriage, which was only designed for goblins smaller than him, he then helped Vanilla down. He felt how light she was, nothing to her; all skin and bone.

He made his way into the common room where an old-looking wizard sat at one of the tables explaining magic theory to a very pale goblinette. When he saw Coffin he stood up, excused himself from his student, and greeted the ork.

'Pleased to meet you Captain Coffin, my name is Pharaoh Henry, and this is Prudence Pepperhill. I am so glad we have met at last. I visited the telepathy office yesterday evening, and you are the subject of a great deal of inter-planetary communication.'

'A bad thing I presume.'

'In parts, well for the most part actually, especially for you. I think you need to know the orks and the dwarves have been sending messages about you all day, and they both want you sent back to their home planets to be tortured and killed.'

'Is that news? Dwarves and orks have been trying to kill and torture me all my life,' replied Coffin with an indifferent shrug.

'I have eavesdropped in on Dwarven telepathic communications. They know Starcatcher protected your escape pod from the dwarves at your last battle. That dragon wants you to go to Hell for him and has ordered a legal contract to be drawn up by a lawyer by the name of Adam Scryer. The upshot of it is that he wants you to rescue a lady star dragon called Moondancer.'

'You are well informed as to my business Mr. Henry.'

'If its anything to do with Hell, and it concerns the Metropolis, then it is my business as well.'

'Well maybe I shall renege on the deal with the dragon, after all, his part was to rescue all of us, and Sally is dead. You wizards and dragons have agendas that generally don't suit the rest of us. What do I get out of this legal arrangement?' said Coffin.

'You have dishonoured your clan Captain Coffin. Your clansmen are to be exiled from Caragula. I could offer them citizenship here, and a large house for you all to live in on Peccadillo Street.'

'And why do I deserve your generosity?'

'If you do decide to go to Hell, I want you to bring me back a book called *Nomina Vera Daemoniorum*. Besides if Princess Sting has gone to Hell, you could go to Hell and rescue her and bring her back to the safety of the Metropolis. Vanilla could find out for you.'

'How will she find out where my princess's soul has gone to?'

'Because she is the finest scryer in the Metropolis. If you have an arcane connection to the princess please place it on the table. Vanilla will use it as a focus while scrying for Lady Sting's soul,' said Henry.

He took the envelope from his pocket, removed the lock of his beloved princess's hair and her necklace, and a dragon scale given to him by Starcatcher, and placed them all in front of Vanilla.

Jevington the butler entered the room with a teapot and two small china cups. He poured out the hot mauve liquid into one of the cups from which Vanilla drank. Vanilla sipped the tea, and very soon she lost her worn-out look. Invigorated she picked up the dragon scale, which was to be the arcane connection to Lady Moondancer. She held the scale next to her heart.

Vanilla used the arcane connection to augur where the soul of Moondancer had gone.

'In the arena of Hell, where no pity or compassion is shown, a

Princess cycles between birth and old age, at the hand of the cruel demon Asentana that eats her over and over,' moaned Vanilla, her eyes now shining with starlight.

'That is the soul of Lady Moondancer, and we already knew she was in Hell,' said Henry.

Vanilla put down the scale and picked up Sally Sting's necklace.

'A fierce warrior queen rejected heaven for cruel sports and infernal delights. She storms through Hell as she did the world,' said Vanilla.

'My love is in Hell,' said Coffin despondently.

'Coffin, would you chance a rescue into Hell itself?' asked Henry.

'Can that be done?'

'It has never been achieved before, at least not to my knowledge. It is a mission that should lead to damnation, with only a gossamer shaving of a chance of success. Only a reckless berserker, intoxicated with love to the point of stupidity would attempt it. Would you try it Coffin for Princess Sting?'

'I will go. Why not? After all, my soul is already damned by my deeds.'

'Jolly good my fine ork. There might even be a demon to help you on the other side; a succubus Euphoria is in contact with. But we need information to help you with your mission. Vanilla must drink more alapania, and you must drink some too. The drug will cause your soul, and that of Miss Catchpenny's, to leave your physical bodies and take a trip to the astral plane. After drinking, lay down on the bed. Vanilla will guide you from there,'

Jack Coffin drank it down. It tasted slightly bitter, but he quite liked it. It was not long before the alapania took effect. He fell into a trance. His soul left his motionless body. Coffin was in the astral plane, standing in a square, most of the metropolitan buildings had disappeared, but not all; All Souls Church remained, and a temple now stood in the place of the Central Post Office.

He could see Vanilla, who no longer looked strange or ghostly, and her strange eyes had turned to regular goblin eyes, each with a white surrounding a black pupil in a violet iris. She looked the picture of health; clearly the astral plain suited her. All around them, going far into the distance, were hundreds of small balls of light, like glowing bubbles of gas.

'This is the astral plane?' asked Coffin.

'Yes.'

'What are the lights?'

'Souls of goblins mostly; a few ogres, elves, cats and other creatures. We cannot see their bodies without concentrating, but we can see the lights of their souls,' said Vanilla. 'If you concentrate on a light you can see the form of the goblin who owns it, but I don't recommend it though because if you do you will not see the creatures of the astral plane who might creep up on you while you do.'

'What creatures?' Coffin asked.

'The astral plane has its own creatures, and we will be meeting one of them soon,' said Vanilla, 'I shall introduce you to the Sphinx. Perhaps she can tell you how to rescue your beloved from Hell itself. We need the strong brave Captain Coffin, the terror of dwarven shipping if you are to stand any chance of success in a mission to Hell.'

Coffin knew who the sphinx was, everybody did. The Queen of the Satyrs was Penelope the Sphinx, Lady of the Riddle.

'Will the Queen ask me a riddle?' asked Coffin.

'Do you know a riddle?' replied Vanilla.

Coffin nodded.

'That is the correct answer. You must ask her a riddle, and it must be your riddle, one you composed, so not copied or just repeated, and if she likes it, she may help you. Queen Penelope may let you ask her a question if it amuses her to do so, but she will only answer in riddles, so do not request a straight answer from her, as she will be offended.'

Vanilla led Coffin across the square, where five angels danced around the clock tower of the church of All Souls in the Wardrobe.

'What are the angels doing?' said Coffin.

'They are mending the fabric of space. We know the vampires and their allies created a gate to Hell; that is why they stole that book from Scribble's. It seems they punched a small temporary hole in the fabric of space-time with a powerful spell, and the angels are repairing it,' said Vanilla.

'It must take a great deal of magical power to create a doorway to Hell,' said Coffin.

'A larger more permanent gate would need a lot of power, which requires the emotional presence of a large number of souls involved in the spell cast. Master Henry cannot fathom how they are doing it. It is not as if we have a huge crowd of diabolists in Dragonfair each night, with every goblin singing and chanting around some infernal alter, and that is what is typically needed to create a gate to Hell,' said Vanilla.

Vanilla led Coffin to the astral component of the Central Post Office on Arcadia Square, which on the astral plane appeared as a small temple in the style of the ancient Greeks. They entered the temple, and as Vanilla had indicated, came into the presence of the Sphinx herself. Queen Penelope lay on a large throne. She was in goblin form, with golden hair and feline beauty. But she was also expressionless and strangely terrifying to anyone capable of feeling fear, which fortunately, was not Captain Coffin.

Vanilla and Coffin curtsied and bowed respectfully to her majesty.

'Tell the queen your riddle,' said Vanilla to Coffin under her breath.

Captain Coffin, stood up straight, and recited his riddle as if he were giving a speech.

First I catch my servant,

Who takes my lady across the sea,

To where I find my place of rest,

Then wrapped in my lady's arms I sleep.

The sphinx thought on the riddle for a while, then she said, 'Jack Coffin, I must concede I do not know the answer to your riddle, please reveal it.'

'The answer to my riddle is the sail on a sailing ship. The sail's servant is the wind which the sail catches. The sail's lady is the ship itself and the wind blows the ship across the sea. When the ship arrives at its destined port it rests. While in dock, the sail is wrapped in the ship's masts, which is expressed by the line, 'wrapped in my lady's arms I sleep.'

The sphinx smiled faintly, then said, 'I like your riddle my orkish captain. Ask me a question and I shall give you a riddle in return.'

'How can I rescue my beloved Princess from Hell?' asked Coffin.

'Now that is a good question. A deliciously dangerous and subversive question. Do the angels know you intend to rescue someone from Hell? Aren't people in Hell sent there for a good reason? Orks are usually so boorish, full of violence and cruelty and not much else, but I am starting to like you Captain Jack Coffin. You like to upset the order of things. I assume you have brought an arcane connection of her with you?'

Coffin passed Sally Sting's necklace and Moondancer's scale to Queen Penelope. Penelope held the necklace and the scale in each of her hands, caressing them gently with her fingers, all the time looking into the blackness beyond her third eye until an image formed. Penelope then gave Captain Coffin a riddle:

> *'The law commands we strike the guilty,*
> *But they did not as guilt is in all of us,*
> *If cast I snare hypocrisy*
> *When uncast I bestow forgiveness,*
> *Demons can smell guilt, yet clemency blinds them,*
> *Hell deals in pain and harm,*
> *Yet mercy burns a devil's skin.'*

'Thank you for your riddle your majesty', said Coffin.

Jack bowed and Vanilla curtseyed, and they walked backwards out of Queen Penelope's presence, and made their way back to their bodies on the material plane.

28

Gaiety Seelykin, wife of Grand Master Jeremiah Seelykin, was killed in a tragic ornithopter accident, thereby ending his marriage to her under the 'to death us do part' clause of the matrimonial contract. Distraught at losing the spouse he loved so much, Master Seelykin resurrected her as a zombie, by way of an illegal 'raising the dead spell'. He then went through the marriage ceremony with her a second time. But this court annuls the marriage as the union between a goblin and a zombie amounts to necrophilia under section 43 of the Ungodly Lusts Act, and considers such consummation with a corpse to be unlawful; as such their second marriage was unconsummated and annulled.

Ratio Decidendi, case of **Rex vs. Seelykin 1888**

***

Just off the corner of Great Goblin street and Arcadia Square, goblin costermongers gather in great number. The evening air was cut through with the trader's cries carried across the market, 'Here's your moonfruit', 'Rootneeps sold by the pound', 'Starflowers - penny a bunch', and 'Fine fresh koboldroots'.

The peddlers had been selling fruit and vegetables from their bright green and red barrows since early morning. Even though the sun had set a couple of hours past, the hawkers were still trying to make just a few last sales before turning in for the night.

Arm in arm with Pharaoh Henry, Prudence strolled by the costermongers as if she had no care in the world. She wore a fashionable perfume she had stolen from Euphoria, and her scent spliced into the sweet smell of fruit, all tunefully accompanied by the noisy scramble of trade.

The second moon Selonia was still almost full; it lit up the square with a silver shine as the church clock struck 8 pm. Small groups of dribblings sang and danced with flower fairies, to the sounds of fiddles and drums of goblin buskers. Around them goblins bought fruit from the barrow traders to give to the dancers and musicians.

'Grand Master Henry, please would you allow me to ask you an important question in law,' asked Prudence.

'Well this does sound grave, how could I refuse you, especially when you have instilled in me such intrigue and curiosity about a question you have not even asked yet,' replied Henry.

'Can a vampire goblinette marry a shape-changing cat?' Prudence asked as she skipped a little to the fiddler's melody.

'That is indeed a very interesting point of goblin law, Miss Pepperhill,' replied Henry 'I would say no, and here are my reasons. The fact that Lampwick is a shape-changing cat is neither here nor there, and does not stop him getting married because he is capable of speech, so thereby considered legally sentient under the Goblin Rights Act, and so, in turn, is eligible to marry. Any goblin can marry any living member of any sentient race providing the proposed spouse is of the opposite gender and made from animal flesh.'

'Made from animal flesh?'

'Animal flesh in the biological sense. You can't marry an intelligent vegetable such as a tree troll for example, or a rock troll, or a golem for that matter. Animal flesh is the flesh from any animal, and goblins are biologically animals.'

'I admit Lampwick is a bit dim-witted, which is why I feed him fish, but he is a cat, not a vegetable, so why can't I marry him under the law?'

'Because as I said to you earlier, you are not strictly alive my dearest and marriage must be between two living sentient creatures,' explained Henry, stressing the word 'living'.

'Is there any way around that silly restriction?'

'If you were to be cured of vampirism, and your heart started to beat again, you would be considered alive and able to marry Lampwick.'

'Well my heart threw a few beats just before dawn.'

'While that is encouraging my dear Miss Pepperhill, it is unlikely to be considered enough to prove you are alive. Your heart needs to beat regularly if you want to be sure a judge would give you legal status as a living goblin.'

'You have mentioned a cure of vampirism before, but how can that be done in practical terms? I thought that once you were undead, then it is undead until proper dead, upon which event the soul migrates to Hell,' said Prudence.

'Not quite. As I have told you, your soul is still capable of compassion, so you are not quite damned yet. As to a cure for vampirism I have absolutely no idea. But one of the goblins we will meet soon may know a way. A goblin by the name of Reverend Noah Bentley. You will like him I am sure, as he is a fine gentlegoblin of the highest moral calibre, and a leading authority on vampirism to boot.'

'Well that would be a help, you are being very kind to me Grand Master Pharaoh Henry. Furthermore, if I do ever become alive again, I would like to marry Lampwick in this church and I want you to give me away to my new feline husband. What's the name of the church we are going to?'

'All Souls in the Wardrobe.'

'Really? What a peculiar name. Why would anyone name a church such?' asked Prudence.

'There is a history to that question, the complex of buildings is known as the *Wardrobe*,' said Henry, while pointing to some buildings around the church. 'They are so called because it's primary use is to store the robes and uniforms of state. It holds the King's clothes, and also those of his household, and retinue. The formal uniforms are for the opening of parliament, coronations, and embassies from foreign dignitaries, military parades, and a host of other ceremonial events at which the Goblin King and his government must attend. The *Church of All Souls in the Wardrobe* was built on what was once the Wardrobe's gardens, hence the church's name.'

'So is All Souls in the Wardrobe usually open to the general public, or is it just used by the Goblin King and his retinue?' asked Prudence.

'Well at one time the church used to be just for the King's retinue. It still happens to be the King's favourite spot for saying his prayers. But the good old King noticed that goblins in the neighbourhood of the Wardrobe had to travel some distance to go to church, so he ordered that All Souls be open for public service and prayer. We are going to meet the King in the vicarage not the church as such,' explained Henry.

'We are meeting the Goblin King in a vicarage?' Prudence asked with astonishment.

Henry led Prudence through a narrow lane between No. 127 and No. 128 Arcadia Square that led to the entrance to All Souls. 'All the other parts of the Wardrobe except the church are off-limits to the general public. The Goblin King purchased number 127 Arcadia Square as a vicarage for the church, and its current resident is the

Reverend Bentley. He was once a famous vampire hunter you know. He is often summoned by his majesty for advice on theology, ethics and extermination of the undead. He was instrumental in planning the recent destruction of the vampire colony on Peccadillo Street.'

Henry knocked on the rear door of the vicarage. The housemistress answered. She ushered Pharaoh and Prudence into the drawing-room, where the King and Bentley were enjoying tea and muffins.

'Henry my stalwart demon hunter, with his lovely lady friend. Please sit down the both of you. Is there any news for us?' Asked the King.

After Henry and Prudence had sat down the housemistress poured them some tea, and Bentley offered them some freshly toasted muffins.

'Rather too much news. Please let me introduce Miss Prudence Pepperhill, a magical memory manipulator extraordinaire,' said Henry.

'Welcome Miss Pepperhill.' said the King, at which Prudence stood up again, and gave his majesty a long, low and befitting courtesy.

'Welcome Grand Master Henry and Miss Pepperhill,' said Reverend Bentley, holding his teacup in one hand, while propping himself up with his dragon tooth walking stick with the other.

Pharaoh Henry then narrated the tale of the demon attack, Coffin's arrival in the Metropolis, the attack on Prudence, and the transformations of Euphoria Fireheart.

'Miss Pepperhill, you tried to manipulate a demon's memory, did it work,' asked the King.

'I am afraid not your majesty,' said Prudence.

'Theoretically speaking it should be impossible to manipulate the memory of demons, as demons themselves are the very essence of deception. It would be inconsistent with their essential nature if you could read truth directly from their minds. Also planting false memories into a demon would be trying to deceive the great deceiver; which while a theological contradiction rather than a hermetic one, is a contradiction never the less, and therefore also impossible. But it is reassuring to know your empirical test of actually trying to do it failed, and so confirming the theoretical view currently held as canon,' said Bentley.

'Can't say I follow you,' said Prudence.

'Me neither,' added the King.

'We also need to protect Miss Pepperhill against being arrested for vampirism by giving her a royal pardon,' said Henry, as he passed the King the document for his signature.

'I am very grateful for protection, but I seek a more permanent solution to my infection. How can I be cured of vampirism?' Prudence asked the Reverend Bentley.

'That's a difficult one. Medicine based on the standard hermetic model just will not work because vampirism is a disease of the soul rather than the flesh or mind,' said Reverend Bentley.

'But can it be done?' insisted Henry.

'Have you ever killed anyone by draining their blood?' asked Bentley.

'No, never, I just drank a little bit each from a lot of goblins, so no-one died, and my bite is not infectious,' answered Prudence.

'As long as you have not killed a sentient creature in the role of a vampire, it should be possible to cure you, theoretically speaking at least. But I must admit I do not know of such a spell that will do the trick,' said Bentley.

'What do you suggest? That I invent a spell to restore my soul?' asked Prudence.

'I just told you; you cannot use the standard theory of magic to cure vampirism. If I were in your shoe's young lady, I would look to the angelic powers. Ask an angel for help, or maybe a virtuous creature such as the sphinx, or a unicorn. Remember that freewill is an issue when dealing with creatures of virtue; they must give you their power out of their own choice. So, for heaven's sake do not go plucking out angel feathers for a potion without their owner's permission because it would render the item useless as well as incur their wrath,' said Bentley.

'I wouldn't dream of it,' said Prudence, who found the very thought of stealing an angel's feather most disagreeable, 'but you have given me food for thought. I shall keep my eye out for an angel, just in case they drop a feather or two by accident.'

'There is another matter I would like to raise, that of Jack Coffin,' said Henry.

'My clerks have been getting requests from the Orkish Ambassador and the Dwarf Trade Delegate all day, they both want Coffin,' replied the King.

'So, any suggestions gentlegoblins, and Miss Pepperhill?' asked the

King, hastily adding Prudence after remembering there was a goblinette present.

'Well it turns out Mr. Coffin is in love with a princess whose soul was condemned to Hell. He wants to go there and rescue her,' said Henry, 'Unfortunately, he wouldn't last long if he tried without help and equipment I should imagine. So, I sent him with Mrs Catchpenny to visit Queen Penelope the Sphinx. She liked him, and gave him a riddle to help. Let me read it out:

> *'The law commands we strike the guilty,*
> *But they did not as guilt is in all of us,*
> *If cast I snare hypocrisy*
> *When uncast I bestow forgiveness,*
> *Demons can smell guilt, yet clemency blinds them,*
> *Hell deals in pain and harm,*
> *Yet mercy burns a devil's skin.'*

'Does anyone have any clue what the riddle means?' asked the King.

'I think it's to do with a Bible story,' said Bentley, 'I think the lines: **The law says we should strike the guilty, But they did not strike as guilt is in us all** refers to the uncast stones in the bible.'

'Ah I see, and so **When uncast I bestow forgiveness** means the stones have captured the essence of forgiveness. A stone could fish a soul right back out of Hell again,' said the King.

'I do hope **mercy burns a devil's skin** means they can be used as a weapon against the demons,' said Henry, as his eyes filled with enthusiasm.

'It might make a raid on Hell itself possible. The uncast stones, would make someone holding one invisible to a demon. If a demon that touches one suffers pain and injury, it would make a good weapon. If Coffin went to Hell, he could create quite a fuss with the stones. But how are you going to send Coffin to Hell?' said Reverend Bentley.

'I plan to use the two mirrors that are a door to Hell we recovered from the vampire's nest. I will arrest Coffin myself. and with his permission, send him to Hell through the mirrors,' said

Henry.

'We should offer Jack Coffin and his woman sanctuary in the Metropolis from the forces of Hell. All he has to do is steal the **Nominae Verae Demonorum,**' said Henry to the Goblin King.

'Domino who?' asked Prudence.

'**Nominae Verae Demonorum**, it's the book containing the true names of all the demons in Hell. We can use it to amplify the power of a demon warding machine and keep the city safe,' explained Henry.

'I will have the royal secretary draft a few passports for the citizens of Hell you rescue, let us say ten of them. If you rescue more souls than that just ask the passport holders to explain there were not enough to go around, but they have my permission to stay in the Metropolis anyway. So that's that.' said the King, who smiled at the thought of tying up so many loose ends.

29

'Master' is usually the correct honorific for a high wizard, except for a very senior wizard where 'Grand Master' is used. Low wizards or hedge wizards prefer to be called 'Mother' or 'Father'.

From **Required Etiquette for Wizards**, 4th Edition, Anon, Green Dragon Press.

***

Prudence and Pharaoh linked arms as they strolled along the cobblestones of Summerfair Lane together. She was going to her first lecture at the Imperial School of Magic and she was so excited that she could not stop smiling. She had done a lot of being happy since escaping the nest

She wore emerald green elfin kimono embroidered with a design of a phoenix, which she had purchased with some of the money Henry had given her as an advance against her wages. She was now a trainee demon-hunter.

They made their way into the school and then into the lecture theatre. It was brimming with magicians of all kinds and abilities, all of whom fell silent at the sight of the Grand Master Henry and Prudence. She felt every eye in the huge hall fall upon her. She was famous now; every goblin knew of the beautiful vampire who had become Pharaoh Henry's student.

Because of his rank, Henry had a seat reserved for him at the front of the hall, and one for his guest. He led Prudence to her place after she had sat, he bowed to her and requested permission to sit next to her later, which made Prudence feel like a queen.

Pharaoh Henry then walked to the podium to introduce the speaker for the evening:

'My dear friends, both magical and mundane. It is my greatest honour to introduce you all to the Metropolis's foremost weather wizard; who will talk tonight about the new weather machine, which as you all know, is the foremost concern of the city. Gentlegoblins and goblinettes, I give you Grand Master Jeroboam Nettlebed.'

Nettlebed stepped onto the podium to the excited applause of the audience. He shook hands with Henry, who left him to take his place next to Prudence. He was a tall and painfully thin goblin. Above his head floated a tiny weather system of clouds and a moon, with shafts of moonlight peeping through and onto his scalp.

He addressed the audience and gave the speech that began with the following:

'Our government set up a parliamentary commission on manna pollution, of which I am the chair. The commission's findings are that in the interests of magical hygiene the pollution levels in the city should be reduced by the construction of a Municipal Weather Machine. The machine will maintain a pleasant living environment and blow pollutants out of the city.

This machine has become necessary as the Metropolis is now the workshop of the galaxy, making every conceivable magical device for domestic use and trade. The discharge from the chimneys of the city's many factories has thrown queens of manna into the air, creating the manna fog. It is this polluted fog that has in recent times, mutated many of the city's goblins.

This commission acknowledges that in some cases such mutations can be beneficial for the goblin. A case in point would be that of Mr. Darius Cheapside, a sewage worker who worked for long hours in the deepest and darkest of the city's tunnels. One day at work, Mr. Cheapside was bitten by an infected wererat; in response to this trauma, Cheapside grew large light-catching eyes that enabled him to see in pitch-black darkness. He has since supplemented his wages by finding lost coins and jewellery washed up in the sluice channels, which he returns to their owners for a substantial reward.

The commission notes many examples of oppressed goblins who have been transformed by the manna fog. Previously possessing no magical ability, post mutation, some were able to evade their oppressors by the spontaneous development of a breakthrough skill.

But mutations are not always advantageous; take the case of a dribbling known only as 'Oliver'. Oliver was an orphan who fed himself by stealing bread from ogres. One day when cornered by an aggrieved and angry ogre, he risked being eaten alive. Under this threat he mutated and developed the ability to become magically invisible, which allowed him to escape. Thereafter he put his invisibility to good use as a successful shoplifter, until he was eventually run over and killed by a number 36 triple-decker tram on Spreadeagle Street. The post-mortem established that the poor tram driver was blameless, because he had been unable to see Oliver; however, he was so traumatized by the guilt of having killed a young dribbling, he had to have his whole memory of the incident magically removed from his mind to restore his sanity.

As things stand the degree of mutation due to magical pollution has become far too hazardous for the public good. Manna pollution has led to magical diseases; goblins that were parasitic by nature have developed vampirism, and those prone to bad temper, lycanthropy. These diseases are spreading to other innocent goblins by the bites from those already infected.'

My bites are not infectious, thought Prudence.

'In summary, the defining feature of the modern urban goblin is that he will magically adapt to his environment, but may do so only when, firstly he is in the presence of a strong magical aura, and secondly under goes a traumatic event.

The recommendation from the Parliamentary Commission on Pollution is that a municipal weather machine is to be commissioned to clear the city's atmosphere of the magical pollution that has accumulated from its many industries. The pollutants will be blown to a reclaiming factory that will extract the manna and clean the air.'

Nettlebed continued with a technical specification of how the weather machine worked, which Prudence found difficult to follow.

The speech concluded and the audience applauded.

'I now invite the audience to ask questions,' said Nettlebed.

A goblin student stood up in the audience and asked, 'In the winter months, where will you get all the heat from to warm the city?'

'The Metropolitan Council has purchased land from the satyrs just to the North of the city, from which the weather machine will draw heat when necessary. Unfortunately, it will make the land extremely cold, so the satyrs will no longer be able to live there. But with the money they have bought a large palace in the Metropolis where they can spend the winter in comfort,' answered Nettlebed.

Prudence put up her hand, and Nettlebed pointed to her.

'If it no longer rains in the Metropolis, how will the trees and flowers in the gardens and parks get watered?' she asked.

'A very good question. The weather machine can create small clouds which will be manoeuvred over the city by the weather machine operators and will rain only over the gardens and parks, and the trees that line the roads. They will do this at a time just after midnight, when there are very few if any, goblins out in the streets, to minimise the chances of them being rained on,' replied Nettlebed.

Prudence had never before enjoyed such a wonderfully interesting evening in her life. After the lecture, Henry and Prudence dined at the Prancing Unicorn restaurant.

They took a cab back to Oakensoul's. As they arrived, Euphoria Fireheart was waiting for Henry outside the main door.

'What's wrong Euphoria,' asked Henry.

'High Constable Euphrates Glock has arrested Daddy on the charge of treason,' she said, then burst into tears.

30

"They said unto him, Teacher, this woman was taken in adultery, in the very act. Now Moses in the law commanded us, that such should be stoned: but what sayest thou? This they said, tempting him, that they might have to accuse him. But Jesus stooped down, and with his finger wrote on the ground, as though he heard them not. So when they continued asking him, he lifted up himself, and said unto them, He that is without sin among you, let him first cast a stone at her."

John 8: 4 to 8:7 **The Holy Bible**

Yellowrind is a kind of citrus fruit, sweet in taste, but as the name suggests, yellow in colour.

From **Modern Goblin Cuisine** 2nd edition by Miss Elegance Woodheart

***

Vanilla Catchpenny was still wearing pyjama's as she shook Jack Coffin's head and then shouted in his ears, by which method she eventually woke him. Coffin thought Vanilla to be a rather good looking but curious creature, largely due to her small size (compared to an ork) and her pale blue skin, and Vanilla thought of him as her guard dog.

'Big news,' said Vanilla to Coffin, 'He made deals with both the orks and the dwarves to send you to Hell. In return he's getting two panship hulls from the dwarves, and the orks agreed to give your entire clan safe passage to the city and asylum. The plan is for you to escape Hell with Sally Sting and Lady Moondancer, and that you will both join his crusade against the forces of Hell.'

'I can think of worse things to do,' said Coffin. 'I am an ork captain that abandoned his ship, so I can never return to Caragula. Consequently, my career opportunities are somewhat limited. I think my chances of surviving Hell are small.' Quick as a snake, Coffin reached out and grabbed Vanilla by the base of her tail, which was most disconcerting for her.

'Let go! You must listen to instructions! When you get to Hell you may get a little help from a succubus called Pandamonia, but I would not rely too heavily on her if I were you. Euphoria Fireheart managed to get herself in some sort of mind share with the demoness, who wants to escape and live here. In my opinion it would-be a big mistake to have too much to do with her as demons are invariably unreliable,'

'There is no such thing as a reliable demon that is for sure. But what about you, what does the great Pharaoh Henry the Grand Master Wizard want from little Miss Vanilla Catchpenny?'

'I would have thought that was obvious, I am a seer who can navigate the astral plane. He wants me as a magician in his new college of demon hunters,' said Vanilla.

'He wants you? But hasn't your mind been damaged by drinking soothsaying tea?' asked Coffin.

'Henry thinks your strength of mind is repairing mine, that I am becoming my old self again. He thinks your presence helps me, but he is wrong, you drive me mad!' said Vanilla, as she stamped her tiny foot.

Coffin still did not release his grip on Vanilla's tail.

'What does the riddle mean?' insisted Coffin.

'Buy me breakfast and I will tell you,' replied Vanilla, her hands defiantly back on her hips.

'Is there anywhere in this city where I can buy meat?' said Coffin.

'The Metropolitan Chop House on Cat Fishing Street is popular with the ogres, and as ogres are stupid meat eaters then it should be popular with orks too,' replied Vanilla.

'Then I shall buy little Miss Catchpenny breakfast at the Chop House,' said Coffin as he finally released her.

After washing and dressing, the pair made their way to the café. Outside a paper boy shouted the headlines, 'Zebedee Fireheart Arrested. To Face Trial for Treason!'

Jack Coffin sat outside the Chop House on one of the ogre-sized tables. An ogre wife served him a large plate of lamb chops with mashed rootneeps and sautéed greens, and an ogre-sized glass of stout. Vanilla sat opposite Coffin with a bowl of mixed nuts, a bowl of porridge, and a glass of yellowrind juice.

Vanilla said, 'Well the riddle goes like this:

> *'The law commands we strike the guilty,*
> *But they did not as guilt is in all of us,*
> *If cast I snare hypocrisy,*
> *When uncast I bestow forgiveness,*
> *Demons can smell guilt, yet clemency blinds them,*
> *Hell deals in pain and harm,*
> *Yet mercy burns a devil's skin.'*

'What does it mean?' asked Coffin.

'Have you heard of Jesus?' asked Vanilla.

'I have, everybody has. He was the one who gave lots of people some bread and fishes to eat and didn't charge them any money for it,' said Coffin.

Vanilla rolled her galactic eyes in exasperation at Jack's biblical knowledge, or rather lack of it.

'Well there is a story about a goblinette who is about to be stoned for adultery, but Jesus saves her life by saying to her would be executioners, *He that is without sin among you, let him first cast a stone at her'*

'So what? Can't you save the religion for Sunday?' said Coffin.

'So, the uncast stones are the answer to the riddle. The uncast stones are the way to raid Hell itself and escape with souls enslaved to the Devil. The stones are the very essence of forgiveness from sin. Holding one will make you invisible to any demon. A demon can only sense guilt so the forgiveness of sin will make you invisible to them. If you touch a demon with one you are touching it with the mercy of God, which will burn the brute,' said Vanilla.

'Very good Miss. Catchpenny. You are not as stupid as you look,' said Coffin. 'But where in the galaxy would I get my hands on Jesus' uncast stones?'

Vanilla accepted the small barbed complement the ork gave her, and kept quiet about the fact that Noah Bentley had interpreted the riddle first, he had told Prudence, who had then told him.

Vanilla pointed to the museum building opposite the café.

'Well we could try asking at the intergalactically famous Municipal Museum of Biblical Artefacts on Cat Fishing Street over there, or didn't Captain Jack Coffin, the great orkish intellectual think of that?'

On the outside, the museum was an ochre-coloured stone building in classical Draskan style. It was a bewildering web of external arches and flying buttresses that carried away the stresses and loads of the masonry and roof, so that on the inside it was a palace of glass, space and light.

As Coffin entered through the huge front doorway, he was impressed by the giant skeleton of a fish hanging from the ceiling. 'What is that?' he asked Vanilla, pointing to the fish bones.

'That's the fish that swallowed Jonah,' explained Vanilla. 'I like those fish bones, big and impressive like your muscles. Shame about your orkish intelligence though. You need to eat a fish that big, because fish is brain food.'

'That's not nice Miss Catchpenny, I did say you were pretty,' said Coffin.

'You also said I was stupid.'

'Well you're pretty stupid then,' said Coffin, laughing at his puerile humour.

As all reasonably educated goblins know, the head curator of the Museum of Biblical Artefacts was a lady goblin by the name of Mme. Utopia Moon. Vanilla eventually found her standing by the exhibit of the last few remaining gopher wood planks from Noah's ark. At Vanilla's request, Utopia guided them to the exhibit of the uncast stones.

'We need to borrow these stones, Madam Moon,' said Vanilla.

Utopia looked bewildered and horrified, she said, 'You can't have them. They are irreplaceable.'

'But we will bring them back. Who do we ask to get permission to borrow them?' asked Vanilla.

'You must ask me for my permission and I say you most definitely cannot borrow them. Oh no, absolutely not,' shrieked Utopia, 'Who in this world would give you the right to borrow these precious stones?'

'This order from the Goblin King; it gives me permission to borrow the stones for a trip to Hell,' said Vanilla.

Utopia Moon took the order, then after studying it carefully, an expression of absolute dread crawled all over her face. She opened up the display case, and then one by one, and with painful reluctance, she passed the stones to Vanilla.

Vanilla led Coffin out of the museum as quickly as she could, just in case Utopia changed her mind.

'I want to give you a present Captain Coffin,' said Vanilla, as she handed Jack a charm. 'It belonged to my late husband, given to him by his mother. It is a ward against firearms; you may need it when you get back to the Metropolis.'

'How do you know I will return from Hell.'

'I can't be sure, but my inner voice tells me you will, and I am a seer.'

Vanilla and Coffin took a tram back to Oakensoul's. They made their way to the lounge where Henry and Prudence were eating crackers and cheese and drinking cocoa, in front of an open fire.

'Jack! Good to see you my fine ork. I can't stop and talk as Prudence and I are just off out to the Goblin King's Ball. But I am glad to have caught you, as I have arranged for you to be arrested tomorrow in exchange for the safe passage of the Coffin clan from Caragula, and some dwarven hulls. When they arrive, they can live at the house on Peccadillo Street where the vampires stayed. I do hope your journey to Hell will not be too unpleasant,' said Henry cheerfully.

'And I hope the Coffin boys bring troll hammers with them, those battlecasts look wrong to me.' said Jack.

31

An 'undead' creature was once alive, and now dead, but still animated by magical or infernal power. Undead creatures include zombies, ghouls and vampires.

The legal definition of 'Undead', originally formulated in **Diseases of the Soul**, by Dr Stygian Lovejoy.

***

The court of the Goblin King was a smaller, simpler and less ornate affair than the wizard's parliament; its walls were plastered and painted plain white, without the slightest magical pigment to colour it up. The King liked a simple plainness that contrasted starkly with the competition for ostentation so typical of the *nouveau riche* wizardry. To the King's mind, plain meant not having to prove anything to anyone, and understated décor indicated authority.

He sat at the centre of the western wall. His throne was a wooden chair raised on a podium. At the base of the podium below the King, sat the clerk of the court. Under goblin law his royal majesty was the highest judge in the city.

On the King's right sat a jury of 12 goblins. Usually the goblins were chosen from ministers that were appointed as representatives by wizards so to act according to their interests. In front of the King was an aisle that ran the length of the court, with benches on either side of it.

Facing his majesty, to his right sat the accused, Mr. Zebedee Fireheart and Captain Jack Coffin on a front bench; to the left sat the prosecution, in the personage of Euphrates Glock for the prosecution of Zebedee, and Pharaoh Henry for the prosecution of Captain Coffin.

Spectators sat at the back of the court, and included souls who hated Jack Coffin and wanted him brought to heel. One such enemy was Aldergund Roggerbrood for the dwarves, and yet another was Kasper Scratch for the orks.

The clerk of the court stood up to address the court, 'Your Majesty, ladies and gentlegoblins of the jury. The matters to be dealt with at this session are: His Majesty will appoint a goblin to be the

Goblin King's advisor on demon bottle safety, he will judge the trial of Mr. Coffin on the charge of piracy on the high space lanes, and the trial of Mr. Zebedee Fireheart for the publication and distribution of treasonous literature.'

'Before we start, why is the jury made up of elves? Come to think of it, why do you look like an elf?' The King asked the clerk.

'It's the latest thing in magical cosmetic surgery your Majesty, all the best goblins look like elves nowadays, it's the fashion,' replied the clerk.

'Well I don't look like an elf and I'm the Goblin King, and neither does he,' said the King pointing to the very goblin looking Zebedee Fireheart, 'there are a few orks,' pointing to Jack Coffin and Kasper Scratch; 'and dwarves,' pointing to Aldergund Roggerbrood and his associates; 'lots of little elves pointing to everyone else; but the only goblins at my court are myself, old Pharaoh Henry who never changes, and that gentlegoblin', said the King nodding at Zebedee.

'Well all the ministers look like elves nowadays your Majesty,' said the clerk.

'Are you telling me that I will shortly have to appoint someone who looks like an elf to be Minister for Demonic Safety in the goblin city? Because that will not do!' said the King.

'With your permission your Majesty, may we proceed to the cases of Captain Coffin and Zebedee Fireheart?'

'Proceed,' agreed the King gruffly.

'First case, that of Captain Coffin,' shouted the clerk.

'Captain Coffin is accused of Piracy on the space lanes. What do you plead?' Said the clerk.

'I am a pirate alright. I did it,' confessed Coffin.

'Well that was easy. Captain Coffin, you admit your guilt eh? I do like a goblin who takes a pride in his work, even piracy, what is the sentence?' the King asked Adam Scryer, the prosecuting lawyer.

'We have negotiated the sentence with the orkish and dwarven authorities, and we agree Jack Coffin should be sent to Hell,' said Scryer.

'Sent to Hell? Seems a bit harsh. How long for?' the King asked Scryer.

'Well any goblin sent to Hell goes there forever; after all that is the nature of Hell,' replied Scryer.

'I am not sending a goblin to Hell forever, even if he is an ork, that would be most ungoblinlike, unconstitutional even,' said the King, 'Any requests before I pass sentence?'

'I request that should I escape from Hell, that you would you grant me, and also any souls I can rescue, asylum in your city,' said Coffin.

The jury and audience of the court laughed at the idea of escaping from Hell.

'A prison break from Hell eh? Alright, I sentence you to Hell until such time that you can find your way out again, at such time you will have served your sentence, and have paid for your crimes. You will be a free goblin of the Metropolis, and so will any soul who escapes with you. Place him into the custody of Mrs Vanilla Catchpenny, and arrange for execution as soon as possible,' said the King, bashing his gavel on the arm of his wooden throne.

'Second case, that of Mr. Zebedee Fireheart,' shouted the clerk.

'Mr. Zebedee Fireheart your majesty is accused of printing and distributing treasonous literature,' said the clerk.

'What do you plead?' asked the King.

'I plead this is a case of injustice and I am a free goblin bound in the chains of tyranny,' shouted Zebedee at the top of his lungs.

Everyone in the courtroom looked at each other in silence, each trying to understand what Zebedee was actually pleading.

'Go on' said the King, his expression was one of cautious curiosity, as he could not yet decide if Zebedee was an original thinker, or a madman, or both.

Euphrates Glock stood up and walked to the front of the court, then said 'Perhaps I could explain your Majesty. Mr. Zebedee Fireheart was caught with a treasonous newspaper called the **Revolutionary Goblin** on his premises. Furthermore, he had possessed a printing press, ink, paper and other sundry materials for the publication of the said newspaper.'

'And what's so wrong with that?' enquired the King.

'Perhaps if you let me read you an extract from the disgusting and seditious magazine **Revolutionary Goblin** your Majesty,' Glock replied, who then proceeded to read the paper out aloud, 'In the Metropolis all political and economic power is now held by an elite class, namely the class of wizards. Only wizards may vote for, or sit in the wizard's parliament, which is the legislature. Although in law, any noblegoblin can theoretically be appointed a minister by decree of the Goblin King, in practice only goblins who are wizards, or the representatives of wizards may take such office.'

'So, I can appoint anyone to be a minister?' asked the King.

'Technically yes, any noblegoblin with a title that is, the alternative is of course to appoint a wizard. But that is not the point your Majesty, this treasonous literature, written and distributed by the accused, undermines the very foundations of the rule of wizards,' explained Glock with a furrowed brow and sour tone.

'Well call your witnesses,' said the King.

'I call Abraham Moon the postman,' said Glock.

Mr. Moon took the stand.

'Sir, have you seen or heard any act of sedition at Fireheart's newsagents,' asked Glock.

'Every day when I picked up the letters, someone had stuck the stamps on the envelopes with the King's head upside down,' replied Moon.

The audience of the court gasped in horror at such an awful felony.

'I call the defendant,' said Glock.

'Mr. Zebedee Fireheart. Are you trying to undermine the rule of the wizards?' asked the King.

'Yes,' said Zebedee.

'Why?' asked the King, his curiosity aroused.

'Because wizards are bossy and don't let anyone else have a say in any matters of importance to do with the government of our city,' said Zebedee.

'You make a good point,' agreed the King. 'They try to boss me about as well, and I'm supposed to be the King. About time these wizards were put in their place. Never the less I find you guilty of treason, and sentence you to be Minister for Demonic Safety by royal decree.'

'You can't do that!' shrieked Glock.

'Yes I can, I'm the King,' said the King.

'Your Majesty, with respect there is a constitutional issue to consider. You can only award an office, such as that of Minister for Demonic Safety to a goblin who has a title, such as a lordship, or a graduate wizard. Besides we are here to punish Mr. Fireheart, not give him a job,' said Glock, trying to regain his composure.

'Mr. Zebedee Fireheart, I am going to make you Lord of Dragonfair, and Minister for Demonic Safety,' corrected the Goblin King.

'You can't make me a lord. I'm a socialist!' said Zebedee, holding his head in shock at the indignity of being thrust into the aristocracy 'So you don't want to be a lord, you wouldn't like to be a lord, is that right?' said the King.

'Certainly not Sir, the aristocracy and wizards are parasites who suck the lifeblood from the goblin workers!' replied Zebedee with good dollop of revolutionary zeal.

The King thought for a moment and then asked the Jury, 'Members of the jury do you find Mr. Zebedee Fireheart guilty or innocent of the charge of treason?'

The members of the jury mumbled in deliberation for a few moments and then the head juror said, 'Guilty as charged your Majesty.'

'Well then Mr. Zebedee Fireheart, in my capacity as the Goblin King, I hereby punish your naughtiness by sentencing you to be Lord Fireheart of Dragonfair, and Minister of Demonic Safety. I hope that is sufficient chastisement for your treasonous acts, and I do not want to see you before me here again. Next case,' said the King, then he banged his gavel while laughing maniacally.

Zebedee Fireheart stood as still as a stone with the shock.

'Court dismissed,' said the Goblin King, who looked very pleased with himself at tying up all the loose ends.

32

*The **Law of Infernal Limitation**: 'Magic cannot fathom infernal deception'.*

Excerpt from **Magic Theory and Practice** 4th Edition

***

Just after sunset, Prudence rose from her bed. She washed and dressed, then went out onto the green and sat on the iron bench, to eat and chat with Oakensoul, her favourite tree. Dinner (or more accurately breakfast as Prudence was nocturnal) consisted of toasted crumpets, served with black pudding and bubble and squeak, washed down with coffee, limony juice, and a pint of sheep's blood; all freshly prepared and of the finest quality.

The tree troll had taken quite an interest in Prudence, after all, it wasn't every day one could discuss the meaning of life with a member of the undead.

'How are they looking after you Prudence?' asked Oakensoul.

'Very well thank you sir. I cannot go out without an escort, but apparently that is for my safety. Master Henry is worried that I might get kidnapped, but it is comfortable and safe here. I went shopping with Vanilla and bought some new clothes. Her pet ork kept us safe. I have plenty to eat and drink. I have a room to myself which is very spacious and free from sunlight. All I have to do in return is learn magic, which is actually rather interesting, and I enjoy the study.'

'Pharaoh Henry thinks you are important, and so do the diabolists he is fighting.'

'Diabolists? Do you know who they all are?' Prudence asked Oakensoul.

'We do not know all of their identities, in fact that is precisely what Master Henry is trying to discover. We know what they are; they are goblins that deal with demons in exchange for power, usually magical power. We know they exist, because Mercy Beanstock of the Municipal Demon Ward, told us that a powerful demon, along with escorting imps, was conjured into the city, despite the demon ward. We also know that Captain Buckle is really a demon who entered from an enchanted mirror; that is a gate to Hell. We know that your former employer, Ephemeral Wormsong is one of them because Henry found demonic books on raiding her house. And we know there must be others; Wormsong would have lacked the magical knowledge to build a door to Hell by herself. The reason I bring this all up is it looks like another member of their coven is about to reveal himself.' Oakensoul rang his bell to gain attention from the college staff.

'Who is going to reveal himself? What is going on Oakensoul?' asked Prudence.

'The reason Pharaoh is so concerned about your safety is because the diabolists want you destroyed. They will try to get at you by any means, and it looks as if they have chosen a legal attack. The trees tell me some policemen are at the college gates and they want to arrest you Prudence. But do not worry, Pharaoh is on his way down, and he has just summoned some soldiers.'

Ten soldiers scurried around the cloisters to take up defensive positions, with lines of fire over the courtyard. Henry walked over to Prudence with a rather large document in his hand.

'Let's see what they have cooked up for you eh?' Oakensoul said to Henry and Prudence.

Three policemen marched out of the shadows of the arches that led to the main gate. They walked hesitantly over to Pharaoh Henry, while Prudence nervously took shelter behind him.

'Grand Master Henry Sir my name is Sergeant Witchson and I have a warrant for the arrest and summary execution of Miss Prudence Pepperhill for vampirism. Please stand aside in the name of the law,' said Witchson trying to sound authoritative as anyone could while shaking with fear.

'Sergeant Witchson I advise you not to attempt to harm Miss Pepperhill in any way until we establish the legality of your position do you understand me?' said Henry calmly.

'I have a warrant Sir,' said Witchson holding up a roll of paper.

'And I have a royal pardon for Miss Pepperhill, I suggest we exchange documents to check their validity before the use of force, agreed?' said Henry holding out his roll of paper.

Sergeant Witchson's large bushy eyebrows furrowed with worry. His instructions from his superior were clear and unambiguous. He was to destroy Miss Pepperhill and under no circumstances was he to show the warrant to Pharaoh Henry. The only thing that could legally prevent him plunging a stake into Miss Pepperhill's heart was a royal pardon, and that was precisely what Henry claimed he had. He belatedly realized that Henry had anticipated his arrest warrant, and now he was legally obliged to show it. He could not turn away, or make an illegal attempt to destroy Prudence as he was up against ten soldiers and the most powerful wizard in the city. He did the only thing he could, the thing he was forced to do was the very thing he wished to avoid the most; he reluctantly handed Henry the warrant in exchange for the royal pardon.

Witchson carefully checked to see if the pardon was in order, and it certainly appeared to be. It was a bona fide royal pardon for Miss Prudence Pepperhill regarding her status as a vampire, and was signed by none other than the Goblin King himself. Henry examined the arrest warrant; it correctly cited the relevant section 15 of the Undead Persons Act 1865 but that was not what Henry was looking for. The question on Henry's mind was: Who had ordered a warrant for Prudence's destruction? Their names were at the bottom of the death warrant:

By Order of
Mistress Venus Sparkle, Member of Parliament
Master Zacharias Potioner, Member of Parliament
Master Darius Hexward, Member of Parliament

Sergeant Witchson had no choice but to leave without finishing his mission, and in the knowledge that embarrassing questions were going to be asked of him when he got back to the station. Purple-faced, he turned on his heels and left the college.

'Thank you, Pharaoh,' said Prudence.

'They will come back for certain Prudence. Whoever wants you will try a different way. I will do my best to keep you safe. I have been expecting this, and it has told me who wants you destroyed.'

Prudence looked confused.

'The signatories on the warrant for your arrest were three junior members of the Green Coat Party, so the goblin behind it must be none other than Cornelius Hand. He is a powerful political wizard, but who else is with him? You are being stalked by a demon Prudence, so how do we turn the tables and hunt the demon?' said Henry.

'Well the demon must be hiding somewhere, so we could use magic to look through its illusion spells to see where it is?' suggested Prudence.

'Goblin magic cannot see through infernal illusions, neither can elfin nor dwarf magic for that matter,' said Henry.

'Why not?' asked Prudence.

'Think of your magic theory, what is the essential nature of a demon?' suggested Oakensoul.

'To steal souls for Hell?' said Prudence.

'No that is a demon's goal, but not its essential nature,' replied Henry.

'Demons are cruel, they are malign, they deceive. That's it! The essential nature of a demon is to deceive. As any magic based on the standard theory cannot alter an entity's essential nature, so then it cannot be used to fathom a demonic deception,' said Prudence as the penny dropped.

'Very good Prudence, you are learning fast. High magic cannot see through infernal deception by the limitation of the law of essential nature, but fairy magic and hedge magic have been known to, albeit rarely and inconsistently. Despite the best efforts of magical researchers, no satisfactory theoretical explanation for this anomaly has yet been put forward. Euphoria Fireheart's ability to see through the disguise of a demon cannot be explained by magic theory, though it must be stressed, magic is unpredictable; therefore, theories to explain it are never exact. So, getting back to our problem, how do we snare a demon?'

'Grand Master Henry, you are the foremost demon hunter in the Metropolis, please tell me as I am in suspense,' said Prudence.

'I also want to know how to snare a demon. Very interesting Pharaoh, how intriguing, please tell all,' said Oakensoul, with a rustle of his leaves.

'You set a trap for it.'

'And have you set a trap for a demon Pharaoh?'

'No, my dear Prudence, you did.'

'I did? When? How?'

'Do you remember planting that horrid and unsavoury memory in Dr. Apricot's mind? Well that was the bait, and because of tonight's attack, we know the demon sprang the trap.'

'Delightful Pharaoh, a wonderful tactic,' said Oakensoul.

'Please explain Pharaoh, as I do not understand,' said Prudence, who felt left out.

'Demons hunt by sensing guilty memories. Just think about it for a little while. The whole reason for a demon's existence is to separate mortal souls away from the one true God with sin. Creating sin forms the core of a demon's world. They can sense sins as we sense music or good food. Each sin has a place in a demon's palate of sensibilities. To a demon, gluttony tastes as does the finest cuisine. They smell the perfume of sweet vanity, savour the visceral excitement of unnatural lusts, and listen intently for the infernal drum beat of wrath. A guilty goblin is easy prey for a demon to root out. Then what to do to catch a demon? Well, the answer is: I get you to plant a nasty but completely false secret into Dr. Apricot's head. A memory so embarrassing he would never willingly divulge it to any goblin. That way the only people who would know about it would be us, Apricot, and any demon that just happens to sniff his guilty mind on passing by.'

'I see, but how does that help us snare the demon? After all Apricot would be unaware that a demon had rumbled him,' said Prudence.

'We will pay another visit to Dr. Apricot, and you are going to look into his mind again, and see who has tried to blackmail the poor doctor on account of his unearned guilt.'

'And the blackmailer will put us on the trail of who the diabolists are,' said Prudence as her face lit up with mental joy as she grasped the trick. 'Oh, Pharaoh you are so very cruel to poor old Dr. Apricot!'

'I think it may be your unique ability to implant and destroy memories that upsets the diabolists. By manipulating memories, you can hide guilt, which confounds the demons. Perhaps that is why they are so eager to destroy you,' said Henry.

'I have given some thought to this memory manipulation Master Henry. I have an idea of how to magically hide a memory. Not destroy it, just make the owner unaware they have a particular memory until it is reawakened by some subsequent event,' said Prudence.

'I look forward to seeing that. You are displaying such promise as a mentalist wizard my sweet Prudence.'

Prudence curtseyed to demonstrate her gratitude at the compliment.

'Please ready the horses,' said Henry to the passing butler.

Soon Henry and Prudence were on their way, riding in a carriage along the underground cobbled streets. On arrival, and even with the late hour, Dr. Apricot's surgery was still open for business and full of rich goblins. The topic of conversation buzzing around the surgery waiting room was the new 'elfin look'.

'Euphoria has started a trend with the new elf thing,' said Prudence.

The overworked receptionist almost missed Prudence and Henry as they crept passed her desk, but she saw them just in time.

'Sir and Madam, where are you going? You cannot visit Dr. Apricot without an appointment,' called the receptionist.

As she started to rise from her chair, Henry raised his left hand in a subtle gesture to ensorcel her. The entranced receptionist sat down, and continued her previous work as if nothing had happened.

'What do you call that spell?' Prudence asked Henry.

'I call it *'The Appearance of Proper Authority'*. It gives people the idea that you have every right to be doing whatever it is you are doing. I will teach it to you someday,' said Henry.

'That spell sounds useful. I will hold you to that Pharaoh Henry,' replied Prudence.

Henry opened the door to Dr. Apricots surgery for Prudence to enter, and they both walked in on him just as he was about to cast a spell on a patient. Dr. Apricot turned to Henry but before he could make any objection Henry stopped him fast with a magical wave of his hands.

'What do you think you are doing?' The patient demanded.

Henry sent the patient to sleep using a spell called *'A Few Minutes Slumber'*.

'Prudence, please look at Dr. Apricot's memories for me. Find who knows about the memory you put in his mind. Who did it, and what did they ask?' Henry said to Prudence.

'He was visited by the singer in the opera, Miss Delilah Twotemples,' said Prudence.

'What did she ask him?'

'She threatened Dr. Apricot saying she would expose him by publishing his guilty memories in one of Solomon Golemaker's papers, so he agreed to answer her questions. She wants to know where Captain Coffin is staying, but Apricot did not know. She wanted to know where I was staying, and he told her. She asked if I could manipulate memories. Apricot said not to his knowledge.'

'That's interesting Prudence, I wonder how Delilah suspected you could?' said Henry.

'Miss Twotemples wanted to know if anyone had asked about the opera, but Apricot said no-one had. Then questions about you Henry, how many demon-hunting wizards did you have at hand, and what were the mundane and magical defences of Oakensoul's college. Apricot told her you had PC Pinch, Euphoria Fireheart, and me. Questions about soldiers, weapons, battlecast golems, fighting ogres, numbers and types of bo staffs, small arms, demon wards, all of which Apricot did not know. That is about it,' said Prudence as she finished reading Dr Apricot's mind.

'Thank you, Prudence,' said Henry as he flicked his hands to release Apricot from the spell.

Dr. Apricot looked extremely embarrassed. 'Did you read my memories? Do you know the revolting thing I did?' said poor Dr. Apricot, almost in tears.

'Yes, but don't worry my good goblin, you never really did it in the first place, it was just a falsehood. It was all just a little ruse to flush out the demon,' explained Henry.

An expression of fury slowly spread itself across Dr. Apricot's face as the realisation of just how far he had been hoodwinked took hold in his mind.

'How dare you? You have violated me!' shouted Dr. Apricot.

'Prudence, I think we should leave the good doctor to his business, but first I ask you to remove all memory of our visit, and the false memory you planted in his mind,' said Henry.

Prudence made a fast but effective modification to Dr. Apricot's memory, after which Dr. Apricot sat in a stupor while Henry and Prudence made a speedy retreat.

The receptionist stared at Henry and Prudence as they quickly passed her, both wizards affected expressions of sincerest innocence which were accepted by all present.

Once clear of the building both Henry and Prudence broke out in laughter.

'You bully!' Prudence called Henry mockingly.

'I would not make an appointment for treatment until Dr, Apricot has had some time to calm down,' said Henry, while climbing into the carriage.

'Let's go for some ginger beers you doctor hating Jezebel! I know a café on Riddle Street; it is Delilah's favourite resort,' replied Henry, as he tried to control his laughter.

'So how are we going to speak to Delilah Twotemples?' asked Prudence.

33

A demon bottle contains its own piece of space time; within which a demon, or some other powerful magical entity, is trapped by a ward. The demon is harvested for magical power. Demon wards are the cheapest methods of providing magical power for spells. The difficulty is that demons are extremely old and cunning, so they can often subvert the demands made on them to escape, and when they do, they are always furious.

Excerpt from **Magical Artefacts** by Grand Master Jeremiah Seelykin, Emperor Phoenix Press.

***

By order of the Goblin King, Jack Coffin's execution was to take place in Arcadia Square, which was packed full of goblins who had turned up to witness the spectacle of him being cast into Hell. Hangings are a favourite spectacle for goblins. Many goblins take their dribblings for an entertaining day out, as goblins consider it a necessary part of any youngster's ethical education to see a naughty goblin swing and kick until dead.

Those goblins condemned to hang get to enjoy their few minutes of fame, indulging in a degree of attention that most of them were deprived of throughout their lives. Many dress up in their finest clothes, and give a speech in their final minutes, usually to the approval of the audience.

But Coffin's sentence was even more spectacular than a hanging, as he was to go straight to Hell. It was a popularly held belief among goblins that Saint Peter could be a bit slack on the job when working the Pearly Gates. This meant that even a goblin sentenced to death had a slim chance of getting into heaven, as Peter often made mistakes when checking if the name of the fresh goblin soul was entered in the book of life.

But even such a slim chance would not be available for Coffin. He was going directly into the fiery pit. This was harsh, so a small group of republican goblins led by Tobias Wandwright, and a larger group of enthusiastic anti-damnation goblins had formed there, to protest.

Vanilla Catchpenny arrived punctually to attend the execution. As she alighted from the triple-decker tram, one of the protesters handed her a leaflet with the headline, **Only God may send a soul to Hell!**

Soon after the police cart containing Captain Jack Coffin arrived. Two policemen dismounted from the front seats then made their way to the rear of the cart to unlock its door.

'Shame on you!' cried a protesting goblinette. 'Don't send Jack Coffin to Hell!' shouted another. But a much larger crowd of goblins on the green (who favoured the sentence) cheered as the police led Captain Jack Coffin out of the cart.

'COME ON JACK AND SAY FAREWELL, OFF YOU GO ON YOUR WAY TO HELL', sang the jubilant crowd.

Coffin despite being handcuffed and in leg irons, still managed to give the crowd a deep bow.

The crowd yelled their approval, 'You show 'em, Captain Coffin. You ain't scared of Hell,' called one, 'Old Jack ain't scared of anything!' shouted another.

Vanilla presented her papers to Sergeant Appleduff, who was one of the escorting officers; they stated she had permission from the Goblin King to walk with Jack. While Appleduff was reading the papers, Coffin pulled the policeman's helmet off of his head and threw it over his shoulder. Once again, the crowd yelled their approval, 'He's a boy, he don't care,' and 'What a naughty lad!' Appleduff and the other police officers hit Coffin with their truncheons, but their blows bounced off his powerful muscles.

'I think that policeman is trying to massage me with his little wooden stick,' announced Jack, which sent the crowd into peals of laughter.

Coffin pushed the policeman to the ground, and then showed his immense strength by tearing apart his iron manacles as if they were made of paper. As three other policemen started to intervene Coffin let out a terrible orkish war cry, and they fell back in terror. Now the crowd did not know what to think, was this uncontrollable warrior ork going to turn on them next?

'I think those police officers just plopped themselves,' said Coffin, as he held his nose.

The crowd broke into laughter once again, relieved that Coffin was on their side. Vanilla gave Coffin the hardest slap she could. Of course, Coffin played on it, with the pretence that her blows could actually cause him pain. Vanilla grabbed Coffin's coat and led Coffin onto the execution platform.

The amused crowd took to chanting, 'JACK COFFIN! JACK COFFIN! JACK COFFIN!'

'Well I hope you enjoyed your theatrics,' said Vanilla.

'Sorry about that Vanilly, I just couldn't help myself.'

At the centre of the platform, stood Pharaoh Henry, a dwarf sorceress, and an orkish witch, and to each side of them, the two mirrors. The onlookers, be they goblins, orks, dwarves, and the great and the good of the city, had a good view of the proceedings.

Coffin noticed that each mirror was 4 feet wide and 9 feet tall, he seemed to remember his cousin, Molly Coffin, explaining to him that ratio corresponded to Hermetic geometry. The mirrors had plain redwood frames, and reflected images with unnatural perfection, without even a speck of dust or distortion. Each of the mirrors was mounted on casters so they could both be moved.

Vanilla gave Coffin the bag containing the uncast stones.

'So how are you going to send me to Hell?' asked Coffin. He placed one of the stones into his jacket pocket.

'Just walk into the mirror,' said Henry.

Henry rolled one of the mirrors until it stood directly opposite the other. Each mirror reflected into the other, creating an image of a mirror in the other mirror, and so on. In one mirror it was an infinite number of reflections, but not in the other. In one of the mirrors, in the centre of the nested images, was a small black rectangle.

'That black shape in the distance is a door to Hell itself. You will pass through it,' explained Henry.

Henry turned to the orkish witch and said, 'Please satisfy yourself that the door in the reflection leads to Hell.'

The witch stood in front of the mirror then she stretched out her arms, and danced and chanted for a few seconds. She nodded to Henry, and turned to Ambassador Kasper Scratch in the audience and nodded to him. Scratch smiled and nodded back. The orkish witch walked over to Jack coffin, and whispered close into his ear, 'I will always love you Jack.' She gave Jack her final kiss.

'Please satisfy yourself that the door in the reflection leads to Hell,' said Henry to the dwarf sorceress.

The dwarf made some magic gestures. She produced a small bag of runestones, then randomly cast a few of them in front of the mirror. She read the runes carefully. She turned to Meister Aldergund Roggerbrood to nod her confirmation.

Coffin put his arm into the mirror, and then his leg, and when he did so the surface of the mirror seemed to shimmer like the surface of a liquid. He stepped entirely into the mirror, and then onward to the distant door. The door was unnatural and foreboding; it was perfectly smooth and completely unreflective. He turned its brass handle, and it opened up into a well-furnished room, it was a study, with a desk and a rather tasteful armchair.

While the room seemed comfortable enough, the air itself was unpleasant, perhaps not as stale as it was inside the escape pod, but even less wholesome somehow. Jack Coffin strode across the room to the windows and looked out over a view of Hell itself. It was a seemingly unending city. It was grey and smoky, and full of slums, with the occasional beautiful mansion, like little islands of opulence in a vast sea of squalor.

He left the study and made his way down the corridor as quietly as he could, which was surprisingly hushed for a six-foot two inch tall, powerfully built ork. Coffin heard the squeals of excited lovemaking almost immediately, but it became louder as he approached the bedroom it was coming from. He carefully looked around a door into the room where he saw a high elf making love to a succubus. The elf was far too engrossed in exquisite pleasure to be aware of Coffin's presence, but the succubus noticed Coffin in an instant. She was a beautiful demon, with dark red hair and green eyes. She clearly recognised Coffin. He quickly made his way down the rest of the corridor, then down the stairs to a large door that looked like the exit.

He stepped out of the mansion and onto the streets of Hell. From the road, he could see that the house was on top of a hill, and so had given him a panoramic view over a large city that extended further than the eye could see. Even at a distance, he could see it was teaming with souls, who were as physical here as they were in the mundane realm. And he could hear them too; screams of excitement, cries of pain and fear, and the distinctive tone of cruel laughter that attends the delight in the suffering of others.

34

"Demons hunt by sensing guilty memories. They can taste gluttony, smell envy and vanity, see avarice, feel lust, and hear wrath. And a guilty goblin is easy prey to a demon. So, what to do? Well the answer is simple my good gentlegoblin wizards; remove guilty memories and so blind the demonic parasites. With the application of modern magic, we can do it."

Extract from **Mind Control, Demon Control** a paper presented by Grand Master Pharaoh Henry to the Symposium of Mentalist Wizards, held at the Royal Hermetic Society.

***

Prudence furrowed her brow as she paced the dining room of Oakensoul's college, 'Euphoria will be so cross.'

'I had to ask her, for the safety of the whole city,' said Pharaoh Henry.

Prudence considered Henry's dilemma, 'Well I am not convinced of any of this. She is going to think you tricked her, which is true, and you know how hot-tempered she can be.'

'What am I supposed to do? I had to ask Euphoria to invite Delilah for dinner. Delilah trusts Euphoria, and would not trust me. Besides I am convinced the opera is the key to an impending demonic attack.'

'Why the opera?'

'Well I am not sure I understand it all. I cannot put all the pieces of the puzzle together, but everything goes back to the opera: The poem found at the vampire nest by Assyria Neepfield, it was called *'The Hubris of Draska'*, which is the same name as the opera. Mr. Neepfield is the opera's librettist. It was Delilah herself, who plays Queen Anatitia, who also tried to blackmail Dr. Apricot. She must be obeying orders that ultimately come from a demon. It is Solomon Golemaker, who finances the opera, and he also finances the Magical Philosophers Party, of which three of the party's members of Parliament, are the signatories on your destruction warrant.'

'You make a persuasive argument, I must say.'

'If I was to speculate, given that Assyria Neepfield is such a fine poet, I would guess that the song he wrote is magical,' said Henry.

'Magical? To do what?'

'Well let's speculate; remember your magic theory Prudence, what is the Law of Similarity?'

'I can't remember.' She felt Henry expected her to learn magic theory far too fast.

'An ornithopter works by the Law of Similarity, so how does an ornithopter work?' said Henry.

Prudence spoke slowly and carefully as she went through the logical steps from first principles, 'By flapping its wings, it imitates bird flight, and in doing so enhances the magical spell that enables it to fly. So, I suppose the Law of Similarity is that something that is similar to the desired effect of a spell, can then be used as a focus to magnify that spell.'

'Exactly so, Prudence. It is by that very same principle a star dragon's wings allow it to fly in the vacuum of space.'

'The opera spell I assume is to open a gate to Hell into the Metropolis, in the same way they infested old Draska, so an opera about the fall of Draska would harness the Law of Similarity. But why use an opera to cast a spell? Isn't it rather too public for a spell designed to invoke demons into a city?' said Prudence.

'Perhaps because of another magical law, the Law of Emotion.'

'I see your reasoning now, the spell will feed off of the emotion of a large audience, and in effect become a ritual spell. A clever set up when you think about it.'

'Never-the-less the set-up still should not work in theory, yet it clearly does so in practice so we are missing some pieces of the puzzle. It still should not be powerful enough to break through the field of the Municipal Demon Ward, or the dimension wall between Hell and our mundane plane. The spell will need more power than seems to be available in order to create a permanent gateway to Hell. Where will they get enough manna to do that? That is also one of the many unanswered questions,' said Henry.

'And the other question?'

'Why have they gone to all the trouble and expense of putting a genuine Draskan demon ward on set when they could have used a mock-up?'

There was a knock on the door; Jevington entered and announced Euphoria and Delilah had arrived.

'Let them in, let them in,' said Henry.

Delilah and Euphoria entered the dining room, and all four of them sat down to eat. Euphoria and Delilah chatted away as to the wonderful day they had spent going shopping, and how they had enjoyed watching the Annual Boat Races on the Bone River. Prudence did not say much, and Henry said nothing at all until he said to Delilah, 'So you visited Doctor Apricot?'

'May I ask what this is about?' said Delilah, her demeanour instantly changed to one of defensiveness.

'You visited Dr. Apricot and attempted to blackmail him,' said Henry.

Delilah was taken aback, but her fighting spirit soon came back to her, 'Have you any idea what that disgusting pervert gets up to?' She glared at Henry in defiance.

'Don't be rude to my guest,' Euphoria said to Henry.

With a wave of his hand, Henry put a spell on Euphoria that stopped her from speaking or moving. Without her friend, Delilah now realised she was alone in a room with a powerful and ruthless wizard, and a vampire; and they did not seem friendly anymore.

'I know what you think Doctor Apricot is guilty of but you are wrong. My question is who told you about him?' asked Henry.

'Solomon Golemaker did,' said Delilah after a pause, her voice now quivering with fear.

'I thought as much, but I need to be sure you are telling me the truth, so I need Prudence to look inside your memory,' said Henry.

'And if I object?' said Delilah.

'I will just cast it anyway, so it would be much easier if you acquiesced.'

'Well, I still object,' said Delilah.

Henry gestured a spell on Delilah to hold her still. Then he said, 'Look into her mind for me please Prudence, and tell me what you see.'

Prudence looked deeply into Delilah's eyes, 'She agreed to help Golemaker take over the city in return to become a famous singer. Now she realises she has inadvertently made a pact with demons, and she is frightened and regretful,' said Prudence, 'She knows the Metropolis is to come under demonic attack, she would help defend the city against it, but she does not know how to pull out of her situation.'

'You must rewrite her memory Prudence. Place your new memory of with the modified last verse of Anatitia's song as we discussed, then destroy her memory of ever being here. When she goes home make sure she does not know what you have placed in her mind; demons will read her memories and emotions. So be careful to make sure she remembers nothing of tonight.'

Prudence erased the memory of the dinner from Delilah's memory, and replaced it with an evening of pleasant conversation. Then Henry called Jevington, and asked him to escort a happy but forgetful Delilah out of Oakensoul's, put her in a cab, and sent her back to Golemaker Hall.

Euphoria was still paralysed at the dinner table when Henry and Prudence got back to her. He removed the spell, and she slowly returned to normal.

'How dare you!' she shouted at Henry. She left the room in a rage, returning to confront Henry again.

'You manipulated me. You tricked me into bringing poor Delilah here, and then you violated her poor mind,' she said; then she started to sob.

'I had to do it Euphoria. The safety of the city depends on it.'

'Well I am going home, and I am not going to train as a wizard anymore.' Euphoria stamped her foot.

'Euphoria, it will turn out for the best. I know I have upset you, but I will make it up to you I promise.'

'How? How will you make it up to me after doing that? And how will you make it up to Delilah? You are underhand and hurtful.'

'I owe you a favour, and you may call on me to keep my promise.'

'I want a fairy promise.'

Henry and Prudence were shocked into silence. A fairy promise was a magical thing, and dangerous to make. While the standard theory of magic could not explain them, the whole of fairy magic rested on promises, and breaking one would have dreadful repercussions.

'Now Euphoria…' stammered Henry.

'Don't you *Now Euphoria* me! I want a fairy promise or I will not help you find demons,' said Euphoria.

Henry made a fairy promise, and as he did it became physical by turning it into a small golden heart, the size of a chestnut. He gave the promise to Euphoria as a tangible token.

Euphoria snatched the promise then stormed out of the room.

35

The matter to be decided on is what we understand to constitute marriage under goblin law. We know that marriage is the union of two goblins, one male and one female, and consummated by their carnal knowledge of each other. Mr. Balshazzar Inchpin has been accused under the Section 4 of the Ungodly Lusts Act 1875, on the grounds he had biblically known his former wife, Elegance Inchpin, who had died and since been resurrected as a zombie. Mr. Inchpin's defense was that he was still married to his wife. But the court holds that marriage ends at death, and physical intimacy between a goblin and any member of the undead cannot be defended under marriage. The jury held Mr. Inchpin is guilty of necrophilia under the Ungodly Lusts Act, so I sentence him to three years imprisonment at Oubliette.

Ruling of High Court Judge, The Right Honourable Enoch Licktoad, in **Rex vs. Inchpin 1880**.

***

Jack Coffin looked back at the mansion from where he had entered Hell. It was a palatial affair, so he assumed it must be the home of some important person of infernal society, a powerful demon perhaps. He made his way to the centre of a street which was filled with souls of all species: Goblins, dwarves, satyrs, even the occasional elf, but all of them loud and uncouth.

The crowded streets chattered with the constant babble of discord; a cacophony that rang through with indignation and blame, unleavened by even the smallest encouragement or forbearance. As he passed a tavern, a prostitute grabbed Coffin's arm and clung to him. She looked beaten up and was dressed in cheap clothes, she tried to make up for this and was experienced enough to know how to make herself look as desirable as she could from what little charms she still possessed.

'Want some business love?' She said as she gently caressed Coffin's face with one hand and lifted her skirt up with the other.

As an orkish pirate Jack Coffin was by nature an instinctive fighter, so he sensed danger was just behind his back. With the agility of a dancing satyr, Coffin spun around and toppled the pimp who was about to stab him, throwing the attacker onto his own dagger, who then cried out in pain from the knife in his shoulder. At the sight of her owner and business manager's injury, the prostitute screamed with fear.

'Would you like to escape Hell?' Coffin asked the prostitute.

'Clear off and leave us alone,' she shrieked.

Coffin re-joined the crowded street that led down to the slums of Hell below. He put his hand into his pocket and gently felt Sally's necklace in his hand. It occurred to him there was a real danger he might never find her or a copy of the Nominae Verae Demonorum.

It was not long before he passed one of Hell's many inns, which as always, was filled with argumentative drunkards. Whatever pleasure it was that they took from drinking there, it was not in each other's company.

'Lend us a penny for a pint Alf; you know I'll pay you back,' begged a goblin, desperate for more beer.

'Get out of it. You never pay me back, how could you, you never work you lazy dog,' replied Alf.

The beggar looked around; all the other drinkers were laughing at the impoverished goblin; they raised their glasses to show they had the drinks he wanted but went without. They enjoyed their beer almost as much as they enjoyed his discomfort and the very last thing they were going to do was buy him what he craved for.

The beggar was fraught for the want of alcohol. He noticed Jack Coffin was looking at him, so he scampered over.

'Please lend me a penny for a beer Sir? Penny for a beer? I was robbed, and all my wages stolen, I haven't eaten or drunk all day. Please Sir, please,' whined the beggar in a pitiful tone.

'If you take this pebble and you can get out of Hell,' said Coffin as he offered the beggar one of the uncast stone.

'What would I want to get out of Hell for? They don't have beer in Heaven, do they? It is a drink I want, not advice from a do-gooder!' he hissed.

'Oi lads, a do-gooder, want to rescue us from Hell? Let's get him,' shouted a troll with a bottle of gin.

'Punch up!' cried an Ogre, as he thumped the troll between his eyes. The whole pub exploded into a tangle of fighting bodies, each belligerent trying to expunge his frustration by harming a stranger. Of course, none of them had any good reason to fight, but they all seemed to be enjoying themselves, or at least they did until they themselves got hit. Even the alcoholic goblin managed to steal the beer from its felled former owner. Coffin did not want to stay around for this, so he made his way past the drunken melee, and continued onwards towards the city centre.

'Buy your tickets for the arena. Come see the gorefest tonight, watch the criminals get their just deserts,' cried a barker on a pedestal. Behind him was a line of terrified victims chained together. A crowd of buyers had sprung up, all interested in seeing a spectacle of pain, and trying to barter with the salesman.

Coffin recognised one of the downtrodden victims; it was young Oskar Mortimer, the orkish lieutenant he had killed in the escape pod. 'Mortimer, it's me Coffin. I can get you out of here, do you want to go?'

'Coffin! I can't say I am surprised to see you here. What are you going to do to me now?' said Mortimer.

'Nothing bad. I can get you out of Hell,' replied Coffin with a tone of hopeful enthusiasm that seemed so out of place in Hell.

'Oi, you! Don't talk to the criminals, you can buy a ticket to see them tortured tonight, but discourse is not allowed,' growled the barker.

Coffin ignored the order, and continued with his explanation to Mortimer, 'I have some stones, they have divine power, and can make your sins disappear, at least while you hold them. They will send you back to the natural world.'

The barker, angry at being disregarded, caught hold of Coffins coat, and two Ogre bodyguards appeared as if from nowhere to back him up, 'I said no talking to the prisoners or you will join 'em,' shouted the barker.

Coffin struck the barker hard in the stomach, folding him over.

Without hesitation, the ogres closed on Coffin; with effortless skill, he sidestepped them both so they struck each other, and were knocked unconscious. The crowd recoiled at the sight of an ork that could defeat not just one, but two Ogres in unarmed combat, just in case he turned on one of them. But one soul stood her ground, a tall elegant lady dressed in a silk scarlet dress

Coffin took the key that hung from the barker's belt and freed the criminals, one or two escaped immediately; others looked at Coffin with astonishment for a few minutes before leaving themselves.

'Why do they stare at me Mortimer?' asked Coffin, referring to the crowd.

'Because you showed compassion Coffin. That should not exist here, and from what I remember of you, it was not characteristic of you back in the mortal realm either,' replied Mortimer.

'Do you know where I could find Lady Sting, or a copy of a book called the True Names of Demons,' Coffin asked Mortimer.

'No I don't,' said Mortimer, shaking his head.

'I do,' said the lady in scarlet, 'But we had better get off of the street. The guards of Hell will be here soon and you will not want to be here when they arrive.'

Coffin ignored the woman, and turned again to Mortimer, 'If you take one of these stones, the demons cannot sense you or harm you, and if you recite the Lord's Prayer while holding it, your soul will return to the Goblin Metropolis.'

Mortimer took a stone and placed it in his jacket pocket, but all the other criminals of Hell shuffled away.

'Do you want a stone?' said Coffin offering one to the woman in scarlet.

'No thank you, that might burn me.'

'So you are a demon then,' said Coffin, 'why don't you attack me?'

'Let's get off of the street and into the relative safety of my home where I shall explain everything.'

Coffin nodded.

'Let me introduce myself, my name is Pandamonia, a succubus and former Countess of Hell. Please follow me.'

'I have been told about you,' replied Coffin.

She led Captain Coffin and Mortimer down a cobbled alleyway off of the main road to the centre of the city of the first level of Hell. At the end of the alley was her modest house. Pandomonia looked around to check she was not being watched and then ushered them inside before shutting the door. The parlour was a reasonably comfortable affair, with a small dining table, two large ox-blood coloured armchairs and a settee, all in traditional infernal style. Coffin found it all surprisingly tasteful considering they were in a place reputed for eternal torment.

'So tell me, why would a demon want to help me?' asked Coffin.

'Because I want you to give me safe passage out of Hell, and sanctuary in your city.'

'Caragula?' replied Coffin.

'No, the Goblin Metropolis, so much more cultivated, progressive and comfortable. More suited to a former countess of Hell.'

'Former countess?'

'But now in reduced circumstances, since I fell from grace with the Devil, or should that be disgrace? I will take you to the lady you seek, and to the book you want. Afterwards, I will aid you in your escape to the best of my abilities, and in return, I ask you take me with you, and give me sanctuary with the goblins.'

'My name is Captain Jack Coffin, formally of the Orkish Navy. I am on a mission from the great goblin. I have authority from the Goblin King to offer amnesty to any soul who wishes to escape Hell and is willing to behave him or herself afterwards in an ethical manner. However, I am not sure whether 'any soul' refers to a demon. Besides could you really behave yourself with your infernal nature?' asked Coffin cautiously.

'I know who you are, I have seen you through Euphoria's eyes, and for you, I can behave myself,' said Pandamonia in her full seductive beauty. 'Do we have a deal?'

'Don't do it Coffin. You are dealing with a demon, it is wrong and you know better than that,' warned Mortimer.

Jack Coffin knew better alright. He knew that in any society that had a body of laws based on even the most elementary of ethical standards, dealing with demons was strictly forbidden. In Elfish law it was the worst crime imaginable. Of all the known sentient species, elves, goblins, dwarves, satyrs, even orks did not consort with devils, at least not legally. He knew that he should not enter into this deal, especially as an agent for the King of the most powerful city in the known universe. He also knew that he would never find his beloved Sally Sting without the help of someone who knew Hell. That meant dealing with a demon, even a demon in reduced circumstances.

36

And said unto them, what will ye give me, and I will deliver him unto you? And they covenanted with him for thirty pieces of silver.

Mathew 26:15 **The Holy Bible**

***

Zebedee Fireheart was a busy little goblin. Between working his newsstand and writing seditious journals, he had little time left. But he did make time for something that was very important to him; the Revolutionary Goblin Party.

Attending party meetings was an arrestable offence and the punishment severe. Activities of the RPG were regarded so treasonous by the city's Metropolitan Police that a special unit called the Counter Agitation Squad had been established, and their job was to be on the lookout for revolutionary activists. So, all said and done, secrecy and safety were of the highest importance to Zebedee and his fellow revolutionaries.

Tonight's party meeting was held in a hidden hall at the very bottom level of the city, and lookouts were posted along all the routes leading to it. The hall they used was accessible by many narrow brick tunnels. The plan was to use them as escape routes in the event of a police raid.

Zebedee walked into the meeting and sat down.

'Hello Jerusalem, Hello Zachary,' said Zebedee trying to strike up a conversation with two comrades. They returned half-hearted grumbles for greetings. Zebedee felt rejected.

Tobias Wandsmith, the well-known goblin firebrand, stood to deliver his speech:

'Brothers and Sisters of the Revolutionary Goblin Party. We live in a city noted for its enterprise, whose manufacturers are talented and whose workgoblins are renowned for their hard labour. The soil in the countryside around our great city is fertile, and the climate pleasant.

Since our arrival at the planet all those years ago, we have all strived to create a prosperous city. The Metropolis creates more magical devices than any other city in the history of the known galaxy. But is that wealth shared Brothers and Sisters?'

'No!' The audience shouted in reply.

'The working goblin is poor, while the wizards and factory owners are rich! In the old days, we were the servants of the high elves of Draska. We did all the dirty and hard work that the elves felt was beneath them, and we are suffering the same oppression all over again, but now for our new masters the goblin wizards! We must fight for a parliament whose members are voted in by a *one goblin one vote* election. We must take ownership of the factories from the owners who idle their time in cafes, and give it to the goblins who work it, so they can enjoy the fruits of their labour.'

'Well said Tobias,' shouted Zebedee.

'Thank you, my Lord Zebedee, the approval of your Grace is of so much importance to me,' Wandsmith replied with enough vitriolic sarcasm to ignite the humour of the gathered goblins.

'No need to be like that Tobias, we are both revolutionary goblins,' said Zebedee, who felt his face become hot and red with embarrassment.

Tobias Wandsmith bowed low and said, 'Of course my Lord.' Now the crowd roared with laughter.

Dejected and humiliated, Zebedee made his way out of the hall, to the jeers of his former comrades. As he made his way back to the surface of the city, he heard a young goblin girl call to him. It was young Felicity Scoops and her brother trying to catch him up.

'Mr. Fireheart Sir, I do hope you don't take the insults of that ignoramus Tobias Wandsmith too much to heart. He's been stirring up feelings against you ever since you became a Lord,' said Felicity.

'It's all right little Felicity. Tell you what, Euphoria and Mercurial have just got new jobs at the Telepathy Office, and I am under the orders of the King who calls me up at a whim, so I need people to help me with my newspapers. As you have just turned 16 now and are old enough to work, why don't you come and work at the newsstand with Lampwick? You and little Gideon could have Euphoria and Mercurial's old rooms. Gideon could go to school,' said Zebedee.

Felicity was actually only 15 years old, but needed a regular income and a place to stay to look after her brother. 'Oh, that would be lovely Lord Fireheart.'

'Please call me Brother Zebedee.'

37

'It is a crime to covenant with a demon. The statutory authority being section 12 of the Demon Act 1845.'

Excerpt from **Goblin Common Law**.

***

'Pandamonia…' said Coffin.

'Call me Pandy.'

'I have a few questions to ask you Pandy,' said Jack Coffin.

'I thought you might. But first I must dismiss my servants, we don't want them listening into our dangerous conversation. The first lesson you need to know about Hell is that everyone will turn you over to the authorities if it advances them, at least if they can get away with it,' replied Pandy.

Pandy rang a small silver bell.

'Why ask a demon questions Coffin, do you think you will get an honest answer?' said Mortimer.

Jack Coffin shot a glance that told Mortimer to 'Shut up'.

One of the goblin serving girls walked in and placed a pot of tea and three cups on the dining table.

'Fanny I want you and Bunny down here at once,' commanded Pandy imperiously.

'Yes madam,' said Fanny, who then disappeared through the door for a few minutes and then returned with her colleague.

'You can both have the afternoon off. Needless to say, neither of you lazy and useless halfwits deserve it. I don't know why I employ either of you, as there are far superior goblinettes out there, who would jump at the chance of employment in my house. Here are two sixpences, one for each of you. I expect you to be back here between ten o'clock this evening at the earliest, and twenty past ten at the latest. If I hear either of you have been telling tales about this household, or who I have for visitors I will find out about it, then you will be discharged but only after I have paid for you both to be professionally flogged as tattletales, and nobody wants to employ a tattletale, do you hear?' said Pandy as she threw stern glances at them.

'Yes Mum,' said both serving girls in unison. They gave their mistress deep curtseys. They took the money and turned to leave.

'Get out of my sight the both of you, and quickly!

Fanny and Bunny rushed to the door, grabbing their coats off the hooks, both of them overjoyed at the unexpected luck of a paid afternoon off, but also half expecting their mistress to change her mind, and that this unexpected offer of a holiday would turn out to be a cruel joke.

When the servants were safely out of earshot, Pandy then turned to the ork and said, 'So Captain Coffin. You have questions?'

'Please explain to me one thing, why do none of the souls here want to escape Hell?'

'Several reasons; some like it here, others have made a deal with the Devil and their soul will simply come back here after they die anyway. So, if they escape, when they die, they will be back here and in for trouble.' answered Pandy dismissively.

'Some like it here? How can anyone want to be in Hell?' asked Coffin in astonishment.

'Because these souls enjoyed evil when they were mortals; they took pleasure in cheating others, and in causing or watching other souls in pain or humiliation. They spent their lives getting stupidly drunk or stealing, and making fools of themselves and others if they could. They loved fistfights, particularly when it involved hitting people they knew could not, or would not, hit back. They basked in hot arguments, and in falsehood and harm. All the very things they took delight in when they were mortals, are now readily available for them in Hell. That is why most of them don't want to leave. They would hate to be in heaven where every soul's heart opened up not only to the view of every other resident but even to God. Could you imagine what it would be like for such souls? Having the whole of heaven looking into their shrivelled black hearts, just think of it. That would be worse torture for them than even being a victim in this place, and the nastiest souls in Hell are not victims, they are the bullies and they enjoy being bullies, and would not trade it for all the peace and love in heaven,' explained Pandy.

'Well I had expected Hell to be a place of torture and pain,' said Coffin.

'In a sense it is. Admittedly not torture by demons with pitchforks, and instruments and the rest. That version of Hell is just imaginative speculation from people who had never been here, although a few made it here later on in their careers. In truth, the souls torture each other, all day and every day. The cheats, the liars and the bullies torment the cheated, the lied to and the bullied, who in turn go on to do the same to other souls. It is true that some souls are tortured by demons as described by the pictures in old churches, but it is done in an arena, and for the amusement of the citizens of Hell who pay good money to see it. But all these things are incidental, and none of them captures the true essence of what Hell is,' said Pandy.

'So what is the essential nature of Hell?'

'Hell is the place where there is no God, or not the benevolent creator God at least, but of course we have Lucifer, who is our God.'

'What about you? Do you enjoy harming other souls? Why do you want to go to the Metropolis?' asked Coffin.

'I used to enjoy evil, but it has lost its appeal. I am bored with it. Can you imagine how long I have seen so many petty souls inflicting pain and harm on each other? For thousands upon thousands of years, and it is not clever to cheat, it is dull. It is not brave to bully; it is soul grindingly tiresome. The same small-minded acts of maliciousness performed by souls who think they have come up with something new. Well let me tell you, there is nothing new about evil, it is the same old tedious nonsense repeated over and over again, ever since Satan's rebellion, and it is just so boring,' said Pandy as she gasped out a small puff of ennui.

'You were rather ill-tempered to your serving girls,' said Mortimer.

'I gave them the evening off. If I had done so with kind words, they would have taken it as weakness, and in Hell, that is an invitation to subjugation,' said Pandy.

'So why are you so dismissive of souls who do evil, haven't you enjoyed your evil deeds?' asked Coffin.

'I did once, there was a time I loved it, that's how I got here, and the cruelty gets worse in the deeper Hells, much worse than this. But what you must understand is that the whole point of Hell is to pervert goodness into evil; that is the goal behind the dishonesty and cruelty. The souls here can die and go to a deeper nastier dimension of Hell; they just have to become more wicked,' said Pandy.

'How far down the levels of Hell did you go?'

'Down to the very bottom of the pit,' said Pandy as she stared into Coffins eyes with open invitation.

'How did you find it?'

'Delicious, and exciting,' said Pandy.

'So why stop?'

'I could not help myself. My curiosity just got the better of me. It happened quite out of the blue. One day when I was watching the mortal realm with a view to creating a little mischief, I inadvertently saw a goblinette give a hungry goblin a bowl of soup at no profit to her. I just could not understand why she seemed to be happy about it.'

'You could not understand that?' asked Coffin.

'I still can't. No demon can, charity is a mystery to us, as is any kind act for that matter. But just being curious about goodness was enough to get me thrown out of the heart of Hell.'

'Just like that? And now you are here?' said Coffin sceptically.

'Captain Jack Coffin, please never stop being stupid, somehow it makes your mind almost as attractive as your body. Obviously, it was not *just like that*. I crept up the planes of Hell, layer by layer, life incarnation after incarnation, all the time vexed by this inconvenient curiosity about goodness until I got here, just one layer below the mortal plane. So here I sit, watching the new souls arrive from the material realm above. All of them eager to display their malice, as they rub shoulders with worn-out old demons like me. I am a has-been. I have lost my authority, wealth and stature. All I am left with is this small house, two maids who would shop me to the infernal police if they could, and a self-destructive curiosity as to why some people take pleasure in kindness. I am cursed with a wonder about compassion that will not go away and it is sinking me further into infernal poverty. And this awful mind-connection with Miss Euphoria Fireheart does not help; she has hope and a desire for self-betterment that amounts to torture here in Hell where such ambitions are impossible. So, I must understand what it means to take pleasure in the happiness and welfare of others and that Captain Coffin, is the reason why I must leave Hell.'

'What do you hope to gain by understanding pity and compassion?' said Coffin.

'Maybe it would help if you learned a thing about compassion Coffin,' interjected Mortimer.

Pandy ignored Mortimer's interruption. 'One of two possible outcomes Mr. Coffin. One is that I can get this obsession out of my mind, so I can get back to the delights of evil for the rest of eternity, and be an aristocrat of Hell once more.'

'And the other way is?'

'That I can change into a creature that is able to enjoy compassion, and so escape Hell forever. I could be reborn a mortal and try again in a fresh life, to be a good soul, and have hopes and aspirations.' Pandy stopped short in her flight of fancy, and changed the subject, 'Enough about me, what about you, what are you doing here in Hell, apart from disrupting the place with compassion that is?'

'I have been sent here to find and retrieve a book called **Nomina Vera Daemoniorum**. Do you know where I could find a copy?'

'Yes, I stole one for Grand Master Henry, it was a dangerous and difficult thing to do,' replied Pandy.

'Good, so all I have left to do is rescue an orkish princess, a lady called Sally Sting, and a star dragon queen by the name of Lady Moondancer,' said Coffin.

'Again, I am in the position to help you. Sally Sting has made quite a name for herself since she arrived. I can take you to where she now lives, as for Queen Moondancer, she will be eaten by a demon called the False Mother tonight on the arena to the amusement of all present,' said Pandy.

'Sally Sting has risen in the society of Hell?'

'Oh yes, your precious Sting is quite the up and coming lady. But down to business. The deal is: You get me out of Hell, and give me sanctuary in the Metropolis, by order of the Goblin King, and I take you to rescue Lady Sting and Moondancer.' asked Pandy.

'Possibly, it all depends if you can hold one of these stones,' said Coffin as he reached into his bag and pulled one out, 'This stone is a holy relic. It is one of the stones that were going to be cast at the adulteress. It is mentioned in the Bible, *He that is without sin among you, let him first cast a stone at her.* Then the angry accusers dropped the stones, and as they did these rocks assumed the very essence of forgiveness. If you take this stone, and if you hold it and say the Lord's Prayer, it will transport you to the mundane world in an instant. But you are a demon, and the way out involves holding a stone that should burn the flesh of a demon, so the question becomes, can you hold a stone?' asked Coffin.

'You have read the Bible Captain Coffin?' said Mortimer in astonishment.

'Let's try,' said Pandy. She held out her palm warily. Coffin placed a stone on her hand, and she held it without pain or injury.

'I am surprised,' said Coffin.

'There are two kinds of demons, those that were made, and unclean spirits. Made demons were once angels, and unclean spirits are those that worked for it. I was once mortal and earned my station by sinful thoughts and deeds, so maybe I can change,' said Pandy.

'So, you feel no pain?'

'No pain at all, rather something I should not feel, something no soul here in Hell should ever feel, a strange sensation that I have not enjoyed for thousands of years,'

'Really, and what is that?' asked Coffin.

'Hope,' said Pandy, as she displayed a long-forgotten childish vulnerability now rekindled. It was as if her soul that had been tanned and hardened by an infinity of cruel acts had, in an instant, softened just a little, just enough to feel something good. Her sensibilities, so long numbed by her chosen society of the wicked, had opened up to the possibility of forgiveness and friendship, and the terrifying risk of rejection of those very things. It was a fragile and strangely intimate moment that caused both Pandy and Coffin to remain silent for a few moments.

Pandamonia thought for a second, and then corrected herself regarding the presence of hope in Hell, 'Very occasionally, Jesus comes down from Heaven and rescues a soul but they are usually souls who have only just got here. I prayed to Jesus to rescue me once, but no luck,' she looked despondent.

Mercifully Coffin eventually changed the subject, 'Do you know the Lord's prayer?'

'I know the Lord's Prayer. I know the entire Bible off by heart and have recited it many times, admittedly out of context for the purpose of trapping souls for Hell of course, but I know the whole Bible cover to cover, as many demons do, except maybe all those begets near the beginning, too boring to remember them,' said Pandy.

'I am surprised anyone in Hell knows the Lord's prayer,' said Mortimer.

'It's an eye opener as to how many clergymen we have in Hell, and they are priests who have earned their place here I can tell you. But will I be allowed to stay in the Metropolis?' said Pandy.

'You will need a grant of asylum from the great goblin, as without one they will simply cast your soul into a demon bottle for the rest of eternity. I have been given permission to rescue the souls from Hell, there was no stipulation as to how wicked they are; if there were, then no one could be rescued. If I were to guess at your conditions, it would be that you will be paroled to a wizard called Pharaoh Henry. He will check you behave properly for a time, then after that, you will be a free citizen of the Metropolis.'

'Pharaoh Henry indeed, I must say I am impressed,' said Pandy.

'With Grand Master Henry?'

'Of course. The whole of Hell, top to bottom knows of Pharaoh Henry. Old Satan himself never stops moaning about that goblin!'

'Really? Well Henry the demon hunter would be happy to hear that I'll wager. But let's get back to the point, do we have a deal. Because if we do, all you need do now is help me rescue the ladies Sting and Moondancer, and then take a copy of the book of demon's names back to the Metropolis with you.'

Jack Coffin glanced at Mortimer who scowled back in disapproval.

'If and when I get to the Metropolis, I will make my own life there, and I want you to keep well away from me Captain Jack Coffin. Well away! Understood?' said Mortimer.

'We have a deal Mortimer.' Said Coffin as he held out a stone.

Lieutenant Mortimer took the stone, and held it in his hand, he recited the Lord's Prayer; when he had finished saying 'Amen' he disappeared to the popping sound of the air filling the vacuum his body had left behind him.

Jack took out one of the Goblin King's passports and filled it out for Pandy. He looked up to hand Pandy the passport, and one of the stones.'

Jack Coffin thought to himself: *Have I just damned my soul by striking a deal with a demon?*

38

'The pipes that make the clouds dance'

Literal translation of the Kobold word for The Municipal Weather Machine.

Befuddlement: *Confusion, intoxication, stupefaction. Most commonly used to describe a confused mental state that magicians can enter when a spell backfires.*
Etymology: *First used after Master Baptisms De L'eau's spell to walk on water malfunctioned. De L'eau was disoriented for a week afterwards, during which time he thought he was a duck, and could only partially communicate in quacks. One quack for yes, two for no.*

From **The Goblin Dictionary** New Edition 1896, City University Press

***

Grand Master Jeroboam Nettlebed was the foremost weather wizard in the Metropolis, and he had a very distinctive sigil: A miniature weather system floated just above his head, and it told of his mood.

Parliament had bestowed on him a commission to solve the pressing need of pollution. The Metropolis stood in a river valley, and on days of little or no wind, manna fog would accumulate to high levels. It presented such a danger to goblin health, that Jeroboam was tasked to build a Municipal Weather Machine to blow it away.

There was no doubt that he was the right wizard for the job. Weather had preoccupied Jeroboam Nettlebed all his life. As a mundane goblin, he built a barometer to measure air pressure, he used a jar and ruler to jot down rainfall measurements, and recorded daily hours of sunshine in his weather diary. One day he got it into his head to conduct a series of dangerous experiments that involved flying a hot air balloon into a manna storm. The inevitable happened, with a bright flash, he was struck by a powerful bolt of magical energy. Miraculously, he did not die, rather he received the gift of magic, and his crown of weather.

No wizard, who knew anything about the subject, was under any illusion as to how difficult the task was. The Municipal Weather Machine required powerful and complex magical spells to work, often requiring research into unexplored and dangerous areas of weather magic. On more than one occasion his spell misfired, damaging machinery, and befuddling Jeroboam. At each episode of befuddlement, a thick opaque mist would form above his head, then float down his face, obscuring his vision and muddling him yet further.

For Jeroboam the Municipal Weather Machine was his labour of love. He had spent a year designing it, and two years building it. And after a huge expense in manna and effort, he started operating it under test conditions a week ago.

Parliament assigned Grand Master Jeremiah Seelykin to evaluate the machine's performance. He was to audit the acceptance tests to determine that the machine was safe, and worked to specification. On the basis of those criteria, he was to sign off (or otherwise) the approval report. Seelykin took his job seriously. He recognised the crucial need for clean air, and so undertook his experiments with the utmost rigour. He was always professional and committed to his work, to the point of sternness. At no time did he indicate his thoughts to Jeroboam as to the machine's efficacy. Jeroboam was curious as to Seelykin's opinion, but would have to wait to see his report.

Jeroboam was in his office when the report arrived on his desk. He opened its large envelope, while above his head puffs of wind blew grey clouds around in unsettled foreboding.

First, he read the final sentence, '*The Weather Machine is fit for Purpose. Immediate operation recommended.*' The clouds disappeared, and the wind settled. Then he read the report from the start. It was highly complementary, stating, '*...the Municipal Weather Machine performs impeccably.*' and '*...it is a masterpiece of modern magical engineering*'. The report put Jeroboam in a radiant mood, and a small warm sun shone down on him, against a bright blue sky, complemented by wisps of cirrus clouds. The Municipal Weather Machine was the greatest accomplishment of his life.

There was a knock on the door, 'It's open,' said Jeroboam.

Master Ebenezer Bluevein entered the office. 'Ah please sit down,' said Jeroboam. His sky turned darker.

This was to be the last day of Bluevein's apprenticeship to Jeroboam, and he had come for his Masters Certificate, 'I need my papers Sir,' he said.

Jeroboam had them ready and handed them to him, 'Well done Bluevein. I hope you find a suitable position.'

Bluevein worked and studied hard. He was good at magic; but that was not enough, he wanted to be outstanding. Deep down in his soul, he knew that no matter how hard he practised he was just not gifted enough to become an exemplary wizard. Still he was now a master wizard, and was soon to become a grand master; a fact he made sure everyone knew about.

He bullied those wizards junior to him; not physically, but emotionally. He was good at noticing any insecurity they might have, and then he played on that, all the while trumpeting his own ability beyond its true merit. Jeroboam saw this and he did not like it, so he took him aside and explained that his behaviour was unfair, hurtful and potentially damaging to a junior wizard's magical development. Bluevein promised to stop it, which he did to an extent; but he could not stop himself undermining his juniors when he could do so with a level of subtlety that would be difficult to detect and criticise.

But Jeroboam could still see it and he was disappointed with Ebenezer Bluevein's demeanour, which placed him in a dilemma: He did not want to stymie the newly graduated wizard's ambitions for a career, but on the other hand he had to protect his junior apprentices from Bluevein's spite. He decided to give him a good reference to reflect his hard work, but not give him a job on the weather machine following his apprentice's graduation. He felt conflicted about this compromise, both for Bluevein, who clearly imagined himself as a great weather wizard, and for Bluevein's future work colleagues who needed to be warned of his malice, but now would not be. The glances between them betrayed both Jeroboam's distrust and Bluevein's resentment.

'I am disappointed you did not see fit to offer me a job on the weather machine,' said Bluevein. Without waiting for an answer, he left the office in bitter silence.

A few minutes later there was a further knock on the door, Captain Nineveh Fogarty of the Royal Footguards entered without waiting to be invited, 'Grand Master, I have orders from the King.' Jeroboam had been told in advance from Pharaoh Henry that the Army was coming. Henry had been tasked by the Goblin King, with the hasty preparation of the city's defences against imminent infernal invasion. He recognised the strategic importance of the Weather Machine, so he had warned Jeroboam that an impending attack was likely, and dispatched Fogarty to help defend it with a company of infantry. 'Good to see you Captain, if there is anything I can do please let me know,' he said.

'Thank you, Grand Master, I must set to work,' said the officer.

Fogarty set about his assignment with energy and due diligence, he posted guards around the weather machine, and pickets along access roads to warn of an attack. He set the remainder of his men to build barricades to give cover from small arms fire.

No sooner than the last sandbag had been laid, a picket ran from around the corner and cried out the alarm.

'How many of the enemy?' asked Captain Fogarty.

'At least four companies of militia with ten battlecasts. Approaching quickly down The Old Pagoda Road,' replied the guardsman.

Fogarty barked orders for the reserve platoon to join the front rank on the barricade. Opposing them, the militia lined up behind the battlecasts, and together they advanced on the guards.

Fogarty ordered his men to open fire. Some shots bounced off the armour of the battlecasts, clattering and sparking on starsteel, most missed completely, a few hit the militia tearing into their bodies and knocking them down.

The militia levelled their muskets and returned a huge volley of fire. The guards ducked safely behind cover, as a hail of lead balls thudded harmlessly into the sandbags of the barricade.

Jeroboam joined the soldiers. Unfortunately, his mood was about to change for the stormier. He was protected from shot by a magical amulet and he had to help defend the guards from being overrun. He raised his arms and cast a spell to throw driving rain into the militia. The wind blew them off balance, while the rain wet their black powder making it impossible for them to fire their weapons.

But the battlecasts kept advancing, the musket balls from the guards bounced off their armour to no effect. Jeroboam cast the spell called **Winter's Wind** which froze the rain on the road into a sheet of ice. Unable to keep their balance, the battlecasts slipped to the ground. He then cast the spell, *Javelin of the Storm's Rage*, shooting a lightning bolt from his hand. It hit the closest battlecast, its armour could not protect it from the electricity that heated its shell to glow a cherry red. The demon inside yowled in agony. As magical bolts of electricity flew from his fingers, tiny flashes of lightning crackled down from the black cloud above his head into his scalp.

He lifted his arms to cast another lightning javelin when an unexpected bolt hit him from behind. Bluevein had attacked him and betrayed his master. The bolt stung a little, but he had plenty of magical defence, so it did him no real harm. He turned to Bluevein, intending to retaliate, but before he could, Bluevein flew into the door of a nearby house.

Angered at his treachery, he chased Bluevein through the door. Once inside he could see Bluevein escape through yet another door beyond. He ran to it, but when he opened the second door it led to the room that he was already in. He realised that he had been tricked into entering a pocket dimension. He was trapped there with no means to escape.

Without the mage to help defend it, the weather machine would fall to the militia and battlecasts. He realised all was lost and he felt deep sadness. A small angry black storm cloud formed over Jeroboam, and tiny hailstones of regret fell onto his head.

39

Orks are a species of large muscular fighting goblins, created by elves for their army, before battlecasts were invented for the same role. Though not as strong as an ogre, an ork could fight with the agility of a fairy ballerina. But the advent of black powder weapons evened things up; a goblin armed with a musket could simply shoot an ork down at long range. Because of the threat of firearms, most orks covet magical talismans to ward off musket balls.

From The History of Elfin Warfare by Felicity Basilisk.

***

Pandamonia gripped onto Jack Coffin's arm as she led him through the streets of Hell. Coffin looked a dangerous proposition in the eyes of the small, petty damned souls, who scrambled to get out of his path. But she frightened them even more. She was exceptionally desirable, so to prevent unwanted advances, she used the tactic of sprouting small bat-like wings from her bare shoulder blades, and the tiny horns of a succubus. This display of infernal power served to dissuade any unwanted advances of familiarity from the plebeians of Hell. It was a fair assumption that someone as irresistible as Pandy had to be a high-class demoness, and in Hell it is always a good policy to avoid a more powerful soul.

'Do you know the invasion of the Metropolis has already begun?' said Pandy.

'Really?' said Coffin.

'Demons have inhabited some battlecast golems ready for the fight. I do hope Pharaoh Henry manages to repel them.'

'Grand Master Henry is the wizard to do it if any goblin can, that's his job. Our job is to find Lady Moondancer,' said Coffin.

'The Circus of Pain is about half a mile from here, where the souls are tortured for the amusement of the masses. A very popular sport in Hell.'

Jack Coffin was a fighting ork who could instinctively tell when he was being stalked, 'There is an elf following us at a distance. Who is he?'

'Well that would be Aether Coroman,' said Pandy.

'Why is he following us?'

'He is not following us Jack; he is following me. He has grown tiresomely attached to me. He says he wants to marry me, and unfortunately Lucifer promised me to him as part of his deal, along with great wealth and a mansion. The very same mansion you entered Hell through actually,' said Pandy.

'Why don't you marry him? He lives in a mansion; he must have done something clever to get that rich in Hell.'

'He exposed the defences of Draska to the infernal legions, not so clever really, just treacherous.'

Coffin sensed Coroman as he followed them using the crowd for cover, then for a few moments they caught each other's eyes, and so the game was up: Coffin knew Coroman was following him, and Coroman knew Coffin knew it.

To Coffin, Coroman looked like a cowardly weasel of an elf, and to Coroman, Coffin looked like a brutish, savage ork, so it was fair to say they both got the measure of each other. Now that Coroman knew he had been seen, he had no choice but to summon up his courage and present himself to Pandy and Jack.

'Pandamonia my dearest, it is so wonderful to see you. Please introduce me to your escort,' said Coroman.

'This is Jack and he is an occasional employee of mine. I hire his services as a bodyguard, and today he is keeping me safe while I go to the Circus of Pain,' lied Pandy.

'Well I can escort Miss Pandamonia from here, my good ork. Here have some payment and be off with you, and be quick about it if you know what is good for you,' said Coroman. He thrust a ten-dollar note at Coffin.

Coffin ignored the money and said nothing.

Coroman was unhappy with this insolent mute ork, and wanted to deal with his rudeness, but Pandy distracted him, 'Aether, what did I say to you about your controlling nature! If we are to get married you must allow me my simple pleasures. Your jealousy is most disconcerting.'

'But Lord Lucifer gave you to me Pandy, and I love you,' said Coroman.

'If you love me you must allow me to go to the Circus with my bodyguard. I will return to you later my darling,' said Pandy. She started off again, leaving Coroman behind alone.

When they arrived at the circus, outside the doors there were long lines of souls queueing to see the spectacle of torment.

But Pandy was not interested in queuing; rather she marched past the waiting souls and straight up to the doorman, 'Allow me to pass, I am a Countess of Hell,' she said.

'No one is allowed in without a ticket,' said the doorman sternly.

A demon with scarlet coloured skin and flamboyant clothes, walked through the door with his entourage of imps, and no ticket. The deferential doorman jumped out of his way. Pandy tried to follow the aristocrat, but the doorman grabbed her and pulled her back.

'Get out of it, you are not the VIP you once were, so it's the back of the queue for you,' sneered the doorman.

She was beside herself with indignation at being talked down to by a mere doorman, but Coffin put a consoling hand on her shoulder, 'Let's not make a fuss,' he said. She followed Coffin all the way to the back of the queue.

'Your showing a level of restraint to provocation that is uncharacteristic of an orc,' she said.

'I have a job to do,' said Jack.

'Ah the ork speaks! And what work is that,' said Aether, who had reappeared as if from nowhere.

Jack did not answer.

'Oh, back to the silence eh?' said Coroman.

'Aether, take us inside please,' said Pandy.

With her acquiescence, Coroman felt he was back on top, and he showed it. He strode up to the doorman with Pandy and Coffin right behind him. 'I am Aether Coroman, and I have the favour of Lord Lucifer himself,' said Aether. The doorman knew who he was and jumped out of his way, giving a long deep and respectful bow.

'I am the elf who hid the essence of betrayal in the demon wards of Draska,' said Coroman smugly.

Jack Coffin was not stupid. He might not be a magician, but like every other ork, goblin, or dwarf, he knew certain terms referred to magic, even if he did not understand what they meant. He got the feeling the phrase *hid the essence of betrayal*, was significant, so he made a mental note of it.

'What torture would you like to watch my dearest,' asked Coroman, holding out his arm for Pandy to hold.

'I want to see the False Mother my darling,' said Pandy.

'You remain here,' said Coroman to Coffin.

'No, he must be with us at all times,' said Pandy.

Coroman looked at Pandy with irritation, so Pandy gave him a long seductive smile in return. Reluctantly he consented.

The three of them made their way to the part of the Circus where the false mother performed.

Coroman caught the eye of an usher, he said, 'I will require a private balcony.'

Getting a balcony was an unexpected piece of luck as far as Coffin was concerned, it could not be better for throwing stones and was only six feet off the Circus floor, an easy jump down for Coffin.

'Who gets to be tortured by the false mother?' asked Coffin.

'It speaks!' said Coroman.

'The souls captured by the collectors,' answered Pandy.

'Collectors?'

'Collectors catch the souls of those who try to wriggle out of their deals with the Kings of Hell.'

A ringmaster stood on a podium in front of Asentana. 'Welcome to the false mother show,' said the ringmaster, 'As a mortal Asentana sacrificed her children to Lord Asmodeus for worldly power, and now she gives birth to souls and then consumes them in a never-ending cycle. These are souls who are too proud to know their place in our society, my good citizens. They deserve their torment as you deserve the entertainment of watching their punishment. Enjoy the spectacle proud citizens of Hell.'

The false mother was a mass of stinking flesh the size of a small house. At the bottom of her body there were five slits. A new born squirted out from one of the slits in a vile parody of childbirth. The mother had no head; rather at the top of her body was a huge mouth.

A baby emerged covered in a viscous slime. Immediately several of many arms grabbed the child. Her goblin progressed up her torso, passed from arm to arm, as she bit pieces from the infant with her sharp little teeth, from her many mouths. On each bite the baby grew in age. A goblin was finally dragged to the top of the mother, and then, while crying for mercy that would never come, he was pulled into her mouth. Finally, aged and in pain, it was swallowed by the mother, to be reborn into a new short life of agony.

Immediately after eating her child, Asentana gave birth to it again. Her fresh offspring was dragged up her loathsome body in the same manner, and all the way small pieces were bitten out of her body.

Then more babies were born, one after another, each enduring the life-cycle of torment.

'Please let me go! I beg you to stop this! Help me!' screamed an agonized goblinette, to the laughter of the crowd.

Yet another baby was born out of another slit, and then another; this time it was a female dragon in elfin form. She looked like a high elf, but with scales instead of skin, and taller, at least 7 feet in height.

'That must be Moondancer,' said Pandy.

'Who is Moondancer, do you know the victims?' asked Coroman.

Ignoring Coroman, Coffin took a stone from his satchel, and then he threw it at the mother. It was a good shot; the stone hit the mother just above the arm that held Moondancer. As it struck, it burned, searing her flesh into black charcoal. The wretched demon screamed in pain from all of her many mouths.

Jack threw another stone, and then another. A stone fell straight into Asentana's huge topmost mouth. Asentana's agony was deafening. She shuffled off away from where the stones were coming. She vomited, spewing out all the victims she gave tortuous birth to.

The mother retreated away from Coffin and his dreadful stones. The confused audience chattered.

Jack Coffin jumped from the balcony and ran over to Moondancer. She was dazed. Jack helped her to her feet. She looked at him in confusion and gratitude.

'Lady Moondancer, I have been sent by Lord Starcatcher to rescue you, hold this stone and say the Lord's Prayer, it will transport you out of Hell.'

Coffin reached into his coat. He handed Moondancer a stone and a passport.

'I am most grateful to you brave ork,' said Moondancer.

Moondancer held the stone. She did not recite the Lord's Prayer, but rather, as is the custom with dragons, she sang it. She sang a sublime melody, while Coffin memorized every note. Moondancer said the last Amen, on which she disappeared with a popping sound.

There were now six other wretched children of Asentana laying in their mother's vomit. On seeing Moondancer's escape, they clambered towards Jack Coffin.

'Please give me a stone Sir,' said one.

As quick as he could, Coffin gave them each a stone and passport.

As soon they had said their prayers they too escaped from Hell.

Coffin climbed back to Pandy, and together they rushed out of the Circus, leaving Coroman standing in his balcony.

The False Mother crouched in the corner of the circus, whimpering in pain. She had spewed out some of the stones Coffin had thrown at her; other stones had burned through her body. Coroman saw one of them laying in her filth. He jumped down to the Circus sand, then covering his mouth with a handkerchief to mitigate the acidic stench, he picked it up. He placed it in his pocket, and followed after his beloved Pandamonia.

***

'Euphoria, I can do telepathy,' said Mercurial.

'Really? How did you learn that?'

'When I made love to Sebastian last night, he tried to enter my mind. Apparently high elves do that; they send their consciousnesses back and forth between bodies. Before I knew it, I could go into his mind, and experience his perspective. Since then I have been able to send him messages telepathically, and I am getting better at it,' whispered Mercurial.

'What does Sebastian think about it?' said Euphoria.

'He worries that a Miss Urania Rego will find out and be cross with him. She is his telepathic link on New Draska.'

40

The many universe theory states that our universe is one of many created by the one true God; where the laws of physics are enforced less strictly than most. In truth, nature in our universe is violated far more frequently than creatures of more mundane universes could deal with. Some inhabitants have taken advantage of this lax interpretation of the laws of nature, and learned to change the world around them by their thoughts and will alone; a practice commonly referred to as 'magic'.

Extract from **Magic Theory and Practice** 4th Edition

***

Pandamonia led Jack Coffin to an up and coming suburb of Hell.

'The whole of Hell will be looking for us now, and they will torture us if they find us,' said Pandy.

'Is this where she lives?' asked Coffin.

'Yes,' said Pandy, as she viewed the mansion with an appraising eye, 'Given this orkette of yours only got here a week ago I must say I am impressed at her social advancement so far.'

'Well she is good at that. She started on Caragula as a slave girl from a rival ork tribe, and she was a princess before she died. But still, her house is smaller and less sophisticated than Coroman's.'

'That is not a fair comparison. Coroman made a deal with Lucifer to betray the whole city of Draska for his mansion; with a few other things thrown in of course,'

'What other things?'

'Aristocratic status, fabulous wealth, any female he wants,' said Pandy.

'You will not be his in the Metropolis. You will be a free goblin. I want to thank you for your help Pandy. God-willing I will see you soon in the Metropolis,'

'I have not been free for over a thousand years,' said Pandy.

At the thought of parting Pandy's face assumed a look that suggested a trace of sadness and affection. It lacked the intensity and persuasiveness of her repertoire of expressions that she employed as part of her role as a succubus. Instead it had an understated quality most out of place in Hell; that of sincerity. Pandy placed herself against Coffin. In return he held her in his arms and felt the gentle trembling of her body.

'Please come back to me soon,' whispered Pandy. She abruptly broke off her embrace, held a stone in her hand, and by the time she had finished saying the Lord's Prayer, she had left Hell without permission for the first time in a thousand years.

Jack Coffin was going to miss having Pandy around, what he was not so sure of was whether that was a good or bad thing. He knew a succubus was a lure used by the forces of Hell to seduce souls into evil. Clearly she had been instrumental in enlisting Coroman as a traitor, and he was an intelligent and sophisticated high elf. Jack held no illusions that as a simple ork, he would be easy prey to a skilled temptress such as Pandamonia. Yet for all that, he was still going to miss her company.

He heard another implosion of evacuated air. He did not spot where it had come from, but he knew from the distinctive sound that someone else had left Hell. In fact, it was Aether Coroman, who had forsaken the infernal rewards of his treachery to follow his beloved Pandamonia.

Coffin banged with the large iron knocker on the front door of the mansion. The butler opened the door; strangely he seemed to recognize Coffin.

'Captain Coffin, you are expected. Please follow me,' said the butler, and led him to the music room.

On seeing him, Sally leapt from her chair and threw herself into his arms, 'Jack, it is so good to see you again,'

'How did you know I was coming?' asked Coffin.

'Because the whole of Hell is talking about you. You have been as discreet as an ogre prima donna in an elfin ballet company and broken even more toes. Besides, one of your succubus's servants ratted on you both. But never mind all that, come sit down with me, we must talk.'

'I am here to rescue you Sally,' said Coffin.

'Well that's what I want to talk to you about Jack.'

'Listen to me Sally; I have some stones that will help us escape from Hell,'

'Well I heard about the stones. Satan, Lucifer, and the other five kings know about the stones, and by all accounts, they are far from happy that you have brought them to their realm.'

'Who cares what Satan thinks, we can escape from Hell itself Sally.'

'But Jack, I want to stay here, and I want you to stay with me.'

'Stay here in Hell! Why would anyone want to stay in Hell?' said Coffin with incredulity.

'Because it is fun here,' she said.

'You think Hell is fun?'

'Yes of course I do, everyone here does, except maybe the victims, and that befuddled strumpet of a succubus you have been keeping company with, but they are weaklings, and they don't matter to us Jack. When we live together here in Hell, we will have adventures, bigger and more reckless than anything we did on Caragula. But I would keep away from that Pandamonia if I were you. Her standing is going downhill in demonic society fast and she might just drag you down with her,'

'Everyone in Hell wants to be here you say?' asked Jack.

'Almost everyone, yes,' said Sally.

'Really!?' asked Coffin.

'It is like this, we all get escorted around Heaven first, but some souls choose Hell. In Heaven your whole being, mind and soul, is opened up for the inspection of the good souls and angels. There are no secrets in Heaven; and no excitement either. Not unless you think singing hymns and being friendly is a thrill, and from what I remember of you Jack, murder and pillage was more your idea of recreation,'

'Yes I enjoyed piracy once.'

'You were the terror of the dwarven trade lanes Jack. You stole, you fought, you terrorised. You would not like Heaven Jack. There is no sport in that place for the likes of you and I. No delight of the fight, no pirate's adventure, no joy of the kill. I want you here my Captain Jack Coffin, with me, for me.'

'There is another life, Sally. I want you to escape with me to the Metropolis,'

'The Metropolis? The Goblin Metropolis? Why would I want to go to the Metropolis?'

'They have refreshing ice cold ginger beer for a start,'

Sally Sting's face dropped in disappointed astonishment, 'Are you telling me that Jack Coffin, scourge of the dwarven mercantile starfleet, would rather be drinking ginger beer? What other wonderful things have you found to do with the goblins?'

'I joked with a lovely goblinette called Vanilla Catchpenny, I heard the sweet melody of an opera, and I'd bet you don't have fairybean soup down here either.'

Sally looked at Jack in dismay, 'So, Jack, I cannot persuade you to stay in Hell?'

'Of course not, I have come here to rescue you from Hell,'

'Then I think we need to go our separate ways Jack. But before you go, I would appreciate a kiss for old times,'

They embraced for the last time and Sally kissed him. But it was a poisonous kiss, from a new magic she had learned from the Devil's book. It was a craft of harm and betrayal. Jack's body quickly stiffened and paralyzed, then he collapsed to the ground. On his neck, where she had kissed him, his skin was blackened in the shape of her lips. She opened a drawer, took out a length of rope and tied him up with it.

'You are not the Captain Jack Coffin I knew and loved. You have grown weak Jack,' said Sally.

Sally went to the drawing room door and called down the hall for the butler.

'Strangeway, go and fetch Lord Azezal. Tell him I have captured the once great Jack Coffin,' Sally said with contempt.

But Strangeway the butler did not leave the mansion, rather he transformed into the demon Azezal. A powerfully built devil, he stood on two hoofed legs, and sported a demon's tail and horns on his head. His skin was scarlet red, and his eyes shone amber yellow.

'Thank you Sally, once again you have shown your great worth to our cause,' said Azezal.

'What are you going to do with Jack Coffin my Lord?'

'What would you have me do with him?' said Azezal.

'You can boil him in fairybean soup for the rest of eternity for all I care. Jack Coffin is less than a dribbling to me now,' said Sally.

'Well that would be amusing, but there is no fairybean soup in Hell. Besides Hell must be rid of Jack Coffin, he and his stones are a disruptive influence,' said Azezal.

'What do you mean?' said Sally.

'Souls have already escaped Hell with his stones. Souls that rightfully belong here. And there are still stones left in the arena. We demons cannot collect them, and we cannot trust the souls of the once mortal creatures as they might use the stones to escape,'

'Escape from Hell! Who would want to?' asked Sally.

'Those wretches who were being tortured by the false mother for a start. Also, Aether Coroman, who gave up his riches and his status in Hell to follow that fool Pandamonia, and the ork Lieutenant Oskar Mortimer. They have all gone back to the mundane world. How long will that poison keep Jack Coffin paralyzed?' asked Azezal.

'About another 15 minutes,' she said.

Jack Coffin's world was destroyed. The one woman that he had loved now despised him in return. He had loved her so much he had dishonoured himself in battle, and betrayed his clan. His heart was deeply wounded, but not broken. Although Jack Coffin the Orkish pirate had died, something new had just begun to grow in him. It gave him a tiny appreciation for respect for others, and just a little care for their well-being. It was a small and delicate thing, but it was alive, and he could feel how much it disconcerted Azezal. It was just a drop of compassion, but it was completely out of place in the desert of Hell, and the demons hated it.

Azezal picked up the bound Jack Coffin. He carried him outside and dumped him into a cart. He called for his body guard. He dragooned a passing ogrewife into pushing the cart. Then the whole party made their way back to the arena. On arrival they found the false mother cowering in the far corner of the pain pit, terrified of the stones. He cut Jack loose, 'Find the stones and get out of here,' said the demon.

Jack started to search among the filth of the torture pit, until he eventually found four stones.

'Four stones will do,' said Azezal.

'But I cast five,' said Jack.

'Coroman stole a stone and escaped to the Metropolis. Never mind, he will be back here soon enough, and when he is, his contract with the Devil will be rendered null and void for having left Hell without permission. So now it is your turn Captain Coffin, get out of Hell, you do not belong here, at least not yet, so go. But remember, your soul is dammed too, so when you die, you will come back, and you will be here forever,' said Azezal.

Bunny had been Pandy's maid, it was she who had betrayed Jack to Azezal in return for better living conditions, and then she had followed Azezal and Coffin to the arena. She had kept out of sight the entire time, which as a small goblinette, she found easy to do. Now she realised she could get out of Hell altogether if she just had a stone. She saw Jack was about to leave, and seized her chance. She summoned up her courage, and in spite of the danger of defying a demon, she ran over to him.

'Please give me a stone,' pleaded Bunny.

Two of Azezal's body guard rushed on Bunny, daggers drawn, but Jack intercepted them, and with a deft throw, used their own weight to throw them both to the ground.

'She must stay here, or we do not have a deal!' demanded Azezal.

'We have no deal, but if you want, I could throw you a stone to show you what it does to a demon's flesh,' said Coffin.

Azezal fell back in fear, as did the rest of his bodyguard.

'Just hold a stone, and say the Lord's Prayer,' said Coffin.

Bunny did as she was told; Jack Coffin and Bunny Gravewish popped out of Hell and into the Metropolis with a rush of air. Jack drew in a long deep lungful of sweet oxygen, enjoying his first wholesome breath for days. They found themselves in the garden of the vicarage of All Souls in the Wardrobe.

In the distance, Jack could hear the crackle of massed musketry in all directions, *there are battles going on*, thought Jack.

Noah Bentley came into the garden with a dozen orks.

'The Coffin Crew are here; they have awaited your return and orders,' said Bentley.

'Did they bring trollhammers?' asked Coffin.

'Lots of them,' replied Harry Throatbite.

41

It is a well-established principle that many magical artefacts, over time, often grow egos of their own to go alongside their own magical effect. The ego of an infernal artefact is always malevolent.

From **Magic Theory and Practice** 4th Edition

***

To conceal his hypocrisy, the firebrand revolutionary, Tobias Wandsmith took his instructions from the exploitative plutocrat Solomon Golemaker in utmost secret. It gave Tobias a sense of importance to be the goblin chosen to carry them out. As ordered, he had called a meeting of all supporters of the Revolutionary Goblin Worker's Party, to be held outside the front gates of Golemaker's demon bottle factory.

His mission was to arm the goblins that had turned up to form a militia, and then wait for ten battlecast golems to arrive at half-past seven. With this force he was to storm Oakensoul's College and take it for the Green Coat Party.

It was now twenty minutes to seven. A cart-full of rifled muskets had arrived that needed unloading, and a large crowd of assembled goblins eager to take ownership of them. But the battlecasts were still nowhere to be seen.

Wandsmith was under strict orders to wait for the battlecasts, but he twitched with impatience. *I can get a glorious victory without their help,* he thought to himself.

'Break open the ammunition boxes and pass the arms to the militia,' Wandsworth bawled to his lieutenants.

Tobias stood on the cart, surrounded by four of his bodyguards, to address the crowd.

'The call for revolution has come my Brothers, and we have been asked to storm Oakensoul's college, that the stronghold of Wizardly oppression. Take up your rifles my Brothers and Sisters, and let us take Oakensoul's!'

As the militia applauded Wandsmith, just behind them Pandamonia popped into the mundane world.

Unfortunately for her two militiamen saw her, 'Halt,' shouted one of them.

Pandamonia turned and ran down a side road, but in her haste, she dropped her copy of *Nomina Vera Daemoniorum*.

As a demon accustomed to sneaking in from Hell, Pandamonia knew what to do; once she was around the corner, she magically disguised herself into the body she had been born into those thousands of years ago, that of a primordial elf.

One of the militiamen picked up the book and looked around the corner for her. He looked at the new elf suspiciously, but he heard his new orders from his leader:

'Follow me goblin Brothers!' said Wandsmith. He led his newly formed company of revolutionary militia down Phoenix Street.

'But Brother Wandsmith, our orders were to wait for the battlecasts,' said Sergeant Jerusalem Pickles.

'No need sister, look how many we are! We attack immediately,' shouted Wandsmith cheerfully.

As they spoke, right in front of the company, and quite out of the blue, Aether Coroman entered the Metropolis with a loud pop of displaced air. The company halted in confusion at such an unexpected sight.

'Grab him, he is a traitor to the cause!' shouted Wandsmith.

Two bodyguards leapt on the hapless Coroman and tied him fast.

'Take him with us,' ordered Wandsmith.

The company picked up their step now as they marched down Troll's Bonnet Street and were soon at the front gates of Oakensoul's college, where they waited, eager for the order to attack.

'Form line and fix bayonets!' barked Wandsmith.

The militia formed a shabby line as best they could. Each fixed a bayonet to his rifle.

The gates of Oakensoul's opened and then Grand Master Pharaoh Henry walked out with a college guard on each side of him.

'To the gates my goblin comrades!' screamed Wandsmith from the rear of the group.

The line of militia raced towards the main entrance of Oakensoul's. They looked formidable as they charged forwards. As they reached just a few yards from Master Henry, the old wizard cast a spell, there was a crackle of small arms fire from inside the college. Two goblins in the front rank fell dead; Jerusalem dropped to the cobbles, blood squirted in pulsating jets from her throat. The militia's exuberance switched to fearful panic in a moment; the attackers fled back down Troll's Bonnet Street as fast as they could.

Tobias Wandsmith had remained safely at the rear to offer leadership without the distraction of being shot at, now he ran after the routing militia.

Pharaoh Henry, accompanied by Pinch, strolled over to the wounded Jerusalem, her throat was gashed and bloody; she looked up at Henry with a shocked stare. Henry kneeled in front of her and put a comforting hand on her shoulder. He muttered magic to pull the round from out of her flesh. He stopped the bleeding with another, then he took a handkerchief from his pocket, and used it to clean her wound; finally, he sprinkled some Merryfield's healing potion onto the gash.

Pharaoh Henry looked kindly at Jerusalem and placed the healing liquid in her coat pocket, then said, 'Just sprinkle some more, should your wound get worse.' She said nothing, but remained stock still, expecting to die.

'Shall I arrest her,' asked Pinch.

'No, I would invite her in for a cup of tea, but I don't think she is in the mood for fraternising with the enemy. Never mind though, she should be right as rain soon.'

As the potion took hold, Jerusalem climbed to her feet, and she staggered away.

The staff of Oakensoul's collected the rifles dropped by the revolutionary militia, Henry walked over to the ammunition cart, where he found the bound Aether Coroman. He broke the knots to release him.

'Those goblins that attacked you turned out to be rather cowardly,' said Coroman.

'Just before the guards fired a volley, I cast a spell on them, **Panic of the Terrified Herd.** Luckily the magic worked because had it not, they would have taken the college. There were just too many of them to hold off,' said Henry.

Henry led Coroman to Oakensoul's common room. He rang a bell to summon Jevington.

'My name is Pharaoh Henry; I am a grand master wizard, dean of this college of Oakensoul's, and in overall charge of demonic safety in the Metropolis. May I ask your name Sir?'

'My name is Homer Tacit,' lied Aether Coroman.

'I must insist you tell me what you were doing on the battlefield,

Mr. Tacit?' asked Henry.

'I am here from New Draska to investigate opening up an import-export business,' said Coroman.

Pharaoh Henry suspected the elf before him was lying, 'I shall order up some food for you Sir, but unfortunately, I must read your mind first. I realize this is an intrusion, but I do hope you see the necessity of it. After all, I just found you on a battlefield so you may well be an infiltrator,' said Henry.

'Certainly not! I object to my mind being read in the strongest terms. I am a high elf of Draska, and you have no right to do such a thing.'

Henry gestured with his hand clenched in a fist to cast a spell to hold Coroman still. Coroman tried to resist, but to the elf's surprise, the goblin was the more magically powerful of the pair. Henry looked into his eyes and started to scan through his memories. He saw Coroman landing in a pan ship at the docks an hour ago. Behind that were memories of business meetings on New Draska, all about opening up an import export business in the Metropolis. *This is a strong memory, perhaps too strong*, Henry thought to himself. He noticed the memory was without detail, he could not see images of the docks, just a narrative. *There is something not right about this elf and his history, I must get Prudence's opinion.*

'Guards, please escort Mr. Tacit to the brig and lock him in with something to eat and drink,' ordered Henry. The elf complained and argued at the top of his voice as he was led away.

'Jevington, please ask Mercurial to telepath Sebastian Valancy at the Telepathy Office. Tell him I have a high elf in my custody by the name of Homer Tacit,' said Henry.

42

Trollhammers are magical warhammers designed to shatter stone trolls, but are also effective against armour. They were invented by dwarves who needed them to destroy trolls while mining caverns infested by those creatures. They can break through the starsteel armour of a battlecast golem

From **The History of Dwarven Warfare** by Felicity Basilisk. Emperor Phoenix Press

***

Henry studied the battle map of the city. He had been taking reports from treetrolls, the using them to build up a picture of how the fighting was going; unfortunately, the war was going badly. The royalist forces were being overrun by the green coat militia supported by battlecasts. *We have no answer to starsteel armour,* thought Henry.

Vanilla scryed for demons, and found plenty, mainly inside battlecasts. Prudence looked on but she could not help much, so she just did what she could, she made tea and sandwiches, and passed on messages from Henry to the soldiers on guard.

Mercurial emerged from her telepathic trance, 'I have important intelligence from the Telepathy Office. Sebastian has contacted New Draska as to our Mr. Homer Tacit. The real Tacit is alive and well on New Draska, so the elf in the brig must be an imposter. Sebastian has been talking to Euphoria; who, from sharing her mind with a demon Pandamonia, added that it was Coroman who had betrayed Draska using cursed silver coins.'

'What do the elves make of Pandamonia's story?' asked Henry.

'It is causing quite a stir on New Draska. They knew Coroman had died, and that his soul had not been sent to a new body by a soul migration machine, but to find him an aristocrat in Hell was very big news to them,' said Mercurial.

'I can imagine. But let's not get ahead of ourselves. Pandamonia is an evil demon, and not to be trusted. Let's go and visit our elfin guest,' he said to Prudence and Vanilla.

When they entered the brig, Coroman was sitting on a wooden limony box.

'I am very sorry to have detained you Mr. Coroman,' said Henry.

'My name is Homer Tacit,' said Coroman.

'Prudence please find out who he really is.'

'Do not read my mind!'

Prudence paid no heed to his complaints; she stared through Coroman's eyes and right into him. Diligently she searched each and every corridor of his mind, and everything seemed in order. But that was the problem, it was just too orderly. Prudence, who had read hundreds of minds, knew that very fact meant something was wrong. Then she saw something strange, a glimpse of a silver coin just for an instant, then just as soon as it had appeared, it was gone again.

She searched the pocket of Coroman.

'Madam I must object. You are interfering with my privacy!' said the elf.

She removed one of the uncast stones from Coroman's right pocket, and a silver coin from his left, and gave them to Henry.

'Where did you get this stone from Sir,' asked Henry.

'I saw someone appear out of nowhere. She dropped the stone and ran away, so I picked it up,' said Coroman.

Henry gave the coin to Vanilla, 'what do you think of it?'

Vanilla examined the silver coin carefully. It was very old and worn, so it must have been held in the palms of thousands of goblins. The only marking left on it was a faint outline of a goblin's head on one of its faces.

Without the coin to help him, Prudence began reading Coroman's memories again. Now it was clear he had been hiding them, but was no longer able to do so. He was strong-willed, but she was a marvellously skilled mind reader, who could dance around the mental walls he threw up to block her probes.

'He betrayed Draska to the forces of Hell. The demon wards he designed to defend Draska are defective. They are worse than useless; they act as gates to let the demons in. Is the coin infernal?' said Prudence.

Vanilla placed the coin on the table and touched it with her silver spoon. It turned black, 'It is infernal alright,' she said.

'Can you tell me anything else?'

Vanilla held the coin in her right hand and felt its aura.

'It is magically powerful, with a mind and ego of its own; a wicked ego of a traitor. There are more like it, and it speaks to them. This is a dangerous infernal artefact,' said Vanilla.

'You violated my mind! You had no right to see my memories,' wailed Coroman.

They left Coroman in the brig, then made their way to the common room. Henry put the silver coin in a small demon bottle.

'What does this all mean?' Prudence asked Henry.

'It means we mostly know how Hell intends to open its door; it will be through the demon ward at the opera. They have three of the four elements they need to attack. They have the similarity from Neepfield's opera about the fall of Draska to the invasion from Hell to create sympathy, the emotional content of the audience to Delilah Twotemple's song to clarify the spell. The demonic portal that looks like a demon ward on the stage is the gate, but what they still lack are the queens of manna to power the pathway from Hell. So where will they get it from?' said Henry.

Henry heard a ringing in his ears from Oakensoul.

'We have been summoned to speak to Oakensoul ladies. Battle reports from the other treetrolls I assume.'

They made their way down an underground tunnel that led to some of Oakensoul's roots.

'I have reports of attacks across the city. Goblins and battlecast golems mainly, but also the demonically possessed plants that escaped from the Xenological Gardens. The Parliament of Wizards, the Weather Machine and the Goblin King's Palace have fallen. The King is missing. An attack on the Municipal Demon Ward was repelled, but it is now under siege. Cornelius Hand has declared the Green Coat Party the emergency government and told everyone to go about their business as usual. They have declared free entry to the opera tonight in celebration,' said Oakensoul.

'The opera, always the opera. Anything else?' asked Henry.

'I have received a secret message from a tree near the Municipal Weather Machine. He says the revolutionaries who control the machine are no longer sending the manna pollution to the recycling factories.'

'Really? What are they doing with it?' asked Henry.

'They are using the Weather Machine to swirl it around in the sky in a large circle centred on the Opera House,' explained Oakensoul. 'There is the missing piece of the puzzle, the manna pollution will power a bridge to Hell!' said Henry, 'We have to sneak into the opera Prudence. You will find Delilah Twotemples and change her memories, and I will look at the warding stone.'

'What should I change her mind to?'

'Something disruptive,' said Henry.

'How do we sneak in?'

'Invisibility; I will give you an invisibility cloak. Let us make our way to the Telepathy Office to see what help we can find there. I just hope that we can get there, the whole city seems to be falling to these infernal rebels.'

An army officer ran into the room. His scarlet uniform was covered in dirt and black powder soot.

'Twenty battlecast golems supported by militia are advancing on Oakensoul's, they will be here within ten minutes, what shall we do Sir?' he asked.

'Every man to his post,' commanded Henry.

'How can we hold back the battlecasts? Rifles and musket balls bounce off of them,' asked Vanilla.

'I am not sure we can. We need a brave volunteer to scout out their approach, anyone?' asked Henry to the soldiers.

Now surrender had long been on PC Pinch's mind, and he saw his opportunity to get away from the fanatic Pharaoh Henry and turn himself over to the militia. 'I volunteer to go out there,' he said to Henry, trying to hide his cowardice.

'You're a brave goblin Pinch,' said Henry, who was completely taken in.

***

Tobias Wandsmith was planning a fresh assault on Oakensoul's. He stood on a table to address his troops.

'I told Sergeant Pickles not to attack before the battlecasts arrived, but she was too impetuous. Which is why I have sent her to guard the Opera House, while I lead the attack.'

The militia did not appreciate Wandsmith's lies. They knew he ordered the attack without the golems. But now they had the golems with them, they did not like that either. Although unaware of the demons they contained, they could feel there was something unwholesome about the creatures.

'Now we can attack Oakensoul's safely, so stay back all of you. Keep well behind the battlecasts,' said Wandsmith.

He wanted to say more, especially about how it was not his fault the first attack failed, but the twenty battlecasts had formed a line across the road, three ranks deep, and advanced ahead of the militia. Militiamen had heard of how battlecasts did not take prisoners. They tore goblins apart, even innocent civilians who could not get out of their way in time. Even militia had been killed by battlecasts.

'Follow me,' Wandsmith said heroically, but the militia ignored him and stayed put.

The battlecasts closed on Oakensoul's unsupported.

Suddenly orks charged from out of the alleys, either side of the golems, outflanking them. It was Coffin's crew. Swinging their trollhammers, they smashed through the battlecast's armour. The battlecasts knew they were being attacked, and lashed out wildly, but none of their blows landed.

Pinch had approached the battlecasts and was about to surrender to them when the orks had attacked. *The battlecasts cannot see the orks,* he thought.

Wandsmith watched on in confusion for a while, trying to understand what was happening. The carapaces of the golems rang out like bells as the trollhammers struck. The battlecasts flayed wildly in retaliation, big powerful swings, but they could not hit anything. Jack Coffin smashed repeatedly into a battlecast, taking long powerful blows at it, breaking a hole right through its armoured shell. He threw a stone into the hole, and a terrible demonic scream came from within. Its shell broke apart as it burst its way out, shrieking in agony, until it was in the open air, then it evaporated into nothing as it fled back to Hell. Now the other battlecasts turned and ran. But orks are faster than golems, and they were onto them, striking at them as they fled, until all that was left of them was shards of starsteel armour.

Tobias Wandwright had run away and was nowhere to be seen.

The militia stood alone and unled in front of a crazed ork crew, and its notorious leader Jack Coffin who even Hell could not tame. The orks turned to stare at them; then through their ranks came PC Pinch.

PC Pinch trembled and shook, a paralysing fear gripped him so hard he could hardly speak. The orks frightened him almost as much as the militia. He wanted to explain to the militia that he had been tricked into supporting the royalists by the mad goblin Pharaoh Henry; that he sympathised with the green coat cause, and wanted to join them, and they mustn't kill or hurt him; and all he wanted to do was surrender, but he was so terror stricken the only word he could get out of his throat was: 'SURRENDER?!'

Well that was it; the militia had enough. Jerusalem Pickles, the leader they had trusted, had been replaced by that windbag martinet Tobias Wandsmith, who had now run away leaving them leaderless. They had found out how dangerous it was to fight wizards and orks, and there had been howling demons in those now destroyed battlecasts. Now some crazed police officer, who shook with rage and was so fearless he could stand alone in front of them, demanding their capitulation. It was all too much. They did what any rational goblins would do in the same situation, they threw down their rifles and surrendered to Constable Babylon Pinch.

43

A modern goblinette should expect gifts from all of her many suitors. She should receive chocolates and bouquets, especially sealysuckles and goldentoes, which are the most beautiful and expensive of flowers.

From **Chanson's Instructions on Modern Etiquette and Good Manners**

***

Pharaoh Henry and Prudence wore invisibility cloaks so as to approach the Opera House unseen. It was a windy evening, the first since the Weather Machine had been in operation, but this was a wind that none of them had felt before; it had a magical feel to it. Henry looked up into the night sky, a great cloud of manna fog swirled directly over the Grand Opera House. It brightened the night with spectral light that brought out the colours of the flowers in the gardens; the reds and purples of the sealysuckles, and the yellows of the goldentoes. Henry knew that the Green Coat militia had taken the weather machine and that the cloud hanging overhead was under their control. *The manna cloud will provide the required magical energy.*

Pharaoh felt a tremble in Prudence's cold hand as he led her through the front doors of the theatre. They made their way down the central aisle. The whole house was filled with opera-loving goblins eager to share in the tragedy of the fall of Draska. *The emotion of so many hearts will create a ritual spell, how cunning!* He knew full well that after he had let go of her then he would be unable to contact her again until the mission was over; he also knew how much danger she was in. She would be on her own, and he would no longer be able to help her. *Am I sending yet another brave soul to oblivion?*

He let go of Prudence's hand.

Now she would need to find the changing room of Delilah Twotemples by herself, to awaken the memory she had planted in her unconscious mind.

But Pharaoh Henry had his own job to do. He climbed the small staircase at the side of the stage, and made his way to the demon ward. He looked behind him and saw the entire audience looking at the stage he was on, but were unable to see him.

The elfin made demonward was sculpted from scarlet starcoral, which was widely prized for its special properties to enhance demon fighting spells. Etched across every inch of its surface was the warding spell itself, written in Enochian script. He moved his hands carefully around the ward until he felt a slight tell-tale tug of an infernal aura. *There is something hidden here. A secret compartment in the ward containing an infernal artefact perhaps, but how to open it?'* He pressed carefully around the spot but could not find anything. *I must not panic; I must search carefully and persistently.*

The orchestra began the overture, and the curtain's opened. Delilah Twotemples stepped out centre stage. She set the scene in song, describing the great elfin city of Draska, elegant and powerful, that had entrapped demons in magical bottles to tap them of their power. She sang of the Draskan elves and their misplaced confidence in their defences against the dangers of Hell.

Five hundred pairs of eyes focused on Delilah, while the invisible wizard next to her frantically searched for the trick to unlock the ward. With a lucky press, the compartment sprang open with a click. Henry felt inside, his fingers touched cold metal; it was a silver coin identical to the one he had found on Aether Coroman. He pocketed it, and in its place put one of the uncast stones. Then he shut the compartment and made his way off the stage.

Henry sneaked back down the central aisle, but he could feel magic attacking him from the coin in his pocket. It was chipping away at his invisibility spell, but he fought back, resisting its magical sallies. The coin had an ego; a nasty personality all of its own and it was using its power to undermine Henry.

He thought he could hold off the coin's attack and make his escape, he was almost there; then suddenly and unexpectedly his invisibility spell gave way. He appeared as from nowhere, standing in the foyer of the Grand Opera House in plain sight of God and goblin.

A militiaman, who had been posted at the front entrance, stared in incredulity at the wizard. Henry tried to cast **The Confident Appearance of Proper Authority** on himself, but nothing happened.

Pharaoh Henry, one of the finest magicians in the city, now realised that he was without any magical ability whatsoever, and he correctly surmised that this new situation had everything to do with the troublesome coin.

'Halt,' ordered the militiaman, pointing his musket at Henry.

Pharaoh Henry stood still, knowing full well that even his magical wards against musket rounds would fail.

'Stand down soldier. I will take him from here,' ordered Sergeant Jerusalem Pickles.

Jerusalem pointed her revolver at Henry. 'Get outside, it is off to prison with you!' she shouted.

The guard obeyed his sergeant and stepped aside. Jerusalem pushed Henry through the front doors of the Opera House, and down the path towards Arcadia square. Once out of earshot, Jerusalem spoke to Henry in a soft voice.

'We were tricked, Grand Master Henry. Tricked by Tobias Wandwright, most militiamen do not realize this yet, and so are still loyal to him, but some are learning.'

'So where are you taking me?' asked Henry.

'To hide Sir. I am in your debt and at your service. The private will have reported us by now, and they will be coming to find us.'

'We must run to the Telepathy Office; we can take refuge there. But I must ask one thing, where is Prudence Pepperhill?' asked Henry.

'I am not sure but we were ordered to look for her, vampires can feel the presence of their former slaves. There is nothing you can do for her now. We must escape, we must fly,' said Jerusalem.

'There they are,' shouted a militiaman behind them.

Pharaoh and Jerusalem ran towards the Telepathy Office as fast as they could. Muskets barked from close behind. Pharaoh heard the sizzle of a ball shoot by his ear.

Golly goblins that was close. Suddenly Pharaoh Henry was knocked to the ground. He felt pain in his back, he tried to reach to the wound, but before he could he had passed out.

Jerusalem knelt beside the old wizard as he lay bleeding. She placed her ear on Pharaoh's chest and listened for his heartbeat.

The militia men gathered around her. Pharaoh Henry was renowned across the city as a kind wizard. Every goblin knew a goblin who had been helped by Henry. He gave money to poor goblins, interceded on the part of goblins that had been treated unjustly, and found fair paid work for idle goblins. Admittedly, wizards avoided him because of his habit of dragooning them into dangerous crusades against the forces of Hell, but the common goblins loved him even for that.

The militia goblin who had fired the shot now regretted it, 'Will he be alright?' He asked.

'Grand Master Pharaoh Henry is dead,' said Jerusalem.

44

"For what shall it profit a man, if he shall gain the whole world, and lose his own soul?"

Mark 8:36 **The Holy Bible**

***

Captain Buckle and Ephemeral Wormsong shared a box at the opera. The Opera House roof was folded back and open to the night sky. Above them could be seen the huge magical cloud that hung ominously above the theatre.

'Our golems are being destroyed, they cannot see the orks that attack them because of the uncast stones,' said Wormsong.

'I don't care. It is too late now for the goblins, the gate will open soon and demons will overrun the city,' said Buckle.

'Won't Azezal mind that his demons are destroyed,' asked Wormsong.

'Azezal matters not, it's the Boss that matters, and the Boss will be happy when the city falls to us,' said Buckle. By the 'Boss' he meant Lucifer.

'I look forward to becoming a demon. I cannot wait to see the looks of surprise on the stupid faces of all those goblins that supported us. The fool Golemaker gave us this city, and all he wanted was wealth. He will be rich for the rest of eternity. I hope he enjoys his wealth, it has cost him his soul,' said Wormsong.

'He does not enjoy wealth, he enjoys being wealthy while others are poor, which as every demon knows is the difference between the sins of pride and avarice,' said Buckle, 'What about the others? What payment did they want to betray their city?'

'I promised Cornelius Hand absolute political power in Parliament for the rest of time, and that is what he shall get. I shall transfer the Houses of Parliament to its own pocket dimension. He will grow old there, lord of no-one but his own bitter soul, where he will become sick and lonely, but never die. After a century, his flesh will have rotted and he shall cry out for the society of others, he will beg for an end that will never come.'

Captain Buckle smiled in amusement at Ephemeral's cruelty,

'And Delilah Twotemples the singer?'

'Fame was her weakness, though she did not sell her soul as such' said Ephemeral, 'Solomon Golemaker arranged for her to become the Prima Donna of the finest opera ever to be performed in the Metropolis. An opera that is a spell to open the gates of Hell, and will plunge this goblin city into oblivion.'

'I just heard Aether Coroman escaped from Oakensoul's. He was spotted heading towards the docks. But it is of no consequence. When he dies his soul will be back in Hell soon enough,' said Buckle.

'Prudence Pepperhill is wrapped in web silk and stowed in my ornithopter. After the opera I shall drop her into the woods just before dawn's first sunlight to cook slowly,' said Ephemeral.

'And the great Pharaoh Henry is dead,' laughed Buckle.

'Well everything has come together. The Palace has fallen. The Weather Machine is ours, and that manna cloud floats above us,' said Buckle pointing to the ominous glowing ring in the sky directly overhead.

'An elegant plan Captain Buckle. The cloud is the power, the demonward the Hell Gate, the emotions of the audience the ritual, and Anatitia's song the spell, which Delilah will sing in just a moment,' said Ephemeral.

As Delilah sang the first verse of Anatitia's song the demon ward glowed red. The story of the demonic infestation of Draska struck a magical sympathy with her story. The manna cloud overhead now assumed the shape of a huge anvil, which sparkled with spectral manna. A massive manna bolt struck down from the cloud, smashing into the demon ward with a deafening crack. It tore out a hole in the fabric of space-time that led right the way down to Hell. Out of the hole, came demons. Some of the terrified audience turned to run; others froze on the spot, most just fell to their knees and screamed in terror.

But unbeknownst to Ephemeral, just before capture, Prudence had managed to refashion Delilah's memory, replacing the last verse of Anatitia's song with a new one. Delilah sang the Lord's Prayer to Lady Moondancer's melody. As Delilah's crisp clear notes played across the theatre, it was the demons turn to scream in agony. The song of hope and God's grace burned through their infernal ears, and seared into their damned souls. The demons turned in terror and pain. They fled back into the Hell Gate even faster than they had entered.

Captain Buckle chased after them and he was the last demon to jump back to Hell before the gate snapped shut.

Ephemeral Wormsong shrieked at the sound of prayer, she fled out of the Opera House.

Two militia members stared incredulously at the whole scene of confusion. They now realized they had been tricked into becoming the Devil's soldiers, and they did not know what to do. They simply stood and looked on as Ephemeral fled.

Ephemeral climbed into her ornithopter. Its wings flapped rhythmically as it took off. Her vampire servants watched her fly away, for the first time since they had become undead, there was no-one to tell them what to do. In the morning the sun would rise, but with Ephemeral now gone they simply awaited orders that would never come.

45

Demons cannot go to heaven because they hate and fear goodness. Neither can they reincarnate into the material world as mortals because through their evil deeds they have only acquired bad karma. Should they acquire mortal form, and are killed, their souls can only return to Hell.

Extract from **The Demon Hunter's Handbook**, by Pharaoh Henry, Green Dragon Press

***

Pharaoh Henry knew he was dead when his soul left his body. He found himself floating above his corpse and looking down at the militiamen who stood around his dead flesh. Jerusalem was kneeling down beside the abandoned carcass that once housed his soul.

Pharaoh rose upwards, away from the corporeal world. He felt peaceful and carefree; the troubles of the world were now far from him. He floated through a tunnel in space-time, moving towards a distant light. As he got closer to the light, he saw an outline similar to a goblin; it was a sentient being of some kind. The light wrapped itself around his soul, and filled Pharaoh with a sense of safety and security; he knew the light soul loved him unconditionally.

'Pharaoh Henry these were your deeds,' projected the light being.

In an instant, Pharaoh remembered every event of his former life, everything. He saw his infancy as a happy dribbling playing with his friends in the gardens of old Draska; as an eager schoolboy learning to read and write, and learning the wonders of mathematics; then as a young goblin drinking ginger beer with his beloved Utopia on a boat, floating on a lake filled with coloured fish that swam to the surface to greet them. He remembered kissing Utopia on their wedding day; her belly swollen with their egg, and both of them watching with delight as their egg hatched.

He remembered the terrible scourge of demons who had invaded the city; the hollowing sadness of seeing his beloved Utopia killed, to see her resurrected as a feral zombie.

He remembered the evacuation. A brave butler had taken matters in hand, a clever butler who organized the escape, a wise butler who was to become the Goblin King.

He remembered scavenging for food, requisitioning pan ships, and voyaging across the star lanes to help found the Goblin Metropolis.

He remembered watching from the windows of his study the goblin artisans and ogre labourers toiling to build a new city; and the days and nights he spent studying magic to ward, hunt down, and destroy the demons that followed them.

He remembered the delightful conversations as to the ontological underpinnings of magic theory with Seelykin, Nettlebed, Silverwings and the Reverend Bentley.

'Has the Metropolis fallen?' Henry asked the light being.

'No. You and Prudence saved it. You turned the gate back into a demon ward. Demons are fleeing back to Hell, Samuel Golemaker is running to his Pan Ship with Tobias Wandsmith, and Ephemeral Wormsong is escaping the city in her ornithopter. The militias are throwing down their weapons now they know they were misled,' telepathed the light being.

'Is Prudence safe,' asked Henry.

'Prudence has been captured by Ephemeral, who means her harm.'

'Poor Prudence,' said Henry. 'Did my wife make it to heaven?'

'No. Her soul is still trapped in a zombie corpse in Draska.'

'I wish I could go to Draska and destroy her corpse to free her soul.'

Henry heard a soft thud. 'What was that?' He asked the light being.

'It is your heart restarting. Jerusalem is trying to bring you back to life,' telepathed the being.

'How could she do that?

'With the healing potion you gave her, she used it to cast a spell to save your life. She is a healing magician now'

'Good for her,' said Henry. He fell into a dreamless sleep.

46

This book teaches the standard theory of magic. It is the high magic of the elves, dwarves, goblins and orks. But there are other magics that it does not cover. We know little about fairy magic, or the many strands of hedge magic. We do know that certain beasts of virtue share the magic of the angels, often referred to as Enochian magic.

Excerpt from **Magic Theory and Practice** 4th Edition

***

The ornithopter's wings thudded softly as it flapped along over Ecclesdown forest. Ahead was a small clearing in the trees where Ephemeral Wormsong came to land. She climbed down from the cockpit, and with strength disproportionate to her size, she pulled the silken bound body of Prudence out of the storage bay, and threw it under the shade of a tree. It landed with a painful thud.

She wanted to hurt and humiliate Prudence, and she thought long and hard about taking that option, but reluctantly she decided against it. It would take too much time, and the sun would be up soon. She knew it would involve cutting some of the silk threads that bound her, and that meant taking unnecessary risks with this memory manipulating vixen. Prudence was wrapped up tightly in silk and so unable to move. *She was safe under wraps. No point in taking a chance.*

She stooped down beside Prudence, and whispered, 'When the sun rises in about one hour's time, my spell will end and the magical silk that binds you will disappear into nothing. You will be free to run through the forest to escape the sun's burning rays. Do you know what the most painful thing for a vampire is? Thirst is unbearable I know, but there is something worse. The most painful thing our kind can endure is God's pure sunlight, and soon you are going to roast away in agony. Each ray of Spring sun will peep through the gaps in the leaf canopy above, to burn your lovely pale skin. Little by little, your beautiful white flesh will scorch to charcoal. I would love to stay and relish your final torment, but I have a safe cave I need to go to, so I must say goodbye to you my pretty little traitor. I assure you that the next time we meet it will be in Hell where I will torture you some more.'

Wormsong climbed back into her ornithopter, its wings started to flap rhythmically. She flew away.

Prudence was cocooned, helpless and without hope; she knew destruction would come soon. She recalled the few hours she had spent with Lampwick the cat she loved so much. She remembered the jokes, and laughter and the cocoa.

She looked back at the hope and kindness that Grand Master Henry had given her. How interesting she found his knowledge of magic; and the promise of a new life at Oakensoul's college.

Her mouth was bound in silk, so in her mind she thought a small prayer to thank the one true God of mercy and compassion, for those precious moments of joy before her long future of eternal damnation.

But none of us should be too certain of our fate, because we have no fate. Our future is made up as we go along, fashioned by our deeds interleaving with the whims of an unpredictable world. And the universe is sometimes ironic; as if it has a sense of humour all of its own. Now it was going to give poor Prudence a long overdue piece of luck.

She lay on the ground, with her ear pressed to the soil. She could not see anything because of the silk around her head that held her tight and blinded her, but she could hear, and she heard the feint thud of distant steps. The creature was coming closer, and she could tell by its sound it was swift and had four hooves, that it was probably the size of a large deer or horse. In the Old Forest it could even be a centaur. But trussed and blindfolded in magical silk she could not be sure what the creature was.

She heard its whinny; it was not a centaur. Soft droplets hit the silken shroud over the side of her head. The liquid from the creature magically burned through her bonds, and then ran down onto her face, over her nose and into her mouth, they were salty warm tears. Her body pulsated and warmed as its benign magic ran through her.

Quite unexpectedly, things seemed to take a change for the worse. She felt physically sick, her stomach started to reach, but her silk bindings held her fast. Vomit rushed up from her belly, acidic and foul, it burned her throat. It forced its way out of her mouth. Its corrosive evil even melted its way through the silk web. Her head unbound; she could look around.

239

She glimpsed the black filth she had spewed out, and she just managed to catch a breath before she threw up again, and then again. There seemed to be gallons upon gallons of the oily bile gushing out of her. She could not understand how her small body held such a volume.

Eventually there was none left. She had emptied herself of it. Prudence lay exhausted in a rancid evil pool that smelled worse than the rot of death itself. Even the silk cords that held her had melted away where ever the pollution touched it. But now she could free herself, so she crawled out of the filth, exhausted and nauseous.

She looked up. She saw the creature that cried the tear that liberated her. It was not a horse, but a unicorn. It galloped away from her. She lay there awhile, her skin and hair caked with black slime. After a few minutes, when she managed to get her breath back, she started to feel something small but very important, something she had long lost the sensation of: Her small goblin heart pumped again, as regular as clockwork, and warm blood flowed through her veins.

She shivered in the cold air because her flesh was warming up. Now she was no longer undead, and remembered how cold it was just before dawn, for a creature with living flesh. She was covered in stinking bile that was the parasitic evil that had been inside her, but now she was alive again.

It started to rain. Each raindrop felt cold, but they washed the demonic filth off of her until she was clean of it. She had been born anew by virtue of a unicorn's tear freely given. She took a long sweet breath to oxygenate the blood in her beating heart. She was alive.

Miss Prudence Pepperhill was no longer a vampire.

47

For a spell to work the caster requires the proper mental attitude. This can be broken down into several parts, the first being the principle of assumption: He must assume nature has already accepted the changes created by his magic; though he must remember that nature has no real preference as to how it unfolds itself, as any outcome is equally acceptable to nature. Even so, the more improbable the outcome asked by the spell, the more difficult it will be to cast. So what does this mean for the caster? It means he must believe the outcome of his spell has already happened with all his mind and heart; there cannot be the slightest room for doubt.

Excerpt from **Magic Theory and Practice** 4th Edition

***

Months had passed since Henry had cast the demons back to Hell. At the King's insistence, Mr. Zebedee Fireheart had been reappointed first minister at the Department for Demonic Safety, whose headquarters was at the very Northern end of The Old Pagoda Road.

He had taken over the position from an ostentatious Green Coat Party predecessor, whose name he did not know, nor want to, but whose office was too grand an affair by half.

The surface of his desk was a huge polished piece of yellow wood, cut long ago from a giant tree in the Steam Jungles of Tindalos. His chair was backed with magically dyed leather the shade of a red dragon's belly. Across from his desk was a much plainer set of chairs for the guests, a setup which nettled Zebedee's egalitarian principles.

The office floor was tiled with dwarven crystalstone of vibrant deep green. It had been telekinetically mined from far below the surface of a distant gas giant world, where it had lay for epochs under intense heat and pressure, to be fashioned into the most beautiful and expensive flooring known to goblin. The room was lit by a single large semi-circular window, offering a panoramic view over the North of the city. In all, Zebedee's office was far too unproletariat for his socialist sensibilities; little did he know but it was furnished in much the same style as Coroman's former mansion in Hell.

He had a personal secretary, a Miss Aurora Moon, whose appearance matched the lavish expense of his decor. She stepped into the office, her stilettos clacked on the floor, sounding out her presence. She stood as straight as she could on her impractically high heels. Aurora's crimson dress complemented her dark Chestnut hair, blue eyes, and her magically transformed elfin body, so recently set in vogue by Euphoria.

My daughter has a lot to answer for! **He thought.**

She placed a pile of papers on his desk. 'These are the intelligence reports regarding the escaped Luciferians. Sightings, cross intelligence from the high elves, star dragons and gnomes, divination reports from stars, cards, and tea leaves. Also, you have an important meeting this morning Sir. Grand Master Pharaoh Henry and the Reverend Noah Bentley wish to discuss the escapees. Less significantly, Miss Euphoria Fireheart wants to discuss the fate of a particular captured Luciferian, that awful beast Miss Delilah Twotemples'.

'Please send Grand Master Henry and the Reverend up as soon as they arrive. Further please tell Euphoria I will see her after work, and send her away as politely as you can,' said Zebedee.

'Yes, Your Lordship,' said Aurora. Zebedee squirmed.

Aurora left the office. Zebedee looked at the top document on his pile; it read: *'Tasseomantic search results for Ephemeral Wormsong unsuccessful'*. Zebedee scanned through the document, reading: *Vampires gone to ground are almost undetectable; Vampire deep sleep of death defeats divining; Conclusion: Ephemeral Wormsong unlikely to resurface for decades to come, and therefore untraceable. Recommendation: Search should be suspended as unlikely to be successful.*

Quite unexpectedly Euphoria entered the room and placed a large paper scroll on her father's desk.

'Daddy, I must speak with you.'

'Euphoria, how did you get in? I asked Aurora to tell you I was busy.'

'Yes I know you did, and that was horrid and uncaring of you. But fortunately, I recently learned a spell from dearest Prudence called **The Confident Appearance of Rightful Authority**. It is a most useful little incantation, most especially for dealing with sales assistants and debt collectors. Those shop girls at the high-class haberdasheries can get quite above themselves when demanding settlement of accounts.'

Before Zebedee could reply, Pharaoh Henry entered the room with Noah Bentley

'Zebedee my good friend, and Euphoria too!' said Henry.

'Any news of the escaped diabolists?' asked Bentley.

'Samuel Golemaker escaped on the Golden Phoenix and took a huge amount of stolen manna with him. Delilah Twotemples turned herself in. Aether Coroman was reported having jumped ship in Sterwyck. Ephemeral Wormsong was seen escaping North on her ornithopter. They cannot find her. Vanilla tried to divine her whereabouts; she even riddled Queen Penelope, but no luck. They cannot say for sure, but they think she has gone to ground in a secret coffin; she could hide out in a deep sleep of half death for centuries. It is very difficult to divine location,' said Zebedee, who now felt resigned at having Euphoria infiltrate the meeting.

'Well at least we have Tobias Wandwright and Delilah Twotemples locked up in Oubliette,' said Bentley.

'It is Miss Twotemples' welfare I have come here to discuss. Poor Delilah is imprisoned in Oubliette. She is all alone in her cell, without any friends for company or convivial conversation,' said Euphoria.

'She signed a pact with a demon for fame. She was tried, sentenced and justly sent to prison under goblin law,' said Bentley.

'That's true. Besides she could have escaped with Mr. Golemaker, but chose to remain in the Metropolis. She did not even try to escape, which means she is innocent,' said Euphoria.

'But she has been convicted of consorting with demons, the punishment is life imprisonment, what would you have us do?' asked Henry.

'Free her. Ask the Goblin King to give her a pardon,' said Euphoria.

'Just let her run around the city again? We cannot do that; she has sold her soul to the Devil. If we showed such leniency others might be tempted to do the same,' said Zebedee.

'Quite right, we must keep Miss Twotemples under lock and key. By the same token, I am very unhappy about having that succubus Pandamonia walking the streets, we must get her out of the city somehow,' said Henry.

'We cannot expel Pandamonia. The King gave his word that every soul Coffin rescued from Hell would be allowed sanctuary in the Metropolis,' said Zebedee.

'Well the dwarves are kicking up a fuss over Jack Coffin again, and it has escalated into a diplomatic argument. Aristotle has been in contact with the dwarven authorities, they will only extradite the Luciferians in exchange for Jack Coffin. Solomon Golemaker and Ebenezer Bluevein have escaped to the Dwarven Federation, where they have been given sanctuary because we will not send them Coffin,' said Bentley.

'Giving up Jack to the dwarfs is quite out of the question, he is a hero who went to Hell and back to save our city. I will not send Coffin to the dwarfs. We owe him a great debt,' said Henry.

'I do not want to give him up either, but the dwarves want Coffin and they are going to cause trouble when they cannot get him. Already they have persuaded the gnomes to impound the ship they paid us for sending him to Hell. They say they will return it only when we send them Jack Coffin,' said Zebedee.

'The gnomes have impounded *The Dancing Nymph*? She was loaded full of Star Coral needed to build demon wards for the Star Dragons. We must have the ship back.' said Henry.

Zebedee, Henry and Bentley sat in a silent dilemma. The peace was eventually broken by Euphoria: 'I have the solution'.

'What do you suggest Euphoria?' said Henry.

'I will tell you the answer, but in return, you must let Delilah go free,' she said, crossing her arms and raising her eyebrows in a gesture of intransigence.

'Miss Twotemples cannot be freed to roam the city at will, and that is final.' said Henry.

'Well would you let her stay with us at Oakensoul's, and only be allowed out under supervision?' asked Euphoria.

'Are you suggesting we parole her under license?' said Zebedee.

'She could even learn magic with us and help us fight demons. I am sure she is very sorry for what she did,' said Euphoria.

'Alright, if we parole Miss Twotemples, what is your suggestion?' said Henry.

'I know how to free your ship; mend the diplomatic differences with the Dwarven Federation; honour the contract to build the demon wards for the Star Dragons, send Lady Moondancer home, and get Pandamonia out of the Metropolis,' said Euphoria.

'How will you get the gnomes to give up *The Dancing Nymph*?' said Bentley, looking intrigued.

'You owe me a promise,' said Euphoria holding up the small golden heart Henry had given her, 'And I want your promise that Miss Delilah Twotemples will be paroled.' Euphoria stuck her nose in the air to indicate her obstinacy on the matter.

'You have my word,' said Henry, taking back his promise.

'Tell the Dwarves you are going to arrest Coffin, but before you do, get Captain Coffin to sail to the gnomish port, and steal *The Dancing Nymph*. He can then sail her to the Star Dragon station,' said Euphoria.

'Steal the ship?' said Bentley.

'Yes, steal the ship. After all he is a pirate; and he has his whole clan with him now: Billy Snatch, John Coffin, Harry and Bert Throatbite to name a few, and all their orkettes who are even more obnoxious and unfashionable. They are a rough lot who cause trouble because they are bored and have nothing better to do except get drunk, bully goblins and fight with ogres. So, I suggest you give them some invisibility cloaks so they can steal the ship, and then they would be happy again; sailing around the galaxy smuggling and thieving from the dwarves. When he is safely out of goblin jurisdiction, you put a warrant out for Jack Coffin's arrest. You cannot arrest Jack Coffin, nor would you want to, but you can use it as an excuse to placate the dwarves,' said Euphoria.

'Well that would get rid of the Coffin clan, and restore diplomatic relations with the dwarves, just as long as they do not suspect we are involved in the ship theft, but what about Pandamonia, how do we get rid of her?' asked Henry.

'I would have thought that was obvious. If Coffin goes, so will Pandamonia. She will follow him anywhere, I know this because my mind is still in union with hers. She would even risk dying away from a reincarnation machine and being sent back to Hell, to be near her beloved Jack.'

'How do we get the starcoral to the Metropolis to make the demon wards?' asked Zebedee.

'You don't bring the coral here. You don't make the wards here. Instead, you put a warding witch on *The Dancing Nymph*, along with Lady Moondancer. She could make the wards on the way to the Star Dragon's kingdom. After she has set the wards in place, we send another ship to pick her up again,' said Euphoria.

'Where would they rendezvous with the orks?' asked Bentley.

Euphoria had anticipated the question. She opened up the scroll on the desk, which turned out to be an elfin star chart.

'Here is gnomish Sterwyck, where *The Dancing Nymph* is impounded, and here is the dragon station at Salin, where you need to take the warding stones,' said Euphoria pointing to the places on the chart, 'here is a small asteroid called Cavenstone. It was once a trading stop between old Draska and Tindalos, but it also lies between Sterwyck and Salin. Since the fall of Draska it is no longer in use, but it is still habitable and maintained by elfin golems. Aristotle has telepathed the chief golem, who told us we can use it to rendezvous with the orks. You can drop off Lady Moondancer and the warding witch on the way to Salin, and after setting up the wards. And pick her up again on the way back to return the witch to the Metropolis.'

'Well it does seem plausible,' said Henry.

'So glad you like my plan; when do I pick up the parole papers for Miss Twotemple's release?' asked Euphoria.

48

Oubliette Prison holds the most depraved souls known to goblinkind. Consider the case of Dolly Strangle, once believed by all to be a sweet mannered librarian, but in truth, she is a hag-witch who sucked the souls out of goblins to feed her wicked magical power. Also, Herod Longtooth, a glue maker by day, but during the nights when our moon was full, he roamed the deep tunnels as a werewolf, hunting for lost goblins to gobble up. But by far the most dangerous inmate of Oubliette is the traitor Delilah Twotemples. Twotemples is now sentenced to spend the rest of her life imprisoned at Oubliette, for selling her soul to the Devil in return for fame. The once celebrated opera singer performed the 'Hubris of Draska' at the Grand Goblin Opera House, but it was a secret ritual spell that harnessed the emotions of the audience. Powered by a bolt from a manna cloud built up by the weather machine, the spell tore apart the fabric of space-time, opening a portal to Hell itself. Only the heroic repair of the demon wards by Grand Master Henry rescued our wonderful city from the infernal betrayal of Delilah!

From *Oubliette – Home to our most dangerous criminals*, a feature article in the Metropolitan Herald, Sunday 22nd April 1898.

***

Delilah had lost count of the days she had been in her cell. She felt subdued by the loneliness and boredom of her imprisonment. Each day her jailor asked if she wanted to mix with the other prisoners for one hour, 'association' he called it. Mostly she refused as she knew from bruising experience that the other prisoners would beat and bully her. Still, after a few days alone, even that oppression gave her some comfort against her crushing loneliness.

Her cell was a pocket dimension just ten feet in diameter. Instead of walls, there were misty curtains at the boundaries, which if passed, would simply take her to the other side of her very confined space. Some days she just ran in the same direction, crossing through her dimension time and time again. She often sang to herself; the tone of her voice always sounded unnatural in her small world, but at least it broke the silence. She had a table and chair, a toilet, a water tap, a float bed, a bookshelf with five books and several long out of date copies of the Intelligencer. She could not remember how long ago it was that she took a wash; she knew if she wanted to wash again, she would have to risk the violence and violation of the association.

When she had discovered that her song was part of a covert spell to open a gate to Hell, she felt horrified and deceived. She remembered Solomon Golemaker asking if she wanted to escape with him, and she rejected his offer. She was arrested, put on trial for consorting with a demon, and sentenced. She remembered entering the terrible prison of Oubliette, seeing the metal double-doors. Doors made from the strongest starsteel, the colour of metallic charcoal; they were the most feared doors in the Metropolis. Oubliette was a prison without windows. Its black stone walls matched the hearts of its most wicked inmates. No goblin escaped from Oubliette, and every mischievous goblin feared it.

Delilah had been delivered to Oubliette in a police wagon. Her guard had knocked on the steel doors; the metal slit had opened, suspicious eyes peeped out, then it had slammed shut with a clank. The mechanisms of the lock clattered, and the inset door opened. Hesitating a moment, she was pushed into darkness.

Her guard had spoken to a jailor who had a wrinkled face that carried the look of acidic suspicion; a face like a lemon, pickled in the wickedness of the prisoners under his custody. The jailor had forced her to strip naked and to wear a prison uniform. Then he led her through the prison's deep corridors. The way was dark, and there were no obvious markings on the floors or walls, so before long she had lost her bearings. He came to a nondescript metal door; he opened it and said, 'In there.' It seemed like an eternity ago that she made the walk, in reality it had only been six weeks. Now the door opened again.

Delilah anticipated the question, 'Association?' But he surprised her, 'Miss Twotemples, come out here'.

She stepped out of her cell into the corridor. Standing with the guard was Euphoria Fireheart.

'It's you,' she said, staring at Euphoria with exhausted apathy.

'I have a parole offer for you Delilah. If you accept it you can leave with me,' said Euphoria.

'Leave? I want to leave here. Whatever it says I will sign it,' said Delilah.

'You should really read any contract before you sign it, that's what got you in here in the first place,' said Euphoria.

'Just pass me the papers,' said Delilah. She took the parole papers then she signed without reading them.

'Follow me,' he said, clearly unhappy at Delilah's parole. He led them both out of the prison in silence. As they approached the exit the guard glared at Euphoria. His face twisted into a scowl, he said, 'What do you want to parole her for? She sold our city to the Devil.'

Euphoria did not reply. 'Do-gooder,' he muttered.

The guard at the door gave Delilah a box containing her possessions.

'I need to change out of this prison uniform,' said Delilah, taking her things. The jailor looked on contemptuously, until Euphoria stared at him, making him turn his back on Delilah. She put on the brown dress she had worn when she entered prison six weeks, and a thousand years ago.

The doors of Oubliette opened for her; clutching the small box that held her remaining possessions, Delilah entered the light of the outside world.

There was a crowd of demonstrators. They held placards demanding that Delilah remain locked up, but they were quiet and orderly. She later learned it was because the newly promoted Sergeant Pinch, the war hero, kept a stern watchful eye on them. Every goblin feared and respected Pinch.

Pinch paraded up and down in front of the crowd to keep them in order. He puffed himself up in his fine new sergeant's uniform; his medals for bravery glinted in the morning sun.

With the help of the police, they got past the jeering crowd. The city now hated Delilah. She could no longer judge how fast the carriages were coming at her, and the noise and hectic sights of goblins going about their everyday life startled and confused her. Euphoria offered Delilah her arm; she linked onto it with a grateful smile, 'Thank you Euphoria.'

After a few steps down the street, Euphoria flagged down a passing hansom cab.

'Oi I'm not taking her!' said the cabby, pointing to Delilah.

'You must take us,' said Euphoria, as she ensorcelled the cabby to put an end to his protests.

With due politeness and careful consideration, Euphoria helped Delilah inside. She climbed in after her. The horse's iron shoes clattered loudly on the cobbles as they drove away from the prison. Euphoria thought Delilah looked relieved at the sound. Delilah felt the movement away from Oubliette was a signal she could begin the long journey of returning to a life worth living.

'Oakensoul's College,' Euphoria said to the cab driver.

'I am most grateful to you Euphoria. I have spent Lord knows how long alone in a cell at Oubliette prison, please could you tell me what the conditions of my parole are?'

'The first condition is that you live at Oakensoul's College. You have been allocated Prudence Pepperhill's old underground rooms. Ever since Prudence stopped being a vampire, she has gone sunlight mad; she has moved her lodgings to a top floor room with a glass roof, but her old rooms are most pleasant,' said Euphoria.

'Well even if I am cooped up in cellar rooms, I am sure it is preferable to a cell in Oubliette,' said Delilah.

'You will not be confined to your rooms Miss Twotemples. You will have the run of the grounds at Oakensoul's, the gardens, the library, the refectory, the communal study. I am sure you will find it to your liking. Also, you may visit anywhere in the city providing you are accompanied by one or more magi and do not visit a known criminal.' said Euphoria.

'Well, that sounds promising. Who are the magi?' asked Delilah.

'The senior wizards are Grand Master Henry, the Reverend Noah Bentley, and a rather strange goblin called Wiggins. But a trainee magus can accompany you too, which brings me to the second condition. You are to train to become a demon fighting magus,' said Euphoria.

'Really? Are you a trainee magus too?'

'I am, and so is Assyria Neepfield, who will be partnered with you to create artistic magic together. We will go to a cafe or theatre tomorrow, and if you have any rudeness from any unruly goblin, I will threaten to turn him into a lizard,' said Euphoria.

'Who else is learning to be a wizard at Oakensoul's?'

'I will study demon hunting with you and Assyria; Prudence Pepperhill as a mentalist, and Jerusalem Pickles as a healing wizard,' said Euphoria, 'Oh and there will be two post-graduate positions,

Vanilla Catchpenny will teach divination, and Felix Lampwick shape-changing. Grand Master Jeroboam Nettlebed will join us as soon as they can dig him out of his pan-dimensional trap.'

On arrival at Oakensoul's, the doorman ran to find Pharaoh Henry, who came to greet the goblinettes.

'Miss Twotemples, I do hope you feel at home here and your diabolism days are over,' said Pharaoh.

'Oh yes sir, quite over,' said Delilah, who found Pharaoh Henry's welcome quite unexpected given his reputation as a zealous demon hunter.

'Come this way,' said Henry. Henry led the goblinettes onto the green, where Prudence and Vanilla sat on the bench opposite Oakensoul. On seeing Delilah, they got up and each gave her a hug.

'I shall leave you goblinettes to catch up,' said Henry, and left.

Euphoria and Delilah made their way down to Delilah's room. Inside her clothes and possessions were still packed in boxes. Unfortunately, the bed was gone.

'Prudence must have taken the bed, but never mind. You can stay with me. And we can shop for a new bed tomorrow,' said Euphoria.

Euphoria's room was on the top floor, so they ascended the stairs. On the first floor they met Prudence Pepperhill and Vanilla Catchpenny, who had been chatting about the new illusionist show that had debuted on Necromancer Avenue.

'No bed? How remiss of me,' said Prudence.

'Let's all sleep together tonight,' suggested Vanilla.

So Vanilla, Euphoria, Prudence and Delilah put on their nighties, said their prayers, and then jumped into bed, where they cuddled and hugged each other, as goblinettes like to do, as they are gregarious and sociable creatures. Just before Delilah fell asleep, for the first time in as long as she could remember, she felt happy, safe and secure.

Printed in Great Britain
by Amazon